Hexes & Honeysuckle

Hexes & Honeysuckle

WISTERIA COVE
BOOK THREE

ERIN BRANSCOM

Audrey, this one's for you. I'm so thankful I get to be your mom.

Content Warning

This book includes "on-page" adult content and language
unsuitable for minors.

CHAPTER 1
Rowan

DON'T STOP BELIEVIN' BY JOURNEY

THE RUSTY ANCHOR is buzzing tonight, and locals call out and wave as I claim a stool at the bar and wait for Finn. Boots scuff the old plank floors of the bar that's older than dirt, the jukebox plays an upbeat rock song, and the air smells like fried food, ocean salt, and spilled beer.

While I wait, I open my dating app and start scrolling, pretending it's not the saddest hobby known to womankind. It's like shopping for shoes that look great in the picture but turn out to pinch, squeak, or are uncomfortable as hell once you try them on. One guy's holding a fish and giving a thumbs up. Always the fish. Not even an impressive fish. And sometimes we can use the term "fish" metaphorically. Sometimes it's not a fish and I really wish it was a fish. Swipe left. Another one says he's "fluent in sarcasm" and "looking for a partner in crime." Left again. I sigh and wonder if maybe I should just marry my air fryer. At least it's consistent and knows how to heat things up.

I hover my thumb over the next when a warm voice leans in from behind me. "Ohhh, hard pass on that one?"

I glance over my shoulder. Finn Bennett stands there, tall and broad, grin bright enough to light up the bar. He looks fresh, like he just stepped out of the shower and is here to torture the world. The problem with Finn is he doesn't even understand how good-looking he is. He's just Finn. The human equivalent of a golden retriever, who is rugged and lovable. Dark blond hair that curls damp under a backward ball cap. Blue eyes soft and amused. White T-shirt clinging to his hard wall of muscular chest. Worn denim jeans that are probably doing the Lord's work for that perfect ass and scuffed up brown work boots that are also oddly doing things for me. He looks like a walking-talking blue collar hottie calendar model without even trying.

And he's my best friend. The real kind. The kind who has been in my life since we were kids. We grew up together in a way that made him part of my daily rhythm. Coffee together on slow mornings. Fixing things around the shop when I get over-whelmed. Showing up for every birthday, every heartbreak, every small disaster I pretend I can handle alone. He knows me better than anyone.

I shouldn't be thinking he looks hot, but I secretly always have. It's the thought that rises in my chest before I can stop it, warm and dangerous, like a spell I never meant to cast.

He slides onto the stool beside me and scoots closer, putting his elbows on the bar and leaning toward my phone. "That guy's a winner."

I say dryly, "That was you, Finn."

The words leave my mouth, but my heart races. Because his profile, smile, and his broad shoulders filling the frame are so natural, like he took the picture without thinking twice. And it hits me in a way I don't expect. A tiny pinch right under my ribs. Finn is on a dating app and out there meeting people, maybe kissing them, maybe touching them in the ways I pretend I never think about.

I shouldn't care, because we're best friends. But the thought of him laughing with someone else over drinks or waking up tangled in someone else's sheets sends a wash of heat through my chest. I look at him, my throat tight, the joke drying on my tongue.

I say nothing about any of that, but the feeling remains.

"I know." He shrugs, but his mouth fights a smile.

I glance at the time and set my phone down. "Why are you so late? Did you finally meet someone and she's not happy that your best friend's a woman?" *Insert biggest fear here.*

"I had a client run late for an estimate," he says as he raises two fingers at the bar. "Mack, can we get a couple of beers and two of the specials?"

We have dinner together here every Thursday night and always order the special. We catch up and he tells me about his week, and I tell him about mine. It's not like we don't talk every day, but I do look forward to these dinners. I won't call them dates, but they are what they are. Dinner dates between friends. *Friends.*

Mack, who is in his late fifties with a gray beard and shaggy hair, has practically been pouring drinks at The Rusty Anchor since the dawn of the Wisteria Cove sea shanties. He gives us a look that lands somewhere between fond and nosy. "How's my favorite couple?"

I roll my eyes playfully. Not this again. "Knock it off, Mack, or I'll curse your jukebox to only play Taylor Swift on repeat from now until Christmas."

He scoffs, looking offended. "But I *like* Taylor Swift."

I hold up my hands. "Hey, I do too. But we'll see how you like it when *All Too Well*, the ten-minute version, plays on repeat for the next six months straight."

Mack rolls his eyes as he puts our orders in and grabs two frosty glasses from the cooler.

Finn grins and says to Mack, "She *almost* swiped right. So close. Maybe next time."

"Don't encourage him, Finn," I mutter grumpily as I swirl a cardboard coaster in circles with my finger.

Mack snorts and places beers in front of us. "If I had to place a bet, I'd say you'll be married before the end of the year. Send me my invitation and I'll bring the kegs."

I flick a peanut at Mack, and he cackles before wandering off toward the game playing on one of the big TVs on the wall behind the bar. Finn lifts his glass and clinks it against mine like this is some kind of quiet celebration between us.

With us, it is always like there is this invisible pull that drags us right back to the same place. No matter how far life scatters us, we shift toward each other without thinking. No one knows me the way Finn does. He has known every version of me, from the quiet kid hiding behind stacks of library books to the woman trying to build a life that sometimes feels too big for her own hands. Maybe that is why I have never let myself look too closely at what I feel around him. Because it has always been there. Soft, quiet, and dangerous. A little spark under the surface that I pretend not to see between us.

We made this unspoken agreement years ago. Best friends only. Safe territory. No crossing lines that could break what we have. And I have stayed inside that boundary like it is a spell I cast on myself.

But sitting here now, watching the way he looks at me, I feel that pull in my chest again. Stronger than I want to admit. His smile is lazy and warm and something a little wilder, like he knows exactly what he does to me even if I refuse to say it out loud.

And for one breath, I let myself feel it. All of it. The bond, the history, the quiet ache I have spent years pretending I do not carry.

"So," I say, resting my chin on my hand, "how's your dating life, Contractor Ken?"

Finn is a general contractor and basically a genius at fixing or building anything. I joke he has a tool belt around his waist most of the time as a permanent accessory. But the truth is that he's good at what he does. I call him Contractor Ken to give him shit because he looks like he could be a Ken doll. The blue-collar hottie Ken version. I gotta keep my friend humble, and he does the same to me.

"Actually," he says, eyes locked on mine like he is trying to read me, "I have a date tomorrow."

The words land softer than they should, but something tightens in my chest anyway. Finn doesn't date a lot. Not seriously. So, hearing it out loud sends a strange little pinch through me, sharp enough that I feel it in my throat. I tell myself it's fine and I don't care. I try not to think about him getting dressed for someone else or smiling at someone else the way he smiles at me.

"Do you now?" I arch a brow, forcing a teasing tone. "Look at you finally swiping right."

He laughs, warm and easy. I smile back, but there is a quiet ache under it. A small twist of something I don't examine too closely, because if I do, I might have to admit what it really is.

"I'm a catch, Rowan. What can I say?" he says as his eyes meet mine and he winks.

"Well, I actually have a date tomorrow, too." I take a sip of my beer and wipe the foam from my mouth with the back of my hand. Classy.

What I don't say is that I matched with someone who isn't really a serious date at all. But Finn doesn't need to know that.

But every time I try to picture myself on a date with someone or if there'll be chemistry or anything past the first drink, my brain drifts right back to Finn. To the way he listens to me like I'm the only one in the room. Or to how safe he always makes me feel. To how easy it is to be around him and just be myself.

I had swiped right anyway. Because I should be dating. Because I should be trying. Because I refuse to let myself sit here and wait for someone who isn't mine.

But even now, saying it out loud, I can feel how halfhearted it is. A tiny part of me wonders if I'm doing this to distract myself from the way Finn makes me feel. I ignore that thought and take another drink.

We share a look that's tender and warm between us. I clear the air and say, "Want to compare notes afterwards over lunch the next day?"

"Sure." He leans back as if planning time with me is the most natural thing in the world. Then it hits me that I'm looking forward to lunch with Finn more than looking forward to the date.

"Where are you going on your date?" I ask him curiously, trying to get back to the discussion and not let my mind wander to places it shouldn't.

"I don't know yet." He shrugs. "I'll figure it out."

I scoff. "You have to put some effort into these and plan something, Finn."

He leans in and says, "Where would you like to go if *you* were my date?"

Something stirs in my lower belly when he says this. I swallow and brush it off quickly, trying to be casual. "Maybe Marco's to split a pizza, then take a walk down by the harbor. And get some ice cream at The Dairy Witch. That's what I'd choose."

"Hmm, that's a good idea. Is that where you're going?" he asks with a smirk.

"As a matter of fact, it is," I say. "Are you going to copy my date?"

"Maybe. Sounds pretty great, actually."

Mack brings out our burgers and a mountain of fries on a tray to share with various dips that we like. A cheese cup, garlic aioli sauce, and ketchup. We like variety. We fall into our usual and familiar rhythm that has always been there. Finn tells me about the floors he's restoring at his new house that he bought from our childhood friend, Tate. He bought it last fall and is fixing it up, and he's so excited about it. He asks me for my opinion on everything, but he hardly needs it. He talks about the mudroom, the built-ins he's restoring like other men talk about their favorite sports teams. It's exciting to see Finn's house coming together. It's a big old home on Main Street just down the road from my apothecary shop, Salt & Root.

He's also been helping me with my shop I got up and going last winter, but I haven't been able to get the permit from the mayor's office to run my yoga studio on the top floor. That's the last piece I've been waiting on, and I've been waiting for months for city hall to approve. I took a break for a while from teaching yoga during the winter to get Salt & Root up and going, but now I'm ready to do classes again.

I was teaching classes three nights a week at the community center, but they said that Marilyn and Vanessa have been teaching Pilates classes in my class spots now and there's no room for me to teach mine. Which makes no sense because I get texts, emails, and people stopping by every week asking me when I'm going to resume classes again.

My studio above Salt & Root is completely ready. I have all new mats, blocks, straps, and it's beautiful up there with freshly sanded and stained wood floors. Honestly, a dream space to practice yoga with bright sunlight, plants, and it's so calming up there. Just need that stupid business permit from the city that honestly makes no sense that I even have to have in the first place. Seems like a giant hoax to me. Vanessa and Marilyn both work for city hall and I suspect that they are keeping me from being able to open my studio. For reasons that I don't understand.

"Thanks for reinforcing the shelves in the shop, by the way," I say after the conversation moves from his house to my shop. "Now I don't have to worry about coming into a giant mess of herbs and glass now."

He waves me off. "No problem. I'll build you whatever you need."

My stomach flutters and I chase it with a sip of beer. That is just Finn, and he's always saying things like that. He's my best friend, I remind myself. Best friends help each other. That's all this is.

"Well, you did pretty much do everything in the shop," I say as I lean in and bump his shoulder with mine.

He reaches over, and our forearms touch as he drags a fry through the cheese sauce and eats it. His eyes are happy, with wrinkles at the corners, as he grins at me in return.

We start a roast session on each other over the dating app because I need to laugh about my non-existent love life. And Finn and I have the most epic roasts. Our banter back and forth is one of my favorite things to do. He's funny and always down to call me on my shit when needed. He's one of the few people I can be myself around. Finn scoots closer to see my screen. Our shoulders touch and heat curls low in my stomach at his warmth. And he smells so good, too.

I swipe to a bio that reads: Looking for my forever fishing partner.

Finn groans. "That's every guy in Wisteria Cove."

Another proudly calls himself The Crypto King.

I deadpan, "Oh yes. Nothing says romance like fake money and zippered hoodies. All he needs is a thick gold chain around his neck."

"Oh, he has one!" Finn says excitedly, pointing to the next picture and throwing his head back and laughing.

"Oh my gosh." I groan and laugh.

"Swipe left. Now," Finn instructs, jabbing a finger at my phone.

Mack wanders back just in time to witness our chaos and lifts a brow. "If you two spent half as much time flirting with each other as you do with chasing these poor souls on an app, you wouldn't have to worry about swiping."

"Go away, Mack," I tell him, but I'm smiling. Mack loves to give us shit.

The door swings open and in saunters Marilyn and Vanessa, aka the mean girls of Wisteria Cove, wearing matching leggings, crop tops, and ponytails. Of course, they spot us and Vanessa leans toward Marilyn and says loud enough for the entire bar to hear, "Still no permit for the witch."

I set my burger down with care. My smile goes flat and sharp.

"Hey, Marilyn and Vanessa," I call sweetly to them and am met with glares.

Finn's jaw tightens. He keeps his voice gentle as he practically growls, "Rowan."

"It's fine," I tell him and keep my eyes on the two of them. "How's your Pilates studio coming along? I can't wait to see it."

Killing them with kindness. That's what I tell myself as I stand there smiling like the calm, collected business owner I'm trying so hard to be. On the outside, I'm polite. Pleasant. The picture of someone who believes in community collaboration.

On the inside, I'm two seconds from throwing my beer all over their stupid designer leisurewear and watching it soak into their matching handbags. I can practically hear myself saying, "Acting like Grade-A bitches at forty is embarrassing. It was pathetic in high school too, sweethearts."

I smile though, teeth gritted together so I don't voice what I really want to say. My jaw hurts from the effort, but I do it. I remind myself that I'm running a business now, not casting curses behind the bleachers. I remind myself that losing my temper gives them exactly what they want.

When I'm with Finn, the restraint drops. With him, I don't have to pretend. I can say what I actually think. And what I think is that if they push me much harder, I'm not above putting them in their places.

He doesn't even flinch. He knows this version of me and he likes her. He's the only one I let see her without apology.

Marilyn gives me a thin fake smile. "We're trying to create a welcoming environment."

"Same," I say sweetly. "Minus the mean-girl soundtrack that you two are playing on a loop. I don't know if you know this, but there can be more than one fitness studio in town."

Okay, so maybe I can't completely bite my tongue. Oops.

They huff and drift away. Finn shifts, narrowing his gaze.

"I really don't like those two," Finn mutters as he pushes his empty plate away.

"You and me both," I say, shaking my head. "I'm convinced they're in on it with Mayor Sammy Briggs about holding up my permit. I can't prove it, but I'm pretty sure they're sabotaging me."

"If I find out they are…" Finn bites out, shoulders tense as he trails off, letting me fill in the blanks of his warning.

"They probably are," I tell him. "I just have to do my thing. Let them do theirs."

"You're pretty calm about this," he says, eyes narrowed as he studies me.

I shrug. "I'm trying to be good. I'm a Wisteria Cove business owner and I want people to take me seriously."

"You eating okay?" he asks, changing the subject, looking down at half my burger still on my plate. "You were also picking at your lunch when I stopped by the shop yesterday."

There it is. The soft moment that he always has for me. "I'm fine."

"Want me to talk to the mayor?"

I frown and shake my head. "I can fight my own battles."

He nods, but his eyes say he's going to quietly fight them anyway.

We get back to the app. He critiques how I rarely make it to a second date until I remind him of his own dating issues. "Please, you never even make it to a second date with anyone either."

"Maybe I have standards."

"Maybe you just get bored," I say dryly.

He drags his gaze over my face and mouth, and right now, he doesn't look bored at all. After a beat, he looks away, focusing on his empty plate like it holds the secrets of the universe. My pulse races, and I pretend it doesn't.

"Oh, hey, I forgot your song for the day," he says as he slides off his stool. "I'll be right back."

I watch as he crosses the bar to the jukebox. He flips through songs and retrieves quarters from his pocket. He leans against the wall and waits for it to load. He has to jiggle the side of the jukebox, and why that looks sexy, I don't know, but it does. Finn is a big guy with wide shoulders, and I hate that when I look at him, I have all these feelings. Feelings I shouldn't be having and chase out of my mind every time.

Don't Stop Believin' fills the room and I laugh. Of course he'd pick that one. For years, music has been a thing for Finn and me. Every time we see each other, we take turns picking a song and either texting it to each other or playing it for each other. Finn usually brings a performance into the mix and sings it to me in his off-key voice. I pretend to be annoyed, but it's funny. From rock classics to silly pop songs, we pick songs we think the other one might like or that remind us about something in our lives at that moment. I've been compiling a playlist of all our songs since we've been doing this. It's a really long playlist now, but I listen to it sometimes, and each song reminds me of a memory of him.

Mack takes our plates and refills our beers as Finn slides in next to me.

"What do you think about your song?" he asks as he sings the lyrics, looking into my eyes. He offers his fist to me. "Here, hold my microphone."

"Stop it." I laugh and wave his hand away.

He continues to sing softly, tapping his boot on the bar stool to the song.

"It's a good song, a classic. I'll have to think up an even better one for your song tomorrow," I add, sipping my beer.

When it's time to head out, we slide off our stools, and the entire bar seems to tilt an ear as we head for the door, and it's not even subtle. Wisteria Cove never is. It's full of meddlers and nosy neighbors. On our way out, Marilyn says something snarky that I can't make out. Vanessa pretends not to look at us, but I see her side eyeing us. I give them both my brightest smile and pat Finn's chest like he's my trophy. He's busy talking to a buddy of his and doesn't seem to notice. Then his hand slides over my lower back and he guides me out of the bar. I almost trip because I can barely focus with him touching me.

Outside, we head down Main Street. His hands slide into his pockets. He walks me to the door of Wisteria Books & Brews, where I'm living above my sister's bookstore in her loft apartment for now. I have a small cottage I rent where I grow all my plants and have a greenhouse, but I like to be closer to the shop. When the cottage kept getting mold and everything broke down inside, I turned it into a little micro farm instead of living out there. The heat was sketchy last winter and when Willa moved out to the tree farm with Tate, I took her up on her offer of staying above the bookstore.

Finn leans in and says, "Have fun on your date tomorrow night."

"You, too. Maybe you'll make it to a second date with this one," I tease.

"That a challenge, Maren?" he asks.

"Maybe. Let's see if we can both make it to a second date." Highly unlikely on my end, but he doesn't need to know that.

He steps closer, near enough that I feel the heat of him before I even register the movement. His chest brushes mine for just a second, light enough to pretend it did not happen, heavy enough that my breath stutters anyway. I can smell cedar and soap on his shirt. It wraps around me before I can blink.

He reaches past me to open the door, his hand near my shoulder, his arm practically caging me in. His face is close, and his voice drops just a little, warm and sure. "I'll see you at lunch on Saturday."

His words move across my cheek like a touch. I swear the air changes. I nod, but my fingers curl around the strap of my bag to steady myself. My pulse races.

He holds the door there, waiting, watching me with this soft, unreadable expression that sinks right into the center of my chest. For a heartbeat, I wonder if he feels it too. This spark, this pull, this thing we have spent our entire lives pretending we do not notice.

"Sounds good." I smile. "Hopefully, my date won't turn out like the last one."

That guy was super creepy. He asked me how big my toes were and kept staring at my feet. That was when I excused myself to the ladies' room and called Finn who somehow made it there in record time and pulled me out the window by my ass. We still laugh about that story. That night he played *Getaway Car* for me on repeat, and we laughed the whole way home singing at the top of our lungs.

"You won't win the worst date wager," I say. "I still hold that title."

"That's for sure." He nods and flashes a grin, the easy kind he uses when he wants everything to seem fine. "You never know. Maybe tomorrow night you'll find the one."

There is something in his tone that doesn't match the grin. It's light and teasing but edged with something I can't quite place. His eyes hold mine for a second too long, like he's waiting for an answer I don't know how to give. The words sound like a joke, but the look... the look feels like worry or something close to it. Something warm and complicated that tightens the air between us for a breath before he clears his throat and turns away.

And I tell myself I imagined it, even though I feel it settling under my skin.

"I challenge you to find someone worse than Toe Guy," I say, trying to ease some lightheartedness into the conversation.

We shake on it. His hand's big, calloused, and comforting. The second our palms meet, a spark races up my arm like a live current. My breath catches before I can stop it. His touch feels grounded, steady, but there's something electric underneath, something that makes my pulse trip over itself. I tell myself it's just the magic reacting, but deep down, I know it's him.

"Night, Carpenter Ken," I call as he walks away.

He half turns, that grin catching the glow of the streetlamp. "Night, Hexy Barbie."

The sound of his voice hangs in the air long after he's gone. I stand there, pretending the chill crawling over my skin is from the breeze and not the way he said it.

But as his silhouette disappears down the street, the lie settles heavy in my chest.

Because no amount of small talk or first-date smiles could ever make me feel the way his goodbye just did.

And I already know that I'm in trouble.

CHAPTER 2
Finn

I WILL SURVIVE BY GLORIA GAYNOR

I TELL myself I'm a grown man who can go on a normal date without thinking about the beautiful witch with flowery ink winding up her arms like it was drawn just for me to trace. About the way she moves when she's stretching, laughing or bending over that damn yoga mat—nope, not going there. Absolutely *not* picturing that.

It is better than picturing her sitting across from some guy who thinks he's good enough for her, because he won't be. Not even close. Some guy who won't understand how Rowan works, how her mind spins three directions at once and somehow lands in the right place every time. Some guy who has never sat with her on the cliff at fifteen, sharing a bag of stale marshmallows while she talked about all the things she wished she was brave enough to want. Some guy who didn't fall in love with her the moment he saw her marching into homeroom in eighth grade wearing combat boots and holding a stack of books almost as tall as she was.

He won't know her the way I do. That she's guarded because people she trusted taught her to be. That she cares harder than anyone should have to. That she's my person. My constant. My home. And I hate every part of pretending I am fine with these dates. I say it out loud like it is my personal mantra.

"You're fine."

But the lie hits the shower tile and echoes back at me. Pathetic.

Date day. Sure, everything's fine. It actually isn't fine at all.

I shower and shave and try to convince myself this is progress and not punishment. That maybe if Rowan dates a few of these guys, she will eventually look up and see me standing right here in front of her. Available and ready to hand her the whole damn world if she'd let me.

I pull on a white T-shirt that is soft from too many washes, then grab a flannel that smells like detergent instead of sawdust for once. My jeans creak a little because they are still too new. I'm supposed to look date-ready, not like a man quietly losing his mind over a woman who has been part of his heartbeat for more than half his life.

But when I meet my own eyes in the mirror, all I can think about is how Rowan would give me shit for trying too hard. How she'd tug on my collar and tell me I look better in older jeans. How she'd tilt her head and look at me with those soft, knowing eyes that always see more than I want her to.

God. I wish she saw everything. I wish she saw me.

But for now, all I can do is pretend I'm okay while she goes out searching for *the one*.

Even though I've known for years that *she's* the one for me.

It's fine. Totally fine. Except it's not. Not even close. I text Rowan.

Are you ready for your date?

My thumb hovers over send, like I'm a teenager and not a grown ass man with a massive crush on his best friend. I hit send. My phone buzzes a minute later.

Rowan: Send me a selfie. I need to approve the outfit.

I snap a selfie and send it.

Where's my selfie?

Another buzz. She sends a link to a song for the day. *I Will Survive by Gloria Gaynor.*

Solid song choice. Again, where's MY selfie?

Rowan: Looking like the poster boy for Small-Town Tinder. Don't break too many hearts tonight, Carpenter Ken.

Rude. She didn't send me my selfie. I send back a winky face emoji and slide my phone into my pocket.

I walk down to Marco's and when I'm halfway there, my phone buzzes in my pocket. I pull it out and it's a selfie of Rowan leaning over, blowing a kiss towards the camera in a black dress, and *damn.* She looks absolutely gorgeous. I wish I was picking her up right now for a date. It makes me beyond pissed some asshole will be picking her up and taking her to dinner and I hate that it's not me. But this is the game she wants to play, so we're playing it.

The minute I open the door to Marco's, it smells like garlic, tomato and cheese, and my stomach rumbles at the familiar smells. It's literally one of my favorite places to eat, minus my older brother Remy's pizza nights he puts on every Friday. Marco has him slightly beat, but I'd never tell Remy that. They're both winners.

The dinner crowd noise hums through the room. Serena, my date, seems like a nice woman from her text messages. We probably have nothing in common based on her profile, but she asked me out, so I figured why not.

And there she is, waiting near the hostess stand, scrolling on her phone with her lips pursed. She's pretty with dark hair curled around her shoulders and a white blouse that looks like it probably requires dry cleaning. She has an expensive-looking watch, and jewelry on her fingers and wrists that look like they're worth more than my truck. She tucks her phone away when she sees me and gives me the once-over like a manager checking over an employee.

"Hi." I smile warmly and hold out my hand. "I'm Finn."

"I know," she says with a small smile, looking at my hand and back at me, not taking it to shake. "I recognize you from your pictures. You look taller in person."

"Thanks." I don't know what to do with that statement, so I just tuck my hands in my pockets.

Bart, a college kid with a small mustache, leads us to a booth near the window. Marco isn't on the floor. You can always tell when he's here. The volume in the room bumps up, and people laugh more. Marco treats you like you are family when you eat at his restaurant. I wait for Serena to choose which side she wants to sit on and wait.

"So," she says, opening her menu as if it's a file when Bart walks away. "What do you do exactly? Your profile said construction, but that could mean a lot of things."

"I build and remodel houses," I say, not even bothering to look at the menu. I know it by heart. "Kitchens, decks, bathrooms, that sort of thing. I also do custom cabinetry out of my wood shop, and sometimes I do the less pretty stuff like gutting, framing, and electrical rough-in. It depends on the day."

She nods as if this is satisfactory, and she's taking notes. "And do you plan to keep doing that long term?"

Damn. This feels like a job interview. "I love it." I shrug with a smile. "I'm good at it, and I take pride in making something that lasts. It's art for me."

"Sure," she says. "But what's the big plan? In five years, where do you see yourself?"

"Still building. Owning more equipment, taking on bigger

projects, and teaching apprentices. Probably buying property to flip."

She opens her phone while I am still talking, and the light reflects in her dark brown eyes. She angles the camera toward herself, smoothing her hair and lifting her chin, and snaps one photo, then another, then a third, then checks them, scanning and flipping to add in filters. I glance around nervously, not sure what to say to this.

"Sorry," she says. "I promised my group chat I would update them. We have a thing where we rate first impressions."

"Really? What's the update?"

"We just talk about whether we are wasting our time," she says. "You know, the usual girl talk."

The usual. That's essentially what Rowan and I do. Honestly, I don't even care how I rate to her and her friends. I don't even want to be here. But my mom raised me right, so I'll be polite and nice.

"What if we split a pizza? Do you like pepperoni or are you into something else? Marco also does good garlic cheese knots."

She tilts her head as if she's giving me a test and waiting to see if I'll pass it or not. "Garlic knots have too many carbs. We can do half with ham and pineapple. I know people fight about pineapple, and I don't care. I like it."

"Half and half works." I don't care about what people want on pizza. People can eat whatever make them happy.

Bart swings by with a notepad.

Serena lights up like she is on stage. "*Ciao,*" she says. "*Possiamo avere una pizza grande, metà con peperoni e metà con ananas. E due bicchieri di vino bianco.*"

Bart blinks. "Uh," he mutters, looking back and forth between Serena and me with confusion. Then he glances toward the kitchen like he wants to make a run for it.

"Hey, Bart," I say cheerfully. "Can we get a large half pepperoni and half pineapple with ham? A white wine for the lady, and a beer for me."

Serena frowns with disappointment at Bart. "You don't speak Italian?"

"No, ma'am, I'm from Ohio," Bart admits with a sheepish laugh. "Sorry. And yes, I can get that put in."

Serena sighs. "Nobody in this town cares about authenticity. Except Marco. Everyone else is uncultured."

"I can go get Marco," the kid says, eyes wide like a deer caught in the headlights.

She waves a hand. "Never mind."

He leaves and I keep my mouth shut, but I can feel the edges of a headache forming. I glance at my watch discreetly to check the time.

"So," I say, trying to make conversation. "You work at the bank?"

She perks up. "Assistant branch manager," she says proudly. "I've been on a leadership track to have my own branch by next year if my numbers hold and if no one blocks me with internal politics. Which is probable because men get weird about women in leadership. You know."

I shake my head, smirking. "Not me. But I see it all the time, and I get it. The world doesn't exactly roll out the red carpet for women bosses, and men can be assholes sometimes." I was raised by a ballsy single mom who didn't take shit from anybody, but I also saw how she was treated by some people precisely because there was no man around. Ignorance and sexism are universal, but not in my mom's house.

She tucks a piece of hair behind her ear and leans forward. "You know, you could do more than construction if you wanted. You have presence, Finnegan. You could get into finance or real estate. There are so many options."

"I like what I do," I repeat. "It makes me happy. And I go by Finn."

My mind starts to wander, and I wonder what Rowan would think of Serena and her trying to change me into a corporate fella. She and I will probably joke about it tomorrow at lunch.

"Happy is what people settle for when they don't have ambition," she says lightly, as if this is a joke and not an insult. "And Finnegan is so much more worldly. People will take you more seriously." She snaps another selfie. "Smile," she adds, and turns her phone camera toward me without permission and takes a picture.

I blink and grit my teeth.

"I am not great at photos," I say, as I take a sip of the water that Bart just set down with the beer.

"Anyone can be great at photos," she says. "Angles and light. You just need to practice, and I can teach you."

I'm thirty-two and I know my angles. They are the corners of the cabinets I mitered last week until the seam was soft as a fingertip. I don't care about photos for social media. I don't even remember the last time I even checked my social media. I'm too busy working and living my life in real time with the people I love. Annoyance rolls through my chest, but I smile anyway because I'm at Marco's where the pizza will be the best and maybe if I'm lucky I'll catch a glance of Rowan here in that black dress.

Serena takes a picture of her wine and asks to do cheers. I pretend to clink and miss because she is busy finding the right filter and she doesn't notice. The pizza lands on the table with a heavy thud. The pepperoni curls at the edges and my mouth is practically watering. The pineapple glows like little suns.

"Thanks, Bart." I give him an appreciative nod.

He glances at Serena and gives me a smile. "Let me know if you need anything."

"So what do you do for fun?" she asks as she ignores Bart, already holding the slice up for a photo. Cheese drips in slow motion. She's barely put her phone down since we've been here.

"Sometimes I go out on my friend's boat when the weather lets me, and I help my friends and family with their house projects. And I'm working on restoring a house I bought from a friend. It keeps me busy, and it's good."

"That doesn't sound like fun," she says, wrinkling her nose. "What about travel and fashion? Or wine tastings? I am planning a trip to Napa in the fall."

I chew and swallow, closing my eyes. The pepperoni hits perfect as usual. "I love this pizza," I say, ignoring her question because I could care less about fashion. Traveling sounds fun, but probably not the kind of travel she'd be doing. My idea of traveling is restoring a camper van, hitting the open road, and stopping at all the cool places. I'm guessing hers might be a little more glamorous and involve first class flights.

She shrugs as she looks down at the pizza. "It's okay."

Wow. Seriously? It's the best food in town, and I'm surprised she's not into this. It's her loss.

She sets her slice down and wipes her fingers. Then she picks up her phone and looks at me like an evaluator again. "Where do you see yourself in ten years?"

Okay, so we're back at this again.

"I'm living in the house I'm remodeling," I tell her, the words coming out of me as I picture it all. "There's a big kitchen island with crayons and puzzles on it, a long dining table where game nights and amazing meals happen with all my family and friends. Outside, there are rocking chairs on the back porch, facing the water, and the old shed's a wood workshop where I tackle all my projects. I get home before dinner every night because we cook together as a family. There's a dog waiting for me in the driveway, a bunch of kids running through the yard, and the most beautiful woman there who's living her dream too. She's got dirt on her hands from gardening and a smile that makes the whole place feel like home."

She blinks, looking bored. "That sounds very domestic."

"Yeah," I say with a smile. It sounds like pure heaven to me. This is everything I'm working towards.

"I'm not sure I want children," she says, examining her nails like she's daring me to argue. Which I won't. Anyone can do what makes them happy.

She adds, almost to herself, "I just can't risk my career for kids." She says, "kids" as if they're bugs or something gross, like they're completely repulsive.

There's a lot of things I want to tell her. Specifically, that statement is wildly derogatory. I know plenty of women who have amazing careers and families. I do work for a lot of them and even work alongside many. And they're killing it and seem happy. I work around a lot of fathers who are also doing great at having both a family and a career, like my brother Remy. But I say nothing, because I truly don't care. She could say the sky is purple right now and I'd say of course it is. I truly don't care.

"I get it. People want different things. Nothing wrong with that," I say instead.

She picks up her phone again and checks her reflection in the camera. She turns the phone slightly and smiles, snapping another. I sip my beer and let my eyes wander the room. The door of the restaurant opens, and in comes a small cluster of voices. I feel her there before I see her. Rowan.

She's in that black dress that ties at the waist. Her thick, long dark hair is up in a messy knot that looks sexy as hell, a few pieces hanging down over her cheeks. I love it when she does her hair like that. She's with a much older man. A pale crown of white hair around a bald top. A crisp brown button-down shirt tucked into pleated pants. He looks like he is old enough to be her grandfather and reminds me of a professor.

Rowan and Professor Midlife Crisis get a high-top table near the center. He sits with his back to the kitchen and Rowan sits across from him, setting her bag on the seat beside her. She gives the host a kind smile. The man keeps staring at her while she talks. It makes my jaw go tight. *Don't even look at her, you crypt keeper.*

"Hello," Serena says, waving to me.

"Sorry," I say. "Someone I know just walked in."

She twists and follows my gaze. "The woman? Do you like her?"

"She's a friend."

"That guy she's with looks really old," Serena says wrinkling her nose, watching them. "Is that her grandfather?"

I don't answer. Serena makes a small sound that could be a laugh and takes a bite of pizza.

"She's pretty." She lowers her voice and adds. "He's okay, but looks kind of boring."

I choke. "Harsh."

"I'm not wrong," she says. "Also, she could do better."

She's damn right, Rowan can do better. She's mine.

The human retirement plan lifts his glass and leans in. He says something that makes Rowan tip her head and look at her menu again. She gives a polite smile, and her fingers tap the table, three soft taps, the way she does when she's trying to be patient. I have the urge to walk over, take her by the hand, and march her out of here. It wouldn't be the first time I've sprung her from a bad date.

Serena watches me watch Rowan and then sighs. "I knew it. You have it bad for her."

"Hey, I'm on a date with you," I object with a grin.

"You're on a date physically," she says. "The rest of you is over there. Which is fine. I'm not offended."

I sit back and hate that this is true.

"Look," Serena says. "You seem nice. You also seem like you want a wife, kids on a porch, and a dog. I want a bonus and a penthouse with a wine fridge. We'd hate each other. Also, your friend owns Salt & Root, right? The witch store?"

"It isn't a witch store," I say out of habit. "It's an apothecary."

"See," Serena says softly, and it's the first time her voice doesn't sound like it came from a boardroom. "You talk about her like I want someone to talk about wine and traveling with me."

I rub the back of my neck, unsure what to say to that. "I'm sorry."

"Don't be," she says. "You're honest, and that's admirable. We can wrap this up."

"Let me get the check and walk you out."

She nods and reaches for her phone again. She takes one last selfie, checks it, and then drops the phone in her bag with a little sigh. "For what it's worth," she says. "You and her would make a beautiful couple."

"Thanks." I glance back at Rowan again. She looks over at me and gives me a small smile, then turns back to Mr. AARP.

We'll discuss him tomorrow.

Serena stands and I toss cash on the table before flagging down Bart to box up the pizza. I want to leave it, but Rowan loves cold pizza for breakfast, so I'm going to take it for her.

We walk toward the door. I keep my eyes forward. I fail and glance left. Vintage Ken leans even closer and tells a joke while wiggling his eyebrows. They dance like thick caterpillars. I cringe as Rowan laughs out of politeness and lifts her water to take a sip.

We could be having fun.

I turn and hold the door for Serena, and she gently touches my arm. "Thanks for dinner, Finnegan."

"No problem. I hope you have a great time on your Napa trip. Stay safe."

Outside, the air is bright, and I walk her to her car around the corner. At her door, she pauses and looks me over again, but softer now.

"You really are handsome," she says, giving me a small smile. "I hope your apothecary friend sees it."

"Thanks." I grin. But Rowan doesn't see it. She's made it clear that I am in the permanent friend zone. Meanwhile I want to bulldoze that friend zone.

Serena unlocks her car and slides in. "And hey, tell your friend that her shop is amazing. My friend and I were there a few weeks ago and bought tea blends from her. We had a lot of fun."

I smile. "I'll tell her."

She pulls away with a wave. I stand there for a beat and my phone buzzes. A new text from Rowan.

Rowan: How's it going? Do I need to send an extraction team?

I look through the glass of Marco's window. The older man is talking with his hands and leaning in again. Rowan is nodding but isn't smiling with her eyes, and keeps glancing at her lap where she's trying secretly to text me. I type back.

You look like you need the extraction team more than I do with Sugar Pension.

Rowan: Haha, very funny. He's very nice. He's telling me about all his grandkids.

I'm heading out. My date was fine. I saved my leftover pizza for you. Don't keep Grandpa out too late.

She replies with a skull emoji, then a heart.

I put my phone in my pocket and step off the curb. I tell myself to be good and leave her to her date with Sir Wrinkleton. She'll never choose him anyway. He's not her type. It's me. I'm her type.

CHAPTER 3
Rowan

I STILL HAVEN'T FOUND
WHAT I'M LOOKING FOR BY U2

"FINN'S HERE." Willa's voice floats from the front of the shop, cheerful as she waves out the big storefront window of Salt & Root.

I lift my head from the counter and pause for a breath, letting my gaze drift across the space I built with my own two hands. The morning sunlight pours through the glass, soft and golden, warming the wooden floorboards I helped sand myself. The shelves along the far wall are lined with amber bottles and glass jars, each labeled in my handwriting. Lavender buds. Rose hips. Wild honey. Dried orange peel. The air smells like bergamot, vanilla, and eucalyptus.

The counter behind me is cluttered in the way I like it. A stack of worksheets from my last workshop. A bowl of citrine I put out for "prosperity" even though I know half the customers only come in because they think the crystals are pretty. Freshly poured lotion cooling in ceramic jars. Tea blends waiting to be packed into brown paper bags. Every piece of it is a little part of me. Hours of stirring and measuring and testing. Late nights at this very counter with a cup of chamomile while I tried to believe I could actually make this dream work.

Salt & Root is small, but it feels alive. It's my special place.

I hear the familiar sound of Finn's boots outside the door. Heavy, warm, steady. The kind of footsteps that make the floor feel grounded beneath me.

I straighten, suddenly aware of the smudge of dried calendula oil on my wrist and the way my braid is slipping loose. My heartbeat changes. Not faster, just deeper, like it knows him before my mind catches up.

The bell over the door jingles, and the air shifts. It always does when he walks in. Like Salt & Root inhales at the exact same time I do.

Finn steps inside, bringing the smell of cedar and a blast of warm air with him. For a second the shop feels even more like home.

Suddenly the music in the shop changes, and *I Still Haven't Found What I'm Looking For* plays over the Bluetooth speaker.

I snort because that little shit hooked his phone up to my speaker system. He sets down a pizza box, then breaks into a performance of him dancing and then singing into his fist like it's his imaginary microphone. He dances around the shop, sidling up to me, singing, bumping his hip into mine. He leans back against the counter, and still sings to the song, making me laugh even harder.

Willa laughs from the doorway between our shops and dances to the music, singing along. Finn dances over to her and sings to her as well. Both give it an all-star performance.

"You're both ridiculous." I shake my head. But I secretly love it.

I put my hands on my hips over my shop apron and shake my head, trying not to giggle. He does this to make me laugh, putting on these pretend performances. I don't think he cares at all that people can see us and that he looks ridiculous.

He stops performing and leans against the counter. "How was your date with the fossil? Did he tell you stories about the Great Depression?"

"Finn," I warn but crack up laughing.

He holds up his hands. "Hey, Grandpa Honeysuckle might have it going on. What do I know?"

"How was *your* date?" I ask as I turn the questioning back to him.

Tom was a very nice widow who didn't quite understand how the dating app worked. He was thrilled he got to go to dinner with someone young and fun to talk to about his family with. The man was sweet as pie and we made plans to go out as friends again. He said he doesn't see his family very often because most of them are scattered around the country. Tom was interesting and loves gardening. We talked a lot about plants, and he had some great tips for me. His profile photo that he used on the app was over twenty years old, which still makes me laugh that I fell for it. But as far as dates go, he was a super nice fella.

"Oh, no. We're still talking about your silver fox special."

"Are you done with the jokes, yet?" I snort laugh.

"Not even close." Finn shrugs, scooting the pizza box closer to me. I reach over and pull out a cold slice and take a bite, moaning with delight. Marco's the day after, and cold, might be the second-best thing to hot and fresh out of the wood fire. Finn watches me with an unreadable expression. Last night I got the pasta, and I didn't have leftovers to take home. Finn is the best for thinking about me.

"That's gross," Willa says as she shudders. "Who eats cold pizza like that? At least let me make you a breakfast sandwich that's warm."

I shrug, enjoying it and not caring. "I'm good." I didn't realize how hungry I was. Lunch isn't for a few more hours and the shop's been so busy this morning.

Finn flips through the new tea blends I've been sorting.

"What's he talking about, anyway? Who did you go on a date with?" Willa gives me a confused look.

I look at Finn and mutter, "Big mouth."

Finn practically cackles. "She had a distinguished gentleman caller."

"Stop it," I clip, but giggle.

"Row, he probably has loafers older than me."

"I'm going to kill you." I shake my head at him, continuing to enjoy my cold pizza.

"Nah, you won't. Who'll bring you cold pizza and grease your back door so it won't squeak?" he says as he roots around behind the counter and produces a can of WD-40 before heading over to spray the back door.

"Now I won't know when people come in. The squeak was the warning," I protest.

He shakes his head at me and sprays the door hinges on both sides.

"Thank God. The squeaky sound was so annoying," Willa says. "Thanks, Finn!"

He smirks my way. "At least someone appreciates me."

"I appreciate you and your pizza very much," I say as I take another piece out of the box. Breakfast of champions.

He turns to the sink to wash his hands. "Did he at least pay?"

"Of course he did."

"Bet he had to write a check."

I laugh so hard my stomach hurts. "You're the worst."

"Wrong," he says with a shrug. "Baby, I'm the best."

We won't talk about the way my stomach dips when he calls me baby.

"And what about you?" I ask. "How was your date? Did Miss Influencer get enough selfies for her social media?"

His mouth twitches. "You know exactly how that went."

"Boring?"

"Worse. She tried to speak Italian to Bart."

"Maybe she's cultured."

He nods, "She was something."

I snort. "Okay, fine. I'm sorry your night wasn't as exciting as mine."

I'm actually not sorry at all.

He grins, that slow, easy one that makes something in my

chest twist. "It's not that it wasn't exciting. It just reminded me of what I don't want and reminded me of what I do."

I don't ask what that means because I'm too busy pretending I don't care.

I sigh and reach for my planner to look over my to-do list for today. I'm so overwhelmed. "I'm not sure I can get away for lunch today. I've got orders to pack and a wholesale shipment to finish. And only three hours to get it all done. Then, this weekend, I have to work on my plants when my part time help arrives."

He shrugs. "That's fine. I'll grab sandwiches for us."

"You don't have to do that."

"Didn't say I had to. Said I wanted to. See you at lunch. Bye, Willa." He waves to us and heads out to the front porch.

"Bye!" Willa calls from the bookstore side of our businesses. There's a doorway between us that we keep open so we can help each other out.

And that's Finn. Blowing in here like a tornado, making me laugh so hard it hurts. He makes it feel lighter, more fun, and thinks about me. Like bringing me his leftover cold pizza. Might be gross or dumb to some, but the fact that he thinks of me like that means everything to me. He pays attention to everything I like and don't. Once, I caught him with a whole list on his phone of my favorite foods and the ones I dislike. He shrugged it off like it was no big deal, but no one has ever done anything like that for me before.

"Why are you going on dates with a grandpa?" Willa asks as she brings me a steaming latte with a plant design in the foam.

"That's so pretty," I say, hoping to change the subject. "Thank you."

"Uh uh, I know what you're doing." Willa places her hands on her hips and waits for me to answer.

"Finn and I both had dates last night at Marco's. He was giving me shit about my date, who happened to be an older man." I shrug as if it's no big deal.

"You guys are so weird. Why you're fighting this, I'll never understand." Willa shakes her head and sits on a tall stool at my counter.

"We have been over this," I say, waving her off like the whole thing is ridiculous, even though my stomach twists. "Finn is my best friend. Why would I mess that up?" I try to sound light, teasing. "Do you know how hard it is to find a best friend who brings you his cold pizza leftovers from his date the night before? I am telling you… no one."

The joke slips out easily, but it covers the truth sitting heavy in my chest. Finn is not just my best friend. He's my anchor, and the person who shows up at my door on the nights I can't breathe. The one who fixes shelves without being asked and the one who steadies me when my world leans sideways. Losing him would break something in me I couldn't put back together.

And under all of it, there's that other fear. The one I never say out loud. That I would ruin everything if I reached for more. That I would take this beautiful, quiet, safe thing we have built and light it on fire with my own clumsy hands. What if he doesn't want me the way I want him? What if I'm not enough? What if love is something I'm not built for, no matter how badly I want to pretend I am?

So, I laugh and make a joke about leftover pizza, because it's easier than admitting the truth: I'd rather starve for him in silence than lose him by trying.

"Do you know how insane that sounds? The fact that he's thinking of you while he's on a date in the first place is wild," she says, eyebrow arching.

I just shrug.

Willa has a customer and hurries back to her shop but shakes her head as she mutters, "You're both delusional."

———

The bell above the front door hasn't rung in half an hour, and the shop finally smells like lavender and lemon balm instead of stress and caffeine. I'm labeling tinctures when I hear the low rumble of a truck out back.

I glance out the window and see Finn swing in and park like he's done it a thousand times. The bed of his truck is piled high with lumber, buckets, and what looks like building supplies. He climbs out, flips his ball cap backward, and adjusts it with an effortless ease that should not make my stomach flip. He grabs a brown paper bag, tucks it under his arm, and balances two drinks in his hands.

When he's strolling up to the back door, his eyes find mine through the window, and he smiles, wrinkles fanning from the corners of his eyes, warm and easy. It's like he already knows I've been working too long and didn't even need to ask what I'd need. He just knows like he always does.

I push open the now quiet back door and hold it for him as he ducks and folds himself in. The doorframe's too low for him. Always has been.

"Hey, Row," he says. "Get caught up?"

"Almost. Trying to stay productive before my next mental breakdown."

He sets the bag on the counter and pulls out two sandwiches. "You need better coping mechanisms."

"This *is* my coping mechanism," I say, gesturing to the herbs, the scales, the entire witchy chaos of my life.

He gives me that half-smile that does dangerous things to my pulse.

We eat at the counter. He tells me about helping his brother Remy fix a fence in the goat pen that a recent storm took out. I tell him about a woman who asked if my herbal pain salve could cure her husband's erectile dysfunction.

"She was serious?" he asks with a chuckle. "Poor dude."

"Dead serious."

His laughter intensifies, nearly having him choke on his sandwich, and then he wipes his mouth with the back of his hand.

The laughter fades a little when I mention what I heard earlier.

"Mayor Briggs was doing one of his fancy tours this morning," I say, sipping my drink. "He pointed at the bookstore entrance to the apothecary and told his group that 'a shady witch runs this place.'"

Finn stops mid-bite. "He said that?" The words are calm, but something in his face changes. His jaw tightens just enough to make a muscle jump and his eyes go darker, sharper, like a storm rolled in. He sets his drink down slowly as if he's fighting the urge to stand up and go find the guy right now.

I know that look. It is the same one he gets when someone cuts Junie off in a crosswalk or when a tourist is rude to Willa at the shop. Protective, controlled, and a little dangerous. I've seen both him and Remy with the same demeanor.

But this time it's for me.

His voice stays steady, but the anger leaks through the cracks. "Rowan. He talked about you like that?"

And God help me, my heart does something it should not do when he looks at me that way.

"Oh yeah, real professional, right? Probably thought he was being funny."

"What'd you say?"

I smirk. "I asked if he wanted me to turn his toupée into a familiar."

Finn groans, grinning despite himself. "You made fun of his toupée again? Are you trying to never get your permit?"

"I don't care," I say, my voice sharp and cool. "If I have to kiss that man's ass to get what I need, he can keep his permit and his bald spot."

"Row," he says, amused but cautious, "you're a menace and probably the reason why he has no hair."

"A witch never tells her spells," I say, crossing my arms.

He laughs again, but I can tell he's half ready to step in before I start an all-out war. Which is fair. I'm halfway there already. I'm sick of him messing with my business and my livelihood.

I pull out my phone. "You know what, I'm calling his office."

Finn leans against the counter, watching me as he chews. "This should be good."

The phone rings twice before a chipper voice answers. "Mayor Briggs's office."

"Hi, I need to schedule a meeting with the mayor about my permit."

"Let me check his calendar," Marilyn says, her voice dripping with customer-service sugar.

I wait, phone pressed to my ear, pacing behind the counter. For a second, there is quiet shuffling, keys clicking. Normal. Professional.

"This is Rowan Maren."

And then I hear it. The change. That tiny inhale, the pause that lasts a beat too long.

Her tone cools instantly, like someone opened a freezer door. "He's... busy this week."

Of course he is. He's always suddenly booked solid the second Rowan Maren calls. My irritation sparks fast and familiar. We've done this dance before. Marilyn pretending the mayor is available for everyone but me. Acting like she's protecting the town from some kind of apothecary-related uprising. I can practically picture her expression right now, that tight little smirk she gets when she thinks she's won something.

I grip the phone tighter. My pulse flicks with anger I'm trying to keep under control. I need this meeting. I need answers. I need the damn town council to stop keeping me from running my business.

And Marilyn knows it. I can hear the smugness creeping into her voice, soft but unmistakable, as if she's savoring every second of making this harder for me.

I swallow hard, trying to keep my own tone polite, but inside my frustration is coiling tight, sinking deep. This is not just a scheduling conflict, it's personal.

"Then squeeze me in somewhere, please," I say.

"He has several very important appointments."

"Like his daily nap between ego inflation and donut consumption?"

"Excuse me?" she asks.

"Never mind," I say, hanging up before she can reply.

Finn blinks. "Getting sick of this?"

"She's trying my patience," I say, grabbing my bag.

"Where are you going?"

"Up there."

"Up where?" he asks, setting down his sandwich.

"City Hall."

He follows me to the door. "I'm coming."

"No, you'd only try to stop me from what I'm going to do."

"Row—"

I hold up my finger. "If you want to help, you can watch the shop for me. If I don't come back in thirty minutes, come get me. I'll probably need bail money."

———

City Hall smells like stale coffee, a cheap candle, and someone's stinky lunch. The fluorescent lights buzz overhead in a way that makes my teeth itch, and the air tastes like old paperwork and grudges. My heels click down the hallway with a rhythm that feels like purpose, like anger sharpened to a point.

Marilyn looks up from her desk the second she hears me. Her eyes widen, then narrow into a smug little sliver. Her blouse buttons are off by one, the fabric slightly askew across her chest, and for a moment she looks startled that I noticed. A soft blush creeps up her neck. Interesting.

"You can't go in there," she says, voice clipped and tight.

"Watch me," I say, and push open the door.

Mayor Sammy Briggs's office hits me like a wave of cheap cologne and clutter. The blinds are half-closed even though it is midday, casting slanted shadows across piles of unfiled paperwork. A half-eaten sandwich sits on his desk, next to a crumpled napkin with Marilyn's glittery handwriting on it. His tie is askew, and he slouches behind his desk.

He's not doing paperwork or reviewing permits. He is hunched over his phone, the bright glow of the screen reflecting off his glasses. The sound effects from his game chirp through the room. He's playing Candy Crush. While my business sits in limbo because of him.

My blood heats. "Real busy with appointments, huh, Mayor?" I cross my arms, letting my voice carry.

He jerks so hard he drops his phone. It clatters across the desk. He fumbles for it, then freezes when he finally registers me standing there. "Ms. Maren. This is highly inappropriate."

"What's inappropriate" I hiss, stepping farther into the room, "is waiting three months for a made-up permit while you give tours about witches ruining the town aesthetic, and spend your workday banging your assistant who is also helping you block my business."

His face goes bright red. He glances at the door in a panic. Marilyn is out there, pretending to be on the phone, but absolutely listening. His eyes are darting between us like he is calculating the fallout.

"You need to leave," he sputters.

"Sure," I say. "But maybe focus on your job instead of Candy Crush."

His jaw snaps tight. "You are out of line."

"Maybe," I say, leaning on the desk. "But at least I'm not shady. That would be you. And maybe I should hire an attorney to sue you and the city for blocking my ability to run my business. I have plenty of documentation. How would that headline look, Sammy?"

He stands up like he wants to scold me, but I am already moving. I stop in the doorway long enough to let my words land.

"I'll be in touch. But probably not through your assistant. She's just as crooked as you."

I turn my gaze to Marilyn. Her face is blotchy, her lips thin, and she fumbles with the phone in her hand like it suddenly weighs ten pounds. I walk past her without another word.

Outside, sunlight hits me full in the face, warm and almost blinding after the gloom of City Hall. My hands are shaking. Not from fear, but from adrenaline and righteous fury. With the realization that I've been patient for too long.

I'm being sabotaged. And I'm done playing nice. Some people get my good karma.

But people like Mayor Sammy Briggs? They get my bad karma.

———

Finn's sitting behind the counter when I walk back in from the mayor's office, his work laptop open, pencil tucked behind his ear. It makes me laugh because Donna, his mom, does the exact same thing when she's deep in her writing. I move to slip past him, but he shifts and suddenly his solid chest bumps right against my breasts. His eyes go wide and he turns bright red as his arms reach out to steady me. His thumbs graze my breasts, sending tingles through my body.

"Sorry," he rushes out, voice a little too high, looking embarrassed.

"It's okay," I say, holding back a nervous grin. "Thanks for watching the store and feeling me up."

He glances out the window and back at me. "Do I need to get bail money? Are the cops coming for you?"

"Not yet," I say, shrugging. "But give it time, it's still early."

He raises a brow. "That bad?"

I sigh and set my bag down. "Last week someone from the city told me if I don't get the permit, it could put Salt & Root at risk too. These new permits are ridiculous. We need a new mayor."

"I can talk to him if you want," Finn offers, looking genuinely concerned.

"Good idea. Ask him how his medical coverage is."

He leans on the counter, watching me with that half-smile that makes my pulse skip. "Remind me never to get on your bad side."

"Too late," I say, but my lips are twitching.

"We'll get it figured out, Row," Finn says as he shuts his laptop and tucks it under his arm. "In the meantime, just focus on your business. They won't get away with this."

"Thanks for watching the shop," I tell him as I tie my apron back on.

"Stay out of jail," he calls as he heads out the back door.

"Thanks," I say as I step into the café inside the bookstore. The smell of espresso and cinnamon rolls wraps around me like a warm and cozy spell. The afternoon light pours through the big windows, the sunlight reflecting across the beams and around the shelves of books. Ivy is sitting at a corner table with Donna, Finn's mom, the two of them leaning over a stack of notebooks, coffee cups, and what looks like a rainbow explosion of colored pencils.

"Hey," I say, walking over. "What are you guys doing? Feel like scheming with me about something?"

Ivy grins but tilts her head toward Donna. "Always. We're plotting fun things for my children's book. Wait till you see it."

I smile, genuinely happy for her. "I can't wait. It's going to be amazing."

She beams, eyes bright and full of that new kind of confidence she's been growing into. She started this whole new brand called *The Good Witch*, a mix of her art, her children's book, and these adorable birthday parties she's been planning for kids all over Wisteria Cove. I swear it's going to be a massive hit. Everyone's already talking about it. I told her she could use my apothecary shop anytime she wants to host them.

Donna looks up from her notes over her glasses, smiling my way. "We were just saying once we finish this next chapter, we'll help you plot how to take down Mayor Sammy Briggs so you can get that permit of yours. Finn filled us in, sweetie."

I snort. "Perfect, and of course he did."

Donna smiles, her red lipstick curling up at the edges. "We'll make a list. He won't know what hit him."

I pull out a chair and sit with them for a few minutes, listening to Ivy describe an illustration of a little witch helping her friends make potions for confidence. Donna's already talking about marketing ideas, theme songs, and merch, and I swear she's about two minutes from pitching a movie deal. It's impossible not to feel proud of Ivy. She's finally found what makes her happy. Her new business and her new fiancé Remy, Finn's brother.

Everyone gives Finn and I crap about not getting together but it's not just our friendship that would be awkward if we didn't work out. My sister and his brother are together. And not just together, but *together.* And they're perfect. Remy's daughter Junie is the funniest kid ever. She's six and hilarious. Finn's such a good uncle, too. So, if things with Finn and I became awkward, it would make it awkward for everyone. And I'm not risking that.

After a bit of chatting, I head to the counter to order a coffee. I spot my best friend Jessica by the pastry case, her blond hair in a sleek ponytail. I haven't seen her all week, which is weird for us. We usually text daily and she visits me when she comes to get a coffee in the bookstore cafe. She's probably been busy. I wave as I walk over.

"Hey, girl! I didn't know you were coming by," I say, smiling. "Want to hang out later and catch up?"

She looks up from her phone as if she wasn't expecting me. Her smile doesn't quite reach her eyes. "Oh, um, I have plans tonight. I'm going to a Pilates class."

I pause, surprised. A tiny pinch hits me low in the chest before I can stop it. "Oh." I force a smile, light and easy even though it feels tight. "Okay. Have fun then. We'll catch up soon."

Inside, it stings more than I want to admit. The only Pilates studio in town is the one run by Vanessa and Marilyn, the she-devils of Wisteria Cove, queens of condescension and passive-aggressive sabotage. Of all places for Jessica to go, it had to be theirs. And she sounds excited. Like it is no big deal.

She's one of my best friends. She knows what those two have put me through. A part of me expected her to avoid that place out of solidarity, out of loyalty, and the quiet, unspoken way best friends protect each other.

Still… it lingers. That soft, unwelcome ache. Because hearing her choose them, even for one class, feels a little like betrayal.

"Yeah," she says quickly and adds, "soon." She tucks her phone away and grabs her latte, heading for the door like she's late for something.

I stand there second-guessing our interaction. That was so weird. Something about her tone sticks with me, but I shake it off and head back toward Ivy and Donna's laughter. If Jessica wants to go to Pilates, that's good for her. I've got bigger fish to fry. Like a certain mayor who's about to learn not to underestimate a Maren sister on a mission.

I pull out my phone and scroll until I find Remy's name. He answers on the second ring.

"Hey, Rowan," he says. "Everything okay?"

"Not really. But I've got an idea, and I need your help."

"Should I be worried?" he asks in his responsible dad voice.

"Probably," I say, smiling to myself as I head back toward my shop. "But it's going to be fun."

CHAPTER 4

Finn

HIT ME WITH YOUR BEST SHOT BY PAT BENATAR

THE MORNING'S QUIET, and sawdust drifts through the sunbeams, catching the light as it falls. The steady hum of my sander fills the shop, low and grounding, vibrating through the workbench beneath my hands. The place smells like cedar, pine, and coffee, the scents settling into every corner the way they always do.

Half-finished projects wait on every surface. A dining table for Mrs. Kline sits clamped beside me, its edges smooth from hours of work. A pair of reclaimed shelves lean against the far wall, still smelling faintly of the old barn they came from. My measuring tape lies open on the bench. A handful of screws scattered beside it. A battered tin of wood conditioner sits next to my elbow, oily fingerprints staining the lid.

This is the place I can go to where everything makes sense. Wood tells the truth if you listen. It shows you where it wants to bend, where it refuses to, where it needs patience and softness instead of strength. I love making new things and I love seeing it all come together.

I like staying busy and trying to keep my thoughts from racing straight to Rowan every five minutes.

And this morning, the hum of the sander is loud enough to almost drown out the thought of her. Almost.

I'm focused, trying not to think about Rowan and how great she looked yesterday. Then I think about Mayor Sammy and the bullshit he's causing. Man, I wouldn't want to be that guy right now. And I can't wait to see what she comes up with. Rowan isn't built for a man who wants quiet. She's full of heat, momentum, a storm that doesn't ask permission before rolling in. She loves too big, feels too deeply, and moves like she's always chasing her dreams. And I love her for it. Every sharp edge, spark, and undercurrent. I love everything about Rowan.

The door to the shop opens, and I nod to my brother, who steps in and slides on safety goggles that hang by the door. He knows I keep strict rules in the wood shop.

"Any idea why I'm delivering goats to the front of the mayor's office at City Hall?" Remy asks as he leans against the doorway, holding his phone, smirking like this is about to be good.

I stop and blink. "Goats?"

"Yep," Remy confirms looking like he's holding back a grin.

I wipe my hands on my jeans, already smiling. "No idea, but I definitely want to see this." There's only one person who would come up with a plan that involves goats and the mayor's office.

Half an hour later, we're parked across the street from City Hall, watching chaos unfold. Goats are wandering across the lawn, bleating and munching on every piece of greenery they can find. People have gathered, phones out, laughing and pointing.

And right in the middle of it is Rowan. She's in black leggings and a dark purple tank top, her hair twisted up all sexy on top of her head. She's standing on a yoga mat and laughing with Ivy and our mom, both of whom are already stretching out on mats as well. About a dozen others are positioned on mats across the front lawn of City Hall. They stretch and pet goats that walk around, curiously eating everything in their path.

"Oh my God," I mutter. "She didn't."

"She did," Remy says, chuckling. "Goat yoga on the front lawn of City Hall. Maybe he'll approve her bogus permit now."

Rowan and her sisters always joke about doing goat yoga and she actually made it happen.

The goats bleat like they're cheering her on. Rowan calls out to the small crowd that's forming. "Welcome to Wisteria Cove's very first of many Goat Yoga Pop-Ups! This is where we'll be hosting our classes until the mayor's office approves my permit for my studio."

I laugh. "She's out of her mind."

"Yep," Remy says. "Mayor Sammy's gonna be pissed."

The goats climb on the mats, and one sniffs Ivy's back, tickling her as she's in downward dog. Our mom laughs so hard she nearly falls over. Rowan steadies her, grinning, and when she bends to pet one of the goats, her tank top rides up just enough to show a sliver of tanned summer kissed skin. My brain practically short-circuits.

Jesus. I feel it sharp and sudden, heat pooling low. Best friends shouldn't give you boners. I yell it silently in my head, *Stop it right now.*

The mayor bursts out the front door, his face the color of a tomato. "What's going on?"

Rowan straightens, her expression perfectly calm. "Goat yoga. Isn't it great? We're here every day until my permit is approved."

He sputters, his tie crooked, his voice rising an octave. "You can't do this on city property!"

One goat nibbles on the flowers by the steps. Another poops right next to the mayor's shiny shoes. I start uncontrollably laughing, no longer able to hold it in, and so does Remy.

Rowan crosses her arms and says to the mayor, "Where else am I supposed to do it?"

"You owe me plants!" he shouts, waving his arms as another goat sneaks past him and chomps on the flowers hanging over the edge of a pot.

Rowan nods her head, grinning. "Good thing I have plenty to

replace them. Though honestly, your taxpayer-funded paycheck could probably cover your own plants, or, you know, whatever else you're spending it on these days."

I don't miss the subtle glance in Marilyn's direction, or Sammy's panicked sputtering, though everyone else seems too distracted by the goat army.

The goat bleats indignantly, clearly offended, and Rowan can't help laughing. She watches Mayor Briggs flail as he tries to shoo the herd away valiantly protecting his foliage.

He glares at the herd, stomping, flailing, muttering, "I'll… I'll make sure you regret this!"

Marilyn hovers behind him, fussing. "Sammy, calm down! It's fine, really!" She tugs at his sleeve, but he waves her off, spinning in a circle as he stomps toward the office door, muttering under his breath, "This isn't over, Ms. Maren…not by a long shot!"

Rowan watches him retreat, chuckling. Today, she definitely won. Tomorrow may be another story.

"No need for threats!" Rowan calls after him, voice sugary sweet. "See you tomorrow, Sammy!"

Remy looks at me smugly. "She's gonna get arrested."

"Nah," I say, but the word barely comes out. I can't look away from her. She's standing there like she just walked out of a battle she won. Her cheeks are flushed, eyes bright, chin lifted in that way that says she has finally had enough and refuses to be pushed one inch further.

My heart pounds hard enough to shake something loose in my chest. God, she looks unstoppable. Fierce. Beautiful. Untouchable. The kind of woman who could topple an empire before breakfast and then show up with homemade teas and salves like nothing happened.

One of the goats lets out a loud, offended bleat behind us. Rowan rolls her eyes like she has conquered both corrupt politicians and livestock in the same hour. Of course she has. She's Rowan.

I swallow, trying to find my voice again. "But if she does," I manage, breath catching a little, "I'm definitely going to be the idiot who bails her out."

She laughs, quick and bright, and something hot flickers low in my stomach. She has no idea how incredible she looks right now. How powerful. How much I want to pull her into my arms and tell her she deserves better than every person who ever tried to mess with her.

Another goat headbutts a tree for no reason at all, and Rowan turns toward the chaos with that exasperated little smile she gets when the world is falling apart but she refuses to let it win.

And standing here watching her, I realize something that makes my pulse trip.

I would bail her out every time. And I would fight beside her.

I would choose her, again and again, even when she is charging into City Hall like a warrior queen. Especially then.

She glances across the lawn, catches my eye, and gives me a little wave, that smug, witchy smile curving her lips and my throat goes dry.

"Mmmhmm," I mutter under my breath. "Totally screwed."

———

On my way home from work, I drive past the back of Rowan's shop and see that her truck isn't there. The place looks closed up and quiet which means she's probably at the cottage working on her flowers and plants.

I take the turn down Honeysuckle Street toward her little rental on the edge of town, the one that's half greenhouse, half chaos. It's like a little jungle that makes complete sense to Rowan. The air cools as I pull up, headlights sweeping across the yard that's been turned into a garden that covers every inch of the property. The house leans a little to the left, paint peeling, porch boards soft enough to buckle. Most people would call it a dump. She calls it her happy place.

Her lights are on, warm and golden through the window. I

park and get out, the smell of damp soil hitting me right away. She's there, surrounded by flowers that seem to bloom just for her, hair piled on top of her head, wearing a faded, ripped up Def Leppard T-shirt with holes and a stain near the hem and dirt on her cheek. She's humming something under her breath and looks totally in her element right now.

I stare at her long enough to make it weird if she catches me, so I grab a pair of pruning shears off the worn wooden table and step beside her without a word. She glances up, smiles, and keeps working. She doesn't need to ask why I'm there. I've done this with her more times than I can count. We move in rhythm, snipping stems and pulling wilted leaves, cleaning up the containers she likes to rearrange around the small yard.

"Mark still hasn't fixed the roof?" I ask, nodding toward the sagging corner.

She snorts. "Mark Briggs doesn't fix anything. I'm pretty sure this place is held together by your fixes and duct tape."

"I'd offer to fix it again," I say, trimming a rose stem, "but last time he told me I was ruining the 'character' of his property."

She rolls her eyes. "Right. Is that what they're calling mold now?"

She doesn't stay here anymore and lives on top of the bookstore apartment. But this is where she grows everything for her apothecary.

I move to the next pot which smells like rosemary. She's always got something growing. Tomatoes in buckets, climbing jasmine on the trellis, flowers spilling over every surface, mostly everything in containers so she can move them around.

"Why so many flowers?" I ask. "You could grow herbs, things you can use for the shop. These are just… pretty."

She stands and looks around, smiling softly. "I just love them. We grow food to nourish the body, and flowers to nourish the soul."

I nod. "That's the most witchy and poetic thing."

"Thank you," she says with a small smile. "I try."

I glance at her, at the smudge of dirt across her cheek and the sparkle in her eyes. She has this spicy little attitude that drives me nuts, and I mean that in the best possible way. She's all sharp edges and has a soft heart. She's unpredictable and beautiful and way too brave for her own good.

"Try not to do anything that'll get you in trouble with the city, Row," I say, mostly joking but not entirely. I don't know why Sammy is out to get her, but I want her to be careful.

She grins. "I'll be fine."

"That's true," I say. "You're the only person I know who could weaponize goat yoga."

"They were adorable," she says, flicking a leaf at me. "And effective."

"Yeah, but the mayor didn't think so."

"Sammy can bite me," she says. "He's such a crybaby. He called the police on me, again."

I laugh, the sound echoing through the greenhouse. The night air smells sweet, and for a second, I forget the whole world outside of this little place exists.

"Real men don't cry," I tease, knowing that Sammy calling the police on her is an empty threat. Number one, my brother is a former attorney. He's not going to willingly participate in anything that will get his future sister-in-law in trouble. And second, that's funny because Rowan has been on a first name basis with every single cop in Wisteria Cove since she was five. And half the police force is probably terrified of her.

She smirks. "They do if you hex them properly."

"Good to know," I say. "I'll keep my emotions locked up just in case."

She sets down her shears and wipes her hands on her jeans. "Here," she says, pulling out her phone. "I almost forgot your song of the day."

Music fills the greenhouse through her small speaker. Pat Benatar's *Hit Me With Your Best Shot*.

She starts dancing, hips swaying as she picks up another plant, her laughter carrying across the yard. I stand there for a second, watching her move in the warm glow of the string lights strung above us and I swear I can feel it, something shifting in my chest, something that's been undeniable for so long.

I set the shears down and join her. "You know this song's a challenge coming from you, right?"

She winks. "Then you better duck, Carpenter Ken."

I laugh, stepping closer, the scent of soil and honeysuckle filling the air. "Bring it on, Hexy Barbie."

She bumps her hip against mine and keeps dancing, and I know I'm madly in love with Rowan Maren. The problem is, she doesn't seem to feel the same. So, if this is what I need to settle for the rest of my life, I guess I'll take it.

———

The house creaks as it settles, the sound low and steady in the quiet. I rinse my hands in the sink and watch the water swirl down the drain. The tile is set, the lines are straight, and everything is coming together. But the air still feels heavy and lonely.

I lean back against the counter and stare out the window. The moon sits high in the sky over the harbor. I tell myself I'm tired, that it's just another night, that the ache in my chest is nothing. But I know better.

I think about what I told Serena last week, about how I see my life in five and ten years. I said it like it was going to happen. Like I wasn't just dreaming. But standing here now, looking at this empty kitchen, I realize I've been building my life like a house without a heartbeat. It's lonely here and I want that dream I described to Serena. I want a family. That's everything that I'm working towards.

I grab a beer from the fridge and step outside. Somewhere down the road, a dog barks, and I hear the faint hum of the ocean waves hitting the rocks. It's peaceful, but it's lonely.

I sit on the porch steps, elbows resting on my knees, and take a long drink. The beer's cold, and it does nothing to fill the space inside me.

Rowan's face keeps flashing through my mind. The way she laughs when she's trying not to smile. The way she stands with her hands on her hips, chin tilted up like she's daring the world to test her. The way her eyes go soft when she's working with her plants, completely lost in her own little universe.

She'd call this porch too plain. She'd tell me it needs color. Flowers, she'd say, or at least a few herbs in pots. Then she'd fill the space with life without even trying. It would probably be insanely chaotic just like her cottage with all of her plants.

I tilt my head back and look down the street towards the shop where Rowan lives above. "You're thinking too much," I mutter to myself.

The phone on the counter buzzes through the screen door. Once, twice, then goes still. I get up, walk back inside, and check the message.

Rowan: You awake?

Her name lights up my phone like a flare in the dark.

I stare at it for a second, trying to play it cool, but my heart kicks hard in my chest. It's stupid how fast I grab the phone.

Yeah.

The reply bubble pops up almost immediately.

Rowan: Can't sleep. Thinking about what's going to happen if Sammy makes good on his threat of getting me evicted. He just has to talk to Mark and I'm done here. I don't know what I'll do.

We'll figure it out if it happens. But Mark also likes your rent.

Rowan: True. Thanks for your help today. Why aren't you sleeping? Need me to come read you a bed-time story?

Maybe.

I shake my head and smile. My fingers hover over the keys before I type.

You're trouble, Ro.

Her response takes a few seconds.

Rowan: Good thing you like trouble.

I set the phone on the counter, but I don't move. I just stand there, the glow of the screen fading into the dark.

For the first time in a long time, the house doesn't feel quite so empty. And she's right. I love trouble.

CHAPTER 5
Rowan

CRAZY TRAIN BY OZZY OSBOURNE

MORNING SUNLIGHT CUTS through the blinds and lands right on my face like it has a personal vendetta with my soul. My phone is still beside my pillow, and when I pick it up and check it, the last message to Finn glows at the top of the screen. *Good thing you like trouble.*

I smile before I can stop myself, then groan into the pillow. Trouble. That man *is* trouble for me too, and I have no self-control when it comes to Finn. I say the dumbest things, let my guard down, and I need to stop flirting with him. It's not going to end well. He's my best friend and I need him to stay that way. Just the thought of having a relationship complicates everything. This is why I'm trying my best to date and move on from the idea that Finn could even like me back like that.

By the time I make it down to the shop, the scent of coffee and old paper has replaced sleep, wrapping around me like a familiar hug as the door swings open to my side of the shop. The ocean hums softly down the street, the breeze salty as I push the front door wide, letting the morning air spill inside. I do it every day. It feels like breathing life into the place, like clearing out yesterday so something new can bloom.

Willa waves to me from the cafe on her side of the bookshop, and I know we'll catch up once her morning rush is over. She's always busy first thing in the morning, and this is my time to have quiet time in the shop before I open. Say a few spells, gather a few new ideas, and get ready for the day.

I get coffee going in my vintage percolator in the back of my shop, light a candle, and try not to think about how often Finn has been on my mind lately. He's everywhere I look. The shelf he built for me last month or the door he fixed without me asking, even the memory of him brushing dirt off my cheek. My cheek warms when I think about it.

The phone buzzes on the counter, and it's Ivy telling me she's on her way. I forgot we were having coffee this morning to talk about what's been going on with the yoga studio.

She bursts through the door five minutes later, sunshine and chaos wrapped in a pink floral kimono. "You're glowing," she says, dropping her bag onto a chair.

"I'm not properly caffeinated yet so that's impossible," I answer, grumpily. "And you're the one glowing. It must be all that good lovin' you've been getting from Remy."

She laughs. "That's accurate. I won't even pretend to deny that. But we're talking about you. Have you heard more about the stupid permit stuff?"

"No."

She gives me a look. "You absolutely pissed off Mayor Sammy. Gladys overheard him telling someone at the diner that he is going to do his best to shut you down in every way that he can."

I roll my eyes, pretending to check the register. "That's a strange threat coming from a man who lives in a flammable house."

Ivy grins, leaning on the counter. "You probably couldn't get away with burning down his house, but it would be fun to watch. He's been pulling this crap repeatedly for the past year, and you aren't the only one tired of his dirty politics. People are starting to talk."

"That sucks. But what can I do?"

"Well, Remy had some good ideas. He said to tell you he isn't giving you 'official' legal advice, because he's not a practicing attorney. But he said he looked into it, and you don't even need the permit. He said just go ahead and open your studio under the umbrella of Salt & Root. Keep it one business, instead of separating it, and then there's nothing the city can do as long as you have the appropriate insurance on your end," Ivy says with a big smile.

"That's awesome. Pass on my thanks," I tell her, feeling relieved.

The door opens again, and Donna sweeps in, lipstick perfect, her silver hair shining, like she just walked out of a magazine shoot. "Good morning, my sweet little witches. I bring wisdom and gossip."

"I'll take both," I say, giving her a quick hug as she kisses my cheek.

I've always loved Remy and Finn's mom. Our moms were best friends when Donna moved here with her sons. So, we've known them for pretty much as long as I can remember.

She lowers her voice. "Mayor Sammy is planning a meeting this morning. He's furious about the goat situation and you pushing back. I think you should pop in and watch."

I smile, pleased. "Good. Maybe steam will shoot out his ears like in an old cartoon."

Donna gasps. "Rowan Maren, remember the last time you said something, and it *actually* happened. You're like the perfect manifester. I would love to see that. Also, I can't believe you called him out on his affair with Marilyn. How did you know about that?"

I shrug my shoulders and sigh. "I just figured it out. And judging by the look on his face, he confirmed it. How hard is it to just have his assistant approve it and give me the form? It didn't have to be this way. Ivy just told me that Remy said I don't even need it. They've just been wasting my time anyway. Joke's on them. I'm going to forge ahead with setting up my classes and move on."

Ivy cackles. "Remy says he's still bringing the goats back at two. I can't wait. I've been begging you to do goat yoga for so long. This is so much fun. I can't believe we get to do it again. He's even grabbing Junie early from school so she can participate."

"Well, we can do it one more time and tell everyone that after today, we're moving them to the new studio, but no goats in the new studio," I say with a laugh, sipping my coffee. "Right now, I'm finishing labeling these and mentally preparing for more bullshit from Sammy."

I refuse to address him as mayor now. He needs to be replaced by someone who actually cares about this town and their local taxpaying businesses. If he worried more about that, than bullying people, I'd have respect for him. He's lost that.

Donna exchanges a look with Ivy. "She's going to need backup for that meeting."

Damn it. I knew these two were going to conspire against me.

"I'm—"

"—calling Finn," Ivy finishes. "I'll call him for you."

I roll my eyes but grab my phone, anyway. "Don't do that. He's probably busy. I'll fill him in later."

"He's not busy," Donna says, conspiracy laced in her voice like she's scheming something.

Finn answers on the second ring cheerfully. "Hey, Row."

Just hearing his voice makes something warm flicker in my belly as I ask him hesitantly, "Are you busy?"

"Why, you need me?"

Need him. Of course, I need him. But his mother is standing next to me, so I'm trying to play it cool.

"I think Sammy's about to pull something shady in a town meeting he just called this morning. I think he's hoping I won't hear about it or be too busy to come."

A pause, then that familiar calm in his tone. "I'll go with you."

"No, you don't have to."

Donna and Ivy lean over simultaneously and say, "Yes, she needs you."

"Hi, Mom, hi Ivy," he says cheerfully.

"Finn—"

"I'll be there in twenty."

He hangs up before I can argue.

———

Finn and I push through the glass doors of City Hall with a folder full of printouts that are receipts of the crap Sammy's been pulling. I'm running on very little patience now. Marilyn looks up, clearly already over my existence when she sees me.

"Good morning," I say sweetly, ignoring her sour look. "I heard you have a town meeting going on."

"Who told you about it?" she asks as her eyes dart to Sammy's closed door.

"Cut the crap, Marilyn."

Her lips press into a line. "He's very busy."

"Yeah, I've heard that before."

Before she can respond, the door behind her opens and Sammy himself steps out, face red as he mutters into his phone about something. When he sees me, he freezes.

"Oh good," I say brightly. "You're here and look like you're ready for the meeting."

He scowls. "Ms. Maren, you're officially on notice."

"And yet here we are. Rumor has it you're trying to shut me down."

He sputters. "Rumor?"

"I have sources," I say, glancing toward the hallway. That's when I see Finn leaning against the wall, arms crossed, watching the whole scene like it's his new favorite show. He tips his chin up to Sammy.

Sammy adjusts his tie. "You both can't just barge in here."

"I didn't barge in anywhere. I'm standing here asking your assistant about the town meeting."

"You're not invited," he argues.

"What's your problem with me, anyway?"

He opens his mouth to argue, but the goat yoga photo on his desk catches my eye. Someone must have sent it to him. It's me, with goats surrounding me.

"Nice picture," I say. "Really captures my best side. I'm glad you like it."

Sammy groans. "Ms. Maren—"

"Let's go to that meeting you have scheduled."

Finn bites his lip like he's holding back a laugh.

Sammy rubs his forehead. "I told you that you aren't invited."

I glance into the board room and see Vanessa sitting there, watching us. "It's a public meeting, is it not? What are you being so secretive about?"

Finn laughs quietly. Sammy glares at him. "You think this is funny, Mr. Bennett?"

Finn straightens, all charm. "I'm begging you. Find something else to focus on, Sammy. You won't win at whatever game you're playing at."

Sammy sighs. "You've taken this too far. I have a meeting that you are both not invited to."

"Of course," I say. "Wouldn't want to keep you from important mayoral duties, like ruining small businesses and ignoring actual important matters."

"Rowan," Finn calls under his breath. "Let's go."

"Watch it," Sammy huffs and storms off.

Marilyn mutters something about security, but Finn takes my elbow and steers me toward the doors before I can say or do anything.

Outside, sunlight hits us full force. I squint, pulling my hair up. "I knew Vanessa and Marilyn had something to do with this."

He nods. "Something dirty is going on. He's not going to get away with this."

"I'm not going to let him get away with this. He picked the wrong one to mess with."

"Row, nothing scares me more than the confidence you have when you're mad. You're ready to ruin lives, including your own."

"No, he's going to get what's coming to him," I argue.

"Someone's gotta stop you from hexing the mayor into a frog."

I grin. "Would that really be so bad? He's kind of shaped like one already. And you have to admit, a frog wearing a toupée is hilarious."

He grins, that slow, devastating one that melts all my good sense. "Come on, Hexy Barbie. I'll buy you lunch before you get involved in another political scandal."

I roll my eyes but follow him toward his truck. "You're lucky you're cute."

"Yeah," he says, glancing down at me. "So are you."

My heart stumbles a little. I look away, pretending to be fascinated by a seagull.

As he opens the truck door for me, I think, maybe for the first time, that this man could ruin my carefully crafted independence in the best possible way.

CHAPTER 6
Rowan

PAINT IT BLACK BY THE ROLLING STONES

THE AFTERNOON LIGHT in the shop slants through the stained-glass window, catching the glass jars I just unpacked from a new shipment. The shop smells of sage, lavender, and rosemary. I'm restocking shelves with tea blends that I've struggled to keep in stock and lining up gemstone necklaces and bracelets. I'm also trying to remember that I'm supposed to be calm and professional and not still thinking about the way Finn smiled at me.

Lunch was… good. He made me laugh so hard I nearly snorted iced tea, and then he paid before I could even grab my wallet. Said it was "hazard pay" for keeping him entertained. The man drives me crazy.

I'm arranging a display of teas when the door creaks open behind me. He went back to work and so did I with plans to catch up tonight after we both get off work.

"Welcome in," I start automatically, but the words die in my throat when I see who is standing in the doorway.

Mark.

My landlord. The man who handles the cottage property where I grow half my herbs. And the man who has never once stepped foot inside Salt & Root.

His expression is tight. Nervous. Already guilty about something. That alone makes my stomach pitch. A cold wave of dread rolls up my spine, settling under my ribs like a stone. I know that look. I know exactly what it means, even before he opens his mouth.

A spark of anger flickers through the dread, sharp and hot. The mayor has already blocked my permit, trashed my reputation in town, and wasted months of my time. If he has dragged Mark into this too, if he is trying to choke off my business from the roots, I swear to every goddess in the sea air outside, I am going to lose my mind.

I swallow hard and steady my voice, even though my pulse is thudding.

"Mark," I say quietly. "What are you doing here?"

He shifts from foot to foot, clutching a folder. "I came to tell you in person and I figured it was better than a notice in the mail."

"Tell me what?"

He clears his throat. "You're being evicted and have until the end of the month to get your things off the property."

The words hit like a slap. "Excuse me? Mark, that's less than two weeks. Don't you have to give me at least a thirty-day notice?"

He won't meet my eyes. "Sammy forced my hand, Rowan. I have no choice. He said that if I don't do this, I'll have to pay him out for the rental properties we have together. He also threatened to have my property condemned."

Not actually surprised at that last part. That probably needs to be done to a few of them. Also, if he's threatening his own cousin, that's even more wild.

I stare at him, disbelief turning to fury. "What am I supposed to do with all my plants?"

His face twists in frustration. "You should've thought about that before you pushed him. You embarrassed him in front of the whole town."

"Good," I snap. "He deserves it. He's a bully."

Mark's eyes flick toward the door like he's afraid I'll throw something at him. "For what it's worth, I'm sorry," he mutters.

I fold my arms, voice low and steady. "I'll remember this, Mark."

Something in my tone must land, because he pales a little, grabs the folder tighter, and scurries out like a man being chased by something. The bell jingles, the door slams, and the air feels sharp.

I'm still standing there fuming when the door opens again and my mother's voice floats in. "Well, hello to my favorite daughter."

Lilith Maren breezes in wearing a straw beach hat and smelling like coconut sunscreen. "Just got back from Coconut Beach. The cottage was divine." She drops her bag on the counter and eyes me. "Fill me in, sweetheart. I feel dissension in the ranks."

I blow out a breath. "Well, Mark just evicted me. I have two weeks to figure out what to do with all my plants, Sammy has been terrorizing me, and Marilyn and Vanessa are opening up a Pilates studio and apparently find my yoga studio to be a threat."

Her brows lift. "That's not good. You should put them all in jars and put them in the freezer."

"No, Mom, it's not good. And the freezer is definitely happening. Maybe something stronger. Where am I going to put everything? Almost everything is in containers, but there's no room here at the shop. And your yard is already full."

"What about Donna's? She's got space, dear."

I am not trashing Donna's exquisite backyard, which is fantastically landscaped, and dumping all of my random herbs and flowers I have growing. I'm not even going to ask her because that would be insane.

"What about the tree farm? Surely Remy could find some space for you out there," she suggests.

That's actually not a terrible idea. It's just so far outside of town. I already run the shop here full time, then tend to all the plants at the cottage, and luckily it's just down the road. But adding an extra twenty minutes each way is precious daylight and time I don't have. But it's better than nothing.

"I'll ask Remy. Thanks, Mom." I sigh, sitting back on my stool, feeling defeated. I didn't expect this, but I knew something was coming. How I'm going to fit in yoga classes, the plants, and figuring out how to get everything moved, is beyond me. I need to hire more help but I'm already stretched thin with getting my business up and running and don't really have the money for that right now.

She glances around the shop, trying to be positive and find something to distract me. "Well, you're going to really need that rest and relaxation at Coconut Beach when you go. Have you packed yet?"

I blink. "What?"

Oh, no. I forgot that I had a trip coming up next week.

She looks at me with worry. "Your trip with Jessica. Don't tell me you forgot."

I close my eyes and press my fingers to my temple. "Oh no. It completely slipped my mind." A breath rushes out of me, thin and frustrated. "And Jessica has been acting weird lately. I do not even know if she still wants to go."

The truth is, it has not just been recently. She has been off for weeks. Little things that keep snagging at me. She stopped replying to my messages right away, even the ones she usually jumps on. She canceled our standing coffee date three times in a row with excuses that felt flimsy, like she pulled them from a bowl of random words. At the shop last week, she barely made eye contact. She kept smoothing her hair and glancing at the door like she was waiting for someone else.

And there's the way she talks when she does show up. Careful. Too careful. The bright, chatty Jessica I know has been replaced by someone who seems like she is walking across thin ice, afraid to say the wrong thing. She does not ask about the permit anymore. She does not ask about Finn. She does not ask about anything real. It is all surface-level, weather and gossip and nothing that touches who we are to each other.

Each time she pauses too long before she answers me, or forces a smile that looks glued on, I feel something inside me shift. A question I don't want to ask. What changed and if she's still my friend or just playing the part.

I open my eyes with a sinking feeling. "Honestly, I can't tell if she wants to go, or if she's avoiding me altogether."

My mom looks at me and sighs. "I didn't want to tell you this, but I heard she's been hanging around town with Vanessa and Marilyn, lately. I thought that was odd because those two don't treat you very well and you and Jessica are so close."

I stare at her. "Really?"

The word comes out smaller than I want it to. A hot twist coils low in my stomach, sharp enough to make me feel a little dizzy. It hits so fast I blink, like my body is trying to catch up to the sting.

I did not expect it to hurt like this, but it does.

I considered Jessica one of my best friends. And hearing that she's hanging out with people that are actively trying to hurt my business...well, that hurts.

"Yeah, I'm sorry, honey."

"I'll talk to her," I say, but my gut tells me she's not taking that trip with me. We were so close and now she barely comes around, calls, or texts me back.

My mom pats my arm. "It'll work out, honey. These things have a way of sorting themselves out. And you really do need a break. I can't remember the last time you took a vacation."

"That's because I haven't taken a vacation in years," I mutter, trying not to sound as defeated as I feel. "I planned that trip to our family cottage with Donna in Coconut Beach for months. I was actually excited for it. Jessica and I were supposed to have this epic girl's week. I bought three new bikinis like a lunatic. I was going to lie on the beach, sip cocktails, read a stack of books, and do absolutely nothing but recharge with my friend."

My mom's expression softens, the sharp edges of her features easing. She reaches out and touches my arm, gentle in a way she rarely is. "Sweetheart," she says, "you deserve that time. Even if Jessica changes her mind, even if things feel strange, you should still go."

The words hit something tender in me. I swallow hard. I had been clinging to that trip like a lifeline, like proof that I could still carve out space in my life for joy. For rest and connection. And now it feels like the ground shifted beneath me, leaving me standing alone with my suitcases full of swimsuits and expectations.

I open my mouth, then close it again. "I just thought she was excited too," I admit quietly. "It was supposed to be our thing."

My mom gives me a sad little smile, the kind that says she knows more than she lets on. "People change, and plans shift. But you can't put your life on hold because someone else lets you down."

She kisses my cheek, her sunscreen-sweet scent brushing against me as she straightens her purse on her shoulder. "Think about going anyway. Sun and saltwater might be exactly what you need."

Then she flutters out the door in a rush of floral print and mild chaos, leaving me alone in the quiet shop, the silence settling around me. Now I have to figure out the logistics of this trip by myself. Great.

———

By the time the sun sets, I'm still bothered by all of this. I drive out to the cottage to water everything and do some weeding, hoping a little dirt therapy will calm me down and help me figure out what to do next.

But when I pull into the drive, I freeze. My breath catches, sharp and painful. My mouth falls open before I can stop it. Half the plants are gone.

Rows of empty spaces stare back at me from the porch, bare wood where my ferns should be spilling over the sides, where my rosemary and chamomile and sage should be catching the morning light. The pots that remain look lonely and wrong, like teeth missing from a smile.

I sit there, gripping the steering wheel so tight my knuckles ache. A hot rush of panic surges through me, rising fast into my throat. My chest tightens, that horrible swooping feeling you get when you are about to lose something you cannot replace. My mind races through worst case scenarios so quickly it feels like falling.

What if Sammy did this. Or his cousin. What if they threw everything away just to hurt me.

These plants are not decorations. They are my livelihood. They are hours of tending, pruning, watering, talking to them like they know my secrets. They are my business, my craft, the heartbeat of Salt & Root. I grow half of my herbs here. I know every single leaf, every bloom, every stubborn stem that refuses to cooperate. The thought of them uprooted and tossed into a dumpster makes my stomach twist violently.

The porch looks wrong without them. Barren and violated. Like someone walked into my life and ripped out pieces without asking.

My breath shakes as I fumble for my phone, my fingers clumsy. I don't even think, I just dial, pulse thudding in my ears, bracing myself for the worst news imaginable.

Because losing these plants would not just hurt my business. It would hurt me. Right down to the roots.

Someone took my plants.

It takes him less than a minute to reply.

Finn: They're at the house in your new greenhouse. Surprise!

I stare at the screen. What house? And what greenhouse? I'm so confused.

What?

No reply.

I spin the truck around and head toward his place. When I turn down his drive, the headlights sweep across the familiar chaos of his truck, building materials in his garage, and tools. But there's something new in the backyard. A large structure with panels glinting in the evening light, and Remy, Finn, and Tate moving plants and stacking them around the greenhouse that is new.

I park, step out, and just stand there in disbelief. I can't believe what I'm seeing right now.

Remy is hauling a tray of seedlings into the greenhouse onto a folding table. Tate's unloading my containers, spacing them around the property like it's a full-blown botanical takeover. And right in the middle of it all, Finn's setting up a frame of wood and Plexiglas, sleeves rolled, shoulders broad, hair sticking up from sweat.

"Oh my God," I whisper. "What did you do, Finn?"

Finn looks up and waves. "Hey, Row."

Remy leans in and says to me, "Don't yell at him too hard. None of us like Briggs and his shady slum lord cousin. We wanted to help."

Tate sets down a planter and strides over, wrapping me in a hug. "You know we've always got your back."

My throat tightens. "You guys didn't have to—"

Finn walks over, taking off his gloves and slides them in the loop on his tool belt. "Yes, we did. You'd never ask for help, and we wanted to help you. You have plenty of space to grow everything here. Mom heard about what happened from Lilith and she called us."

"I can't believe you did all this." My voice comes out soft, shaky.

He smiles, slow and warm. "You've been keeping that old cottage going on pure magic. You deserve a space that doesn't leak and have copious amounts of toxic mold."

He's right. I haven't been able to stay out there for a long time because the structure became inhabitable. But it was a good place to grow everything, so I kept it going.

I look around, taking it in. The new greenhouse sits on a flat stretch of his back yard, framed with reclaimed wood and panels that catch the last of the light. My plant babies are scattered around the greenhouse, and their leaves shimmer in the sunset and it's perfect.

I whisper in awe, "I can't believe you did all this."

"It'll be fine," he says. "But now you don't have to worry about Mark or Sammy. And all your plants are close to the shop. You can pop in any time, and no one will bother them."

I shake my head, still stunned. "You can't just build me a greenhouse, Finn."

He steps closer, voice low in a challenge. "I can if I want to."

My breath catches. His hand brushes a bit of dirt from my arm, his fingers slow and careful. The air between us hums, heavy and charged.

"Thank you," I say quietly.

He smiles, eyes soft. "You're welcome."

I look up at him, and the world narrows to the space between us. The scent of soil and the feeling of something electric between us. His hand lingers on my arm, warm and steady, and for a moment I think he might kiss me.

But instead, he takes a step back and says, "Come on. Let's get another load in before it gets too dark. We should have everything out of there by tonight. Maybe a few loads in the morning if we need to."

My pulse is still hammering as I follow him to his truck.

And even as the stars come out, all I can think is that my heart might already belong to a man who builds things, especially things I didn't know I needed. And this makes all the feelings I try to shove down really hard. Because Finn is completely taking over my heart.

CHAPTER 7

Finn

DANCING IN THE MOONLIGHT BY TOPLOADER

"UNCLE FINN!"

I look up and there's Junie in pink sparkle sneakers with hot pink safety goggles that are too big for her face. Hair sticking up in a halo of dark messy curls around the strap of the goggles. Her dog, a blue heeler, Lola trots beside her, tongue hanging out, watching every move her little person makes. She was Ivy's dog and now she pretty much follows Junie everywhere. Sometimes when Junie's at school, she'll come hang out in my shop with me.

I scoop her up before she can trip over the extension cord. "What's up, Junie Bug?"

She wraps her arms around my neck. "Ivy said I could come see you before my bus comes. She's over there smooching my dad in the barn. It's gross."

I laugh. "Lucky me that I get to see you," I say, spinning her around until she squeals. "What's the big plan today?"

She frowns. "Stupid school. But then we have pasta night."

"I have questions. First, why is school stupid?"

"There's a boy that keeps being mean to me. Ivy said we can work on a special spell for him," she says with a grin.

"Well, that sounds like he better back off or he'll be in big trouble," I say trying to be serious. "What's for dinner? Can I come?"

"You can always come, silly." She leans close, like it's a secret, holding up two fingers. "Ivy and I are making homemade pasta with two different sauces."

"Homemade pasta?" I whisper. "Well, now I have to come. I won't turn down dinner from my favorite little chef."

She laughs, loud and happy, then pushes at my shoulders until I set her back down. She looks around the shop like she always does, checking out whatever I'm working on. She touches the corner of the cabinet.

"This one's very smooth," she says.

"It's looking good," I tell her. "You still want to work on a bird house with me sometime?"

"Yeah," she says, nodding happily. "And we can paint it."

"Okay, Bug, we can definitely paint it," I promise as I hear Ivy calling for her.

She nods solemnly. "I gotta go to school," she says, goggles slipping down her nose. I keep a special set just for her by the door so she can put them on before she comes in.

When Ivy shows up a few minutes later, she waves as I stand in the doorway and watch Junie bounce toward where her bus comes, little pink shoes glittering in the sun.

She's my favorite kid. I love having my shop out here and being able to see my brother Remy, Ivy, and Junie. Someday I'll move my shop to town, but for now I don't mind coming out here, because I get to see my family and I have all my wood stored, and plenty of room for projects.

I press my palm over the smooth edge of the cabinet faces I'm building for a client. This part is my favorite when something rough starts looking like it's going to make a space look great. I love the thought of someone's kitchen having my work in there for decades to come. The morning sun spills in through the wide doors of the wood shop, and I've got music playing low, just enough to keep the quiet from swallowing me. I finish sanding my cabinets and lay them aside.

I head over to the barn where my brother Remy is already at

work for the day. He looks up from his desk when I walk in, pulling the door closed behind me.

"Thanks for your help yesterday," I tell him as I slide into the chair across from him. He and Tate dropped everything to help me move all of Rowan's plants from her shitty cottage to my backyard which luckily is much bigger than the area she had. She doesn't know this, but I had all of the pieces to the greenhouse waiting for months. I had planned on surprising her but then when she got evicted, it was perfect timing.

"If someone messes with a Maren, they mess with us. We're not putting up with that bullshit," my brother says, like it's obvious.

I nod, trying to keep my voice steady. But inside, I'm boiling. *Way too far, way too personal.* Every instinct in me wants to march into that office, grab that guy by the collar, and make it crystal clear that Rowan Maren isn't someone to be messed with. My fists clench at my sides, my jaw tightens, and I can feel my pulse hammering. I'm already running through ways to shut this down before it gets worse. No one, especially some self-important mayor asshat, is going to make her life harder on my watch.

"I agree. Have you heard from Mom today? Anything on how Pete's doing?"

Remy sighs and leans back in his chair, the heaviness hanging between us. "Hanging in there. His doctors say that new drug he's on is giving him time and he's comfortable so that's what's important. He made the comment the other day that every single day he has right now is so special to him."

Hearing that is like a kick to the chest. "I hate this," I say, looking out the shop window at the rows of trees in the distance. "First Uncle Carl, now Pete? What did those two do to deserve this?"

"Not a damn thing. Life is too fucking short. We gotta live each day to the fullest and love our family and friends. That's it," Remy says as he flips a pen on his desk, looking just as sad as I'm feeling right now.

Pete, the retired old harbor master has been like a father figure to both of us since we moved to Wisteria Cove when we were little kids. Our mom was a single mom to both of us rowdy boys, and when she needed Pete, he put us in line, and took us under his wing like a dad. Those two were never romantically involved to our knowledge but they were best friend companions. Last fall he was diagnosed with cancer and it's not lost on us that he's on borrowed time.

"Speaking of Mom and Pete, they are coming to dinner tonight. Are you coming?" Remy asks, looking up at me.

Trying to lighten the mood, I say, "Well, just so you know, I've already received my official invitation to pasta night from Junie."

He snorts. "I love that kid."

"Me, too. I'll be there," I call as I turn to head out, closing the door behind me.

We're definitely going to live life to the fullest. That puts this mayor nonsense into perspective with Rowan. They need to leave my family the fuck alone. We have got enough that we're dealing with right now.

———

On the way home that afternoon, to shower before pasta night, I stop by the store to grab a few things. I like to bring dessert and drinks when I go to my brother's and not show up empty-handed. I am badly in need of groceries.

There's a new flier displayed by the front windows in glossy pastel pink. *Better Bodies Pilates Studio.* Marilyn's face is right there at the top of the poster next to Vanessa's.

"Finn," someone singsongs behind me and I immediately tense up when I recognize the voice.

I turn and Vanessa's already closing the distance, her perfume hitting me square in the face. She rests her hand on my arm, her bright nails flashing in the light. I pull back just enough to make it clear I don't like it. She ignores me and scoots even closer into my space.

"Did you see?" she says, gesturing at the poster. "We're having our grand opening in two weeks. You should come to a class. I think you'd love it."

I stare at her. "Are you out of your mind?"

She laughs like I'm being cute. "Don't tell me you're scared of a Pilates class. It won't hurt, I promise. You'll have fun." She giggles, covering her mouth with her bright pink acrylic nails, so long they hit her nose.

"You're unbelievable," I say flatly. "I've been wondering why you've been treating Rowan like crap. She hasn't done a damn thing to deserve any of what you and Marilyn have been pulling."

Her smile tightens and she drops the baby act with her voice. "Rowan just isn't a nice person, Finn. She's a bitch."

Something inside me snaps when I see Jessica standing a few feet from Vanessa, obviously a part of this. "First of all, watch your mouth."

She blinks, surprised. "What? We all know how Rowan is."

I tilt my head. "And how *is* Rowan? Enlighten me."

"She is…well you know…difficult," Vanessa says, examining her nails and not meeting my eyes.

"No, I don't know." My voice comes out low, steady, and it hits harder than yelling ever could. "She's done nothing but work her ass off for that shop all while being a good friend to all of you. So if this is about jealousy or whatever game you're playing, find someone else to mess with. She's been supportive of both of you and encouraged you. You both used to take her yoga classes for years. You are the ones who are out of line here."

"And you." I turn to Jessica. "You're actually supposed to be her friend. Some friend," I clip, my eyes not leaving her face as she looks away guiltily.

Her cheeks flush and Vanessa pipes in, looking angry. "You don't know everything about Rowan."

"I know she doesn't need friends like you." I brush past her, grab my bag from the counter, and before I walk out, I turn to them and say, "Rowan isn't even as mean as she could be. And I wish people like you would appreciate that more before she stops tolerating your bullshit. Because that's what she's been doing. Good luck with that when she stops." The door slams behind me.

The warm sea breeze hits the air as soon as I step outside, and it does nothing but add to the heat under my skin. My jaw is locked tight and my hands are curled around the paper bag tightly.

Small towns have their bullies, I get it. Wisteria Cove isn't different from any other small town. But Rowan doesn't deserve this. She's trying to build her business and studio. It's bullshit mean girl jealousy is what it is. I'm so mad right now I can hardly see straight as I drive to my house.

I can't remember a time when I didn't love Rowan. Maybe longer than I've let myself admit. But hearing someone tear her down like that? I want to make the whole damn town pay for saying shit like that about her and harassing her.

I take a deep breath, and try to calm my nerves, but it doesn't help. I still see Vanessa's smug face and hear her calling her a bitch. I know for a fact that is one of the things that Rowan struggles with. She has a Wednesday Addams personality. Always has and that's one of the things I love about her. She is direct and powerful. She doesn't do fake or other bullshit. And for the people calling her a bitch, it really bothers her. It's usually when people figure out that they can't manipulate her or get what they want from her. Then all the sudden she becomes a bitch. It's ridiculous. Rowan has a heart of gold and does a lot for people. She just doesn't go around advertising it and is a good person to the core.

I grip the steering wheel harder than I should. I don't know how to tell Rowan that her best friend is shady as hell. But I know I have to. She doesn't need Jessica.

I don't know what's coming next with Rowan, or with Sammy's little scheme, but I know one thing's for sure. I'm not standing on the sidelines and letting anyone give her a hard time. That's my best friend.

———

Remy's house smells like lemon and clean laundry, and it always feels cozy like a real home. Something I so badly want my house to feel like, someday. Ivy and Junie are in the kitchen when I walk in, rolling out pasta on the kitchen island. Ivy smiles and says, "I'd hug you, but I have messy hands."

"It's okay," I say as I tuck the drinks in the fridge and set a tray of brownies on the counter.

Pete's on the couch next to my mom, dozing, his color looking good today. Sometimes when I see him sleeping like that, I have to do a double take and make sure he's okay. But like Remy has said, every day is a gift and we're going to love him until his very last breath and then keep on loving his legacy even more. He's our Pete.

"Hey," my mom says softly, coming towards me and glancing back at Pete. "He's resting."

I kiss her cheek and lower my voice. "How's he doing?"

"It's been a good day," she says. "He loves being here with everyone."

I nod.

"What's wrong?" she asks, searching my face, never missing much.

I pull my hat off and run my fingers through my hair. "I ran into Vanessa and Jessica at the store."

She snorts. "Oh Lord. What did Tweedledee and Tweedledum want?"

"Invited me to a Pilates class," I say, crossing my arms. "And then had the audacity to talk trash about Rowan to my face."

Mom's eyebrows lift high and her expression sharpens. "Pretty ballsy of them," she murmurs. "I swear, I am putting both of them in one of my next books and turning them into the villains. No one will even question it."

I try to laugh, but it comes out flat. "I do not like those two making trouble for Row."

That gets her full attention. "Sweetheart," she says, "they've hated the Maren sisters for years. Especially Rowan. She shines, and small people can't stand bright women. I'm not surprised."

She steps closer, lowering her voice. "But of all people for Jessica to cozy up with, it had to be them. I know that hurts. Rowan would never admit it, but she feels things deep. And this? This will cut her."

A small ache blooms inside me, heavier now that she names it.

Mom sighs, shaking her head. "I also heard Sammy is an investor for that Pilates studio which means those two idiots aren't just being mean, they're playing games. And if Rowan is in their way, they will push. Hard." She looks at me, eyes full of understanding and something almost fierce. "Make sure Rowan knows she still has her people. She needs that right now more than anything."

And I realize she's right. Rowan may act tough, but this kind of betrayal hits her heart first.

They're trying to keep it quiet, but nothing stays quiet here for long. He's been making trouble because it affects his investment. They're threatened by Rowan. She's always had an amazing turnout for her classes. I can't wait for her to start them back up again.

"Isn't that illegal or something?" I ask, shaking my head. "Conflict of interest for Sammy?"

She gives a small smirk. "Yes, and that's why a lot of towns-people are whispering about getting him removed. He's a shitty mayor. He needs to go."

I think about Rowan and how hard she's been fighting to keep everything going through these stupid obstacles Sammy made up to keep her from her classes. And how Marilyn, Vanessa, and

Sammy are circling like vultures. And now her friend Jessica getting involved in that, too? Ridiculous.

I can feel the restless pull in my chest. The part of me that's always trying to fix things for people I care about. I look over at Pete and Mom, the warm light filling the room, and something settles sharp and clear in my chest. I'd give anything to fix Pete right now.

I'm not letting them push Rowan around. Not without a fight.

———

Later that night after I ate way too much pasta, played the game Trouble with Junie six times, and said goodbye to everyone, I finally got into my truck to head home with a full stomach and heart. I couldn't stop thinking about Rowan for most of the night. I was at the dinner but wishing she was there. Before I pull out, I send her a text.

What are you doing?

Rowan: Working on my plants. How was dinner at Remy's?

I grin the second I realize she's at the house, right where I wanted her. I knew moving all those plants in the house would pull her in closer and it worked. She's a part of the place now, her energy tucked into every corner. I want her near me any way I can get her. If I can't love her out loud, I'll love her in quiet, in the small ways. Whatever it takes until she realizes we're *it*.

I drive home and swing my truck into the driveway. After I put it in park, I head toward the backyard. I whip out my phone and pull up my song. It starts playing as I round the corner and there she is in a tank top, cut off shorts, and hair pulled up in a messy bun looking hot as usual.

"Is that my song?" she calls with a smirk.

"Sure is." I flip on the string lights in the green house and she looks up in surprise.

"When did you put those up?" she asks in awe.

"This morning before I went to work."

"Thank you for all of this, Finn. Really. You didn't have to do this, and I owe you big time," she says as she licks her lips which makes me take a deep breath and look to the sky for support. Fuck me.

"Want to go swimming?" I challenge as I look down at the beach in the distance, hoping she'll say yes. It's a warm summer night and I wish she'd take me up on it and cool down with me. And I can gently break the news to her that her friend is a trash bag.

She looks toward the water longingly. "I don't have my suit."

I give her a look. "Swim in your tank top. And since when has that stopped us?"

"Okay, let's go. Race you," she calls as she takes off to the wooden stairs down to the cove at the back of the property. I chase after her, and she squeals in laughter as she runs faster.

"If you dunk me, Finn, I swear!" she warns over her shoulder. "Let me at least get my shorts off first."

I tug my shirt off with one pull from the back of my neck and toss it, sliding my jeans down, while kicking my boots off. I bend to pull my socks off and can't help but peek towards her.

She slips out of her shoes, peels off her socks, unbuttons her shorts, and kicks them off to reveal black panties that instantly have me hard. Damn it.

She runs in and swims out, floating as she waits. She watches me and smirks. "Nice boner."

"I can't help it," I sputter. "You have an advantage. I can't tell when you're turned on."

She says nothing but smirks and leans back and floats, her breast bobbing through her tank top that I can see her hard nipples through. Maybe I can.

I dive in, coming to the surface next to her.

"How was your day?" she asks, expression relaxed.

I blow out a breath, unsure whether to tell her or not. "Okay."

She glances at me, a worried look on her face. "Pete?"

"He was okay tonight," I say quietly.

"What's wrong then?"

I just say it and get it over with. "I ran into Vanessa and Jessica at the store. I don't think Jessica is your friend, babe. She isn't right. I don't like her hanging around those snakes."

She bites her lip and looks down at the water that's glowing in the moonlight. "I know," she says softly.

"I'm sorry."

"I was supposed to go on a girls' trip with her next week," she says, her voice flat.

"Coconut Beach?" I ask, glancing over at her.

We grew up spending summers there. My mom's cottage sits right on the beach, and for as long as I can remember, our families have shared it with the Marens. It's always been one of my favorite places. Sun, palm trees, late-night bonfires, and lazy days on the beach.

She nods slowly. "Yeah. I was really looking forward to it. Good food, drinks with little umbrellas, lazy days on the sand with a stack of books I've been meaning to read. I actually cleared my schedule. First vacation in what feels like forever."

I study the way her shoulders dip, how tired her eyes look even when she tries to shrug it off. She never lets herself rest. That trip probably felt like a promise.

"Can you still go?" I ask quietly, even though my chest is already tight.

"I texted Jessica about it and she made up a lame excuse about not being able to go," Rowan says, rubbing her arm like she is trying to smooth the hurt out of her skin. "I can't believe she bailed on me like that. But she's been avoiding me. I checked with my sisters, and they are both busy. My mom just got back. I don't know what I'll do."

And still, Rowan's voice stays soft. She's trying so hard to understand. To not take it personally. That is who she is. She has a heart bigger than the whole damn town. Even when people hurt her, she tries to find reasons to forgive them. Fire on the outside, tenderness tucked deep beneath it.

God, I love that about her.

I swallow my anger and try to breathe past it.

She deserves someone who shows up. Someone who does not leave her standing alone in the middle of plans she was excited about.

"I'll go," I hear myself say, shrugging like it is no big deal even though it feels huge in my chest. "If you want. I'll go with you."

Her head snaps up, eyes wide with surprise. For a second, hope flickers through them. Small, bright, fragile.

And seeing it makes every ounce of anger inside me burn hotter. Because she should never doubt that someone will choose her. She should never feel alone. Not as long as I am here.

She glances at me and wrinkles her brow. "You can't just take off like that from work with no notice. It's literally in just a few days."

I shrug. "Why not? I'm the boss. I can do whatever I want."

She bites her lip. "I do have an extra ticket."

"So, let's do it."

"There's only one room, Finn."

"And?"

She looks at me as if she's considering it. "You really want to go?"

I'd go anywhere with you Rowan. "Sure, it'll be fun," I say instead, playing it cool.

And I mean it.

"We can think about it," she says softly.

I don't need to think about it. I can tell she thinks I'm saying I'll go out of pity, but I'm not. I'd follow this woman to the ends of the earth. But a week in Coconut Beach with her? Sign me up.

CHAPTER 8

Rowan

PARADISE CITY BY GUNS N' ROSES

WILLA'S at the front counter, working on her supply order, with a black cauldron shaped mug that says, "Witch Better Have my Latte" beside her. Since my shop isn't busy at the moment and I'm keeping an eye on it through the doorway that connects the two businesses, I'm helping her unpack a new shipment of romance novels, stacking them in tidy piles for her while we talk and catch up.

Ivy's perched on the stool at the counter, doodling cupcakes and confetti in her notebook, looking like she's planning world domination one children's birthday party at a time.

"Okay, so this party theme is 'The Good Witch's Garden,'" Ivy says, scribbling a note next to the confetti. "There will be sparkly potion bottles, decorating witch hats, and a butterfly release. Do you think these kids can handle glitter in their potions?"

Willa groans. "No one can handle glitter, Ivy. Glitter is the devil."

I laugh, stacking another row of books. "Maybe we should put a warning sign up at the entrance to the party. *'Participate at your own risk. You'll sparkle for the rest of your life.'*"

Ivy looks up with a mischievous grin. "Speaking of sparkle.

Let's talk about your trip to Coconut Beach. Are you excited? You finally get to wear all those sexy bikinis you bought."

Oh no. I forgot about the bikinis.

Jessica and I originally planned this trip to find hot beach guys and flirt our way through Coconut Beach. Now? I'll have a hot guy *with* me.

I still don't know if he was serious about actually going. He *seemed* serious. And knowing us, it would be easy. It always is with him, and he'd make me laugh the whole time. We'd probably drink too many fruity cocktails. It would be a good time. It might also break my heart if he meets someone there. Because if Finn comes, there's a chance of that happening. I'll have to smile through it while watching him flirt with another woman like it doesn't gut me a little.

Willa arches an eyebrow so sharp it could slice someone. "Please tell me you are not still considering taking Jessica after she's been acting like a dumbass."

Before I can answer, Ivy gasps dramatically, pressing a hand to her heart like she has been personally wronged. "She doesn't deserve a trip to Coconut Beach," she declares. "She deserves a curse. Maybe she can always step on Legos."

Willa spins toward her. "Legos? Ivy, aim higher. We're witches."

"Oh, I'm aiming," Ivy says, eyes narrowing with mischief. "I'm thinking something that makes her eyelashes fall out one at a time during important conversations."

Willa snorts. "I was thinking more along the lines of a hex that keeps leaving her on read for the rest of her life. Every single message. Radio silence. No dopamine for her ever again."

"That's diabolical." Ivy looks genuinely impressed.

I try to cut in, but they are revving up now, feeding off each other's outrage like it is a coven sport.

"And the mayor," Ivy says, lifting a finger. "We're not forgetting that worm."

Willa nods sharply. "Oh, don't worry. I have ideas for him."

"Same," Ivy says, rolling her shoulders like she is about to go twelve rounds in a magical boxing ring. "I'm thinking a tiny charm that makes him forget every single talking point during public speeches. Right when the cameras start rolling."

Willa bursts out laughing. "Perfect. And I will add one that unties his shoelaces at the worst possible moment. Every time he tries to be dramatic or smug, boom, on the floor."

"I would pay actual money to see that," Ivy muses dreamily.

My head drops into my hands. "Guys. Please."

They both ignore me completely.

"Oh, oh," Ivy says, snapping her fingers like she just discovered fire. "A mild itching spell. Not harmful, just… inconvenient."

"Yes," Willa breathes, eyes sparkling. "Right in the middle of council meetings. The man would unravel."

I groan. "You two are unhinged."

Willa crosses her arms, chin lifting. "We're your sisters. What did you expect? That we'd just let this crap happen to you? Not a chance. We're here for revenge."

"And someone is screwing with our sister," Ivy adds, voice fierce in a way that makes my chest squeeze. "The audacity."

There it is. The heart of it. Beneath the jokes and hex ideas and creative ways to ruin Sammy Briggs's life, they are furious on my behalf. Protective. Ready to start magical warfare over me.

A warmth spreads through my chest, unexpected and a little overwhelming. I feel loved. Supported. Seen. And just a little exasperated because they really might try one of these spells if left unsupervised.

I sigh, but a smile tugs at my lips. "I appreciate the enthusiasm."

They exchange a look that absolutely means there will be hexes.

Willa steps closer and squeezes my arm. "We always have your back. Always."

Ivy nods, slipping her hand into mine. "No one messes with a Maren."

And even though the world is still spinning and the mayor is still a disaster, and my life feels unsteady, standing here between my sisters makes everything inside me settle.

This is my coven. My family. My home.

And they will burn the world down before they let me fall.

I slide the last stack of books onto the shelf, but my hands are shaking a little. The words scrape out of me before I can stop them. "I am one hundred percent not taking Jessica. Not now. Not ever."

It sounds firm, final, almost cold. But inside, something aches.

Because it is not about Pilates. It is not about Marilyn or Vanessa. It is not even about Coconut Beach.

It's the way she laughed along when those two tore me apart, even though her eyes flicked away like she knew it was wrong. It's the way she keeps dodging my calls and pretending nothing is wrong, like I imagined all of it.

It hits me harder than I want to admit. I thought she was my friend. A real one. Not another girl who gets close to me until the town's pecking order tells her she is supposed to choose a side.

I press my palm to the shelf to steady myself. "She flaked on me, Willa. She let them talk about me like I was garbage. And she did not say a word." My voice cracks, embarrassingly soft. "If she can't even defend me when I am not in the room, then she never cared at all."

The truth settles in my chest, heavy and familiar in a way that makes my throat burn. "I should have seen it sooner. She's just another girl who decided it is safer to stand with people who hate me than beside me."

My voice wobbles, but I force a breath. "So, no. I am not taking Jessica. I am done begging people to treat me like I matter."

Willa and Ivy nod in agreement.

"I'm taking Finn," I say, cheeks warming, knowing how much crap they're going to give me after this confession. But it's better to rip the band-aid off and get it over with. Let the teasing commence. They're obviously going to figure it out if he goes with me.

Ivy gasps like I just announced I'm marrying him. She leans across the counter, clutching her pen like this is the juiciest gossip she's heard all week. "You're taking Finn to Coconut Beach?"

Willa's grin spreads slowly and wide. "Oh, this is good." She sets down the pen next to her list. "This is *really* good."

I lift my chin, pretending I'm unfazed even though my stomach is doing that dumb swoopy thing it always does when Finn's name comes up. "He offered to go with me," I say, aiming for casual, but it comes out a little too fast. "Like you said, flights are already booked with no refunds, and I figured, why not? He loves Coconut Beach. And he has time to go. It's practical."

Smooth, Rowan, I think to myself. I sound like a clown.

Ivy snorts. "Practical my ass. This is Finn Bennett. You're going to be in a tropical paradise with the man who looks like a woman's wet dream. Alone. In a cute little one-bedroom beach cottage. And let's not forget that he'll be shirtless all week. Have you seen his chiseled torso?"

I try not to imagine Finn shirtless. It doesn't work. I've seen it so many times, and it never gets old. His body is so ripped with muscle from all the physical labor he does every day. He's a literal wet dream. But I'm never admitting that to them.

"Oh no," Willa says dramatically, clutching her chest and pretending to swoon. "Poor Rowan. Forced to take a beach vacation with a hot, loyal, emotionally stable man who clearly adores her."

"Oh, stop it," I warn, pointing at her. "He's my best friend."

"Uh-huh," Ivy drawls, clearly not buying it. She taps her pen against her notebook. "Friends who just happen to vacation together and have off-the-charts chemistry."

"For the record, Tate is my best friend. And I do dirty things with that man," Willa says with a smirk. "Maybe you need to do those things with your best friend, too."

I roll my eyes, but my face is burning. "It's not like that."

Willa makes a little *mmhmm* sound that has me wanting to throw a cookie from the plate on the table at her. "You're going to come back tan, relaxed, and in love."

"They're already in love," Ivy corrects softly, and that's when I know I've lost. "Right now, they're just in denial."

Willa looks at me thoughtfully. "Maybe we should put a spell on you so that you come back more in love than you ever could imagine." She tilts her head at Ivy, and Ivy nods with approval.

Willa begins to gather items, and I stare at her. "Stop it. We're not in love and you'd better not do any of your love spells."

"Mom probably has already been working on a love spell for the both of you." Willa shrugs. "I'll just add in a little extra touch."

"Great idea," Ivy says, nodding fast like she's had three cups of coffee. "Yes, this is a great plan. Sun, sea, and finally realizing Finn is your endgame."

I nearly drop a stack of paperbacks. "He's not my endgame."

Willa snorts. "Rowan, he literally built you a greenhouse and moved all of your plants onto his property. That's husband behavior."

Just as I'm about to argue, a customer steps up to the counter like she's on a mission.

"Excuse me," the woman says. "Do you have any recommendations for cozy fall reads with magic... but not, like, *too* much magic?"

I flip my hair back like this is the moment I was born for. "Ah. You're speaking my language."

I grab a copy of *Practical Magic*, *Fall Too Well*, and my personal favorite, *The Pumpkin Spice Spell*. I set them down with a flourish as the woman's friends also join us, curious. "These are perfect. A little chaos, a little love, some mild hexing. Basically, real-life small-town magic."

"Okay, I'll take them," the first woman says. Then she squints at us. "Wait. You guys aren't *the* Maren sisters, are you?"

I deadpan. "Depends on who's asking. Friend or foe?"

She laughs. "You're funny and definitely friend."

"Thanks," I say sweetly. "I would have been burned at the stake in 1692 for this personality. And yes, we are, in fact, the Maren sisters."

That gets a full-on giggle fit from her friends. One of them looks at the others and back at me. "Can we take a picture with you guys? You're like iconic."

I glance at Willa and Ivy, who are already smirking like smug little witches that they are. "Sure," I say, sliding between them for the photo.

"Smile, Wisteria Cove's witchy sweethearts," Ivy stage-whispers, and I elbow her in the ribs while still cheesing for the camera.

They wander off to browse more books, still giggling and looking at the picture on their phones and back at us. I plop down on the stool next to Ivy, and Willa slides a mug of tea my way like she's rewarding me for unboxing her books for her, not that I minded in the least.

My phone dings in my pocket. I pull it out and glance at the screen.

Finn: I found a cat. I think I'm keeping him.

"Finn found a cat," I tell them as I text him back.

What? Where?

Finn: Someone dumped him on the edge of town. One of my clients found him.

What kind of asshole dumps a cat?

Finn: I know, right? He's so cute.

Willa lets out a long, dramatic sigh. "The kitty distribution system is working overtime in this town and I'm here for it."

Ivy laughs. "We have barn cats at the farm now. Tate and you have Cobweb. Now Finn's got one. It's almost like…"

"Don't even say it," I mutter as my fingers fly over the phone texting him back as Ivy leans over to read it.

> I'm coming to see it as soon as it's time to close the shop.

Ivy smirks. "You're going to 'see it.' Uh huh."

"I'm going to make sure he didn't find a demon in disguise," I say, standing when I hear the bell over the door ding on my side of the shop. "I'll catch up with you guys later."

"Right," Ivy says, tapping her pen. "Don't think we're done talking about your sexy time vacay with Finn. We'll pick this up again, later. And we'll work on your love spell."

"Yeah, we're going to need to plan this out!" Willa calls.

No, we're not. I shake my head as I hurry over to my shop. But I am starting to get excited about this trip to Coconut Beach.

———

After I closed the shop, I made my way to Finn's house where his truck's out front, tailgate down, and there's a cardboard box sitting on the ground next to it with a piece of screen over the top.

When I look inside the box, it's the grumpiest looking thing I've ever seen. A tortoiseshell cat glares up at me with bright green eyes, like I personally hexed its bloodline.

"Hi, kitty," I say softly. Which makes the cat look like he's glaring even more and blinks at me slowly like he's already over me.

Finn's crouched beside the little grump, sleeves rolled up, sawdust still clinging to his forearms. He looks like he just stepped out of a *blue-collar hottie* calendar shoot with his broad shoulders, forearms that could probably bench press me, and that easy, rugged kind of strength that doesn't need to brag. He's the epitome of big dick energy. *Best friend big dick energy*, I think to myself. Also, I've seen his boners through his boxers. Definitely big dick energy.

When he looks up, that slow, deep grin of his hits me right in the stomach and trickles down to my lady parts. My knees forget what they're supposed to be doing.

"Isn't he cute?" he says, voice warm and low, like he's got no idea he's the real problem here looking like that.

"Why does his face look like that?"

Finn frowns. "What do you mean?"

"He looks angry like he's plotting something. Blink once if you're safe right now, Finn. Has he held you captive or something? Do you have Stockholm Syndrome?"

Finn laughs softly, eyes crinkling. "No, that's just his face. He's misunderstood."

I scoff and cross my arms, pretending not to melt at Finn looking so good with the cat. And he's not wrong. I can't tell you how many times people have called me a bitch and not liked me because I'm quiet, admitted have a resting bitch face at times, and can be serious. It's literally my Scorpio personality. "So, what's his name?"

"Allen," he says, gazing at the cat lovingly like he's a newborn.

"Allen? Really?"

"Yeah, like as in Allen wrench."

I blink. "You named the cat after a tool. No wonder he looks like he wants to murder you."

He grins. "He looks sharp and reliable."

"He definitely looks like he could have sharp claws or a shiv."

He stands, brushing his hands on his jeans, and the look he gives me is too warm, too soft. "Nah, I think he likes me. Don't you, Allen?"

Allen responds with a glare directed at both of us.

I bravely reach into the box and scoop Allen up. The cat lets out a half-hearted grumble but doesn't fight. He's warm and surprisingly cuddly. Finn watches me like I'm picking up his newborn baby.

"You love him already," Finn teases. "I knew you'd love Allen."

I meet his eyes. "He's got attitude and I respect that."

We stand there for a beat too long, just staring at each other while Allen purrs like a tiny engine with his absolutely terrifying RBF. Hmm, maybe he is misunderstood.

"So," Finn says, clearing his throat. "What's the plan for the trip? You still letting me come?"

I stroke Allen's soft head and scratch his ears, the little grump growing on me. "I meant it, you know. You don't have to go."

He pretends to look mildly offended, "I want to go. Do you not want me to come?"

"I just don't want you to feel obligated. Like I'm pitiful and need someone to go with me."

He smirks but gives me a flirty look that he knows works on me when he wants to soften me up. "If it means sunscreening your back and laughing all week with you? Yeah, I'm going."

My stomach somersaults and I remind him, "There's only one room, Finn. You have to be near me like all the time."

He steps closer, enough that I can smell cedar and coffee and something that makes me dizzy. "I'm pretty sure we can figure it out. You were going to share with Jessica." He says her name as if it's a disgusting bug.

"Yeah, but she's a girlfriend and doesn't mind sharing with me."

He leans in a little, eyes steady on mine, voice dropping lower than usual. "Rowan," he says, and my name sounds different on his tongue. Warmer. Rougher. "I definitely don't mind sharing with you."

The air tightens and his tone is suggestive without crossing a line, like he is testing the waters, like he's saying one thing but meaning more. And when he said "you," it hit me low in my stomach, because he's not just being polite.

He sounds like he wants this. He wants *me*.

And the way he said Jessica's name earlier, being dismissive, almost irritated makes this feel even more serious. Sharing a space with Jessica would be tolerable. Sharing with me? That feels like something he wants. Something he's offering.

Heat flickers through me, unexpected and sharp. I try to swallow, but my throat is dry. I should laugh it off. I should say something breezy. But all I can do is look at him and feel that familiar, terrifying pull.

I look down at Allen, whose grumpy face seems to be judging both of us while he's still purring. What an odd cat.

"Who is going to watch him?" I whisper, snuggling him close to my chin, the cat surprisingly purring harder, liking it.

"Remy said he'd be happy to watch his new nephew, Allen. Remy and Tate are also going to check on your plants with your sisters while we're gone. Everything has been worked out."

I chuckle at him referring to Allen as Remy's nephew. Finn's always had a soft spot for animals.

"Alright. Pack your swimsuit, flip flops, and sunscreen because we are going to spend the whole week relaxing, Coconut Ken. I need this," I say, trying to sound breezy.

But the second the words are out, my mind betrays me. Because I know exactly how relaxed I will be with Finn sitting next to me in a beach chair all week. Sun on his shoulders. That warm, steady smile. The way he looks at me sometimes, like he is seeing something I do not know how to hide.

Finn's grin spreads, slow and certain. "Yes."

Allen lets out a tiny meow, like he is adding his vote.

"Welcome to the chaos, Allen," I tell him softly. "You fit right in."

But Finn's smile lingers and it stays on his mouth, in his eyes, in the air between us. Slow. Devastating. Warm in a way that does things to me I am not ready to admit.

I try not to picture the cottage by the beach. Or the one bed. Or how much space Finn takes up without even trying. His body heat beside me, inches away. The softness of sheets and sand and the quiet sound of waves outside the window. Him turning over in the night and brushing against me and his breath on my neck.

I swallow, heat blooming low in my stomach.

One small bed. Just one. Fine for most people. But Finn is not most people. Finn takes up space just by existing. And the thought of sharing that cottage with him burrows under my skin on the drive home, warm and impossible to shake.

By the time I crawl into bed, it is still there, pulsing through me with every heartbeat.

I already know exactly where my mind is going to wander once I close my eyes. And I don't fight it.

———————

I jolt awake in the middle of the night, my heart pounding, sweaty with the heat pulled at my core. The sheets are tangled around my legs, the moonlight leaking through the curtains just enough to paint the ceiling in silver streaks.

For a few seconds, I can't breathe. It's like my body hasn't caught up to the fact that it was just a dream. My skin is flushed and warm, and I can still feel Finn's hands and mouth on me.

God, it felt so real and *so* good. I have never had an orgasm in a dream before. This is a wild feeling.

I roll onto my back and press a shaky palm to my chest, my heart beating so fast. The edges of the dream cling to me, my legs still shaking. It felt so real and I can still hear the sound of the ocean and the taste of salt on his skin.

I close my eyes, and I still feel his breath against my neck before he kissed me. The low sound he made when I touched him and ran my hands down his chiseled torso. The weight of him over me and moving. The way I felt... safe and complete. The way I unraveled in a way I've never let myself before.

I've had great dreams before. Stupid, fleeting flashes that disappeared the second I opened my eyes. But this one felt real, and like Finn and I were at Coconut Beach with the warm sand under our feet, and a soft breeze on our bodies through an open window as Finn made me come over and over. Until I woke up from my dream having a real orgasm.

I swear I can still feel his fingertips brushing down my spine, his mouth on my body. His voice was low and rough, whispering things that send heat curling through every inch of me while I replay it in my head.

God, it was only a dream, but it felt so real. How am I supposed to go on this trip with Finn in a few days and trust myself to sleep in the same cottage as him and not have sex dreams with him nearby? It'll be so embarrassing.

I drag a hand over my face, half mortified, half dizzy from how real this was. This isn't some silly crush anymore. This isn't just best friends and easy smiles. This is deeper and messier like it's been simmering for years, waiting for a crack to push its way through, and tonight it changed something in me.

I shift under the sheet, trying to shake it off, but I can't. My skin tingles where he touched me in that dream. My stomach flips like I'm still there, tangled up with him while the world faded away.

It wasn't just the physical part, though. That's the thing that undoes me the most. It was the way he looked at me. Like I was it for him and he'd been waiting for me just as long as I've been quietly, stupidly waiting for him.

A breath shudders out of me as I press the heels of my hands against my eyes. I shouldn't let a dream mess me up like this. Because if it felt that real in my sleep, what would it feel like if it actually happened?

My throat tightens because it wouldn't just be physical and never could be with Finn. Being with him would be the kind of thing that changes everything. If I was ever with Finn like that it would be impossible to go back to being just friends if anything happened. It would change everything and ruin the friendship.

I turn onto my side and stare at the soft glow of the fairy lights over my small bookshelf. The quiet of the small studio apartment wraps around me, but I can still hear his voice in my head. I can still feel him.

And the scariest part? It didn't feel like a fantasy. It felt inevitable.

I let out a soft laugh that sounds more like a sigh. "God, Rowan," I whisper to the ceiling. "You're so gone for him."

This trip to Coconut Beach isn't even here yet, and my brain is already trying to undo me in my sleep.

My fingers twist in the sheets. If I go… if we're there together… I don't know if I could keep pretending.

Because tonight, in my dream, it didn't feel like pretending at all. It felt pretty damn real.

CHAPTER 9

Finn

YOUR LOVE BY THE OUTFIELD

I WAKE up to the sound of the ocean drifting through the open window, carrying that salty breeze that always makes me sleep so well. Allen is curled against my side, snoring like an old man. He stretches when I move, then curls right back into a little donut shape like he owns the place and isn't new here. I never knew I needed a cat, but here we are.

My suitcase is lying open on the floor. I sit up and look at it, feeling that quiet hum in my chest I haven't felt in a long time. My hygiene bag sits on the dresser, toothbrush sticking out like it's mocking me for how early I packed. I can't even pretend like I'm not ridiculously excited about this trip with Rowan.

Coconut Beach. *With her.* I grin like an idiot just thinking about spending a week with her in paradise.

She'll probably pretend it's no big deal, because that's what Rowan does when something feels too close to the chest. But I know her. She'll love the beach, and I can already see her there, bare feet in the sand, hair blowing wild, sunlight in her eyes, her skin turning a beautiful, golden color because she tans so easily.

I give Allen a lazy scratch behind the ears. "We're in trouble, buddy."

He purrs like he agrees and gives me the most unfriendly stare.

Later that afternoon, I'm in the workshop finishing up the last stain coat on the cabinets for a client, my hands steady as I work. But my brain? It's nowhere near here. It's already in Coconut Beach with Rowan.

I picture her laughing and playfully rolling her eyes at me when I pick a corny song for her on a little speaker we take down to the beach. I can see her walking through the sand in one of those bikinis she bought I overheard her showing her sisters. And for the record, they were hot.

"Hey." Ivy's voice cuts through my daydream. I look up and she's walking toward me with a brown paper bag and an amused expression. She holds it out. "I figured you haven't taken a break or packed yourself something to eat."

"You'd be right." I wipe my hands and take the bag. Inside is a sandwich, chips, a cookie, and an apple. Classic Ivy. She's always taking care of everyone, and she has been the best thing to happen to my brother since Junie.

She hops up on the workbench next to me like she's done a hundred times. We've always had an easy friendship. She knows too much about me, and I trust her with anything. I've been confiding in her about Rowan for months now and she always has solid advice when it comes to her sister.

"So," she says, kicking her feet lightly, "when exactly are you and Rowan going to stop orbiting each other like confused satellites and just become a couple?"

I bark out a laugh as I unwrap the sandwich, suddenly so hungry and remembering I forgot to eat breakfast. "Subtle, Ivy."

She smirks. "I'm serious. It's getting annoying seeing you two be so sexually frustrated when we all know you could just put each other out of your misery."

I lean back against the bench, chewing slowly on a bite of sandwich, trying to keep my voice steady. "I think she thinks we will ruin the friendship if we cross that line."

The words sit heavy in my chest, because I know that is true. Rowan protects her heart. She has to. She has been dropped too many times. And I have watched every one of those drops. I have picked up the pieces when other people walked away or she lost them, like her dad.

But there is more I never say out loud. It slips past my defenses before I can swallow it down.

"And maybe she worries that it is just attraction," I admit, staring down at my hands. "Just heat." My throat feels tight. "She doesn't date much. She hasn't had something real in a long time. Maybe she thinks that's all this is. Something temporary."

I let out a long breath, rubbing my thumb over the edge of the workbench.

"But that is not what I want with her," I say quietly, the truth finally rising in my chest. "I want more than that. More than trying to get something out of our system. With Rowan... God." I shake my head. "With her, I want everything."

The admission lands between us, real and exposed, and I feel the weight of it settle in my ribs.

"That is why I have held back," I say, voice low. "Because I'm scared that she will think it's only physical for me."

I force myself to meet Ivy's eyes.

"But she isn't a fling. She's it for me. And if she doesn't feel the same, I can't risk losing her completely."

The truth leaves me raw and unsteady.

"She's the only person I want," I say softly. "And the one person I'm terrified to lose."

Ivy tilts her head. "That's dumb. Look at Remy and me. Tate and Willa. We're all fine. Beyond fine, actually," she says wiggling her eyebrows.

I shake my head, snorting. "But Rowan's different. She's careful with her heart."

Ivy nods, her expression softening. "Yeah, you're probably right. When our dad died, she started pushing people away. She didn't want to let anyone get too close and risk losing anyone else."

I stare at the floor, letting that sit heavy in my chest. I've always known losing their dad changed everything for them but hearing it directly from Ivy hits different. I nod slowly. "Yeah. Makes sense."

Remy and I grew up without our biological dad. But honestly, we've always had Pete. He was there for us when it mattered. And our mom made sure we had everyone in our life who mattered and treated us well. Last I heard, our dad started a new family a few hours away and never bothered to be a part of our lives. So, we just leaned into the people who wanted to be there for us. But losing your dad tragically and losing your dad who is still living are two different types of grief. I'm not sad about our dad anymore and neither is Remy. We know who loved us and who mattered. But this whole town was devastated when Tate's dad and Rowan's dad went missing on a commercial fishing trip years back and never came back. Their boat was never recovered either and that was even worse. No one truly knows what exactly happened.

She bumps her shoulder against mine, loosening the mood. "For what it's worth, we're all rooting for you to finally get it together."

I let out a low laugh. "No pressure, right?"

Her grin turns wicked. "None at all. Just… passionately bang each other until the town of Coconut Beach files a noise complaint."

I give her a look like what the heck, shake my head, and take another bite of my sandwich, but my brain's already in Coconut Beach. Back to imagining Rowan walking next to me, laughing, sun on her face.

I can't predict what will happen. But something about this trip feels like a shift. And I know what I *want* to happen.

I smile to myself. "We'll see what happens."

Ivy's grin widens. "Oh, I think I know exactly what's going to happen."

I'm not going to even pretend I don't want that, too.

———

The music's loud enough that it vibrates through the still mostly empty house I'm remodeling, my summer playlist full of old rock and a little country. Sweat slides down the back of my neck as I tighten the last screw on the kitchen light fixture that Rowan picked out, my drill grinding over the music. When it finally clicks into place, I step back, grinning like an idiot. I look around proudly at my house. This was my friend Tate's childhood home and when his mom sold it, I made sure it was okay with him before I bought it. Partly I wanted it for the land that backs up to the cove, and partly because it's just down the street from Rowan's shop. I knew over a decade ago I wanted this house if it ever sold. Tate didn't care either way and had no attachment to it. He was happy to see me put the life back into it that it deserved and try to make better memories here than he had growing up. It has great bones, and I dreamed about remodeling this house and keeping the historical parts of it intact. Our uncle passed away leaving his tree farm to us a few years back. I didn't really have an interest in the tree farm but my brother has always loved it. So, he bought me out, giving him the farm, and me the money to buy the house. I have the house but now I need to fund the renovations. I'm fixing it up little by little and we're both living our dreams.

The house sits perched above the rocky shoreline, and feels like it's been here forever, quietly watching the boats come into the cove. The cedar shingles have long since faded to a soft silvery gray, and the salt air has worn the siding smooth under years of storms and summer breezes. White trim frames every window, a little chipped at the corners.

From the porch, you can hear the waves crash against the

rocks below. Not loud. Just steady like a heartbeat. Seagulls drift overhead, their calls stretching across the wind.

Inside, the floorboards sigh beneath every step. I'm replacing a lot of the sub floors but to be honest, I feel like the creaks and groans gives the old house character. The walls are painted a soft cream in Betsy's Linen that feels warm and like a blank canvas that's ready for new life. The windows are wide and a little wavy with old glass, and when the light hits just right, it spills golden across the room like honey. A large stone fireplace anchors the living room, and the scent of sea salt clings to the wood mantel no matter how many candles you burn.

It's the kind of house that feels a little alive. Like it's waiting for someone to come home. Everything I put into this house makes it feel even more like home.

The windows are wide open, letting in the warm evening air that smells like the ocean and Rowan's herbs from the plants in the yard. My tools are scattered across the counter, flooring samples fanned out like a deck of cards. I'm working longer hours to clear my schedule for that week away. I may be the boss, but I still have a schedule to keep.

I wipe my forehead with the back of my arm and grab two glasses of cold water. Through the window, she's out there, barefoot in the grass, black crop top, little cut-off jeans that should be illegal. She's bent over her herbs, murmuring to them like they're her little green babies. She swears talking to them makes them grow faster. Honestly? At this point, I believe her. Everything she touches thrives.

"Hey, plant whisperer," I call as I step outside. The planks creak under my bare feet, reminding me that they're getting a fresh reset eventually, too. By the time I'm done with this house it's going to feel like the kind of home that stays in families for generations to come.

She looks up, a soft strand of hair stuck to her cheek, sunlight long gone but the porch light catching the curve of her smile.

"Hey, Carpenter Ken" she teases.

"Whatever, Garden Barbie." I hand her the glass.

She laughs, a soft belly laugh that hits me square in the chest. I take a long drink of water because it's either that or stare at her legs a second too long.

And of course, I stare anyway. Those legs are tan, toned, smooth. I picture them around my hips, and my throat goes dry, so I drain the rest of my water like it's going to save me.

She drinks her water, herbs fanned out in her harvest basket like a little bouquet. "You're quiet," she says.

"Just thinking," I reply. Then, before my common sense can stop me, I smirk. "About how I'll probably show up in your dreams tonight."

Her eyes go wide. She freezes mid-sip, choking on her water.

Holy shit. Did she really have a dream about me? I was just giving her shit, but I definitely hit a nerve.

I try not to laugh as she sputters. "What?" I ask, all fake innocence.

She guzzles her water too fast and then says, "Nothing."

My grin grows slow and wicked. "Rowan Maren."

"No."

"You had a dream about me."

"No, I didn't," she blurts way too quickly.

I'm enjoying every second of this. "You 100% did."

Her face goes pink. "You're ridiculous."

"Yeah?" I step closer. "So what was it? Something romantic? Something steamy? Was I wearing a toolbelt or—"

She slaps my chest, laughing despite herself. "Shut up!"

"Oooh, you're blushing," I tease, leaning down until I can see the way her pupils dilate just a little. "Was it a good dream at least with a happy ending?"

"I hate you," she mutters, but she's smiling.

I chuckle and brush a bit of basil off her shoulder. "No, baby," I say, voice low enough that it makes her breath hitch. "You definitely don't."

And for a heartbeat, the night air goes still. Just her, me, and the crickets.

Then she rolls her eyes, pushes off the railing, and says way too brightly, "Come on. Show me your updates before I go home to get ready before your ego gets any bigger."

I watch her walk inside with those damn legs and laugh into my empty glass.

Allen sees Rowan and immediately leaves his windowsill to go greet her with his mean ass looking mug. The summer air clings to us like warm syrup, and the second she crosses the threshold, I watch her take it all in the way she always does with excitement and encouragement to every little update that I do.

"Okay, hotshot," she says as she sets her glass down onto a table just inside the door. "Show me."

I gesture toward the kitchen as I place my empty cup next to hers. "Prepare to be impressed."

She follows me in, brushing past close enough that my entire body notices. I flip the switch, and the new light over the counter flickers to life warm, golden, and perfect. It makes the kitchen feel like home.

Her mouth curves into this soft little grin that just knocks the wind out of me. "Finn," she says, low and happy. "This looks *amazing*. I love how you picked out the light I liked."

I pretend to look casual, leaning a hip against the counter, but I can feel my chest swelling like a damn idiot. "Yeah?"

"Yeah." She steps closer, tilts her head up, and squints like she's appraising it for some HGTV show. "It's perfect and I love it."

I love it. Those three stupid words echo in my chest a little too hard. I clear my throat and wave toward the spread of flooring samples on the table. "Okay, next decision."

Her eyes light up. She loves this part. I swear she gets more joy out of this than I do and I love watching her face light up when she lands on the choice that she likes.

I fan the flooring samples out for her. "So," I say, "what's the verdict, Basil Barbie?"

She drops into one of the chairs, tapping her fingers against the samples. "This one's too orange. That one's too dark. This one feels like a dentist office."

I huff out a laugh. "You're very decisive."

"You asked for my opinion." She looks up at me, one brow raised. "And I take your flooring very seriously. You're going to be stuck with this decision for a long time."

She finally taps a warm, honey-toned plank. "This one. It's clean, cozy, not too dark. It'll make this place feel like a home."

She scoops up Allen and says, "What do you think, Allen wrench?"

I nod like I'm considering it. Truth is, I already know I'll pick whatever she chooses. I've done it with every paint swatch, light fixture, and tile sample since she started giving her two cents. It's not just because I trust her taste. It's because I want her finger-prints all over this place.

"I like that one, too," I say, letting a smile tug at the corner of my mouth. "Good choice."

"Come on," she says. "It's Thursday. Go shower. I'll meet you at the Rusty Anchor."

"Bossy," I tease.

She smirks as she gives Allen one last scratch behind the ears and heads out the door, her hips swaying, "Someone's gotta keep you in line."

I shower, clean up fast, and throw on a clean T-shirt and jeans before running a hand through my hair, and try not to look like I care too much.

———————

When I get to the Rusty Anchor, she's already there.

And damn. Her hair's pulled up, a few soft pieces falling around her face, and she's in a dark gray tank top that hugs every inch of her chest in ways that should be criminal. Ripped jeans. Black Converse. No effort at all. Just Rowan. Casual and stunning and entirely too good at wrecking me just by existing.

Mack waves us toward our high-top table like he's been expecting us. "Thursday lovebirds," he calls, smirking. "I heard you moved the honeymoon to Coconut Beach."

Rowan rolls her eyes. "Mack, seriously."

I slide into a stool across from her, grin stretching wider. "He's not wrong."

She kicks me under the table, but there's a spark in her eyes. "Don't encourage him," she mouths.

"You look good," I murmur.

She arches a brow. "You don't clean up too bad yourself, Carpenter Ken."

"Yeah." I lean forward on my elbows. "Did you set up a second date with Sugar Grandpa?"

She laughs, and it's the one that always gets me. "Actually, yes. I'm meeting with him tomorrow. He's giving me a tour of his garden. Speaking of, he mentioned a few handyman things that he needs to have done. Would you want to go with me and help out a charming fella?"

Mack drops off our usual order of two beers without even asking. We've been doing this every Thursday for so long. I give him two fingers and he nods, heading toward the kitchen window.

"Let me get this straight. You want me to join you for a three-some with your fossil?"

She snorts. "Gross, Finn. He's a sweet old man."

I laugh. "Sure, I'll help. But for the record, you're into some freaky shit, Maren."

"I am not!" She shakes her head and takes a sip of her beer, leaning in, making her cleavage pop even more and causing my dick to strain even harder against my jeans.

"So," I say, picking at a coaster, "how's the Sammy drama this week?"

Her lips curve into the mischievous grin she gets when she's about to drop town gossip. "You're gonna love this. Things have actually calmed down."

I look at her with disbelief. "Calmed down?"

"Yeah." She leans closer. "Vanessa and Marilyn are apparently neck-deep in their grand opening. They've been too busy for their usual petty nonsense. Mayor Sammy's been on his best behavior. Apparently, someone put the fear in him that he could be fired, so he's been freaking out."

"Shocking," I say. "I was counting on a Thursday night rant."

She smirks, trying to make it playful. "Do not put that out there. I want vacay vibes from here on out. I need this vacation, Finn. I need peace."

She sounds light. Joking. The same Rowan everyone else sees. But the second she says "peace," something in her eyes flickers, quick and raw, like a spark dying before it catches. She hides it well, but I know that look. I know the tightness in her voice. I know the forced smile. She has been knocked around from every direction lately, and she is holding herself together with sheer willpower and a little bit of spite.

Most people would miss it entirely. I don't.

I chuckle, shaking my head for show. "Yes, you do."

But inside, my chest tightens. Because she is tired. Worn thin by the mayor's bullshit, by Marilyn's smugness, by Vanessa's cruelty, by Jessica's betrayal.

And I want to take all of it from her and give her the peace she is begging for.

I smile back at her, but underneath it is something else. Something that hurts in the best and worst ways.

Because I see her.

And I will burn the whole damn town down before I let her break.

There's a warmth in the way she looks at me, like this thing between us is quietly growing roots, even if we haven't said the words out loud yet.

When we finally step out into the night, the warm air wraps around us like a blanket. She walks a little ahead, swinging her purse, the soft light from the streetlights catching her hair.

I look at her and think about the light she loved in my kitchen. The floors she picked. The way my house already feels less like mine and more like ours, even if she doesn't know it yet.

CHAPTER 10

Rowan

LA GRANGE BY ZZ TOP

"I FEEL like I'm watching a Hallmark movie play out in real life with you and Finn," Ivy says with a sigh as I fold the last of my shorts and tuck them into my suitcase. Ivy's going to be running my shop for me while I'm gone.

I roll my eyes. "I'm definitely not a Hallmark movie."

"What do you want to be? A Netflix special like a true crime documentary? That's not romantic," she says as she scrolls through her phone.

"I don't want to be any cheesy romance. What I want is a week of relaxation. I want to come home and all the drama is over so things can go back to normal."

"Oh, I'm sure it will be. Meanwhile, don't worry about your shop. Junie and I are going to help out and we're looking forward to it," Ivy assures me.

"Thank you for all of your help."

"Hey," Willa greets as she joins us in the loft above the bookstore.

I'm packing and Ivy is apparently trying to give me romantic advice. Which I definitely don't want. We don't need to feed whatever this is festering between Finn and me. It's embarrassing enough that he called me out on my sex dream and I was so shocked I couldn't even play it off.

"I like your shirt," Willa says plopping down on my bed, watching me.

"Thanks," I say. My shirt reads, *"Crows Before Bros."*

"Speaking of, have you seen Ralphie since you moved everything out to Finn's?" Ivy asks.

"No, I'm hoping he finds me there, though."

Ralphie was the crow I had made friends with out at my cottage. He would bring me little treasures. Once, he brought me a diamond ring that we learned was missing from an older woman in town. Luckily, we were able to get it back to her. But I am still holding out hope that Ralphie will join me at Finn's. He's been my little friend for two years now.

Ivy sighs. "How does it feel to live out my dream? I want a pet crow."

"I'm sure you can find one out at the tree farm to be friends with," I tell her.

"So, did it work?" Ivy asks Willa.

"Shhh." Willa gives her a stern look.

"What are you two talking about?" I narrow my eyes, gaze darting back and forth between them.

"Nothing," Willa says too quickly.

"Tell me now," I demand. "I swear. If either of you mess up my first vacation that I've had in years, I will lose it."

"Well, you see…" Willa begins.

"We might have done a love potion spell with Mom on you and Finn. And now we're just waiting to see if it worked," Ivy spills.

I stare at them. "What kind of love spell?"

"It's nothing, just silly. I blame Mom," Willa says. "You know her and Donna are always meddling with all of us and trying to fix us up."

"Finn and I don't need to be fixed up. We're friends." I groan as I zip up my suitcase.

"Raaaaaahr!" Finn calls from the doorway.

We all jump. "Crap, Finn!" Willa shrieks, holding her chest. "What are you, five?"

I stare at him, wondering how much of that he heard.

He turns and looks at me, coming over, kissing my cheek and putting his arm around my shoulders. "Hey, baby. Ready for our trip?"

I stare at him, wide eyed. Willa and Ivy are frozen.

"Did that actually…work?" Ivy hisses.

"No way," Willa whispers back in disbelief.

"You good?" I ask him, staring at him like a deer in the headlights.

"Better than good. Ready for our trip? What do you need help with?"

"I'm…fine." I stutter, confused at his sudden display of love.

"We'll leave you to it," Willa says as she yanks Ivy along with her toward the door. Both look back at us and grin, high fiving each other.

"I love you, Rowan. It's time you finally realize it. It's you, always been you," Finn says loudly.

I swat his chest. "You *did* hear that, Finn."

My sisters giggle as they head down the loft stairs.

He doubles over, laughing on the bed. "Yeah, I did. Your sisters are shit at love potions. We're good, Row."

"Asshole," I tease, tossing one of my hoodies at him.

"Yeah, but you loooooooooooove me," he calls. "What's my song of the day?"

"So glad you asked," I say as I scroll through my phone and pull up La Grange by ZZ Top.

He nods with approval. "Everything good to go on your end before we head out tomorrow? Oh, and Allen wants to know if you'd like to come over tonight for pizza."

I laugh. "Oh, really? Grumpy Allen wants me to come over for pizza?"

"He does," Finn confirms, pretending to be serious.

"We have to run over to Tom's tonight first. I promised I'd check in on him before we go. Still want to help me with a few things for him?"

Finn nods. "Yeah, we can run over to Daddy Warbuck's. Let me throw my tool bag in the truck."

———

Finn and I pull into Tom's driveway late afternoon, the tidy traditional New England style home with a tidy yard. Tom steps out, wearing his usual button-down shirt and suspenders, like some sweet old movie grandpa. He's got his hands tucked in his pockets and he's grinning like he's been waiting for us all day. Becoming friends with Tom has been one of the best parts of my summer.

I step forward, brushing my palms down my jeans. "Hey, Tom. This is my friend, Finn."

Tom's grin widens in that *I've-lived-long-enough-to-spot-some-thing* kind of way. "Friend, huh?" he teases, raising a brow.

Heat rushes up my neck. "Yes. Friend."

Finn chuckles under his breath and sticks out his hand. "Nice to meet you, sir."

Tom shakes it with a firm grip and looks at me. "Tom works just fine. But I like this one already."

Finn gives me a sidelong look that makes my stomach flutter. Tom laughs again, clearly enjoying himself, and gestures toward the back door. "My back door lock has been giving me trouble. Let's see if you're as handy as your girlfriend says you are."

Finn flashes me a stupid, heart-melting smile. "I'll give it my best shot."

While he heads around back to work on the lock, Tom falls into step beside me as we walk through his garden. The air smells like tomato vines and salt from the ocean. He shows me where the basil's grown wild and which herbs need cutting back. His hands are steady, patient.

I walk with Tom through the garden while Finn works. I love how Tom talks about his plants like they're family. And in some ways, they are all he has with his own family scattered around the country. I'm glad I met him and became friends with him.

"You're gonna be gone a week?" he asks.

"Yeah," I say softly. "Coconut Beach. I actually can't believe I'm finally going."

He gives me a gentle smile. "Good. It's important to have a planned holiday."

"Thanks, I think so, too. I'm looking forward to it."

Tom glances toward the back of his house where Finn is replacing the new lock he'd laid out for him. "Are you taking your fella with you?"

I don't even begin to correct him about Finn not being my fella and I just nod.

He looks at his hydrangeas, then back at me. His smile softens, and something nostalgic settles in his eyes. "Well, I hope you two have a splendid time," he says. "Oh, to be young, travel, and have adventures again."

He chuckles, low and fond, then keeps talking, almost to himself. "My Henryetta, which I called Henry, and I used to take trips every summer. Before the kids, and after them too, when we could convince them to get in the car without staging a full rebellion." His eyes go distant, warm. "We camped in the Smokies once. Froze half to death. But Henry made cocoa over a camp stove, and the kids told ghost stories until the fire burned low. Best night of my life."

My chest gets tight in the way it does when someone shows you the softest part of their heart.

Tom shifts his gaze to his flowers again, brushing a petal with a careful hand. "We adopted our girls when they were little. We probably had the loudest house in Wisteria Cove." He smiles, but there is a shimmer of loneliness there. "Now they're grown. One lives up in Portland, the other in Chicago. They send pictures, but it isn't the same."

He inhales, steady and full of memory. "Henry passed five years ago. Cancer." His voice wavers but never breaks. "I miss her every day. But I would not trade a minute of what we built." A soft laugh. "She was my person."

My eyes sting, unexpected and sharp. The way he talks about Henry, his wife, is how I feel about Finn. He's *my* person.

He pats my hand gently. "Love looks different for everyone. But it's worth it. Especially the hard parts."

My throat tightens.

He smiles again, sad and fond all at once. "So, go. Take your trip. Have your adventures. Don't miss out on life."

We circle back to the porch and find Finn leaning against the doorframe, wiping his hands on a rag, the lock fixed. He looks proud and a little sheepish at the same time.

Tom invites us to sit on the porch and have a glass of lemonade. We can't say no and have a good time chatting. Tom and Finn hit it off and make plans to have breakfast together when we get back from our trip. He wants to show him the house he's remodeling. I watch Finn and Tom talk about the Red Sox and how the next game is going to go. It seems like I'm not the only one with a new friend.

We say goodbye and head back to Finn's so I can get the plants taken care of for the night.

"Okay," Finn says, rubbing the back of his neck. "I can't believe I ever felt threatened by that guy. He's... really nice."

"Told you," I say, smirking.

Later, I end up at Finn's with dirt under my nails, a dull ache in my shoulders and thighs from bending and squatting down, and Allen the cat weaving between my ankles while I wash my hands in Finn's kitchen sink. I want everything to be weeded and watered so it's easier for Tate and Remy to take care of my jungle while I'm gone. Finn has a pizza box open on the counter and a paper bag full of garlic knots that smell like heaven.

"Smells so good," I say, grinning.

"Only the best," he replies, sliding me a plate.

We eat out on his back screened in porch in chairs with our feet propped up on the railing. The night's warm and breezy, the ocean humming softly in the distance. Allen sprawls out on the chair next to us like he's lived here forever.

After dinner, I tackle my plants, crouched among terracotta pots, picking out weeds and trimming dead leaves. Finn mows the yard without a shirt, and I try not to stare. He looks so good. I finish watering the rest of the plants while he hauls bags of weeds to the trash.

"This is what bliss looks like," I say, wiping my forehead with my forearm.

Finn tilts his head, a slow smile spreading across his face. "You look really happy, Row."

I pretend to focus on the basil, but my chest does that stupid soft squeeze. "Yeah, I am. Thanks for this."

The air smells like damp soil and freshly cut grass. The fairy lights strung across his porch and green house glow warm against the dark. I can't tell if it's the night or him, but everything just feels so easy.

Tomorrow we'll be on a beach together. And things will be very interesting. I'm nervous.

And even though I've spent the past few days trying to tell myself it's just a trip… standing here next to him, with dirt on my hands and the sea breeze in my hair, it doesn't feel like *just* anything.

It feels like something beginning.

CHAPTER 11
Finn

"SORRY," she mutters, shifting for the third time in ten minutes. She smells like coconut lotion and mint gum, and I swear this middle seat suddenly feels like first class.

Did airplane seats get smaller or did humanity just collectively bulk up?

"It's fine," I whisper, already leaning into her so I don't crush the poor guy on the aisle. He's built like me with broad shoulders, and zero legroom. We're two full-grown men crammed into a row built for toddlers. The tray tables in front of us might as well be decorative. If one of us tries to lower it, someone's losing a rib.

But the thing is, leaning into Rowan doesn't feel like a sacrifice. It feels stupidly good, like it's exactly where I'm supposed to be. Her shoulder presses against mine, warm and soft. Her thigh is flush with my leg, sending these electric little sparks up through me like a power surge.

I could sit like this for hours. Hell, she could crawl into my lap, and I'd gladly be put on a no-fly list.

I try to act normal, like my pulse isn't doing cartwheels, like I'm not thinking about how damn easy it would be to tip my head and rest it against hers.

Best friends. That's what this is. Just two best friends on a flight.

Half an hour in, she let her head fall against my shoulder. My heart does a high five with itself because this is shaping up to be an even better trip than I dreamed it could be.

The flight attendant stops to take our drink orders, and she glances over at Rowan laying on me and gives me a smile, she says, "Will your wife want anything?"

I shake my head, smile, and don't correct her. Because I love the sound of that so much. *Wife.* I dream that to be true. It feels so good to pretend for a second.

At our layover, we're at a restaurant and bar, she's sipping a fruity cocktail with a tiny pink umbrella like we're in the opening scene of a summer romcom where the two idiots at the bar don't realize they're each other's plot twist.

I try to play it cool while she leans her elbows on the counter and props her chin in her hand, all casual and dangerous. It's unfair, honestly. Nobody should be allowed to look that good while holding a drink with a paper umbrella.

"So, Coconut Ken."

I grin and play along with her. "So, Beach Barbie."

Her mouth curves up like she's already plotting trouble. "Should we set our dating apps to Coconut Beach and see what our odds are of meeting the love of our lives?"

I snort. "No."

Hell no.

She tilts her head, teasing. "Why not? I mean, clearly, we're not hitting the jackpot in Wisteria Cove. Maybe we just needed to expand our horizons."

"I like my horizons just fine," I deadpan.

Because my horizon is currently sitting across from me, twirling a drink umbrella and making my brain crash out with the idea of her on a date with anyone in Coconut Beach.

She lets out a soft laugh and lifts her drink, eyes bright. "It's probably for the best anyway. I've decided I'm not wasting time on anyone who doesn't match my energy," she says, voice soft but certain. "I want someone who's just as obsessed with me as I am with them. Mutual chaos. Ride-or-die vibes is what I'm going for."

I nearly choke on my drink. Of course she describes the exact way I already feel about her.

Our server drops a tray of appetizers between us, mozzarella sticks, southwest eggrolls, chicken bites, which is a great distraction from this conversation.

She twirls the umbrella between her fingers, completely unaware that she's short-circuiting my brain with every small movement.

"Coconut Beach is full of hot strangers," she says, flashing that grin that kills me every damn time. "You're totally going to fall for some sun-kissed Barbie named Tinley. Or Savannah. She'll wear those tiny bikinis, have perfect beach waves and a flower in her hair. You'll fall madly on your Coconut Beach Ken face."

I snort. "Sounds so cliché."

She smiles but it doesn't reach her eyes. She doesn't mean any of this. In fact, if I had to guess, she's nervous that I would meet someone and that is what she's afraid of right now. "That's because it *is* cliché."

I lean in a little, voice low. "Nah. I'm more into hexy witches who steal all the cheese sticks."

She pauses, mid–mozzarella stick grab and gives me a look of surprise.

I wink at her, smirking, and let her do with that whatever she will. Because I don't want anyone else. I never have.

Yeah. My horizons are exactly where I want them.

She points her fork at me after she spears a chicken bite, trying to change the subject because she's nervous. "Or maybe we should just have a love free week. Just time to recharge. I'm not wasting my energy on some random dude in Coconut Beach when I could relax on vacation. No more half-assed energy. I want full ass."

My brain: You're the one I want.

My mouth: "Oh yeah? That's a lot of ass."

I don't tell her I want a love free week. Because that's the last thing I want. What I want is for her to see me right in front of her and want me back. But I'll give her whatever she wants.

She laughs soft and low and leans a little closer for the air to shift. "But if you did end up matching with someone who owns a boat, I'm inviting myself. That's non-negotiable."

"Well, that wouldn't be awkward at all." I chuckle.

"We're going to be busy having such a good time, there'll no time for awkwardness," she says bringing her straw to her lips and I have to look away to keep from staring.

"Don't worry," I murmur, my voice dropping into that quiet space meant only for her. "I've already got plans to have a fun week."

Her head tilts, curiosity sparking in her eyes like I just dangled a secret in front of her. "Yeah? Who? Does Cal have someone he's setting you up with?"

I bark out a laugh. Of course, she thinks Cal's involved.

Cal, my cousin, the professional flirt, Coconut Beach's unofficial bad decision mascot. The guy can't commit to a sandwich, let alone setting me up with someone. And also, Rowan is very much off limits to Cal, and I'll make sure he knows it.

I lean in just enough that she has to tip her chin up to keep her eyes on mine. Her breath catches, and I swear the air gets thicker between us.

"If I told you," I say, letting a grin tug at the corner of my mouth, "I'd ruin all the fun."

Her knees brush mine under the table, her coconut scent messing with my ability to think straight. Then her gaze flicks down to my mouth and it's quick, unintentional, lethal.

For half a second, the entire airport melts away. It's just us. That tiny, electric space between wanting and almost... And God, if she leaned in even an inch, I'd kiss her right here. Right in the middle of this overpriced restaurant with bad lighting and plastic menus. I'd make her forget that fucking app and all those losers she's dated on there.

Then some guy two seats down laughs way too loud, snapping the spell. She blinks, laughs softly, and shakes her head like she's shaking off the moment.

"We're going to have so much fun," she says, bright and easy.

I grin, leaning back just enough to keep it light, but my voice comes out lower than I mean it to. "Yeah," I murmur, holding her gaze. "But just so you know... I'm planning on being your favorite part of it."

———

When we drive into Coconut Beach, it feels like walking straight into a postcard. Palm trees sway like they're saying *welcome back*, and the air smells like salty sea air and food from the taco truck parked on the street. I've spent a lot of time here as a kid. My mom has a younger sister who lives here, and my cousin Cal.

"Here's your song," I tell her as I play *In The Summertime by Mungo Jerry*.

She laughs and dances to it, the breeze flowing through our open sunroof and windows.

Rowan pulls her hair up into a messy bun on top of her head and I resist the urge to release it and let it be wild. Her cheeks are a little flushed, lips soft and pink, and there's still a slight crease on her cheek from where she leaned against me on the plane and napped on the way here on our last flight.

She looks like summer: warm, bright, impossible to look away from. And damn if it doesn't knock the breath right out of me.

The cottage is exactly how I remember it, but somehow it is even better now that I am standing here with Rowan beside me.

Heat wraps around me the second I step out of the car, thick and soft like a warm blanket. Humidity clings to my skin, carrying the sharp tang of salt and the sweetness of something blooming nearby. The ocean is close enough that I can hear the waves rolling in slow, steady breaths, each one brushing the shore with a sound like a long exhale.

Sunlight pours through the palm trees, catching on the bright pink bougainvillea climbing the porch railings. The cottage sits beneath it all, small and whitewashed, the paint a little weathered, the blue shutters faded from years of salt and sun. It looks like a place that has stories soaked straight into the wood.

The front steps creak in that familiar way under my feet. A soft breeze moves through the wind chimes hanging from the corner of the porch, sending a light, tinkling sound across the air. The smell hits me next. Sun-warmed wood. Coconut sunscreen left over from who knows how many summers. Citrus from the lemon trees flanking the walkway. A hint of ocean spray drifting in through the open windows.

Inside, the cottage smells like fresh linen and driftwood, like a life lived slowly. Bright woven rugs cover the floor. A low ceiling fan spins lazily, stirring the air just enough to cool the back of my neck. The kitchen counters are tiled in a sun-washed teal, and shells line the windowsill where the light hits them and makes them glow. The old couch is still here, soft from years of use, the cushions sunken in the exact way I remember.

It's different from Wisteria Cove in every possible way.

And Rowan steps past me, her face open and awestruck, hair lifted by the ocean breeze, eyes shining in the golden light.

Cal's already stocked the fridge and left a note taped on the blender that reads: *Don't break it this time.*

I roll my eyes. That was one time. One incident several years back with him. Two margaritas. Three stitches. And suddenly I'm a legend. Cal always has jokes.

Rowan kicks off her shoes the second we walk in, laughs, and throws herself backward on the couch like a happy starfish claiming new territory. "I could live here forever."

I swear the air in the cottage jumps ten degrees. Being here with Rowan, with both of us in fewer clothes than usual, is going to be fun. And torture. Mostly torture.

I lean against the doorway like an idiot already in too deep. She has no idea how much I love her. None. She tosses another paperback into the pile she is taking to the beach, mumbling about options and moods and backup reads, and I cannot do anything except stare like she is the sun.

"Give me ten minutes," she says, grabbing her clothes and disappearing down the short hall to change.

I inhale, steadying myself. Her sandalwood perfume lingers in the air, soft and warm, mixing with the salty ocean breeze drifting through the screen door.

I grab sunscreen, the beach bag, a couple of cold drinks, and try not to think about what she is doing in that little bedroom. Changing. Skin. Bare legs. God help me.

When she emerges, it knocks the breath clean out of me. Her cover-up is loose and light, brushing mid-thigh, and her hair is pulled up, a few strands falling around her face. She looks soft and sunlit, like something the ocean washed up just to torture me personally.

"Ready?" she asks, pretending she does not feel the tension stretching between us.

"Yeah," I manage. My voice sounds like it has been dragged over gravel.

We collect the last few things, her stack of books wobbling in her arms. I take them from her because there is no universe where I let her carry more than she needs to. She rolls her eyes but smiles, and it hits me straight in the chest.

We walk the sandy path from the cottage to the beach, the boards warm under our feet. The afternoon sun hangs low, turning the sky gold and peach. The beach is alive in that soft, lazy way that happens near the end of the day. A family is packing up their cooler. Kids shriek as they chase each other near the tide. A couple strolls along the waterline, hands intertwined. Someone farther down strums a guitar, the music drifting on the warm wind.

We pick a spot between two palms, the perfect mix of privacy and people-watching. I set up the chairs while Rowan shakes out her towel, sending a faint spray of sand into the air that glitters in the light. The ocean stretches out in front of us, deep blue with streaks of orange from the sinking sun.

Rowan sets her bag down and then, without warning, pulls her cover-up over her head.

My brain almost short-circuits. Her swimsuit hugs every curve. Sun-kissed skin, water-ready confidence, long legs that go on forever. She glances at me, unaware of the absolute destruction she is causing, and flips her braid over her shoulder.

I force myself to breathe. This is going to be a long week. A beautiful, impossible, torturous, perfect week.

And I already know I am not going to survive it unchanged.

"Hey, Coconut Ken, want to spray some sunscreen on my back?" she asks, tilting the bottle towards me. "I'll do you next."

I make a strangled sound that comes out as a cough and a whimper.

"What?" She laughs, plopping down on her chair like she doesn't know she just ended me.

"Nothing," I croak as I spray the lotion into her shoulders, trying to concentrate.

"You're being weird."

Yeah. Weird. Sure, that's what we're calling it these days. Not head over heels in love with her.

I hold up the sunscreen bottle. "Turn," I say, and my voice comes out rougher than I intend.

Rowan gives me a look, half amused, half shy, then turns around and lifts her hair off her neck. The tiny movement alone is enough to wreck me. The sun has warmed her skin, golden and soft, and the faint scent of coconut drifts toward me, sweet and dizzying.

I spray lightly at first, but she lets out the smallest inhale when the mist hits her shoulders, and my hand trembles. I smooth the sunscreen over her back, slow circles, letting the lotion sink into her skin. She relaxes under my touch, her muscles softening, her breath catching just enough for me to hear it.

"Sorry," she murmurs. "It's cold."

It is not cold. Not anymore. My hands are warm on her, and her skin is warmer under them. I can feel her breathing, the rise and fall, the tiny shiver she tries to hide. Her shoulder blades shift when she exhales. Her hair brushes against my wrist. Every part of her is doing something to me I am not prepared for.

"Tell me if it's too much," I say quietly.

She swallows. "It's fine. Feels nice."

Nice.

She has no idea how hard I am working not to pull her back against me, not to bury my face in her neck.

I move down her arms, her waist, the line of her spine. I feel her melt a little more with each pass of my hands. When I finish, she turns around, cheeks flushed, eyes bright. She hands me the bottle with a look that makes my stomach flip.

"My turn."

My pulse jumps. "Yeah. Okay."

I stand still while she steps close, so close I can feel the warmth radiating off her. She sprays my chest first, and the cold mist makes me jolt. She bites her bottom lip, fighting a grin.

"Sorry," she says. She is not sorry.

Her hands glide across my chest, my shoulders, my arms. Gentle but firm. She lingers near my collarbone longer than she realizes. Her fingertips drag just slightly, and I have to clench my jaw to keep from making a sound.

She feels it. I know she does. Her breath hitches, barely, but I catch it. Her eyes flick to my mouth for a heartbeat before she looks away again, flustered.

The world narrows down to her hands on my skin, the ocean behind us, the distant voices of kids playing in the surf, and the pounding of my heart in my ears.

By the time she steps back, both of us are pretending this was normal. Casual. Nothing to see here.

It is not normal. None of this is casual. Her hands were on me. Mine were on her.

We settle into our chairs finally, but my body still feels electrified, like her touch left fingerprints on my bones.

I tip my head back, crack open a bottle of water, and try not to combust as she stretches out beside me, sunglasses on, smile lazy and wide. She digs through her bag and produces three books.

"Which one should I read?" she asks, holding them up.

I look at the cover that has two illustrated people on a beach. "That one. *Just Another Summer Escape.* Looks beachy."

She smiles as she tucks the other books away. Then, she rolls onto her front and cracks it open in front of her, that perfect ass on display. "It's about a hot bartender and a runaway bride."

I lose track of time out here with her. The speaker's playing a lazy summer song, the kind that melts right into the sound of the waves. Vacation has officially started. And I'm in so much trouble.

She reads for a while, legs tucked under her, sun warm on both of us. I pretend to look at my book, but I am watching her instead. The way the light hits her cheekbones. The soft rise and fall of her breath. The faint shimmer of sunscreen on her shoulders. By the time she pushes her sunglasses up and stretches, I am already halfway gone.

"Water?" she asks.

"Yeah," I say, even though my voice feels thick.

We walk down to the shoreline, the sand cool near the waterline. The heat clings to our skin, mixing with salt and sunscreen and coconut air. A wave rushes forward and kisses our ankles, cold and shocking. Rowan laughs and grabs my hands, fingers threading through mine naturally. Like they belong there. Like they always have.

We jump through the waves together, her laughter ringing out over the surf, bright and wild. I feel the sound in my chest, in the soft places I keep locked up. She leans back against the pull of the water, hair whipping behind her, and I swear the sun itself leans in to watch her.

Another wave builds behind us, bigger than the last. I see it a second before it hits.

"Rowan," I warn.

She shrieks as it crashes over her hip, and she stumbles forward, straight into me.

And just like that, her body is slammed up against mine.

Her slick skin slides against my chest, her hands grabbing at my shoulders for balance. Her breath rushes out against my throat. Her hair, wet and heavy, sticks to my arm. She smells like sunscreen, salt, and Rowan.

I grip her waist without thinking, the warmth of her soft against my palms, my fingers brushing her ribs. She looks up at me, wide-eyed and breathless, her lips parted, sun catching on the tiny droplets on her lashes. My heart punches hard. Her nose is pink from the sun. New freckles are blooming across her cheeks. Her eyes are a color I swear has no name, some ocean-deep shade the world has not discovered yet.

For a second, neither of us moves.

Her body fits against mine as if the universe designed her just to lean into me like this. Every inch of her is pressed to every inch of me. My body goes hot and tight, and I know she feels it. God help me, I know she does.

Then she laughs, a soft, breathless sound that melts straight into my bones. "Well. That was a wave."

"Yeah," I manage, voice low. "That was a wave."

We try to untangle, but we are both slippery with saltwater, so we end up falling into each other again, laughing too hard to stand upright. Her fingers curl around my arm, and I cannot stop touching her, steadying her, memorizing the shape of her against me.

When we finally pull apart, I already miss her warmth.

Later, back at our spot, we reach for the sunscreen again. The bottle is slick with sand, so she hands it to me, and I spray her shoulders. Her skin glows in the late sun, warm and smooth under my hands. She lets out the tiniest sigh when I massage the lotion in, and I have to look away before my thoughts slip somewhere dangerous.

Then she does me.

Her fingers glide across my back, slow and careful, lingering at my shoulders, the back of my neck. Every touch burns, but in the best way. Her breath fans my skin when she leans in to reach the middle of my spine, and I almost lose it.

When we finally collapse into our chairs again, toes buried in the sand, hearts still racing, the sun is sinking lower, painting the whole beach in gold.

We sit there in silence, side by side, the kind of quiet that feels intimate.

And I know with absolute certainty: If I touch her again tonight, I will not survive it.

The sun sinks lower, and everything feels soft and golden and stupidly perfect. By the time we're ready to call it a day, the beach has emptied out a little. We walk back to the cottage and I unlock the door. She hangs up her towel on the hook in the entryway of the cottage and calls, "Dibs on the shower first!"

"Okay," I say as I hunt down some food. Neither of us have eaten since the airport and we need real food.

Cal left us a little care package in the fridge with burger patties, all the fixings on a separate plate under foil, and a note that says, *Finn, don't burn down my favorite grill.*

I fire off a text to Cal thanking him for the food.

He responds:

Cal: Come see me at Cocktails & Chaos later. Can't wait to see you guys!

A cold beer sweats against my palm as I lean back on the porch railing, the sky melting into shades of pink and orange that look too perfect to be real.

The sound of the shower slips through the open bathroom window. I lean against the porch railing, beer still in my hand, but my focus is shot to hell picturing Rowan in the shower not too far away from where I'm standing.

Then I hear this quiet, breathy sound that slides right under my skin. A moan of pleasure filters quietly through the screen.

My pulse stutters. *Is she?*

Another soft moan follows, and then… my name. Whispered like it's not meant for anyone else to hear. *What the hell? No fucking way.*

Everything in me goes still. My grip on the railing tightens. The air feels hot and heavy, like I'm unable to move.

I can picture her too easily, steam clinging to her skin, water rolling down her body, head tipped back while she makes herself come while she says my name. The image hits me like a punch. I'm rock hard.

Before I realize it, I'm moving. One step toward the door, then another.

Screw the burgers. They can burn straight to hell for all I care.

Her soft moan floats through the air again, wrecking me.

I stop just shy of the door, chest rising and falling like I've just run a mile. My fingers brush the handle. One turn and one step, and I could be inside. I could find out if she really meant it when she said my name just now.

But I don't move. I don't go to her. I do not touch the door.

Because she is not just anyone. She's Rowan, the woman who has her roots tangled through every damn part of my heart. The woman I want in every way a man can want someone, but only if she wants me just as much, and chooses me.

And as much as hearing her moan my name sends heat crashing through me, that is not an invitation. That is not consent. That is not her saying she's ready for me, or that she even wants me in the same way when she is not lost in a dream or a fantasy.

The last thing I would ever do is mistake her pleasure for permission. Or turn something real into a moment we regret, a moment she'd pull away from, a moment that could break everything we have spent years building.

So, I stand there, hands shaking, breath unsteady, wanting her so much it hurts.

But I let her have her privacy.

Because if I finally get to kiss her the way I've wanted to for years, I want it to be because she looks at me with clear eyes and says my name for real.

Not through a shower door. Not through a dream. But choosing me back.

Still… the thought sinks its hooks in. She said my name. Not someone else's. *Mine.*

My heart's pounding like it's trying to escape my chest. Does that mean she actually wants me? Not just in the way I've been torturing myself wanting her, but *really* wants me? Is this finally the thing neither of us has been brave enough to say out loud?

This is when I decide that on this trip I'm going to find out if she wants to end this bullshit game and make it real between us.

Could we finally stop pretending the app jokes and "best friend" crap are what we're doing and really give this a shot?

The sound of the shower keeps spilling out, wrapping around me like heat, like it knows exactly what it's doing.

She has no idea what she does to me. Or maybe… she does.

It's dangerous being here like this with no distractions. No daily Wisteria Cove routines. Just me, her, a sunset that already feels like it's cheering us on, and the growing truth sitting heavy in my chest that she has feelings for me, too.

I'm so far gone for her it's not even funny. I drag in a long breath and push off the door, forcing myself back to the grill. The flames hiss when I flip the patties, and the sizzle is a good distraction from the way my body's still burning for her.

I focus on the burgers and try to get the vision of her in that shower out of my mind. *Don't think about her moaning your name,* I silently tell myself again, the mantra barely working.

The ocean breeze rolls through, cooling the sweat on the back of my neck. I grab plates, line up the buns, add lettuce, tomato, and onion, trying to keep my hands busy.

Inside, I set the small table in the cottage kitchen. Two plates.

Condiments. Beers sweating on the wood coasters with seashells printed on them. I try to ignore the way my heartbeat kicks up at the sound of the bathroom door opening and her walking toward me.

She looks like she's glowing, like whatever just happened in that shower didn't just try to ruin me.

She's wearing a lacy V-neck little purple tank top and cutoff black jean shorts, nothing fancy. But damn if it doesn't make my pulse skip anyway.

"Wow," she says with a content smile, padding barefoot toward the table. "These look amazing. I'm so hungry. What can I help with?"

Well for starters, there's a few things, I think smugly. But I clear my throat, aiming for casual. "I've got it, we're all set."

She plops into her seat, tucking one tanned leg under her. I slide a plate in front of her, trying not to look like someone who spent the last twenty minutes wrestling with self-control.

She picks up her burger, eyes sparkling. "This has been the best day so far, hasn't it?"

"Yeah," I say, leaning back against the chair opposite hers. "It has."

She bites into the burger, and I swear I've never been more jealous of food in my life. She moans, just a little, all soft and content and my knuckles tighten around my beer bottle.

"Good?" I ask, my voice is rougher than I mean it to be.

She nods, licking a bit of ketchup from her thumb. "Perfect."

I take a big bite of my burger like it's a lifeline. I can do this. Just two friends eating dinner. Two friends... who probably shouldn't be thinking about each other the way I am right now. But she's over there having orgasms thinking about me apparently, so this is pretty fair I guess for me to think things as well.

But then she looks at me across the table with that summer-night glow, and my stomach flips.

Yeah. I'm so screwed.

And God help me, a part of me is already imagining this as

more than a trip. "You know," she says, watching the flames catch, "Maybe Willa and Ivy were right."

I glance over at her. "Why's that?"

She laughs, that warm, soft kind of laugh that slides under my skin and makes my chest feel too tight. "They said we're like a Hallmark movie," she says, and takes a huge bite of her burger.

Then she tips her head back with a groan that's half laugh, half moan, like the burger might actually be a religious experience.

"Wednesday Addams," I tease, leaning across the tiny table, "are you admitting that you watch Hallmark movies?"

Her head snaps up. "No," she says way too fast. "Mom and Donna do."

"Uh-huh," I say, smirking. "Sure."

She narrows her eyes at me, sauce still on the corner of her mouth. I lean in to wipe it away with my thumb. She grins and takes another bite. "Keep feeding me like this and I'll stay here forever with you, Finn."

Fine with me.

The breeze off the ocean slips through the open windows, carrying the sound of waves and distant laughter from the tiki bar where Cal works down the beach. I could live here forever if she was with me.

I tap my bottle against hers. "Let's go to Cocktails and Chaos and say hi to Cal after dinner. You in?"

She sits back, crossing one bare leg over the other like this whole night was made for her. "Yes," she says, grinning wide and giving me a teasing look. "Let's do it."

And I swear, right then, watching her this happy, it feels less like a vacation and more like a *plot twist*.

CHAPTER 12
Rowan

CONGA BY MIAMI SOUND MACHINE

"COME ON, SLOWPOKE," Finn calls, his voice teasing as his big, warm, and strong hand slips into mine. It's not just a grab.

Sure, Finn has given me a hand up before. We have gone swimming together, sat next to each other, watched movies shoulder to shoulder on his couch, gone camping in separate tents, done a hundred things side by side. But this is different. New. Quietly intimate in a way that makes my breath stall.

And I will admit to myself that I love it.

Not just the warmth of his hand wrapped around mine, or the steady pressure of his fingers between my fingers. Not just the way our palms fit, like they have been waiting years for this exact alignment.

It's the way his hand grounds me. The way it makes me feel steady, like the world stops wobbling for a second. It's how seen I feel, like he's saying without words that I matter, that he wants me here, right beside him. That I'm someone he chooses to hold onto.

There's safety in it too. Soft but undeniable. Something that settles in my ribs and makes the tight, weary parts of me unclench. His presence has always steadied me, but this... this is different. This feels like a promise. Like a tether. Like something I am suddenly terrified of losing. I tighten my grip without meaning to.

And when he squeezes back, warm and sure, something deep and quiet inside me answers him.

The soft music from Cocktails and Chaos drifts down the beach long before we reach it. Buttery yellow string lights glow across the ceiling of the tiki bar, laughter spilling into the air. Everything here feels calm, easy, and familiar coming back to Coconut Beach. I've been here before with my mom and sisters. But nothing about the way my heart is pounding while holding his hand feels casual at all.

His thumb sweeps over the inside of my wrist, slow and unintentional, in circles. Like he can sense I'm nervous and he's trying to calm me. It's ridiculous how good something so simple can feel.

My mind flashes back to earlier, the heat of the shower on my skin, the way every thought had circled right back to him. The way I imagined his hands and his voice while he touched and talked me through coming so hard in that shower. The memory is a low, warm ache in my belly now, and it makes the way he's holding my hand feel dangerous and intense in the best way possible.

Finn glances at me, a smile curving his mouth like he already knows I'm thinking something I shouldn't be. My heart trips. I squeeze his hand, maybe to ground myself. Maybe to hold on tighter. Either way, it feels like it is more than just handholding. It feels like a promise.

Cal's behind the bar when he spots us, flashing that grin I've known since we were kids. He's only a few months younger than Finn and looks like a younger version of Remy. The way they look so much alike is uncanny.

"Well, well, well," Cal drawls when he sees us holding hands, tipping his chin toward Finn with a mock-serious nod. "You finally land yourself a Maren sister?"

Finn gives him a look I can't quite decipher, something

between *easy, man* and *say something else, I dare you.* Finn and Cal have always been close, and he's come to Wisteria Cove to visit. When Willa, Ivy, and me were kids, Ivy used to have a big crush on Cal. Kind of funny now that she's with Remy and he looks like his cousin Cal. I make a mental note to tease her about that later as a good sister does.

Cal winks as he slides me a fruity drink with a bright blue umbrella tucked in mine and Finn a beer like it's a reflex.

I take a sip of my drink and say, "Oh, he couldn't handle me, Cal. I'm too wild and I'd only corrupt him. He's my best friend."

The look that flashes across Finn's face is *everything*. One eyebrow quirks, his jaw tightens just slightly, and that slow grin spreads across his face like he's already picturing proving me wrong.

Cal whistles low. "Uh-oh. I know that look. That's the *challenge accepted* face. And for the record, my 'best friend' doesn't look at me the way you two look at each other." He fake coughs and says, "Bullshit."

Finn finally speaks, voice low and steady, "I can handle you just fine, baby."

My heart does a full-on somersault, and Cal looks entirely too entertained by this. Damn it. I love it when he calls me baby. Anyone else, I'd probably throat punch. But there's something about Finn saying it like he means it. Not condescending, just sweet and endearing. And Finn has a good sweet. He penetrates my black Wednesday Addams personality armor that everyone else teases me about. But not Finn. He's always seemed to like me for me. I've never had to shrink myself or be smaller for him. He's the one safe space I can be me.

Cal straightens, shaking his head like a man who's seen this train coming for years. "All right then. I'll leave you two sexually frustrated *'just friends'* to it."

I sip my drink, laughing, and twirl to the music on my stool. "Whatever, Cal."

He winks, already backing away. "What? Somebody had to say it."

"Was that a challenge, Row?" Finn's leans over and says in my ear, his voice dropping, meant only for me, and it slides right down to my lady parts, making me tremble.

My pulse skips and my drink suddenly tastes sweeter.

I arch a brow, trying to play it cool even though my brain is not cool right now. And whatever is in this drink is giving me the liquid courage to flirt back with Finn. "What if it was?"

His grin spreads, slow and dangerous. "Then I guess I should start warming up. I never back down from a challenge."

I snort into my drink. "Oh, please. You're going to trip over your own ego."

He leans closer, close enough that I can feel the warmth of him against my bare arm. "Baby, my ego's got great balance."

My heart does back flips, and my mouth feels like it has a mind of its own the way I'm flirting with him recklessly. "Big talk, Casanova Ken."

"Big follow-through too," he shoots back, easy and confident, taking a swig of his beer.

The music dips lower, the beat rolling through the sand like a heartbeat that belongs to both of us. Finn stands, hand out, grin wicked. "Come on," he says, his voice low and rough in a way that makes my stomach flip. That smile isn't just a smile anymore. Nope, it's more like a dare I don't want to say no to.

"What are we doing?" I ask, taking one last sip of my drink before setting it down next to his beer.

"Cal, watch our drinks, will ya?" Finn calls to Cal, his eyes not leaving mine.

Cal nods his head like a man watching a slow-motion love spell unfold. He moves the drinks behind the bar, still grinning.

I slide my hand into Finn's, and his fingers lock around mine. He pulls me close, my feet sinking into the sand, the night thick and heavy around us.

My arms loop around his neck as his hands settle on my waist.

The tiki lights blur, the music hums in my chest, and the world shrinks down to just us in this moment, together. The way his body fits against mine. The heat that rolls off him, like the comfort I've searched for all my life and not been able to find until Finn. Other than my dad, no man has ever made me feel safe and loved like Finn does. I can't explain it. He's always been special.

We start to sway, lazy at first, just a rhythm. Then his fingers press harder into my hips, and he guides me against him like he's not even thinking about it. My hips move with him. The heat spikes between our cores.

His breath skims my cheek, his thigh brushes mine, and we're locked into the beat. Grinding. Every shift of my body drags against him, every small roll of his hips answers mine.

I thread my fingers through the back of his hair and tug, just enough. He groans, low and rough, the sound vibrating against my mouth as our bodies move against each other in ways they probably shouldn't. And honestly, I'd fuck Finn behind this tiki bar right now if I could. They could haul me to jail for public indecency. It'd still be worth it.

"Careful, Row," he rasps against my ear, voice shredded around the edges. "You keep doing that, and I won't be able to play nice anymore."

My laugh is soft and shaky. "Who said I wanted nice? Maybe I want whatever the opposite of nice is."

His grip tightens, pulling me flush to him. His forehead dips to mine, breath hot and uneven. I can feel his heartbeat where our chests press together. His nose brushes mine. "What do you want?" he asks, his voice raspy.

We're one small breath away from kissing.

I tilt up, and his lips graze mine, just barely. Just enough to send a sharp shiver down my spine and set my pulse racing like I've been waiting my whole damn life for this. I moan a little and tremble against him, feeling his hardness against me. God, I want this man. What love potion did Cal serve us? Is this my mom and sister's potion working? Because whatever it is, it's effective.

The world tilts and the music fades. All I can taste is the ghost of how close his lips are and the salt in the air as a warm breeze blows in from the ocean.

His hand slides up my back, his thumb tracing a line just under my tank top, and I melt against him even more without a second thought.

He tilts his head, so close that my lower lip brushes his.

And then—

"Hey, lovebirds!" Cal's voice cuts through the music like a slap, full of smug amusement.

I jerk back half a step, breathless, my heart hammering.

Finn's fingers stay curled at my hips, thumbs brushing against my skin like he's daring me to pretend the last sixty seconds didn't just happen. When he finally looks at me, he's grinning slow, dangerous, completely unbothered.

"Timing, Cal," Finn calls back, voice rough but playful. "Real solid wingman skills you've got."

Cal just laughs and shakes his head, not even pretending to be sorry. "Place is closed. You gotta head out. Go bang it out...or whatever.

Holy shit. How much time has passed and how long have we been dancing? Because this has been the hottest foreplay I've ever had.

Finn leans in, close enough that his breath ghosts against my ear, low enough that only I can hear him. "Don't think we're done," he murmurs. "I'm just getting started. Let's get out of here."

A shiver runs all the way down my spine. My heart's still pounding like the music hasn't stopped.

When I look up at him, his smile is cocky and soft at the same time. Like he already knows I'll let him finish what he started.

We leave the bar barefoot, shoes dangling from our fingers, the warm sand folding around our toes. The tiki lights fade behind us as the music is replaced by the sound of the waves licking the shore. I had a few sips of my drink and I'm feeling the best buzz of my life. But it's not alcohol. It's him. I'm literally drunk on Finn. I don't know whether it's the perfect starlit sky, the music, or just being with him.

Finn starts singing *Conga by Miami Sound Machine*, and doing a Conga on the beach by himself, dancing, and I laugh. It's ridiculous and adorable all at once. He doesn't remember half the lyrics, so he makes them up, leaning close to me like he's trying to sell the performance.

I bump my hip into him. "You're terrible."

He bumps me right back. "Nope. I'm a national treasure, baby. You just discovered me."

We sway a little as we walk, tipsy and loose, his arm brushing mine, our fingers grazing until they finally tangle together with Finn still singing, telling me this is my song for the day. I make a mental note to add this song to our playlist because this night is a memory I never want to forget.

The ocean stretches out beside us, calm and endless. The moon has a soft glow over everything like a warm blanket.

I spin toward him, the sand giving way under my feet. He spins with me, still holding my hand, both of us laughing like we're kids again. My hair falls across my face and the sound of our laughter mixes with the rush of the waves crashing up on the shore.

Then my foot catches in the sand, and I stumble backward. He tries to catch me, but we both go down anyway, tangled together.

I land on my back, sand sticking to my skin, and Finn lands half on top of me, one arm braced in the sand to keep from crushing me. For a second, neither of us moves.

His laughter softens into something quieter, and more serious. He's looking down at me like I'm also a memory he doesn't want to forget, and the air between us turns electric. My heartbeat trips over the sound of the waves blurring everything else.

"Hey," he whispers, still close enough that his breath brushes my cheek.

"Hey," I breathe back, my voice a little shaky, a little wrecked.

His eyes flick down to my mouth, just for a second, and it's enough to make the world tilt.

"What if…" he starts, voice rough, then trails off like he's afraid to say it.

I tilt my chin toward him, my pulse hammering. "What if you kissed me?"

The space between us disappears as his mouth brushes mine, soft at first like a single spark. And then he kisses me deeper, like he's been waiting for this moment as long as I have.

The world blurs at the edges and the only thing that exists between us is the heat of this kiss. His hand slides up my neck, fingers curling into my hair, holding me there like he's afraid I might not be real. I arch into him, needing more of him, and more of this.

The weight of his body settles against mine, warm and solid, and my back sinks into the sand. His chest presses to mine, and the contact sets off something low and electric inside me. He tastes like salt and beer and summer, familiar and dangerous all at once.

I fist his shirt in both hands and pull him closer until there's nothing left between us but heat and skin and everything we've been holding back. His tongue slides against mine, slow and sure, and the sound he makes—low, rough, wrecked—shoots straight through me.

Oh my God! I am kissing Finn Bennett! My mind screams, and my heart is doing a fist pump at the same time.

His thumb brushes over my jaw, then drifts lower, tracing the curve of my throat like he wants to memorize every inch. I breathe him in, my heart hammering, my body already swaying toward him.

The kiss turns messy, urgent. My hands slip beneath the edge of his shirt, and he shudders against me like he's seconds from losing control. His palm slides to my waist, then lower, fingers digging into my hip as if he's anchoring himself to me.

I gasp into his mouth, and he catches the sound with another kiss, deeper this time, stealing my breath, stealing everything. And at this point he can have it all. All of me. Just take it and take me.

The ocean crashes somewhere behind us, the breeze skims across our overheated skin, and the whole world feels like it's holding its breath while Finn makes his move and I take it.

He finally pulls back and his forehead rests against mine, both of us panting, lips brushing with every shaky breath.

"Row," he whispers, as if my name's a secret he's finally allowed to say.

I smile, breathless, my fingers still clutching his shirt. "Took you long enough."

He laughs softly, the sound low and rough in his throat, and it's the best sound I've ever heard from Finn. Because it's with me. Then he presses a lingering kiss to the corner of my mouth that's soft, deliberate, and devastating.

"Baby," he murmurs against my skin, his breath hot and steady. "You're worth the wait."

The words hit somewhere deep. Not just a flirtation, but truth. Holy shit. He wants this and he wants me.

Under the moonlight, tangled up in the sand, everything feels electric. Like the start of something, neither of us will be able to stop once it begins.

He tilts his head back down, slow, like he's savoring every inch between us. I can smell the salt on his skin, the faint warmth of beer on his breath, the sun and sweat and something that's entirely *him*.

When his mouth finds mine again, it's slower this time. Deeper, messier, and his hand skims down my back, fingers tracing lazy patterns on my skin like he's learning me by touch. My hands roam over the hard lines of his shoulders, his chest, and the steady beat beneath his skin.

We stay wrapped up like this, kissing, touching, memorizing. The night disappears, time stretches out, and everything else falls away. At one point I realize I'm matching my breaths to his heart-beat, pressing closer like I could live inside that rhythm.

My fingers trace the ridges of muscle across his back, slide along his chest, over warm skin that smells like sun and saltwater. His hands stroke up and down my sides, every pass slower, deeper, making it impossible to breathe without wanting more.

It's not a game or a mistake. Is this us finally giving in? My brain has so many questions, but my heart has no answers. I can only focus on him, his touch and everything in this very moment.

I can't tell you how long we kiss. Minutes. Hours. All I know is the world shrinks down to the sound of the waves, the heat of his mouth, the way he holds me like I'm his prize and he's memo-rizing me as well.

At some point, exhaustion slips in, soft and quiet. We end up falling asleep right there, tangled together in the sand, fifty yards from the cottage. The sky is turning pale when I wake, and Finn's arms are still around me, solid and warm, like they've always been meant to hold me.

The ocean hums in the distance, gulls stir somewhere down the beach, but I don't want to move. Not yet.

This is the best sleep I've had in my life. And it's because it's with *him*.

CHAPTER 13

Finn

KOKOMO BY THE BEACH BOYS

THE FIRST THING I register is the sound of seagulls squawking next to my head. The second is Rowan's head on my chest.

Her breath puffs against my skin, the heat of it tickling over me. She's tucked into me like she's been here a thousand times before and my body was always meant to be her personal pillow. I blink over at the ocean where the sun is coming up and down at our bodies covered with sand. This is real. Rowan and I kissed all night, and she's into me.

I shift just enough to see that her wild hair is fanned out, tangled, and sprinkled with sand. My heart should not be beating this hard. But it is and I'm surprised she doesn't wake up from the pulse of it.

She stirs, squints at the sun, and groans. "Why's it so bright?" She picks sand out of her hair. "I have seaweed hair. Don't look at me, Finn."

I grin and kiss her forehead. "Too late, I'm already looking."

She peeks through her fingers and narrows her eyes. "How are you not feeling like you're dying?"

"Oh, trust me, I am." I'm just sidetracked by the fact that I'm laying here with the woman I'm madly in love with.

I help her up, and we trudge toward the cottage, sand sticking to everything. Her hand brushes mine once, then again. We stay like that, barely touching, but close enough to feel the current that runs through me when we touch.

"We look like shipwreck survivors," I say as I brush sand from my hair. She's carrying her flip-flops in her hand and winces.

Cal shoots past us with a surfboard under one arm, like he didn't just get off work a few hours ago. He doesn't even break stride. Just calls out, with the smuggest smirk on earth, "Morning, lovebirds!"

And he's gone. A literal drive-by lovebirding. We gawk as he runs down to the water and plunges in with his board, not even looking back at us.

Rowan freezes mid-step. "Did that little surf rat just… lovebird us?"

"Yup," I deadpan.

She blinks. "While looking like a damn sunscreen commercial?"

"Yup."

She lets out this loud, unhinged laugh that makes her wince. "We just got trolled by Cal!"

I groan. "You know he's going to give us shit for this all week."

"Oh, definitely," she says, nodding. "And he will tell everyone that we slept on the beach."

"I can't wait." I snort dryly as we struggle to the cottage porch, the sand feeling like quicksand under our tired feet. Every step feels like a mile.

She cups a hand to her mouth and makes a very bad Cal impression. "'Mooorning, loooovebirds!'"

I laugh. "I swear I'll bury him in the sand and let the tide decide his fate if he gives us too much crap."

"Sure you will," she says, grinning like the menace she is. "Finn, the lovebird, doesn't bury people."

"Finn, the lovebird," I mutter, but I can't stop smiling.

She's not wrong at all.

We rinse off the sand in the outdoor shower and push open the cottage door, tracking through the house like feral beach goblins. She stops and stares at the queen bed in the middle of the only bedroom.

"So…" she says slowly, a little sun-kissed and still flushed from the walk back. "Do you think it's too late to talk about our sleeping arrangements?"

I lean my shoulder against the door frame, trying way too hard to look chill. "I mean… technically, we *already* shared a bed. The beach counts as a bed, right?"

She grabs the nearest pillow and whips it playfully at me. I catch it with one hand, grinning like an idiot.

Her cheeks go pinker. "You're not wrong," she mutters, but there's a smile tugging at her mouth.

"And you drooled on me in your sleep," I say, dead serious. "So, we're basically like broken in now. We could share anything at this point."

Her jaw drops. "I *did not*."

"Oh, you did," I tell her solemnly. "A single, delicate droplet."

"Gross." She laughs.

Then she stops and looks at me seriously, "Finn…should we talk about this?"

I realize I'd let her drool on me every damn night if it meant waking up like this. "We can do whatever you want, baby."

She steps closer to brush sand out of my hair. The touch is small, barely there, but my pulse jackhammers like it's the main event. "Okay," she says softly. "We can talk later. We're good?"

I reach behind me for a towel and drape it over her shoulders. She smells of ocean air and faintly like my cologne. "We're good, baby."

Her eyes flick down to me. Her teeth catch on her lip. I file that away for later, because sweet baby Jesus, that look might end me.

My phone buzzes. I fish it out, still half drunk on the way she's looking at me.

Cal: Volleyball on the beach at 2. No excuses.
Bring your girlfriend.

She leans over my arm to read it. "Girlfriend?"

I laugh, holding up my hands. "Cal is a… creative guy."

"Uh huh." She arches a brow. "But volleyball sounds fun after a shower, breakfast, and a nap. Does that guy ever sleep?"

"Maybe he's part cyborg," I mutter as I respond that we'll be there.

"You care if I shower first?" she asks as she gently touches my arm, eyes meeting mine.

Fuck me. Rowan is going to destroy my heart and I'm gonna let her.

Instead of letting my inside thoughts win, I say, "You go first."

Rowan disappears into the bathroom, and when she comes back out… she's wearing nothing but a huge towel wrapped around her as she bends down to dig through her bag for clothes.

Just a towel and those bare toned and tanned legs, her hair wet and loose, and sun-kissed shoulders.

I feel as if I'm going to black out from my pulse hammering so hard seeing her practically naked, knowing my lips were all over her last night.

"You okay there, champ?" She smirks. The woman knows exactly what she's doing.

"Yeah," I croak. "Just… great."

She twirls a strand of hair around her finger, completely oblivious to the fact that she's now living rent-free in every part of my body and making my cock so rock hard I know that shower is going to have to be a cold one.

For a second, I imagine this with her in my life every morning, making coffee, the ocean outside us. Not just for a week. Maybe forever.

The thought hits me like a hammer to the chest.

I clear my throat a little. "All done in the bathroom?"

"Yeah, it's all yours," she says.

I snag a clean T-shirt and boxers, but before I make it to the bathroom, I stop right in front of her.

She peers up at me, lips a little swollen from earlier.

I slide a hand around the back of her neck, pull her in, and kiss her slowly and deep enough to make her melt into me, soft enough to make it sting when I pull away. Then, I dip my head until my lips brush the shell of her ear, my voice low and rough.

"I'm gonna go finish what *you* started yesterday in that shower," I whisper, letting my breath skate down her throat. "And this time, you're the one who gets to sit here and listen... while I come, moaning *your* name."

Her breath catches and her jaw drops. She looks up at me like I just set the room on fire.

Yeah. She thought she got away with touching herself behind the shower door yesterday while I stood at the grill pretending not to hear every desperate, filthy moan spilling out of her mouth.

She didn't get away with anything. It's my turn to torture her back.

I grin, slow and wicked, and head for the bathroom. She doesn't say a word. She doesn't have to. The look on her face is everything.

The door shuts behind me, steam wrapping around my shoulders as the water hits my skin.

Payback.

I turn on the spray and step in, leaning back to let my shoulders cool on the tile. The water sluices over me, as I run my fingers over my face and lean into the spray.

My hand slides down, wrapping around myself, and the sound that slips out of me isn't quiet. I don't want it to be. I want her to hear. I want her to know exactly what she does to me and just how fast she can undo me without even being in the room.

I pump slowly at first, dragging my palm over the length of me, letting the slick heat of the water add to the ache that's been building all day. My head falls back against the tile, breath coming out rough.

It's not enough. It's nothing compared to her. I picture Rowan's knees braced on either side of my hips, hair damp from her own shower, eyes fixed on me like she owns every shiver I make. The way she always looks at me right before she kisses me... like she's choosing me again.

My grip tightens, hips jerking forward into my own hand. A low, helpless sound rips out of my chest, and the steam swallows it up. I bite back another groan, but it still escapes.

Heat coils low in my stomach. My breath stutters. I'm right on the edge, too close, too fast, and I force myself to ease up, slowing my strokes because I want fantasy more than the finish.

I'm shaking a little as I let go, bracing a hand on the slick wall. I take a second, breathing hard.

When I'm cleaned up, I reach for the handle and push the shower door open, stepping out into the thick cloud of steam. The air hits my skin, cooler than the water, and I drag a towel around my waist, knotting it low on my hips. Droplets run down my chest, down my stomach, and I swipe a hand through my hair, trying to look composed.

Then I open the bathroom door, steam curling out around me like I'm carrying a damn confession into the hall.

Rowan's laying on the bed casually like she *hasn't* been listening to me in the shower. Her legs are crossed, hands twisted in the hem of my T-shirt she's wearing, pretending she's fine. She's not fine. I can tell by the way she's looking at me.

Her eyes drag down my body, slow as sin. She swallows hard. And then she blurts, breathless, "That was the hottest thing I've ever heard in my life."

My grin is slow and sharp. I take a step towards her. She doesn't move.

"You should've joined me then," I murmur, voice low enough to vibrate against her skin as I close the distance.

The moment stretches and her chest rises with every breath, the hem of my T-shirt brushing the tops of her thighs. That's when

I notice the lacy, pale blue panties peeking out beneath the fabric, bright against her tanned skin.

Yeah. I'm fucked.

I lean on top of her, my hand at her waist, balancing my body weight on top of her. She lets out a shaky little breath like she's been holding it since the shower turned on. My towel hangs lower as I press in, close enough to feel the heat between us, but not enough to close it.

My mouth finds hers, and she tastes like salt and sun and everything I shouldn't want this badly. The kiss starts soft but turns into something that's got my blood buzzing slowly, filthy, desperate.

She fists the towel at my hip like she might tear it off. My hand slides beneath the edge of my T-shirt, fingers brushing the bare skin of her breast, teasing her nipples, and she shivers.

I trail kisses down the side of her throat, then lower, tasting the edge of her collarbone. Her breathing stutters, her back arches, and it's so easy to forget everything except her.

And then, between our kisses, she whispers breathlessly, "Finn—wait. We have to talk about this."

I stop, forehead pressed to her neck, breathing hard.

"Okay," I say, voice rough against her skin. I kiss the spot just below her ear, slow and teasing. "Then let's talk."

My lips keep tracing lazy paths down her neck as her hands slide up my back, trembling.

And then it slips out like she can't stop it. "What happens after this week?"

But her voice wavers. Like she already hates the idea of this ending.

I drag my nose along her jaw, down to the spot where her pulse pounds under her skin. "What do you want to happen?" I murmur against her throat.

Instead of answering, her hands slide down to the towel that's still wrapped around my waist, thankfully separating us because my cock is straining so hard right now, aching for her.

Her fingers trail from my hips and up my chest and thread into my hair, tugging hard enough to make me groan. I can feel every ragged breath, every inch of her tight against me as she kisses me—slow, desperate, filthy.

"Finn…" she whispers, lips brushing mine, breath shaking.

I freeze for half a second, chest pressed against hers, my heartbeat slamming into her ribs. "Yeah, baby?"

"I like this, a lot," she admits. And my heart clenches.

I kiss her desperately, gripping her hips with one hand and pushing toward her, the other sliding up the back of her thigh, dragging that thin cotton T-shirt higher. She's warm, flushed, breathing hard, and pulling me tighter, urgently.

Every time I pull back to breathe, she chases me, fisting my towel, dragging me closer. Her mouth is hot and hungry against mine, her soft little gasps shooting fireworks straight through me.

She trembles, and my hand slides down her thigh, hooking behind her knee to pull her against me. The towel is barely hanging on now. The soft fabric of her panties presses against me, and it's a miracle I haven't come just kissing and pressing into her.

Her eyes flick up to mine, wide and terrified and so damn honest. "What if we just agreed that what happens in Coconut Beach stays in Coconut Beach?"

I pull my forehead back and stare at her. Rowan is going to destroy my heart. And fuck, I'm going to let her. Because I love her so much. And she might never be on the same page as my love is for her, but I can't stop. I love her so much. If one week is all she's going to give me, then so be it. I'm going to love her and have the best week of my life even if it destroys me in the end.

"Okay, baby," I answer. But it's not the truth. The truth couldn't be further from this bullshit. A week of fucking. Nah. I'm going to do one better. I'm going to give her something she'll never be able to walk away from.

She nods and moans, trembling, and my hand slides higher up her thigh, hooking her panties and pulling them down. I stare at her bare beautiful pussy and think if a week is all I get then I'll die a happy man.

I kiss my way down her neck, trickling across her breasts as my fingers find her pussy. "You're so wet for me, baby...tell me this is for me."

"Finn..." she moans as I rub her clit fast and feverishly, feeling her tremble, her eyes hooded and staring at mine in desperation.

"You think you can just be my friend, Rowan?"

She moans and pants.

"Answer me, baby," I warn.

She shakes her head as her body starts to give. "No..."

"You think you're just going to get orgasms for a week and that will be enough?"

She shakes her head faster.

"I'm gonna ruin you so that no other man could ever fucking give you what I'm going to give you."

"Finn!" she screams as she comes so hard on my fingers, her body writhing, panting and grasping my shoulders.

Just like that, the line between us blurs so hard it disappears. Because I'm just getting started and I'm going to ruin her pussy for any other cock that could ever *try* to come after me.

CHAPTER 14

Rowan

COME AND GET YOUR LOVE BY REDBONE

THE AIR IS STILL heavy with the sound of the ocean outside, but all I can really hear is the sound of our breathing, uneven and hungry, still tangled up in the heated orgasm he just gave me with only his fingers. And holy shit that didn't disappoint. That was the hottest orgasm I've ever had in my life. And it wasn't even sex. If that's what he can do with his hands, I'm absolutely going to love what he can do with his big dick. He's going to wreck me, and God help me, I'm going to let him.

But that's why I threw out that whole "whatever happens in Coconut Beach stays in Coconut Beach" thing, because I panicked. Because I felt something I wasn't supposed to feel and the second he touched me, it stopped feeling wrong. If felt so right. And I can't let him know that he already means more than I can handle.

Finn's lying on his side, propped on one elbow, the towel sitting dangerously low on his hips. His skin is warm against mine, his heartbeat still pounding fast enough that I can feel it when we touch.

I feel lit up from the inside out. Like someone rang my bell and I'm never going to be the same after this.

He leans in and drags his lips along my neck, soft and lazy, like he's trying to memorize the taste of me. "You like that?" he whispers, voice low and rough, having no idea how much he just obliterated me.

I let out a shaky laugh, because *like* isn't the right word. "Yeah," I breathe. "I more than liked it."

His grin is slow and dangerous, his thumb tracing circles against my hipbone. "And here I thought friends aren't supposed to give each other orgasms."

The way he says it, filthy and warm, makes me shiver all over again. Who knew Finn was so dirty? God, I love this.

I look down, feeling his hard cock. Straining against the towel, his chest rising and falling like he's holding himself back.

My hand moves before my brain can talk me out of it, sliding over his hard abs, feeling every muscle tense under my palm. His breath hitches, a quiet, broken sound that goes straight to my core.

His eyes lock on mine, dark and hot, like he's barely holding on.

"Rowan..." he whispers, voice a warning and a plea all at once.

"Yes?" I say softly, knowing exactly what I want.

God, I love the way my name sounds like it's a warning, and low and dirty.

I lean in and kiss him, slowly and deep, the kind of kiss that erases every line we ever swore we wouldn't cross. His hand slides up the back of my thigh, gripping, holding me there like he can't stand the space between us anymore.

His towel shifts lower and my pulse trips. It's pure fire and heat between us, and years of friendship burning into something neither of us can take back after this moment. We'll probably never be the same ever again. And I'm really trying to consider that. But that all went out the window and now I feel like I have no self-control when it comes to Finn. I need him.

When he exhales against my lips, it sounds like surrender.

The towel is hanging on by a thread. One soft tug and it'll be gone.

"Rowan," he whispers, voice already fraying at the edges.

I shift closer, between his legs, my fingers curling under the edge of the towel. His head tips back, a rough sound tearing out of him. The sight of him like this, so damn big, so hard, makes something inside me snap.

He looks down at me through heavy lashes, eyes dark and wild. "You have no idea how long I've wanted you."

I drag my nails lightly down his hipbone, and his entire body shudders and the air between us crackles with intensity.

"You sure?" I murmur, my voice low and dangerous.

"Fuck yes," he breathes.

His hips twitch, his breath goes ragged, and I know exactly what he wants—what *I* want. I lean in, slow and deliberate, teasing, letting the tension stretch tight enough to make him groan like he's losing his mind.

The first sound that leaves his mouth is raw, deep, and filthy. His hands fist the sheets, knuckles white.

I look up at him, and the way he's watching me, like he'd burn the entire world down to keep me, is enough to make my thighs clench and me almost come just by having my mouth on him and watching him come undone.

"Rowan..." he growls.

It's messy, hungry, and feels reckless. As his hand slides into my hair, guiding me gently, his hips lift in a desperate, involuntary jerk.

He reaches down, grabs my hips, and pulls me up, settling my bare pussy right against him just as he comes. The hot, rhythmic spill of him hits my core, and the shock of it steals my breath.

God.

It feels filthy and intimate and so much like a promise that my whole body trembles.

He grinds up against me, slow and deliberate, coating me in every pulse of his release while keeping himself right at my entrance and close enough to make me shake, far enough to make me lose my damn mind.

A needy sound claws out of my throat. I can't help it. My clit drags against the slick heat of him, and the tease of it—him—sparks through me so sharply I grip his shoulders just to stay upright.

I should be the one in control. I should be teasing him. But right now, I'm the one being undone.

The way he holds me there—bare, open, wanting—makes me ache so deep I swear he can feel it through my skin. I wasn't prepared for how much I'd want him inside me, how hard the need would hit the second I felt him come on me instead of in me.

And I regret it. I regret not letting him fill me.

Because now all I can think about is what it would feel like—his heat spilling into me, his body locked tight with mine, his voice saying my name against my mouth as I break around him.

My heart is a mess. My body is worse. And I want him again. More. Deeper. Everything.

I clench my thighs around him as he reaches down, stroking my clit again, my body shaking as I start to feel close again as he rubs himself into my clit, stroking, fucking me with his fingers and making my clit explode again on his fingers.

His breath saws out of him, uneven and ragged, the sound that makes my entire body clench in response.

I rest my hands on his hips, still breathing hard, and he blinks down at me like he's trying to remember how the world works. Then his hand finds my jaw, warm and a little shaky, and he leans forward, catching my mouth in a kiss that's soft and slow but absolutely drenched in heat.

"Rowan," he rasps, his voice so low it feels like it slides right through me. "Holy shit."

I laugh softly, and it's a messy, breathless sound. "Yeah," I whisper. "Holy shit."

His hand slides down my neck, his thumb brushing the underside of my jaw like he's memorizing every inch of me in a new way. It's a small touch, but it makes my heart trip hard in my chest.

There's this unfamiliar weight in the air between us now. Not just heat or raw unfiltered need. It's more and something that feels dangerous in the best way.

He looks at me like he wants to say something, like there's a war happening in his chest. I beat him to it.

"I can't believe I've been missing this," I whisper, my voice shaking more than I want it to. "Have you been this filthy dirty all along with a giant dick?"

He lets out a soft, rough laugh, pressing a kiss to my temple. "Yeah, well... turns out best friends are pretty fucking bad at pretending they don't want each other."

The honesty in his voice hits low and deep. My chest aches. Part of this conversation I don't know if we're ready to have, yet.

"You wanted me, Finn?"

His eyes tell me everything I think I've always known, and the vulnerability on his face is the sweetest thing I've ever seen. "I always have, Row."

His arm slides around me, his fingers tracing lazy patterns against my skin. Outside, the waves are rolling, steady and soft. I rock against him and he moans into my neck, making me feel safer and more loved than I've ever been.

Here, tangled up in him, I can feel my world tilting just a little. And for once, I don't want to fight it.

The fan hums softly above us, but it's the ocean breeze seeping through the window that keeps everything warm and lazy. Finn's body is solid and heavy against mine anchoring me, like the world outside of this little cottage doesn't exist.

We must've fallen asleep wrapped around each other, because when I blink awake, sunlight is cutting across the bed in golden stripes, and his arm is locked around my waist like he's claiming me even in his sleep.

I stretch slowly, and his chest presses into my back, his breath warm against my shoulder. He shifts, nuzzles his nose into the crook of my neck, and mumbles against my skin, "Mmm. Morning."

"It's not morning," I whisper back, voice still rough from sleep.

He lets out a low laugh when he sees the clock. "Damn. Noon already?"

I grab my phone from the nightstand, squinting at the screen. "Yep."

He presses a lazy, soft, and dangerous kiss to my shoulder. "I'm starving," he mutters. "Let's get lunch and then volleyball. Cal's gonna annoy the hell out of us if we don't show up."

I roll over to face him, my hair probably a wreck, him looking so unfairly gorgeous. This is *so* bad. Because I want to stay here, tangled up with him, forever. Like forget home. We'll just live here now in Coconut Beach. We can move our businesses here. I like *here*.

Instead, I say, "Lunch." Like it's a normal thing you do with your best friend after you had the best orgasms. Like my heart isn't still hammering from thinking about what just happened.

He gets up first, and heads to the bathroom, tossing me a look over his shoulder that makes me bite my lip. And just like that, we're moving through the motions, like we didn't just cross a line that can't be uncrossed.

I step into the bathroom after him once the water turns off, and as I catch my reflection in the fogged-up mirror, my face is flushed and soft and *happy*. That's the part that gets me. I look… *happy*. And I think to myself when was the last time that I actually felt this way? I don't know if I ever have. Maybe before my dad died. When things were easier. But I have never felt like this before and it scares me and exhilarates me all at once.

My phone buzzes on the bedside table, pulling me out of my daze. A text thread with my sisters lights up the screen.

Ivy: How's the trip going?

Willa: Tell us everything. How tan are you? How many fruity drinks have you had? Are there hot guys?

I stare at the messages, and my face gets even hotter. Hot guys. Singular. One. *My best friend.*

I type back, fingers shaking just a little.

Great! Going to grab lunch and play beach volleyball with Cal.

Totally casual. Nothing to see here. Definitely not recovering from the best sex of my life with the one man I swore I'd never fall for.

The bubbles pop up again almost instantly.

Ivy: So, what's really happening? Did you and Finn finally bang yet?

Willa: Yeah, did you two finally give into this friends-to-lovers thing you've had going on?

I laugh under my breath and toss the phone onto the bed, stepping into the shower to rinse away the morning without actually wanting to.

When I step out, Finn's leaning against the door frame, hair still damp, wearing swim trunks and a stupid sexy smirk.

"Ready?" he asks.

I nod, even though ready isn't the word for what I feel. Because ready means this is normal. And nothing about this feels normal anymore as I grab my phone and purse, and I slide my hand into his and we head out.

———

The beach shack next to the sand volleyball court is loud, already alive and people enjoying the beach, sunlight glaring off the water, music floating on the breeze, the smell of fries, salt, and sunscreen everywhere. But all I can really focus on is *him*.

Finn's across from me, damp hair curling at the ends, ball cap backward, sun warming his golden skin, blue shirt unbuttoned a few buttons showing off his bronze, muscled chest, which feels downright illegal. He's lounging back like he owns the damn world, like he doesn't even realize what he's doing to me. He's watching me as if I'm the most interesting thing in the world.

He leans over, slowly and cocky, and snatches one of my onion rings.

I gasp. "Excuse you."

Then I retaliate, grabbing one of his cheesy fries with a dramatic flourish, because if we're starting a war, I'm winning it.

He doesn't even flinch. He just pops the onion ring into his mouth and gives me a look so hot and smug it makes my thighs press together under the table.

"Payment," he says, voice low and rough like sin.

"I thought I already paid for that," I say as I slowly lick my lips and then bite my bottom one. His eyes stay fixated on my mouth.

"Baby," he drawls, leaning closer and whispering as he grabs another, "I made you come so hard this morning. I think I earned the whole damn basket."

I choke on a laugh and a shaky breath at the same time. "Finn."

"What?" He feigns innocence, even as he licks a crumb off his thumb in a way that is definitely *not* innocent. "Gotta keep the books balanced."

"Balanced," I repeat flatly in a whisper. "I made you come just as hard if you don't recall."

He leans closer until his breath skims my ear. "Yeah, so here's the thing. I'm just getting started with you, Rowan."

My thighs squeeze tighter and my pulse trips. I try to glare, but I'm pretty sure my face is on fire.

He knows exactly what he's doing, and I hate how much I love that he knows.

He leans closer, brushing against my shoulder. "You keep looking at me like that and we're not gonna make it to volleyball," he murmurs, so quiet only I can hear.

"Finn." It comes out breathier than I intend.

His hand drops under the table and lands on my knee. It's warm, firm, and steady, and too much. He doesn't stop there. His thumb starts rubbing slow circles on the inside of my thigh, just a little higher than innocent.

My whole body locks up, heat flooding through me like a match just caught fire in my chest.

"You're flushed, baby," he whispers, grin curving wicked. "You thinking about me?"

I try to swallow but my throat's dry. "Definitely."

He dips his head closer, his breath brushing my ear. "I'm starving. And not for food."

Every inch of me gets hot. I can feel the pulse between my legs pounding like it's begging for him.

He steals another onion ring like nothing happened. Like his hand isn't on me and he isn't slowly working on unraveling me in public. He could have all my food for the rest of my life if it means I get just one more orgasm from this man.

Someone a few tables over laughs at something and almost breaks me out of my trance. But the way Finn is looking at me is making me nearly come undone again as his finger strokes closer and closer to my already soaked panties. I tremble and try to focus on his face as his eyes practically talk me through it while I have the quietest and again hardest orgasm of my life as he rubs my clit through my panties in a way that I can't come back from.

He holds me and grips my pussy as I come hard, shaking silently against him in the booth, everyone oblivious around me.

I turn to him and whisper breathlessly, "Are you just going to do this every day, all day? I mean, I'm not complaining, but this is...wow."

He whispers back, "I told you I'm going to fucking ruin that pussy, baby. Ruin it."

And I hate how much I want that.

This is trouble. Big, grinning, dirty-talking Finn trouble. And I'm falling straight into it.

CHAPTER 15

Finn

WORK SONG BY HOZIER

"YO, FINN," Cal calls, tossing the ball. "Eyes on the game, lover boy."

To be fair, I have a valid reason for not keeping my eyes on the game. Rowan's in a black bikini. Not just any black bikini. The bikini that clings to her like it was made to personally ruin me. It's tied at the hips, her hair's down, she's got her legs crossed in the chair like she knows exactly what she's doing to me. I've had years of bad ideas about this woman. Years. And now I'm living out every single one of them.

The sun's hot enough to make the sand burn under my bare feet and melt any reasonable sanity I had left. Cal's been playing like he's trying to impress some ladies watching, the music from a portable speaker filling the court. We're all shirtless, sweaty, and dangerously distracted. We're going to get beaten by the tourist team, and at this point, I don't even care.

"Shut up," I mutter, but my eyes are exactly where they shouldn't be. On her.

She tips her sunglasses down just enough to meet my gaze, smirks, and bites into an orange Popsicle like she's trying to end me.

Cal serves. I jump and spike. A whistle cuts through the air. I turn to look at what Cal is whistling at, and a bachelorette party has just walked up to watch us.

Three girls in matching "Last Fling Before the Ring" crop tops and tiny shorts line up at the edge of the court, drinks in hand, waving like they're auditioning for a music video. One of them giggles. Another yells, "Nice arms!"

Cal grins at them and waves. "Oh, this is gonna be fun."

I barely register them. I'm already looking for Rowan—

And when I turn, she's staring at the girls like she'd happily hex every single one of them on the spot.

A pinch of something tightens in my chest. Not amusement. Not ego. Protectiveness and a need to steady her. I want to make sure she knows the truth before she spirals into thinking anyone else is even on my radar. She's the only one I'm seeing and the only one I *want* to see.

I step closer, lowering my voice so only she can hear. "Hey," I murmur, catching her eyes. "I wouldn't have noticed them at all if they hadn't yelled."

Her expression flickers—surprise, maybe a little relief—and it hits me hard how badly I want to keep giving her that.

The one thing she never expects anyone to offer her.

And that's when it clicks and I'm smiling because for the first damn time, I think she might care even a fraction as much as I do.

Cal jogs past me, muttering, "Please just call it, whatever this is between you two. I want front-row seats to this romcom movie unfolding."

I playfully roll my eyes and wave at Rowan, and she smiles and waves back. I don't know what we're calling this. I know what I'm calling it because I want this. I want everything with Rowan. I want a future, I want a life. I want vacations, and mostly I want every day. I want to bring her coffee every morning just the way she likes it. I want to work with her in her garden every night getting hot and sweaty and laughing. I want to eat dinner with her each evening and not just on our Thursdays at The Rusty Anchor. I want to do big loud holiday dinners with her next to me holding my hand. And I want to get lost in her every single night, making her mine. I want it all and I always have.

The next game's a mess because every time I glance at Rowan, she's doing something else that's designed to make me lose my mind, like flipping her hair, and leaning forward with her elbows on her knees, her tits pushed up in her bikini like she's trying to make me throw her over my shoulder caveman style and drag her back to the cottage.

Cal whistles. "And Finn once again forgets he's in a game and not a goddamn sex dream."

"Bite me," I say.

"Buddy, the only person who's gonna be biting you is her," Cal singsongs.

He's not wrong. I've got plans for her tonight. Now that she's given me the green light, I'm literally in heaven. If this is a dream, don't even think about waking me up.

A time-out's called, and I head over for water, half because I need it and half because I need her. She hands me a cold water bottle out of our cooler bag we packed. And then she does something that shocks the hell out of me. She leans up on her toes and kisses me. Not soft or innocent, but like she wants me just as much as I want her. And it gets the attention of the bridal party sitting on the chairs not far from us as a few of them groan.

Cal yells, "We're in public, horn dogs."

I grin against her mouth, pull back just a little, and say to her, "You doing that to make them jealous?"

She tilts her head, smiles wickedly. "I'm reminding you about who you're spending the week with."

I nearly drop the water bottle. "I haven't forgotten."

Her hand trails down my stomach, feather-light, right above the waistband of my shorts, just enough to make my dick twitch against the fabric.

I lean down and mutter in her ear, "You're gonna pay for making me hard in the middle of a volleyball game, Rowan."

Her eyes flash as if she's enjoying every second of this game that's going to wreck me. "Oh yeah? How am I going to pay?"

I lean down so close that my breath skims her ear. "Later, you'll find out."

She shivers, and I feel it. Hell yes. I glance down at the goose bumps on her arms that are comical being how hot it is outside.

Behind us, Cal clears his throat dramatically. "Do you want us to lose this game? Or should we all just get some popcorn and watch this tale of lovebirds unfold even more?"

Rowan flips him off over her shoulder without missing a beat and Cal laughs.

"Okay, lover boy," Cal says when I step back onto the court, "try not to pitch a tent out there, yeah?"

"You're dead, Cal."

"I'm just saying," he yells, "if I had a girl looking at me like that, I'd have gone home by now."

The ball hits my shoulder because I'm not even pretending to pay attention anymore. And I know I'm not winning this game. I don't even care.

Because the real game's tonight. And I'm going to make the most of every second I have with Rowan Maren.

———

The tiki bar is busy, and full of people. The food is good after a long, hot day in the sun, the drinks are strong, and the music's easy with old songs we all seem to know by heart. Coconut Beach has always been the perfect place to unwind and fully relax. I have a lot of good memories here and have been coming here since I was a kid. And there's no one I'd rather be here with right now, than Rowan.

Rowan's sitting on one of the barstools, her legs crossed, wearing one of my T-shirts over her black bikini, and a pair of cutoffs, which should *not* be allowed. I'm behind her with my arms around her waist, chin resting on her shoulder, both of us swaying to the music like we don't have anywhere else to be.

She tilts her head back against my chest, laughing at something one of the old guys at the bar says about Cal being "the worst volleyball player in recorded history." Cal gives him a look from across the bar, like really?

She fits against me like she's always belonged.

We talk with a few locals, people who've lived here their whole lives. They tell stories about fishing, hurricanes, and weddings on the beach. Rowan listens with a wide, soft smile that makes my chest hurt. Every time she turns her head to say something, her hair brushes my jaw, and I swear I forget how to breathe. I've stepped away a few times and each time she pulls me back in closer, wrapping my arms around her.

This feels like a dangerous game we're playing, but I have no intention of stopping.

After a while, she twists a little in my arms, tips her head up, and whispers, "Want to get out of here?"

I don't need to be told twice. I nod to Cal, who closes out our tab and brings me the check to sign. I slide my card back into my wallet and take Rowan by the hand and pull her toward me, tucking her into my side.

We walk barefoot back along the beach, the late afternoon soft and quiet except for the waves. The tiki bar fades behind us, just a hum of music and laughter now. She looks over at me, hair blowing around her face, and for a second, I forget every reason this is supposed to just be temporary. I don't want that, and I'm beginning to question if she feels the same way. I want to talk about it, but I'm also scared of the answers.

Back at the cottage, we fall onto the bed, the ceiling fan spinning lazily overhead. Her skin is warm from the sun, and she smells like coconut sunscreen and saltwater. We are facing each other, talking the way you only do when the world feels small and safe with your person. And Rowan has always been that person for me.

I heave a big sigh. "Rowan, I love this. I want this. But I also know we have to really talk about things."

She puts a hand to my cheek and leans against my shoulder. "I know."

"Where's your head at with all of this? We went from friends to...I don't know what we are. And now not knowing, that's kind of messing with my head," I admit.

"I've always loved that I can be myself with you, Finn," she says softly, tracing a lazy line across my chest with her fingertip. "Very few people I can feel safe with, and you are one of them."

"Why can't you be that way with anyone else?" I ask, knowing this is big for her to be vulnerable about. Rowan and I have always had a kismet connection and there's no denying that. But until we got to Coconut Beach, we never crossed any lines.

She snorts lightly. "Trust me, nobody is ready for that version of me."

I tilt her chin up, keeping this moment serious. "I love every version of you."

She freezes, and her eyes search mine, and she gets quiet. We're so close to saying it, the words sitting right on the edge of our mouths. But I know we're not there yet; we still have so many things to work out.

"I mean it," I tell her. "You're more than my best friend to me, Rowan. And nothing can change that. I hope you know that. I would do anything for you, and to make sure that never changes."

She nods, twisting her ankle nervously next to my foot. The ocean breeze floats in through the window, bringing in the sounds of the gulls in the distance.

Finally, she whispers, "I don't want a love like my parents had. I don't want to have everything with the love of my life, then lose everything like that. I saw how that made everyone so sad and devastated."

I trace my thumb across her palm, gently. "Rowan..."

She swallows and continues, her voice cracking a little with emotion. "When my dad died, everything broke. It was just a normal day, and he went out fishing when the ship went down, and they never found him or Tate's dad.   The unthinkable happened, and my mom's never recovered. She's just... existed after that. I can't— I don't want to have my heart ripped out like that."

"I don't plan on dying," I whisper. "If I died, I'd just come back from the grave."

She lets out a soft laugh, half choked and half real. "That's gross."

"Romantic," I counter, grinning. "Nothing could hold me back from being with you."

"Isn't that a Hozier song?" she teases. "No grave can hold your body down or something?"

"Yeah," I say. "And it's true. That can be your song for today."

She shifts and presses her forehead against mine, and everything else disappears as I kiss her softly.

We've talked about her dad a lot. I was by her side from the night she found out he was missing, to the months and the years after when she had to process that grief with no real closure. It was hard on all of them. Tate left, he couldn't deal with the grief. Willa, Ivy, and Lilith got through it by clinging to each other, but it left a mark on all of them. So when she talks about her dad, it means something. She's afraid of losing someone, and I get that. With my dad, I never really had a loss. He was just gone when I was really little. And we had other people in our lives who stepped up to be in our lives. But losing her dad not only hurt their family, but our entire Wisteria Cove community.

Her fingers trace lazy circles over my chest, but her shoulders are tight. She's letting me see that part of her, the one that's always braced for the rug to get pulled out.

I push her hair back gently. "Hey," I murmur, "look at me."

She does. And damn, I feel it down to my bones. Her soft brown eyes, vulnerable, and searching mine.

"You can't keep living like you're waiting for the worst day to show up," I say softly. "What if what you're worrying about never even happens? And you miss out on all the good parts of life?"

She lets out a soft, bitter laugh. "I've been the 'strong one' for so long. If something breaks again, I'm the one who has to pick up the pieces and I'm so tired, Finn."

I trace a line down her jaw, my thumb brushing the corner of her mouth. "Then let me help you carry it. You've got me, Row."

Her breath catches, and that tiny sound is going to live rent-free in my mind forever.

"What if we just..." I pause, swallow, then let it out. "What if we stop overthinking every single thing? We get one life. What if we don't waste it hiding from what we want?"

She blinks at me like she didn't expect me to say it out loud.

"We're adults," I add, a little dryly. "If it works, we figure it out together. If it doesn't... we'll still figure it out together. Because that's what we've always done."

She huffs out a sound and loosens something in her shoulders. She shifts closer, pressing her cold toes against my leg to mess with me.

"God, you're always so brave," she whispers. "You believe in things even if they might not work out. How do you do that?"

"Because I know what I want and I know what I'm going to fight like hell for, Rowan."

She shakes her head like she's trying to fight a smile. "You really think it could work with us? For real?"

"Rowan," I say, leaning in until our noses brush. "This already *is* working. You and me? We've been a team since we were kids. This just... adds kissing and more. And frankly, that's been pretty damn great too."

We both know we're circling something dangerous and beautiful here.

I tuck a strand of hair behind her ear as I kiss her neck. "What if we just... try? No what-ifs. No expiration dates. You and me, and whatever comes next."

Her fingers fist in my shirt, pulling me closer. "Finn," she whispers, like my name's the safest thing she knows.

I lean in slowly, like if I rush this, the spell will break. Her lips brush mine, feather-light, and something in my chest stumbles. It's about everything we've never said, everything that's been simmering for years.

When she exhales against my mouth, I feel it all the way down to my bones.

The kiss deepens, piece by piece. Like the tide sneaking up the sand, drawing me under one inch at a time. Her fingers slide into my hair, slow and sure, curling tight like she's anchoring herself to me.

I shift, rolling us gently until she's on top of me, her knees pressing into the mattress on either side of my hips. Her hair falls around us like a curtain, shutting the rest of the world out.

She lets out this soft little laugh against my mouth, half surprise, half joy, and it hits me square in the chest. God, I love that sound.

I look up at her and know, without a doubt, that I'm already done for. I cup the back of her neck, keeping her close. "Whatever happens, we'll figure it out," I promise.

"Yeah?" she whispers, searching my eyes.

"Yeah."

And then there's no more talking. Just the slow burn of her against me, the salt in the air, and the quiet, terrifying, perfect feeling of knowing we're not pretending anymore.

This isn't just one week. This is something real.

CHAPTER 16

Rowan

A BAR SONG (TIPSY) BY SHABOOZEY

THE LIGHT IS soft when I wake up, a hazy gold that always makes everything look a little dreamlike. The ceiling fan hums lazily, the air warm and salty, the waves outside soft like background noise.

And then I realize why my breath is already catching.

Finn's between my legs, the sheet pushed down, his hands on my thighs, his mouth on me. He's slow and intentional and making my body vibrate from his tongue.

I let out a soft, startled sound that melts into something breathless and want-drunk. His grip tightens, and everything inside me pulls taut like a bowstring. It's not just the way it feels—it's the way *he* looks at me when he lifts his eyes, like I'm something he's waited his whole life to have.

I fist the sheet in my hands, trying to stay quiet, but a laugh gets tangled up in the moan that escapes me. Of course, this is how he wakes me up. Of course, Finn is both a menace and a dream.

"Finn…" My voice breaks around his name, shaky and low.

He makes a soft murmuring sound against me that feels like it slides straight up my spine, and I arch up against him, already dizzy from how good it is the way he moves like he knows just what to give me.

And then, right before I feel like I'm going to come harder than I ever have in my entire life, the universe has a sick sense of humor and there's a knock at the door.

I freeze, still breathless. Finn groans low into my skin like he's personally offended.

Another knock. Louder this time. "Rowan? Finn?"

Shit, it's Birdie.

Birdie. The witchy, Stevie Nicks–esque Coconut Beach auntie who's basically everyone's fairy godmother and neighborhood gossip in one. She owns one of the neighboring cottages and I've known her since we were teenagers coming here.

I slap a hand over my mouth, half laughing, half dying. "Oh my God, of course this is the moment Birdie comes over," I whisper.

Finn lifts his head, hair a mess, face flushed, looking like pure sin. "You've got to be kidding me," he mutters, voice rough. "Ignore her. She'll go away."

Please go away, I look up in silent prayer. *I need Finn. Right now, I need this orgasm.*

The knocking continues. "I *know* you're in there, sleepyheads," Birdie sings out. "I brought donuts and coffee."

Of course, she brought my favorite donuts, and it's obvious that she's not leaving.

I scramble, nearly tripping over the sheets, and hiss, "Get dressed."

Finn smirks up at me, still sprawled out, very pleased with himself. "Pretty sure I was in the middle of something."

I throw his shirt at him. "Pretty sure Birdie just heard my almost orgasm, so *move*. Let's get this over with."

He laughs under his breath, a warm, low rumble that makes my stomach flip even now, and hauls himself up just as I peek through the window.

Birdie stands on the porch in her flowy floral kaftan, hair

loose, probably smelling faintly of sage and patchouli like always.

When we're both dressed, I finally open the door. Her eyes twinkle as she looks between me—flushed, probably glowing—and Finn, who is absolutely not hiding his smug grin at all.

"Well," she says, tapping her painted fingernails against the door frame, looking pleased, "I see that you two have finally figured out what we've all known for a long time."

I resist the urge to hide in the bathroom in mortification. "Morning, Birdie."

She breezes past me into the cottage like she owns the place. "I just got back into town. I had to see for myself what everyone has been talking about between you two. How's Donna? Does she know you two are finally a couple?"

Finn chokes on a laugh behind me. I glare at him, which only makes him laugh harder.

"Donna's good," Finn says with a grin as he helps her with the drink carrier. "Working on a new book. And no, this is…new."

"Mmhm, she's going to like this. And of course she's on another deadline. I don't know how she does it. On my way back, I spotted someone in the airport reading her newest book. It's my favorite so far," she adds.

"You say that about every book she writes," Finn teases. He's always had a closeness with Birdie. Her, Donna, and my mom have been friends for a long time, and we always had get-togethers when we'd come down here. She's been up to visit Donna and my mom too.

Birdie gets a little more serious when she says, "And how's Pete?"

Finn gets quiet, and I know Pete has been on his mind every day since we've been here, as well as mine.

"He's good for right now. Just taking every day as a gift," I tell her softly.

"Oh, good. I was hoping he was still raisin' hell. Pete's a good man."

Birdie is already making herself at home like she lives here as she unwraps the box on the counter. The scent of cinnamon sugar and warm dough fill the cottage, making my mouth water. I love the donuts from Boardwalk Donuts, especially when they're still warm and fresh.

Finn and I try not to be awkward like two teenagers who just got caught making out in the backseat of a car. He's wearing low-slung board shorts and nothing else, still flushed, hair mussed from my hands. I'm drowning in one of his T-shirts, hair every-where, thighs still shaky and tender from his touch.

"Nothing like the smell of sugar and sin in the morning," Birdie says, voice all breezy mischief.

Finn actually chokes on the water he's pretending to drink. I whip my head toward him, wide-eyed. He just grins like the smug little shit he is.

"Birdie," I huff, unable to keep from smiling.

"What?" she says, feigning innocence so badly it's practically a performance. "I didn't say anything *specific*. But sweetie, you've got the glow. Don't even try to deny it."

I press my palms to my face. "Oh my God."

Finn leans close to my ear and whispers, "She's not wrong." I elbow him so hard he laughs.

Birdie sets out the donuts like she's hosting brunch for royalty, then plants her hands on her hips. "It's good to see you two together. Been years since you've been down here at the same time. Donna used to say she couldn't tell if you were going to get married or blow something up together. You've always been thick as thieves."

"Both are still on the table," Finn mutters.

I nudge him and he doesn't flinch. Just smiles that soft, wicked smile that gets me in trouble.

Birdie raises a brow like she *definitely* notices the under-the-table shenanigans. "Mmhm. Well, you've got that look of love, Rowan." She waves a hand at Finn. "And this one has the energy of a man who's about to do something about it."

Finn laughs, leans back in his chair, arms folded behind his head, looking entirely too good for someone who was just nearly caught between my thighs ten minutes ago. "Oh, Birdie," he says.

Birdie grins like she can *feel* the tension radiating between us. "Ah, young love. Or whatever we're calling it these days."

"Birdie," I say, dragging out her name, half mortified, half laughing.

She chuckles. "Relax. I'm just happy for you two."

Birdie chatters about her garden, the moon cycle, and some neighbor who has just moved to the beach. Finn listens and laughs. And that's one of the things I love about Finn. He always makes people feel seen and heard. He is almost always present and when you're talking to him, he's really listening. In whatever Finn is doing, he's all in. I love just being with him and talking.

And somewhere between her talking, I catch him looking back at me. Not in the "I want to get you naked" way (though, yeah, that's probably in there too), but in the *real* way. The kind that says: *this isn't just a fling.*

My stomach does that fluttery, terrifying thing.

Birdie reaches for another donut and says, "Well, this is nice. Don't screw it up, kids." Then she breezes out the door as if she didn't just casually light our morning on fire and walk away.

The second the door clicks shut, Finn bursts out laughing.

"She's the best meddler," he says between laughs.

"She knows *everything*." I groan, hiding my face in my hands.

Finn pulls me in, laughter still hot against my throat, but there's something darker underneath it like he's thinking about exactly where his mouth was before we got interrupted. "Yeah."

"So, what's the plan for today?" I ask, pretending I'm capable of a normal conversation when I can still feel the ghost of his tongue on me.

"It's a surprise." He tilts my chin up and kisses me slowly, as if he knows I'm still aching and he's enjoying every second of it. His lips taste like heat and control and the kind of trouble that leaves bite marks.

I try to act casual even though my pulse is pounding between my legs instead of my wrist. My fingers tap restlessly on the mug. "So... about earlier," I murmur, voice dropping into something shameless, "when you were so rudely interrupted..."

I lean closer, lips brushing his ear. "Are you planning to finish what you started? Or are you really going to make me wait through your whole little surprise while I'm still so wet for you?"

Finn freezes for half a breath. His smile is slow, filthy, hungry. I'm in big trouble now.

"Baby," he says, voice scraping low as his hand slides down to my thigh, "if you're still that wet for me, I could make you come right here on this counter before the coffee even cools."

A shiver shoots through me so hard. He grazes his thumb over my lower lip, tugging it down. "You want me to fuck you now?" he asks softly. "Right here?" His hand tightens on my thigh, dragging me a half-inch closer. "Or do you want to spend the next hour thinking about my mouth right where it left off when all you had to do was ask?"

I swallow hard, heat rolling through me so sharp it's almost painful. "Finn..."

He grins, wicked and victorious. "Yeah. That's what I thought." His knuckles brush the inside of my thigh and I actually gasp.

"Tell me," he whispers, "how wet are you for me not letting me finish you?"

I'm trembling. I'm starving for him. I'm one second away from grabbing his shirt and climbing him like a tree and begging him.

I'm in so much trouble for Finn Bennett. So much fucking trouble.

The morning is already warm when we walk down the street, sun streaking across the pavement in gold ribbons.

Finn's got that look, the one that means he's absolutely up to something and absolutely not going to warn me before he does it.

He slows in front of the motorcycle rental shop, and my heart stutters because there it is.

A sleek black bike, polished and growling even while it's standing still.

We both love motorcycles, even if neither of us owns one. We've ridden on friends' bikes before, but this one? This one is ours for the day, and every inch of it screams fun we probably shouldn't be having.

"Wait here," Finn says, eyes sparkling like he's about to commit a felony-level surprise.

I lean against the railing outside, watching him push open the glass door and step inside. Through the window, I catch flashes of him talking to the clerk. Finn's hands move as he gestures toward the bike, the clerk nodding, laughing at something he says.

They move around the shop together, Finn pointing at helmets, then slinging a backpack over his shoulder to test the fit. He signs a form, glances back at me through the window, and winks. My stomach drops straight through me.

A minute later, the door swings open, and he walks out loaded like a man on a mission with two helmets hooked at his fingertips, two backpacks strapped together, and a small cooler bag swinging casually from his hand.

"Got everything we need," he says, smug as hell.

Yeah. He really, truly does.

"This is going to be fun," I say, my heart already racing with excitement.

He tosses me a helmet with a grin. "All-day adventure. Swimsuit, sneakers, and a beautiful scenic ride."

I laugh. "When did you plan this?"

"Cal helped me set it up," he says, adjusting the strap under my chin before he tucks the cooler and extra backpack in the saddle bag and slides a leg over the bike.

I climb on behind him, my legs wrapping around his waist.

The engine roars to life, the sound thunderous and thrilling. The wind whips against us as we ride down the coast, the ocean glittering like it's showing off to the right of us. The smell of salt and the heat of summer fills my lungs, and for a moment, I can't tell if it's the ride or *him* that makes my pulse race. Either way, I'm at total peace right now.

By the time we reach Hidden Cove, my cheeks are flushed and my hair's wild under the helmet. And just like I hoped, the place is completely empty.

I swing off the bike and take it in. The cliffs curve around the water like a secret. The sun hits the ocean and turns it into a sheet of glitter. I feel the grin pull at my mouth before I even realize I'm smiling.

"I love Hidden Cove," I tell him, almost breathless.

He looks at me like he already knew I'd say that. "I know," he says softly, and there's a spark in his eyes that makes my stomach dip.

We hike in, about a mile, our backpacks bouncing against us, the sound of the ocean fading into the sound of rushing water. And then the trees open up, and the waterfall is there, tumbling into a crystal-blue pool, sunbeams cutting through the mist.

I drop my backpack with a little laugh. "It's perfect."

He drops his too, and his gaze lingers on me as I strip down to my black halter top bikini that makes my boobs look amazing. The way his jaw tightens when I peel off my shirt should not feel this good. He strips down to his swim trunks, all muscle and tanned skin, and I suddenly forget how to breathe.

The water is shockingly cold at first, but then it's just *good*. I wade deeper until the waterfall mist kisses my shoulders. Finn's already behind me, hands sliding around my waist, pulling me against his chest.

"God, you feel so good," he murmurs against my ear, voice low and rough.

I laugh softly, tilting my head back against him. "You do, too."

He presses his mouth to my shoulder, the scrape of his teeth making me shiver. The waterfall pounds around us, loud and steady, but his breath against my skin is louder somehow.

When he turns me to face him, I can barely think. He kisses me like he's been waiting all morning, deep and greedy, one hand sliding up the back of my neck, the other gripping my hip under the water. My fingers curl against his wet skin, and everything else just falls away, the world, the sound of the water, even my own heartbeat.

"Rowan," Finn groans against my mouth, and my knees actually go weak, not in a soft, swoony way, but in a *holy-hell-I-might-climb-him* way.

His hands slide lower, rough palms skimming my soaked skin, and every place he touches sparks like it's wired straight to my pulse. The water pounding around us is freezing, but somehow, I'm burning everywhere he touches, everywhere he hasn't touched yet, everywhere I'm desperate for him to touch.

He presses me back against the slick rock beneath the waterfall, crowding in close, the heat of his body cutting through the chill like he's my only source of warmth. His mouth drags down my throat, open and hungry, and my breath breaks apart.

God, I want him. I want him so badly I feel a little feral.

The way he looks at me here, wild, unguarded, like he's been starving for me hits me hard enough that my whole body trembles. Something sharp and reckless twists deep in my stomach, and I can't tell if it's lust or longing or both tangled together until I'm barely breathing.

"I'm on the pill," I manage, my voice shaking. "And I haven't been with anyone. I got checked."

He lifts his head, eyes blown wide, pupils dark as midnight. "I want you," he says, voice thick with heat. His mouth curves into a wicked, possessive grin.

Oh God. A pulse of want crashes through me so fast I have to grip his shoulders just to stay upright. I want it too, not just the physical part, not just the feel of him thick and hard filling me without anything between us, but the *meaning* underneath it.

The closeness, intimacy, and trust that I have with Finn. It scares the hell out of me.

But it also makes me feel alive in a way I haven't felt in years.

"The way you're looking at me right now," I whisper because I can't hold it in, "it's… so good."

His gaze drags over me, slow and reverent and filthy all at once.

"You're the only thing I've ever wanted," he says, and my heart slams hard enough I swear I feel it aching heat between my legs.

My body reacts before my brain catches up, pressing closer, tilting into him, like his gravity is stronger than mine. I'm trembling, shivering, trying to steady my breathing, but it's completely useless. I'm unraveling in his hands, in his mouth, in the heat of him pressed against the cold water.

"This feels…" I swallow, unable to finish the sentence.

"Right," he murmurs against my skin. "It feels right."

And it does. So right I'm ready to take every inch of him, every piece of him, every reckless, breathless second we're about to fall into together.

I gasp as he lifts me against the rock, water dripping down my hair, his hands steady and sure. I wrap my legs around his waist, and he laughs low against my jaw, that rough, dirty laugh that melts every defense I've ever had.

The kiss that follows isn't careful. It's hungry and it's everything. His hands roam, my nails dig into his shoulders, the waterfall pounding against us like it's trying to drown out the sound of how badly we both want this.

He whispers things against my ear that make me tremble, soft filth and promise tangled together. I answer with a whimper he swallows with his mouth, his hips pressing in closer, everything slick and hot and overwhelming. I pull off my bottoms and untie my top and toss them on a rock behind me. I don't care if anyone comes down here, I need this with Finn. Right now.

He grins and slides off his trunks and throws them on top of my swimsuit and melts into me, kissing me, taking his time on each of my breasts as I fist his hair and moan.

When we finally give in, it happens the only way it ever could with Finn.

With the waterfall crashing around us and the sunlight slipping through the trees.

With his hands gripping my hips, his forehead pressed to mine, and our breaths tangling in the cold mist.

The moment he pushes into me, slowly and deep, my breath shatters. Every nerve lights up and every part of me opens to him. Finn groans like he's been waiting his whole life for this. And God… it feels like I have too.

I cling to his shoulders, nails dragging across his wet skin as he thrusts up into me, steady and strong, the kind of rhythm that steals thought and replaces it with pure sensation. Water rushes over us, soaking our bodies, mixing cool droplets with the blistering heat of his mouth on my neck.

"Rowan," he whispers against my ear, voice breaking. "I'm yours. I'm so fucking yours."

My hips meet his, desperate and unrestrained, and the sound that leaves me is nothing soft or pretty. I don't care. There's no holding back now. No pretending we're casual. No pretending this is temporary.

Every movement pulls us closer, deeper, tighter like we're trying to fuse, like our bodies have been waiting for this one impossible moment under a wild cascade in the middle of nowhere. He kisses me like he can't get close enough, like he'll drown if he doesn't breathe me in between every thrust.

I gasp his name, and he tightens his grip on my waist, anchoring me, guiding me, worshiping me with every shift of his hips. My head falls back, the spray of the waterfall hitting my face as pleasure coils low and hard inside me.

"I can't— Finn, I can't—"

"Let go." His voice is a growl against my throat. "I've got you. I've got you, baby."

I fall apart in his arms, trembling around him, crying out into the roar of the waterfall as he holds me through every shaking second.

He follows moments later, burying his face in my neck, his body shuddering against mine, his breath coming in ragged, uneven gasps.

He whispers my name again like a prayer. Like a promise. And something inside me breaks open in the best way possible.

Because this...This isn't a vacation fling. This isn't "whatever happens in Coconut Beach stays in Coconut Beach." This is forever, whether I'm ready or not.

The waterfall still thunders behind us, steady and loud, but everything else feels impossibly calm now.

The sun filters through the trees, warming my damp skin as I stretch out on the smooth rock at the bottom edge of the falls. My limbs feel heavy, boneless, blissfully spent.

Finn lies beside me, water droplets still clinging to his shoulders, one arm draped lazily across his stomach, but the other reaches for me, fingers brushing mine like he can't stop touching me, even now. Even after everything we just did.

I turn my head toward him. His eyes are closed, lips soft with a tired, satisfied smile.

And when he threads his fingers through mine, something in my chest softens and tightens all at once.

I'm ruined. He said it. I tried to deny it. But lying here with him, skin warm from the sun and heart pounding from something deeper than sex...I know it's true.

Finn Bennett ruined me for anyone else. And I'm not sure I want to be saved.

We're both still a little breathless, our laughter spilling into the open air in soft, uneven bursts. My hair's plastered to my shoulders, water trickling down my neck, and I've never felt more alive.

"This place," I murmur, staring up at the sky through the branches, "is magic."

Finn turns his head toward me, that slow, satisfied grin spreading across his face. "Or maybe it's just you."

I snort out a laugh. "Please. You're drunk on waterfall sex."

He chuckles, deep and warm. "Yeah, and it's the best damn hangover I've ever had."

I turn my head too, and there it is, that look in his eyes again. The one that makes my stomach flip. Like he's already memorizing this moment. Like he doesn't plan on letting it go.

"You ever notice," he says softly, "how everything feels lighter when it's just us?"

My heart stutters a little. "Yeah."

His fingers slide over mine fully now, our palms pressed together on the sun-warmed rock. "We don't have to over complicate this, Row. Life's short. And messy. And we only get one shot at it."

"Finn—"

"I'm serious," he says, shifting closer, his voice dipping low but steady. "We could keep dancing around this thing forever. Or we could just... choose it. Choose *us*. No promises of perfection. Just real. Me and you, and whatever comes our way."

I stare at him, and something tightens in my chest in that way it only does with him. This is Finn. My best friend. The one person who's seen me at my worst and still stayed. And he's being vulnerable right now.

"You make it sound so simple," I whisper.

"Maybe it is." He grins. "Besides, I've already proven I can handle you in a black bikini and a waterfall. I feel like that earns me some points."

Something in me melts. I can feel it.

I curl into him, resting my head against his chest. His heart beats steadily beneath my ear, grounding me. I can feel the sun warming our skin, the wind tugging at my hair, the quiet heartbeat of the cove holding us in this perfect bubble.

"Finn," I murmur.

"Yeah?"

"If we were back in Wisteria Cove… if this wasn't just a trip…" I hesitate, but the words come anyway. "Would you still feel like this?"

He doesn't even hesitate. "Rowan, I've wanted this for years. The trip just gave me an excuse to stop pretending."

The breath leaves my lungs in one sharp rush.

He tilts my chin up and kisses me like it's a promise. A slow, deep, honey-sweet kind of kiss that makes everything else fade out.

I kiss him back, fingers tangling in his wet hair, my chest aching in the best, scariest way.

When we finally break apart, his thumb brushes over my cheekbone, and he murmurs, "We'll figure it out. Whatever this turns into. Just… let it happen, okay?"

And for the first time in a long time, I let myself believe him.

I curl back against him, the water lapping softly at the rocks. The cove is quiet, hidden, holding us like a secret. And it's terrifying how good it feels to think that maybe—just maybe—this doesn't have to end here. It's just the beginning.

CHAPTER 17

Finn

SUNRISE, SUNSET, REPEAT BY LUKE BRYAN

ROWAN'S SPRAWLED out in the sunshine, and I'm convinced that she's the most beautiful woman in the world. Her hair's damp from the waterfall, and her cheeks are flushed pink, her lips still kiss-swollen. Her skin gleams in the sun, all dewy, soft, and marked with little reminders that she is just mine.

God, she's so beautiful she could practically knock the air out of my lungs just thinking about how lucky I am right now.

I unpack the picnic like a man trying to pretend his entire world didn't just get rocked. My hands are steady, but inside, I'm a damn mess. For years, I've imagined what it would feel like to be with Rowan. To know what her breath sounds like when she says my name against my skin. To feel her tremble and make her come and have her look at me the way she just did under the falls.

Now I do. And nothing's ever going to be the same. I could die a happy man now.

Sandwiches. A sad little bag of chips. Two sodas I shoved in my bag this morning without a single thought in my head except *don't forget the drinks, idiot.* She props herself up on one elbow, squints at the chips as if she's confused.

"You brought one bag of chips for both of us?"

I shrug, because if I speak too much right now, I'll say something stupid like *I love you*—and it's too soon for that to spill out, even if it's been sitting in my heart for years. "I didn't realize I was picnicking with a non-chip sharer."

Her mouth drops open, all faux outrage, and then she laughs. Not polite or careful. Real. That laugh is a sucker punch to my ribs, a reminder of every night I wanted to hear it this close.

"You're lucky you're hot," she says, swiping the chips like the adorable menace she is. "And that I do share."

I lean back on my elbows, watching her crunch a chip. My heart is still beating too fast, too hard. I've kissed her a thousand times in my head. Touched her in a hundred different what-if dreams. But none of those daydreams came close to the real thing with Rowan, warm and glowing and completely, terrifyingly real beside me.

"Yeah," I murmur, rough around the edges. "Lucky."

She playfully tosses a chip at me. I catch it midair and pop it in my mouth without breaking eye contact.

"This is the perfect day. I love it out here. I haven't been here since I was fifteen. It's funny to think that the last time we came out here was when Ivy had a crush on Cal. I'm going to tease her about that when we get home. It's funny to think she had a crush on Cal but ended up with Remy. I couldn't imagine her with anyone else. Her and Remy are perfect."

"Yeah, they are," I say, grinning. "And I'm glad we came out here."

Her cheeks flush just enough to give her away, and something shifts low in my chest. She bites her lip like she's fighting back a smile, and that's it. I'm gone.

When we finish eating, she peels off her shorts and wanders toward the water like she was born to make me lose my mind. The waterfall sparkles behind her, and she glances back over her shoulder, mischief in her grin.

"C'mon," she calls.

I already know that tone is full of trouble. "What are you up to?"

She twirls her finger in the air. "Let's do the *Dirty Dancing* thing where I run and jump and you lift me up."

I snort. "Absolutely not."

"Finn." She splashes water at me. "You're not scared you can't do it, are you?"

"Oh, I know I can do it." I scoff.

She splashes me again and I wade in. She grins like she's won.

"Okay, Baby," I tease, "don't drop *me*."

She rolls her eyes so hard it's a miracle they don't fall out. "You're Patrick Swayze in this scenario. I'm the one getting lifted."

"Tragic," I tease, but she's already backing up, ready to run.

She charges toward me, laughing so hard she can barely get a running start. I grab her waist, water swirling around us, and lift her straight up. She lets out this *gorgeous*, breathless laugh that wraps itself around my spine and doesn't let go.

She's slick and glowing and completely ridiculous, and I swear I'm going to remember this day for the rest of my life.

"Look at you," I say, trying not to lose my grip as she wiggles.

"Look at *you*," she shoots back, breathless. "You're actually doing it!"

"Don't elbow me," I grunt.

"My boobs are in your face," she says, and we're both laughing too hard to breathe.

"That's the best part," I pant.

When I lower her down, her legs slide against mine in the water, her hands cupping my cheeks like she's already made up her mind about me. She kisses me, wet, messy, *perfect*. My hands find her hips, and for a second, there's no ocean, no world, just her mouth and my heartbeat trying to catch up.

We tumble back onto the blanket, damp and tangled, still laughing. She stretches out on top of me, her cheek pressed to my chest. I trail my fingers down her spine to hear that soft little sigh she tries to hide.

That's when a flash of black catches my eye. A dragonfly lands on my shoulder.

Rowan gasps. "Oh, I love dragonflies. I always see them when I feel like my dad is trying to tell me something."

I glance down at it. "I sure hope your dad didn't see what we just did under this waterfall."

She smacks my chest lightly. "That's *a good sign*. Dragonflies are good luck. Basically, a saying of trusting the change and transformation."

I grin at her. "What does it mean if it sticks around?"

"It means the universe is saying we're going to end up together," she whispers dramatically, eyes wide.

I laugh, pulling her closer, feeling her shake with laughter against me. She tilts her head up, all flushed cheeks and wet hair and the kind of smile that wrecks a man.

"Finn," she says softly, like a secret she doesn't know she's telling, "this has been the perfect day."

Yeah. It has.

I press my lips to her temple, breathing her in like I'll never get enough. And as stupid as it sounds, with that dragonfly on my shoulder and her heartbeat against mine, it feels like something bigger than just a fling.

It feels like the start of something I won't be able to walk away from.

"We're in trouble," she whispers again, forehead resting against mine, breath hot on my lips. "I can't stop kissing you."

"Yeah?" I murmur, tracing my thumbs along the soft dip of her hips, feeling her shiver. "Good thing I've got a thing for trouble."

She rolls her hips enough to make my breath catch and my dick twitch. Enough to make the edges of my control fray. I slide a hand up her back. She's warm, damp, and soft under my touch, and when she exhales, it's a quiet, shaky sound that hits me straight in the gut.

The world doesn't exist anymore. Just me and her, straddling me in the sun with a smug little grin because she knows *exactly* what she does to me.

Her hands fist in my shirt, tugging me closer until our mouths meet again. This kiss isn't soft like the first. It's deeper. Hungrier. Her fingers slide into my hair, tugging just enough to make me groan into her mouth. Her hips rock again, slow and teasing, and I swear I could lose my mind right here on this blanket.

"Rowan," I breathe against her lips, half warning, half prayer.

She grins at me, wicked and sweet. "What?"

I tilt my head, brush my mouth against the curve of her jaw, down her neck. She shivers, letting out the softest gasp, and my hands grip her hips tighter like I need to anchor myself. Her pulse flutters under my tongue. She tilts her head back, giving me more.

God, she's sunshine and sin and everything I've ever wanted.

I shift us lower, rolling her gently beneath me. She lets out a breathless laugh, and I can't help but grin against her throat. Her legs wrap around me without hesitation, like she's been waiting for this just as long as I have.

"Still just want to be my friend?" I rasp against her skin.

She laughs, breathless and gorgeous. "Maybe."

"I said I was going to ruin you for any other man," I say, dragging my lips back up to hers.

She smirks. "You've already done that, Finn."

I kiss her again before she can finish teasing me until the edges between us blur. Her fingers slide up my chest, nails scratching lightly, and I tremble against her. The heat builds fast, like it never really left us.

Her body arches into mine, warm and soft and right. I know this rhythm already because it's *her*. My best friend. My everything. Every kiss, every sigh, every brush of skin feels like it's always meant to happen right here.

The sunlight warms our skin, the blanket rough under my hands, her breath hot against my mouth. She whispers my name again, soft and shaky, and that's it. The last thread of control snaps.

I kiss her deeper, my hands sliding beneath her shirt, memorizing every inch of her. She gasps against my mouth, her back arching, hips rolling against mine in a way that leaves nothing between us but heat and want.

"What do you want, baby?" I whisper against her lips.

Her eyes meet mine and are steady. "You."

And just like that, I slide into her and the world falls away, nothing but her breath in my mouth, her nails in my shoulders, the cool rush of water around our hips, and the sun warming every inch of skin we can't stop touching.

This is years of wanting finally catching fire, burning bright and right and inevitable.

When it's over, neither of us moves for a long moment. The waterfall crashes behind us like a heartbeat, steady and wild, but everything between us is quiet, soft, humming with something deeper than just wanting.

Rowan rests her forehead against mine, her breath warm and uneven. I stroke her back, feeling her shiver, not from the cold, but from what just happened between us.

Eventually, we pull apart, both reluctant. She laughs under her breath, pushing wet hair out of her face, and I swear I feel that sound in my chest.

We climb out together, slipping over the smooth stones. She squeezes water from her hair while I grab our towels from the pack. I hand hers over, but she's already close, her fingers brushing mine, eyes soft and a little dazed.

I towel her off slowly, maybe slower than strictly necessary, my palms gliding over her shoulders, her arms, her stomach. Goosebumps rise everywhere I touch. She does the same to me, dragging the towel down my chest, across my stomach, her cheeks flushed with warmth that isn't just the sun. Every accidental brush of skin feels intentional.

We get dressed in the dappled sunlight, still stealing glances, still smiling like idiots who just learned a secret only the two of us get to keep. She bumps her hip into mine as she slips her boots back on. I bump her right back. It feels natural. Easy. Dangerous in the best way.

We gather our things and hike back to where the bike waits at the tree line.

Rowan runs her fingers along the leather seat, sun catching on her damp hair. She gives me this tiny smile, the kind that hits straight in the gut. When she climbs onto the back, it's with confidence that looks like she was made for this, made for me. She slides her arms around my waist, her chest pressed against my back, her breath warm at the base of my neck.

And I swear I feel her heartbeat sync with mine.

She tugs on the helmet, giving me a look that makes me want to hike all the way back to that damn waterfall and fuck her all over again.

"Ready?" I ask over my shoulder.

She presses her hands to my hips, leans in close enough that her lips brush my ear. "I was born ready."

I swear I feel that sentence in places I'll show her later.

The engine rumbles beneath us, low and steady, and we pull onto the sun-warmed road. The wind rushes past us with the faint hum of the ocean.

Her arms slide around my waist, tighter than before, her cheek resting between my shoulder blades. I could ride like this forever. Just me, the road, and the woman currently making my heartbeat harder than ever.

We stop at a little burger roadside stand that smells like heaven with grease, grilled onions, and summer. The sign's peeling, the benches are wobbly, and I've never seen Rowan look so happy as we stand holding hands and putting in our order.

She tosses her helmet on the picnic table and shoves her sunglasses up on her head. "This place looks like it has the best burgers."

"Maybe you're just so hungry because you worked up quite an

appetite," I tell her, already ordering two double cheeseburgers, a mountain of fries, and two chocolate shakes.

She eyes me when the tray comes out. "You got my order perfect, and I didn't even have to tell you."

I grin. "Please. I know what you like, baby."

She grins and eats a fry and takes a sip of her shake, a look of pure bliss on her face.

I point a fry at her. "See? I just know."

She leans forward, eyes sparkling. "Thank you," she says, and pops the fry into her mouth.

We sit across from each other, sharing fries. She licks a smear of milkshake off her thumb and doesn't notice how hard I'm staring at her mouth.

"You're looking at me weird," she says around a fry.

I shake my head, smirking and whisper, "You're just teasing me with that mouth."

"Yeah," she says softly, almost to herself. "You like it, though."

She's not wrong.

An older couple at the next table leans over, smiling the way people do when they see something good.

"Y'all look like you're on your honeymoon," the woman says.

Rowan nearly chokes on her milkshake. "Oh—uh—"

I don't even hesitate. "Yup. Day three," I deadpan.

The couple laughs and goes back to their burgers. Rowan grins and eats another fry. "Really?"

"Play along," I say again, grinning.

But she's blushing, pink creeping up her cheeks, and it's adorable.

We end up at the pier just as the sun starts setting off in the distance, the sky painting itself in streaks of gold and pink. Rowan kicks off her sandals, walking barefoot along the wooden boards. I follow behind her, watching the wind tangle her hair, the hem of her shorts brushing against her sun-kissed thighs.

She looks back at me over her shoulder with that soft, *you're in trouble* smiling, and yeah, I already know I am.

We sit at the end of the pier, legs dangling over the water. She leans into me without hesitation, her head against my shoulder, my arm slipping naturally around her. Her skin is warm from the sun, and she fits against me like she's meant to be there.

For a long time, neither of us says anything. The waves slap gently against the posts below. Someone's playing music faintly in the distance. It feels... *easy*.

She tilts her head up, and I kiss the top of it without even thinking. She lets out a quiet sigh, like she's been holding her breath for a long time and finally lets it go.

"I can't remember the last time I felt this..." She trails off, eyes drifting toward the water, like the right word is somewhere in the sunlight skipping across the surface.

"Free?" I ask quietly.

She nods, slow, like the word settles into her bones. "Yeah. Free."

And I swear... I didn't realize how much she needed this until I saw it happen.

Rowan acts tough with her quick wit, ready to square up with anyone who tries her, but I know what she hides beneath all that fire. The weight of Vanessa breathing down her neck. Marilyn stirring shit just because she can. The mess with the mayor. The betrayal with Jessica. The pressure of the yoga classes, the shop, the expectations she never asked for. She carries all of it alone, pretending she's fine because she thinks she has to be.

But right now? Right now she's just Rowan. Bare feet and sun in her hair, just breathing like nothing owns her.

And I want to protect that. Protect *her*. I want to fight beside her when we go back and stand with her in every single one of them.

She exhales, light and unguarded, and looks at me. "Free," she repeats softly.

Yeah. If I have anything to do with it, she's going to feel a hell of a lot more of that. I rest my chin on her head. "Then let's not waste it."

She looks up at me, and the way the sun hits her eyes says it's game over. I lean in, slow and steady, and kiss her like the whole world's holding its breath. And when she kisses me back, fingers curling into my shirt, it's soft and sure and *real*.

I didn't mean to fall in love my best friend. But somehow, I can't begin to fight any of this ever again. Sitting here with her, watching the sun sink into the ocean, I know that she is my entire world.

CHAPTER 18
Rowan

WI$HLIST BY TAYLOR SWIFT

THE SUN and the sand are so hot it nearly burns my feet, so when I plop down on my chair, I hurry to pull them up. I stretch out in my bikini, sunglasses on, pretending I live in Coconut Beach and don't have to go back to real life of bills, small town drama, and everyone meddling in my life.

I'm dreading going back to real life in Wisteria Cove, but excited to see my sisters and mom. And my plants. I hope they keep my plants alive while I'm gone.

A woman with long blond hair and a floppy straw hat drops her bag on a chair a few feet away, and a few seconds later, she leans over with a sheepish grin. "You mind if I sit near you? All the good spots are taken, and I really don't want to sit next to the guy wearing socks with sandals over there."

I snort. "Yeah, you're safe here. No sandal socks over here."

She grins. "I'm Savvy."

"Rowan."

Within five minutes, we're chatting like we've known each other forever. She's a licensed mental health therapist from Arizona, who just broke up with her boyfriend of three years, and she came on their planned trip solo.

"I figured," she says, shrugging, "if I already paid for the flight and the hotel, why should I waste it? Might as well enjoy the piña coladas and the view."

The view she's looking at right now is Cal. That makes me smile. He's a good guy, big flirt, but he'd be good for her if she wanted a weekend fling. If she were to have a little Coconut Beach fun, Cal would be the one.

I let out a laugh. "Honestly? I love you already. And yeah, girl, you deserve better than some guy who can't see a good thing when it's right in front of him. I can't believe some of the stuff you've been telling me. Where is this guy? I want to have a little chat with him."

She raises her drink toward me. "Back in Arizona enjoying his single life. To better."

I clink my drink against hers. "To better."

A little ways down the beach, Finn joins Cal and a few other locals. They're tossing a football around, all tan skin, easy laughter, and *absurdly hot in the sun* energy going on. Every time Finn laughs, my stomach does a stupid, fluttery thing I keep pretending isn't happening.

Savvy glances at him, then back at me. "Sooo… where did you order that one from? Send me the link."

I roll my eyes, fighting a smile. "I didn't order him. He just… kind of showed up and never left. He's been my best friend since we were teenagers."

"Uh huh," she says, grinning. "When did you stop being just friends?"

"This week." I grin at her.

She nods with approval.

A few minutes later, Finn strolls toward us carrying two drinks in coconuts with umbrellas, and a grin that should be illegal.

"Ladies," he says, handing over the drinks. "I thought you and your new friend could use fresh drinks. I tried to order a snack, but you weren't on the menu," he says as he leans down, pulling me in for a kiss.

I laugh and kiss him back. "Finn. That was a terrible dad joke."

"Thanks," Savvy says as she watches us in fascination.

"Yeah, but it made you laugh," he says, winking before heading back to Cal and the others.

Savvy fans herself dramatically. "That one could go in the boyfriend hall of fame."

I watch him rejoin the guys, the sun catching in his hair. He tips his water bottle up toward me, winks like he knows exactly what he's doing. Flirting with me. It's working.

"I have no idea what I did to deserve Finn," I say quietly. *Because I know how good I have it.*

What I don't say is that I don't know if I'll ever be enough for someone like Finn. Someone steady, and who looks at me like I hang the damn moon. Because at the end of the day, he's literally perfect. And I'm Rowan. Who struggles with my deep thoughts and black cat personality. I'm fierce, loyal, and direct. And sometimes I struggle to make friends. But sitting here with Savvy has shown me that I can make friends. I have barely thought about Jessica this week. We were supposed to be here together. And we probably would have had an okay time. I don't understand how we could just drift away like that and I've blamed myself. But now that I've been here with Finn, I know that isn't true. Something shifted in Jessica, not me. She decided to partner up with two mean girls who used me, took my business model and made it into their own, which was fine. Like I've said, there's room in Wisteria Cove for more than one fitness studio. But the way they treated me, I didn't deserve. And when I go home, I'll set up my classes and go on about my life because I'm glad that I know what kind of people Marilyn, Vanessa, and Jessica are. Not my friends.

"So, what are you going to do about your ex?" I ask Savvy, trying to change the subject.

"When I go back, I'm moving out of our apartment and starting over," she says as she sips her drink.

"Good for you. And the best part is that you get to go back all tanned, relaxed, and he's going to see that you're just fine. And I bet he'll hate that."

"He's totally going to hate that. I found out he was going out with other women and told me they were just friends. Do I look dumb?" she says rhetorically. "All the gaslighting was terrible."

I groan, dramatic enough to shake the entire damn table. "Oh my God. I hate him even more for you. Like... full-body hatred. Even my spleen hates him."

Savvy snorts into her drink. "Good. Because the last straw? He took my car out and I found a pair of women's panties in the back seat."

I slap the table so hard the silverware jumps. "IN YOUR CAR? No. Absolutely not. Straight to jail."

Savvy wheezes laughing. "It was a whole crime scene, Rowan. I had my car detailed after that."

"He didn't even have the decency to cheat in his own car? He used YOUR car?" I shake my head, disgusted and personally offended. "Sir. Have some shame."

She grins. "Honestly, that poor woman had no idea he was taken."

"Oh, for sure," I say. "She probably thought he was single, and not a human red flag with feet. She was duped. Hoodwinked. Bamboozled."

Savvy cackles. "She probably left pantie-less, unsatisfied, and confused after it was over."

"Absolutely," I say, nodding aggressively. "Meanwhile you're discovering Victoria's Secret CSI-level evidence in your back seat."

Savvy clinks her cup against mine. "To being single."

I hold mine up. "May we heal, may we thrive, and may your ex suddenly go bald."

She chokes laughing. "Oh my God, yes."

I grin. "Tell me everything. I'm ready to hate this man on a professional level."

Savvy wipes her eyes. "You know what? I think we're going to be great friends."

I tip my chin up at her. "We already are. You should plan a trip to Wisteria Cove."

"It sounds amazing, I'd love that. And if you have more men there like Finn, let me book my trip now," she says as she leans back and places her hands behind her head.

"You have a master's degree?" I ask her.

She shrugs. "Yeah, in counseling."

I shake my head "Girl, you have a MASTER'S DEGREE. You are crying over a guy with probably only a birth certificate. This man's biggest achievement is memorizing his Chipotle order. He's the type of guy who borrows his neighbors Wi-Fi. And you have *multiple* degrees. Meanwhile, he's likely still proudly sharing his participation trophy from little league. Who is this guy?" I demand, pulling out my phone. "I need to see what he looks like."

She takes my phone and pulls up his profile, and I look at it, realizing he's already sharing some pictures with a brunette woman. "He's a guy who peaked in high school and he's what, almost thirty now? The only thing he did was waste your time. You are a straight up catch, Savvy."

She looks teary eyed. "Thank you. I'm so glad I sat next to you. I know I deserve better, but I was too scared to leave."

"I'm glad you're here. You're pretty great, friend. I have a feeling you're going to be better than fine. Without him weighing you down, you're going to find a nice man that you deserve."

Later, as the sun dips lower, we all end up in a loose circle near the bonfire pit with Cal, Finn, a handful of locals, me, and Savvy, who is absolutely *not subtle* about making eyes at Cal. And Cal? He's grinning back at her like a man who likes her back.

We start a ridiculous drinking game that someone learned at a bachelorette party. I lose every round because I'm too busy laughing, which means I'm definitely *way too drunk* by the time someone suggests karaoke or streaking and I happily volunteer for both.

Savvy's also tipsy and leaning against Cal's shoulder. I'm

sitting between Finn's legs on a towel, my head resting against his chest. Everything feels warm, blurry, and *perfect*.

I tilt my head back and announce to the group, "This is my Finn." I poke his chest for emphasis. "The best guy I know. He even does electrical work. Like… an electrician. Why they don't call him a Power Ranger, I don't know."

Everyone erupts in laughter, including Finn. He shakes his head, then in one smooth, stupidly hot motion, scoops me up and throws me over his shoulder like I weigh nothing.

"Okay, that's enough out of you, my spicy little comedian," he says, laughing as the world spins around me.

"I'm making a speech!" I protest upside down.

"Your speech is over, baby."

"Hey!" I argue, though my words are slurred from laughing too hard. "I was just telling everyone how much I love you."

"Yeah," he says with a chuckle. "I love you, too. And you're mine. Prize secured. Bye, everyone!"

The group waves as he carries me away down the beach, his arm firm around me. The night air is warm against my skin. My heartbeat won't calm down. Not from the alcohol. From him and how I feel about him. God, I love Finn so much it hurts my heart to think about if I were to ever lose him.

He sets me down gently on the steps in front of the cottage. I curl up sideways in his lap without hesitation. Our fingers find each other and lock together.

I'm tipsy enough to let the truth slip out. "Finn?"

"Yeah, baby?"

I swallow hard and the words taste scary, but either way, I'm feeling courageous. "I'm afraid, Finn."

"What are you afraid of, baby?" he asks gently, searching my eyes, concerned.

I hiccup. "I don't think I can be who you want me to be. I'm not a sweet girl and you deserve a sweet girl. I'm… spicy. Like you said. I'm not good."

He laughs softly, brushing his thumb over my knuckles. "I

love you spicy. And you're more than good. You're great. You are everything I want you to be. You don't need to be anything different."

I look down at our hands, tangled together. "What if I'm not... forever material? You look like the kind of guy who'd like a wife who drives a minivan. Someone who bakes cookies and makes dinner every night. And I'm like...witchy. I am not the sweet girl, and I never will be. And sometimes I eat chips for dinner."

He looks at me and strokes my cheek like he's trying not to laugh but his eyes are soft and gazing at mine.

"I can never drive a minivan," I tell him seriously.

His laugh rumbles through me, warm and easy. "Baby, I don't care what you drive. I'd buy you a semi-truck if that's what you wanted. You can haul babies, chips, plants, dogs, and a marching band for all I care. I just want *you*. You're enough for me. And we can eat chips for dinner anytime you want."

My throat tightens. The world feels soft and a little blurry, but it's clear to me that he means it. Maybe I can be enough. I can be messy and be me and he'll still love me. Or maybe not. But either way, I'm a goner for him.

He kisses the top of my hand, then my knuckles, and I melt against him like I always do.

I whisper, "Don't fall in love with me, Finn."

He murmurs against my skin, "Too late."

The light in the cottage is too bright like a personal attack. My skull throbs and my stomach second-guesses my life choices of drinking way too much last night. I groan into the pillow and pull it over my head and consider becoming a nocturnal swamp creature who never sees daylight again.

"Morning, sunshine," Finn says from somewhere above me. His voice is way too smooth for someone who should also be dying right now.

I peek out from under the pillow, squinting at him. He's standing there shirtless, hair mussed, holding a bottle of water.

"Why," I croak, "don't you look like death too?"

He smirks, crouching down beside the bed with that annoyingly sexy confidence and a glass of water and two aspirin in his hand.

"Because when I saw you having fun last night," he says, setting them gently on the nightstand, "I cut back so I could take care of you, baby. Someone had to make sure you were all right."

I drop the pillow dramatically over my face. "Why do you have to be so sweet? It's rude."

He laughs, tugging the pillow off me and replacing it with a soft kiss to my forehead. "It's my curse," he says, brushing my hair back like he's been doing it for years. "Being devastatingly charming and unable to stop taking care of you."

I groan, half-mortified, half-melting. "You're ridiculous."

"And you're dehydrated," he counters, nudging the water toward me. "Drink up, trouble."

My phone buzzes on the nightstand. I grab it with one hand, blinking at the screen.

Willa: You alive?

"It's my sisters," I say, my throat still scratchy as Finn heads into the bathroom.

Ivy: Give us a wellbeing check or we're calling in five.

I grin. My sisters are nothing if not aggressively nosy and protective. I type back with shaky thumbs.

Sooo, I think me and Finn are a thing??

The little typing bubbles appear so fast it's honestly impressive.

Willa: WHAT.

Ivy: FACETIME NOW.

Before I can practically blink, the screen fills with their chaotic faces. Willa's in her kitchen at her cabin with a mug of coffee, and Ivy's outside with her red hair piled on top of her head.

"HELLOOOO," Ivy singsongs. "Are we talking *thing thing*? Or, like, 'I accidentally kissed him' thing?"

"She looks like she did more than kiss him," Willa says, sipping her coffee like an evil little gremlin.

I groan and flop back onto the pillow. "Why are you both like this? I'm too hungover for your teasing right now."

"Because we're your sisters," Ivy says sweetly. "It's literally our job."

Finn comes out of the bathroom, pulling on a T-shirt, glances at the screen, and raises a brow. "Good morning, witches."

"Hi, Finn," my sisters say in perfect unison, like the world's nosiest choir.

He just shakes his head, totally unbothered. "I'm going to grab breakfast from the diner down the street. Hash browns, eggs, pancakes, the hangover miracle kit. You good?"

I nod, cheeks warming. "Yeah."

He leans down, kisses the tip of my nose, and heads for the door. My sisters immediately explode.

"Oh my God," Willa squeals. "He just kissed you like that? In front of us?"

I cover my face. "Stop."

"And he's going to get you food," Ivy says. "Willa, this is, like, officially boyfriend behavior."

"Full cinnamon roll boyfriend energy," Willa agrees. "We stan."

I peek out from behind my fingers. "I don't know what to say, guys. I'm… really happy."

Last night, I was a disaster. Telling Finn not to fall for me. Panicking like I always do. Terrified I'd mess everything up before it even fully started. But this morning… the way he touched me, the way he looked at me like I wasn't something fragile or complicated or too much and like I'm just *his*, something in me finally unclenched. Finn doesn't look at me like he's scared we won't make it. He just looks at me like he's so happy. And I want that with him.

Ivy softens immediately. "You look happy."

"I am," I admit, feeling that flutter in my chest, not panic, not dread, but something warm and bright and terrifying in a good way.

Willa leans closer to the camera like she's about to perform a psychic reading. "Can we tell people?"

I should protect this moment and keep it just ours for a little longer like I always do. But I don't. Because the truth is that I'm ready. Finn made me feel this morning that it's okay to stop hiding, stop running, stop sabotaging. I'm steady enough to believe that letting people know won't break us. Steady enough to believe *I won't break us.*

So, I shrug, but the giant, traitorous smile on my face gives me away instantly. "Yeah." The reaction is immediate and catastrophic. They scream. Like full-volume, glass-shattering, neighborhood-disturbance screaming.

I panic, shriek, and yeet my phone onto the pillow like that'll somehow stop them.

I can still hear Ivy chanting, "Our girl's in loooove!"

And Willa yelling, "I KNEW IT! I KNEW IT FROM THE FIRST TEXT YOU SENT!"

I feel really good. Like I finally stepped into something I've been afraid to want for years.

Whatever we have and wherever this is going, it suddenly feels right to let the world see it.

And maybe that's the scariest part. But it's also the best part.

They catch me up on everything and then I take the world's best feeling shower while I wait for Finn. Telling my sisters about us will make it easier when we get home. They'll all know and talk about it and hopefully get it all out of their system and treat us normal by the time we get back. Not likely, but I can dream.

When Finn comes back later, balancing a tray of coffee, and takeout containers with the smell of pancakes and grease heaven, I'm sitting cross-legged on the bed, cheeks pink, hair still wet, and grinning like an idiot.

He pauses in the doorway, taking me in with that look that makes my insides go soft. "What's got you smiling like that, Row?"

I steal the coffee from the tray. "My sisters," I say. "They're… excited for us."

He sets the food down on the end table, and sits beside me, bumping his shoulder gently against mine and kissing me. "Good. I'm glad you're happy, Row."

I take a sip of coffee, trying to look casual, but my heart's doing back flips. "They also want to tell everyone we're a thing."

He grins. "Good. So do I."

And just like that, even with my pounding head and dry mouth, the world feels warm and light and dangerously easy.

Finn and I are officially a *thing*.

CHAPTER 19

Finn

HOOKED ON A FEELING BY
BLUE SWEDE, BJORN SKIFS

THE TIKI TORCHES flicker against the night sky, throwing gold light over everything. Cal's laughing at something Savvy said, leaning back in his chair like a man who didn't know he was going to catch feelings this week. Rowan's next to me, one bare knee brushing against mine under the table, and it's so damn comfortable I almost forget this is our last night here.

The table's covered in empty drink glasses and half-eaten appetizers. A breeze rolls off the ocean, and somewhere in the background, someone's playing guitar. It shouldn't feel perfect, but it does.

Savvy looks happy, which is a miracle considering how the trip started for her. She deserves a fun time with Cal.

Her ex showed up earlier at the bar like some cheap romcom villain, sunglasses still on after sunset, and the smuggest face I've ever wanted to punch. Savvy froze, all color draining out of her face. Before I could even stand, Cal was up like it was instinct. He slung his arm around her shoulders, leaned in close, and said loud enough for the guy to hear, "Hey, babe. You want another drink?"

The ex blinked like he'd been punched. "Babe?"

"Yup," Cal said, grinning wide, daring him to do something stupid.

The guy started sputtering some nonsense about "unfinished business," but Rowan stepped right up next to Savvy, and I moved in beside them. That guy didn't stand a chance.

"Time to scram," I told him, voice flat. "She's not interested."

He actually looked at me like he might say something back, but then Cal's grin sharpened a little, and I think the guy saw his life flash before his eyes. He muttered something about a "misunderstanding" and left with his tail between his legs.

Savvy had tears in her eyes, the *holy shit, I'm free* kind. Rowan hugged her like they'd been best friends for years. Because that's how Rowan is. She's a momma bear through and through. You don't mess with her or the people she cares about.

And now… here we are. All of us at dinner, full of drinks, and pretending tomorrow morning isn't creeping closer when we have to go home and face real life. And I'd be lying if I said I wasn't worried about how things are going to go when we go back to real daily life. What if we go back to the way we were and not how we are now? Because I love how we are now.

Cal leans over and says something to Savvy that makes her snort into her cocktail. Her hand brushes his, and he doesn't move it.

Rowan squeezes my knee under the table. "You're a good man, Finn Bennett," she murmurs, and I swear the whole world could stop right now and I wouldn't give a shit.

"Nah," I say, grinning. "Cal's the one who went full knight in shining armor tonight."

"True," she says. "But you looked ready to deck him if he didn't leave."

She's not wrong. I hate guys like that think they can treat a woman like that and get away with it.

———

By the time we ended up at the tiki bar dancing, the night's soaked in warmth and salt air. Fairy lights loop between the palms, and the little band on stage is playing something too upbeat for anyone to sit still.

Rowan tugs my hand and drags me onto the dance floor, her hair catching the light, her laughter carrying over the music. She's barefoot, spinning in the sand like the world is hers, and I swear my chest might crack open just watching her.

I pull her in close. She loops her arms around my neck, looking up at me with that look that does me in every single time.

"You're staring at me," she whispers, her eyes locked on mine in a place of being half buzzed and half in love.

"Yeah," I admit. "And you told me you loved me last night."

She rolls her eyes, but she's smiling. She presses her forehead against mine, and for a second, the music fades out, and all I feel is her. "I love you so much, Finn."

I kiss her softly and murmur, "I love you so much, baby."

Over by the bar, Cal's got an arm slung around Savvy's shoulder. She's laughing, looking up at him like she didn't expect to meet a good guy here. I catch his eye over her head, and he grins at me.

I hold Rowan tighter, swaying with her until the song ends, then another one starts, and neither of us moves to leave. If I could trap this night in amber, I would.

We say our final goodbyes to everyone and head out. We hold hands and take our time walking the beach on the way back to the cottage. Neither of us say anything and enjoy the evening, the palm trees making beautiful shadows against the starry night sky.

Back at the cottage, I look at our pile of packed bags ready to go for our early morning flight. I'm sad this trip is coming to an end, but it will always be a special trip for us. The trip that tipped us over the edge and got us together, finally.

She turns on the shower and steps in, glancing back at me through the steam. "You coming?"

I don't need a second invitation.

The water's hot, and the tile fogs up instantly. She presses her hands to my chest, eyes searching mine. "I can't believe we're really leaving tomorrow."

"Yeah."

Her lips find mine, and everything else falls away. Water runs down her back as I lift her against me, her breath catching when my hands trace her hips.

It's slow, desperate, and beautiful.

She wraps her legs around me and I pound into her, making her moan and pant into my shoulder as I tell her, "You're mine, Rowan. Mine. No matter where we are."

When we finish and the water is starting to run cold, she rests her forehead against mine, both of us still under the spray, breathing the same air.

"I don't want to go back," she whispers.

"I know," I murmur, brushing my thumb over her lips. "But Wisteria Cove's home. And wherever you are, that's where home is."

She laughs softly, watery and real. "We're going home two completely different people."

"Is that a bad thing?"

"No."

"Good," I say. "I don't care who we are, as long as we're together."

She falls asleep in my arms, hair still damp, the sheets twisted around us. The moonlight sneaks through the curtains, soft and silvery. I watch her breathe for a while, wondering how I got so lucky.

She looks peaceful. Maybe a little too peaceful for a woman who's changed my entire life. I hope she always feels like she's enough for me and knows how incredible she is. She's everything to me and I'm going to make sure she knows that.

Our bags are ready to go, and our ride is scheduled. But I've got a feeling that this magic isn't going to wear off when the plane takes off in the morning.

———

The first thing I notice is the smell of rain that fills the air from the open windows. The second thing I notice is Rowan, warm and snuggled into my chest, her knee hooked over my thigh like she's trying to anchor me to her, and I don't mind at all.

The sky is still dark, mostly because it looks like we're going to get a storm. Above us, the fan turns slowly. Her hair tickles my collarbone. I slide my palm along her spine, and she sighs without waking.

Our alarm hasn't gone off yet, and the numbers on the clock glow at 5:11. I kiss the top of her head. She murmurs something that sounds like my name. My entire chest squeezes.

The breeze pushes the curtains, and they sway like they're dancing. The air is cooler, a whisper of rain on hot sand. Rowan wiggles closer until she's nearly on top of me, hand sliding to rest on my stomach.

"Morning," I whisper.

"Five more," she mumbles into my throat. "Minutes. Years. Preferably years."

"Years might make us miss our flight. And we get to go home to Allen. I hope he still remembers us."

"I do miss, Allen." She peeks up, sleep-soft eyes and pillow-creased cheek. "Of course he'll remember us."

We lay there and her fingertips trace idle circles across my ribs. I only know that I can't imagine not waking up like this. Not hearing her little morning-croak voice.

"You're staring," she says, eyes still closed.

"Not my fault." I nudge her nose with mine. "You make it hard not to."

"Flattery accepted." She kisses my chin, my jaw, the corner of my mouth. "Payment due."

"Invoice me."

I roll and pin her gently, sheets sliding, her laughter warm against my mouth. The storm smell deepens, and a shiver runs through the room. Goose bumps kiss her shoulders, and I smooth them away with my palms, slow circles, slow breath. We keep it soft. Lazy. Sunday morning is slow, even though it's not Sunday and it's not morning enough to count, and we're going back to real life today.

When I pull back, her lips are a little swollen, and she looks like trouble I'd gladly sign up for every time.

"What time?" she asks, stretching like a cat.

"Car's at six thirty." I glance at the clock. "We've got time."

"For coffee?" she says.

"For whatever you want." I kiss her forehead. "Always."

She rolls onto her back, hair spilling everywhere, and stares up at the ceiling. "Do we have time for me to stress spiral about what life is going to look like for us back in Wisteria Cove together?"

"No," I say, and hook an arm around her middle. "We have time for me to distract you."

"You're very useful." She pats my chest. "Like a human Swiss Army knife. With abs."

"I'll add that to my résumé, right next to my official title of Power Ranger Ken."

She laughs and we finally peel ourselves out of bed and stumble to the tiny kitchen. The first drops of rain hit the porch while the coffee maker fills. Rowan stands at the screen door, my shirt hanging off one shoulder, watching the rain begin. It starts tentatively, then commits, the way she did with me. I too have been thinking about what life will look like for us back at home, together, and I can't wait. I've wanted this for so long.

Outside, thunder rolls and the cottage smells like coffee and rain and her shampoo, which I'm not above stealing when we get home. We drink, hips touching, and count lightning like kids. She smiles whenever I miscount on purpose just so she'll correct me.

Rowan sighs and leans her head on my shoulder. "Okay," she says. "We do this."

"We do this," I echo.

We move through the cottage like a team that has practiced. I wash the mugs. She folds the blankets. I zip my bag. She tries to zip hers, gets the fabric stuck, and swears in a voice most sailors would respect. I kneel, fix it, look up into eyes that are bright for the wrong reason.

"Hey." I touch her knee. "We'll come back."

"I know." Her mouth tilts. "I still reserve the right to be dramatic."

"Wouldn't dream of stopping you." I stand and kiss her. "Dramatic is one of my favorite Rowan features."

She laughs and sniffs at the same time.

She checks under the bed even though neither of us put anything there. I do one last sweep of the bathroom and grab her forgotten mascara, and we pull our suitcases to the door. The rain thickens, a proper tropical curtain now. Rowan watches it like it's a movie she's seen a hundred times and still cries at.

"It's like Coconut Beach is crying," she says, voice small and a little wobbly. "Because we're leaving and our trip is over."

I step in close and tip her chin up. "Our trip is over." I kiss her. "Our new life together is just starting, baby."

Her breath catches. For a second she searches my face like she's reading fine print on the contract. Then she nods once, decisive, like she's choosing us again on purpose.

"Okay," she whispers. "You're right."

I tuck her into my chest and sway to the rhythm of the rain. Stupid and sappy and perfect. If anyone asked me when exactly I surrendered, I'd say right now. In a wet doorway with her heart thumping against my shirt and the whole island applauding in water.

The car isn't here yet. We've got twenty minutes to kill and a storm to play in.

"Come on," I say, and grab her hand.

"What are you doing?"

"Eating breakfast." I say as I kneel down in front of her and pull her legs down and put my mouth right on that pussy that's wet just for me.

"I'll melt," she warns.

"Then I'd better eat you fast if you're going to melt."

Her eyes flash and she moans. "Finn."

"What." I grin as I lick, suck, and pull her into my face.

She shakes her head like she can't take it and absolutely can. I grip her legs with my hands and keep going until she trembles and comes on my mouth.

"Finn," she murmurs.

Our driver pulls up and I stand, wiping my mouth with my hand, "Go freshen up, baby. I'll load our bags," I say with a smirk.

"You're going to pay for that, later," she mutters.

"I can't wait," I tell her and grab the bags and carry them down to the car while she gets herself together. Yeah, I'm going to have fun with Rowan.

We're in the back of the car headed to the airport when she lays her head on my shoulder and says, "Say the thing again."

"What thing?"

"That our new life is starting."

"Our new life is starting," I say into her hair. "Today. With coffee and rain and an airport that will probably lose our luggage."

She laughs. "I hope not."

"Ready?" I ask.

"No," she says. Then she smiles. "Yes."

Rowan grabs my hand on the seat between us. I turn my palm up and pull her fingers to my mouth. I kiss her knuckles slowly. One, two, three, the rhythm we've invented, the way to say every-thing without embarrassing ourselves in front of a stranger.

She watches, eyes shining in the wet morning light.

The driver asks a polite question about the radio and Rowan picks a station of rock. I pull her closer. She rests her head on my shoulder and watches Coconut Beach glide by through a film of rain.

The island is crying, or maybe it is baptizing us. I just know the road out looks like a path we take together, and my chest feels loose in a way that makes room for the future.

The airport sign appears around the curve. She squeezes my hand once, firm and sure. I squeeze back.

CHAPTER 20

Rowan

YOU MAKE MY DREAMS COME TRUE
BY DARYL HALL & JOHN OATES

THE AIRPORT HUMS with a weird exhaustion where everyone's half asleep or running on caffeine. Finn's hand is warm in mine, and he's carrying my carry-on like it's weightless, the strap slung over his shoulder, while I clutch my purse and try not to cry that Coconut Beach is officially behind us.

He looks ridiculous and perfect at the same time with his rumpled T-shirt, sunglasses hooked on his collar, and a backward ballcap. I look up at him, and he catches me staring.

"What?" he says, grinning.

"Nothing." I squeeze his hand. "Just… you."

He bumps his shoulder against mine. "Careful, you're gonna make me blush."

We stop near the carousel, the belt still empty and clunking as it starts to roll. Finn checks his phone, and the light from the screen catches the edge of his smile. That's when I notice the picture on his lock screen.

"Oh my gosh." I tilt my head. "Finn Bennett."

He looks up, confused. "What?"

"Your background picture." I point, heart melting. "That's us at the waterfall. You made it your phone background?"

He shrugs, a little sheepish but not sorry. "Yeah, well, there's a picture of me playing volleyball shirtless on your lock screen, so…"

My jaw drops. "How do you know that?"

"I have eyes," he says. "And you opened your phone on the plane and fell asleep with it in your lap."

I can't help but laugh. "You got me."

He grins and pockets his phone just as our bags start tumbling down the chute. "Hey, they made it."

When we walk through the sliding glass doors toward the pickup area and I freeze.

Because standing there with balloons, noise makers, and homemade signs, are the people I love most.

Lilith, Donna, Pete, Remy, Junie, Ivy, Willa, and Tate.

And the signs?

Willa's says **"FINALLY!"** in giant pink glitter letters.

Tate's reads **"WELCOME HOME FROM PRISON."**

Donna's, naturally, says **"KISS HER ALREADY."**

Remy's just says **"We took bets."**

Lilith's: **"About time."**

And Junie, bless her mischievous heart, holds one that says **"LOVE SPELL SUCCESSFUL."**

I lose it. Completely. Laughter bursts out of me, uncontrollable.

"Oh my God," I say, covering my face. "You guys."

Finn's laughing too, shaking his head. "You're all insane."

Donna shrugs. "You're welcome, dear."

Remy steps forward, smirking. "You two look tan. And disgustingly happy."

Junie skips right up to me, holding out her hands. "Aunt Rowan! Some of your plants died, but we kept Allen alive!"

"Junie!" Remy groans. "Don't tell them about the plants, yet."

I laugh so hard my stomach hurts. "Oh boy. That's fine, kiddo. I'm so happy to see you."

Junie keeps going, undeterred. "But Allen might've got one of

Dad's barn cats pregnant. He took him in to get the snip-snip. Dad says you owe him child support, Uncle Finn."

Finn's laugh is so loud it echoes. "You're killing me, kid." He scoops her up and spins her around until she squeals. "I missed you."

"I missed you too!" she says, hugging his neck. Then she leans back and studies both of us. "So, you and my uncle..."

Finn and I exchange a look and grin.

Junie wiggles her eyebrows. "When are you gonna make an honest woman out of her, Uncle Finn?"

Everyone *loses it*. Willa's doubled over laughing, Tate nearly chokes, and Remy groans, rubbing his temples.

"Easy, kid," Tate says, ruffling her hair. "Maybe let them get home first."

Donna waves a hand. "No, let her finish! This is the best entertainment I've had in weeks."

I can barely breathe from laughing. "You guys are *the worst*."

Finn's still grinning when he sets Junie down. He slides his arm around my shoulders and presses a kiss to my temple. "Nah," he murmurs. "They're family."

And just like that, I melt. Because damn it, it feels good to be home.

———

The drive back is familiar and strange at the same time with the winding roads, the smell of salt and cedar, the way the ocean glints through the trees. Wisteria Cove looks greener, brighter. Or maybe I'm just seeing it differently now.

Willa takes me to the bookstore and up to my apartment above it. The windows are open and the breeze smells like rain and coffee.

My plants are lined up and thriving. Cobweb, Willa's bookstore cat, meows at me.

I drop my bag and exhale.

Remy took Finn home. And just like that, the apartment feels emptier without Finn now than it ever did before I left for Coconut Beach. I flop onto the couch and text him, already missing the weight of him next to me, the warmth of his hand in mine, the way his laugh lingers even after he's gone.

How do we do life separate?

It takes only a second.

Finn: Well, they've been varnishing the floors here, and it reeks. I was hoping I could stay there for a few days?

I smile so big.

Get over here. lol

Half an hour later, there's a knock at the door.
I open it to find Finn standing there with an overnight bag.
I grab his shirt, pull him inside, and kiss him. Hard.
"Welcome home, Finn," I whisper.
He grins against my mouth. "Feels like it, Row."

———

Finn's backyard smells like cedar mulch, tomatoes, and the faintest trace of rain that we won't turn down. The sun's fading, but it's one of those Wisteria Cove nights that feels like the perfect summer night.

He's kneeling by the raised beds, forearms flexing as he digs into the soil, that little crease between his brows making an appearance. The man looks criminally good in a faded gray T-shirt and worn jeans, dirt on his knuckles and a smudge on his jaw.

I'm trying to work, but honestly, I've been staring more than planting.

He glances over his shoulder. "You keep looking at me like that and I'm going to take you inside the green house and christen it."

"I can't help it," I say, picking up a trowel and poking at the soil. "You're distracting me."

"I'm going to do *something* to you."

"Prove it."

He laughs, that deep, easy sound that settles somewhere low in my stomach. "You're asking for it."

I shrug. "We have new places to break in here."

He sits back on his heels, wiping sweat from his forehead with his wrist. "We need to finish up so we can go back and shower...together."

I aim the hose at the plants. And maybe just a little at him.

He jerks back, laughing. "Rowan!"

"Accident," I say sweetly. "The hose is cursed."

He shakes his head, walking toward me, eyes glinting with mock danger. "You sure you want to play this game?"

"Maybe I do."

Before I can react, he snatches the hose from my hand and sprays me right down the front. I squeal, trying to duck, but it's useless. The water's cool and shocking against my shirt.

"Oh, you're dead," I gasp, lunging for the hose again.

We wrestle for it, both laughing so hard I can't breathe, until it drops between us, spraying harmlessly into the grass. He catches my wrist and pulls me close, both of us dripping and breathless.

"Truce?" he asks, voice low.

"Temporary."

He kisses me and my hands find his chest, warm and solid under the damp fabric. He tastes like sunshine and feels like home.

When we pull apart, I'm smiling so hard it almost hurts. "You're lucky you're cute."

"I'm aware," he says, brushing a strand of wet hair from my cheek. "Also, you look good soaked."

"Finn," I groan. "I can't walk back to the bookstore with a soaked wet white t-shirt."

"What?" He grins. "I'm not complaining."

Later, we're both barefoot in the grass, working side by side. He digs new space for basil; I prune the mint and lavender like it's my therapy, because it is. Every few minutes, he steals glances at me, like he still can't quite believe I'm here.

"What?" I finally ask, not looking up.

"Just thinking," he says.

"Dangerous."

He chuckles. "About how this—" he gestures between us, to the garden, to the house "—feels like the start of something good."

"It does," I admit softly.

He wipes his hands on his jeans, and sits beside me in the dirt. The breeze ruffles his hair, and he looks at me with that same quiet steadiness he's had since Coconut Beach.

"You know," I say, pretending to sound casual, "I could help you redo the yard. Add some plants in the front, maybe some color."

He smirks. "You offering your services, Rowan?"

"Maybe. My rates are high, though."

He leans closer. "What's the price?"

"Coffee. Kisses. You know what I like."

He grins. "That's steep."

"Worth it."

"Yeah," he says, eyes locked on mine. "It is. And you can do anything you want to this yard, Row. Anything."

We finish up as the sun dips lower, the air turning golden and lazy. The garden looks good with the fresh soil, tidy rows, and little markers I made with my handwriting.

Finn comes up behind me, arms sliding around my waist. His chin rests on my shoulder.

"Looks good," he murmurs.

"Yeah," I say, leaning back into him. "Feels good, too."

He presses a kiss to my neck. "Ready to go?"

I turn my head, brushing my lips against his. "Yeah, let's head out."

He smiles, that slow, crooked one that melts me every time. "Guess we finally figured out how to do life together."

"Guess so," I say, grinning.

The breeze stirs, carrying the scent of basil and rain and the faint hum of the ocean in the distance. I close my eyes, sinking into the quiet, the warmth, the certainty of him.

Home isn't just a place. It's his hands, this garden, this laughter that keeps finding me even when I'm not looking for it.

And damn, it feels like the beginning of forever.

CHAPTER 21
Finn

ENDS OF THE EARTH BY TY MYERS

THE HOUSE SMELLS LIKE VARNISH, sawdust, and paint, and not in a good way. It doesn't smell or feel like a home. It feels like a pile of unfinished dreams that I can't wait to be done.

I'm standing in what's supposed to be the living room, only right now it's more of a construction site than home. Half the floor's refinished, edges taped off for the walls. The plastic tarp covers the built-ins I made last spring. The windows are new and still waiting for the trim. There's a stack of reclaimed wood leaning against the wall for the mantle, so much left to do in this place. It's rough, unfinished, stubbornly hanging on, same as me. Everything's halfway done and driving me nuts.

Which is exactly why I'm pacing the room like a caged animal, running numbers in my head. I want this place to be finished. Not for me. For her.

I can see it if I close my eyes. Rowan barefoot in my kitchen on a Sunday morning, wearing one of my shirts and drinking coffee with that look that makes me forget every struggle it's been to finish this house. Her plants are in the windows, and her books are lined up on the built-ins. Her laughter fills these walls and we're together and doing everyday life finally with her, here, like she's always belonged. That's the plan. Step one: finish the damn house.

Step two: Get her to see the same vision that I see and be my forever here with me. I don't just want to tell her I'm serious, I want to show her.

So, when the mayor calls me this morning and says something like, "I've got a contract for you if you're needing work," I don't immediately tell him to go to hell. That's probably mistake number one.

Sammy Briggs has never done anything in his life that wasn't mainly for Sammy, and every person in town knows it. Guy's got ambition like a rash. Always smiling, shaking hands, talking about "revitalizing" and "what's best for Wisteria Cove," which everyone knows really means tearing out anything old and putting in something that'll take a brochure picture or somehow line his pockets.

I don't trust him. And I want to know what he's got up his sleeve and if he's stupid enough to tell me, I can protect our town.

But, the number he threw out at me? That caught my attention. That number could finish out this house and would eliminate ninety percent of my stress right now. It's a three-month project that could cover the rest of the renovations if I took it on. That's the part that keeps making me consider this. My house could be done by Christmas. Curiosity gets the best of me, and I accept the meeting.

My phone buzzes in my back pocket. My brother, Remy. Always on time when I start to spiral. It's like he has a sixth sense about when I need him.

I answer. "Yeah?"

"You home?" he asks.

"I'm not sure we can quite call this a home yet, but sure." I say as I run a hand through my hair and look around at the chaos.

"I'm coming by."

"Why?"

"So I can look you in the eye when I tell you not to do whatever dumbass thing you're currently thinking about doing."

I laugh despite myself. "Get over here, then."

He hangs up. I stare down at my phone for a second, then shove it back in my pocket and look around again. I briefly mentioned to Remy that there was a job I probably shouldn't take but was thinking about it. Remy used to be a criminal defense attorney and he has a sound head on his shoulders, so he's usually the one who is logical on most things.

Finishing takes cash. And right now this job is what's keeping me from getting there. So in order to get that cash is to make a deal with the devil aka Sammy Briggs, the corrupt Mayor of Wisteria Cove.

I mutter to the empty house, "Just let me get this right. I swear to God, I'm trying."

I sweep up construction dust and glance in the fridge and notice it's bare and in need of groceries.

The door swings open without a knock, because apparently boundaries aren't a thing between Remy and me. Remy steps inside, glances around, and grunts. "Still smells like paint and stain in here."

"It'll air out."

"Mm." He eyes me. "You look like you haven't slept."

"Thanks, Mom."

"Don't 'Mom' me. Talk."

"Sammy offered me a contract. It's good money."

Remy laughs, then stops when he realizes I'm serious. His smile dies mid-chuckle. "Oh, hell no. Absolutely not. You can't be seriously considering anything when it comes to Sammy."

"I didn't say yes yet," I mutter. "I told him I'd think about it and those thoughts aren't serious. But he doesn't need to know that."

"Good call. But remember, if you lie down with dogs, you'll get fleas. That guy can't be trusted." Remy gives me a look that's half warning. "Hope you know what you're doing."

I chuckle. "Noted. I'll keep my flea collar on."

"What are your plans tonight?" he asks. "Want to come out to the farm?"

I shake my head. "Nah. I'm taking Rowan out on a proper date."

"Good," he says, waving a hand at me. "Now go shower. You smell like ass."

I arch a brow. "Rude."

Remy laughs, shaking his head. "Go get pretty, lover boy. And think about this Sammy stuff. There's got to be another way."

I wave as he leaves. He's not wrong. My pulse is already racing just thinking about this deal and the choices I have to make soon.

The bathroom's a wreck. The tile cracked near the baseboards, the sink chipped and badly stained, and the grout crumbled from too many "I'll fix it later" plans. Plans that aren't included in the current budget that I'm struggling with. The mirror's spotted with paint and broken in one corner, and the bulb over the sink flickers like it's giving up, too. An accurate representation of my life at the moment.

Remy's words still echo in my head. *There has to be another way, Finn.*

I pull my phone from my pocket when it buzzes and I see that it's Pete.

Pete: How are you doing, buddy?

Contemplating how to finish this house without crashing and burning.

Pete: You'll figure it out. You always do. You're a hard worker. I'm proud of you. I wish I could help you.

My eyes sting when I think of all the projects he has helped me with. His energy isn't there anymore and I hate that we're losing him.

It's okay. What are you doing today?

Pete: Watching the boats come in. Good day.

It's a good day for that.

Pete: I agree. I was hoping you could stop by and see me later and bring your new pretty girlfriend.

I stare at the message longer than I should, letting it sink in. Pete doesn't waste words, but when he says something, it sticks. He knows his days are limited. It makes me remember that stuff like this house aren't really that important. Pete is important. Family is important. This is just a house.

We will for sure stop by.

I set the phone on the counter, twist the shower knob, and wait for the water to heat. Steam curls around the mirror, hiding the mess for a second. I step in, tilt my head back, and let the hot water hit my shoulders until the ache starts to loosen.

I lean on the counter and stare at my reflection. Tired eyes, in need of a haircut, and calloused hands. A man who looks a whole lot older than he did a year ago.

Pete's face flashes in my head, laughing at his own bad jokes, whistling while he works, always finding the good in whatever's left.

He's been saying he feels "fine," but we all know better. The way he moves is slower now. The way Mom hovers, trying to be brave for him.

I don't want to think about any of it. Instead, I throw myself at projects and things I can control when the rest of life's spinning out of control. I fix what's broken. Sand what's rough. Pretend if I keep my head down long enough, I won't have to remember that time is running out and punching me in the face with reality.

The shower hisses steadily now, steam wrapping around me. I step in, close my eyes, and let the water hit hard against my shoulders until it almost hurts.

I press my palms to the tile and breathe. Rowan's the good thing in all of this, and the reason I keep building, keep showing up. For her, Pete, and my family.

I stay under the water until it turns lukewarm, until my skin feels cold. Then I shut it off and stand there for a second, dripping, palms braced against the wall, trying to get my head right.

You can't stop time, I remind myself. But maybe we can make what's left count.

I grab a towel off the hook and wipe the fog off the mirror. My reflection stares back at me, still tired, but steadier now.

Pete wouldn't want me moping around, waiting for the world to fall apart. He'd tell me to get moving, to keep building, to live the hell out of the time we've got. And Rowan would tell me to breathe, to stop trying to carry everything on my back, to just *be*.

So that's what I'm gonna do tonight. Try to just live in the moment and not think about the stress that life keeps throwing at me.

I get dressed, pulling on clean jeans and the dark green t-shirt that Rowan once told me she liked. I run a hand through my damp hair, grab my keys, and head for the door.

The air outside smells like rain and salt. The porch light flickers when I pass beneath it, and I make a mental note to look at it tomorrow. Add it to the never-ending list. There's work tomorrow. There's always work. But tonight, there's her. For now, though, I've got somewhere to be. And that's enough to keep me going.

She texts me that she's waiting down the street at Salt & Root, and if I've learned anything lately, it's that you don't waste time on things that don't matter.

I slide into the truck, the seat creaking under me, and start the engine. The radio crackles to life, an old country song bleeding through the static.

For a second, I picture Pete sitting beside me, humming along. Then I shake it off, put the truck in gear, and pull onto the road.

If I can just finish this house… maybe it'll be enough to hold it all together when the rest starts to fall apart.

———

We go out, and it's nothing fancy, just downtown Wisteria Cove on a Saturday night, where the air smells like fried fish, ocean salty air, and everyone who knows us smiles curiously when they see us together, holding hands. Strings of warm lights zigzag above Main Street, and someone's busking outside the diner, playing an off-key version of "Brown Eyed Girl."

From the moment tonight when she slipped her hand into mine, just like that, the weight I've been carrying gets a little lighter. It's stupid how something that small can make the world feel steady again. I'm focused on the house because it's the one thing that I can control. I'm so afraid of messing this up, that I'm trying to control something and it's not helping. I need to focus on my family and Rowan. People are what matters.

Even old Mrs. Eaton stops, squints at us over her gold glasses on a chain and says, "You two look good together. Don't mess it up."

"Yes, ma'am," I answer, pretending to be serious.

Rowan looks up at me, her cheeks pink, her smile soft. "This is weird."

"Good weird?"

"Yeah," she says, eyes shining. "Really good weird."

Rowan didn't even blink when I asked her if she'd mind going to Mom's for our date. She knows time with Pete is precious and if we get a chance to go, we're going to go.

We barely make it to Mom's front porch and the smell of butter and garlic hits. Rowan groans. "That smells so good."

We don't even get a chance to knock. The door flies open, and Mom's standing there like she's been waiting. "There they are! My favorite couple!" She grins when she says it. I know she's so happy for us.

"You say that to Remy and Ivy, too," Rowan teases.

My mom waves a hand. "And I mean it every single time I say it to whoever I say it to. Get in here before the garlic bread gets cold."

My mom's kitchen is pure luxury in the best way. She lives in an old, restored Victorian that is stunning. I helped her restore everything down to the outlet covers. Music is playing, flour dusted on the counters, Junie drawing horses at the table, Pete pretending he's helping, but really he's eating from the charcuterie board she has laid out. It smells like heaven. My mom hasn't been big on cooking most of her life, but recently she's gotten into it more and she's made some amazing dinners.

Mom moves to the stove, stirring sauce like she's conducting an orchestra. Pete's beside her, trying and failing to look useful.

"Pete, go relax, I've got it," she says as she lays a hand on his forearm.

He looks over his shoulder. "Well, they're here now, so we can eat, right?"

"Yes." She laughs and reaches over to grab a potholder.

He smirks at me. "You hearing this, Finn? She's trying to starve an old dying man."

Pete loves to say things like that to get a rise out of us. We all know he's on borrowed time with his cancer. At first, we'd get upset when he said that, but we realized that's his dark and humorous way of making light of it, so we go with it. He uses it to coerce us into getting ice cream. He'll say, "Let's go get ice cream." And if he needs us to give in, he'll say, "You would deny a dying man?" So now we just laugh and go with it. I think he thinks that when he does die, it will make it easier on us because we talked about it, even joked about it. We're a dark family, what can I say?

"I'm staying out of it," I say fast. "I've seen her swing a wooden spoon."

Mom flicks her towel at him. "You'll thank me when your pasta doesn't taste like drywall."

Pete grins. "Donna, your pasta could never taste like drywall."

She rolls her eyes. "That's what you said right before you lied and ate my burned soft biscotti."

Rowan laughs and grins, and I swear my whole chest aches watching her fit right in as she sits with Junie at the table, talking to her.

Mom finally spins around, hands on hips. "Don't think I don't see you two giggling back there. Everyone get to the table, so I can feed you before you all starve, apparently."

Pete mutters, "Impossible woman," and brings over a basket of garlic bread that could feed a small army. "Deadline," he mouths. "She's been a menace all week."

Mom drops into a chair with a theatrical sigh. "Three chapters behind. My editor's sending me GIFs of ticking clocks. I'm writing something new. It's a small-town romance with a witchy twist. And I have to get it just right."

I nearly choke on my beer. "You're writing what?"

She grins. "Oh, don't look so scandalized. You all inspired me. Love, chaos, questionable decisions. It's the Bennett family brand."

Pete leans in. "You should see her Pinterest board. It's called Wisteria Cove Hotties."

"Pete!" she gasps, smacking his arm playfully with her kitchen towel. "Don't tell them that."

Rowan's laughing and I'm just staring at her, completely gone. "I want to see that," she wiggles her eyebrows at me, knowing that this is at my expense. My mom is notorious for including people she knows in her books. We never know who her next victim will be.

"Anyway," Donna says, cheeks flushed, "it's called Mistletoe & Magic. Due next week, if I can get these last chapters knocked out."

"I can't wait to read it," Rowan says as she passes out napkins and forks.

Dinner is everything I love about this family: loud, messy, full of laughter, and second helpings. Mom fusses over everyone, making Rowan eat more garlic bread, patting my cheek, and getting Junie another napkin.

Junie tells Rowan about school. Ivy calls during dessert just to say that her and Remy will be there in an hour.

For once, it feels like time's slowing down, like maybe nothing's slipping through our fingers. It's easy, and comfortable. But deep down, we all know better.

Rowan fits in and is smiling like she belongs here. Like she's always belonged here right here by my side as my partner.

And right here, I know exactly what I'm fighting for. Because she's it, she's everything.

CHAPTER 22

Rowan

HOLDING OUT FOR A HERO BY BONNIE TYLER

THE FIRST YOGA class fills before I'm even done lighting the candles.

I'm down on the floor unrolling mats and setting out blocks, trying not to panic-sweat through my cute black yoga set, and people just… keep walking in. Not the three or four regulars that I expected. Not even the pitiful turnout of friends and family that I can count on to fill classes if no one shows up.

No. Like. Packed. I'm so excited to be back to teaching.

There are about half a dozen women from town. Plus, there are two tourists who "saw the chalkboard sign outside and thought this was so aesthetic" are making videos, setting up, and looking excited. There's also a teenage girl who will not stop whispering, "Oh my God, I'm obsessed," and Willa in the corner, already on her mat with her water bottle like she's moral support slash security as she smiles at everyone.

"Are we… full?" I whisper to her.

She stretches her arms over her head and smiles. "Baby, we're over capacity, but I'm not making anyone leave."

"Oh my God."

"We might need to start a waiting list for your next class," someone says from behind me.

I turn around and blink. "I'm sorry, what?"

A woman near the romance shelf raises her hand. "If you're doing this every week, can we sign up in advance? My sister wants to come, but she's working today."

My heart does this weird warm flip. "Yeah," I say, trying to play it cool even though I want to scream into a pillow. "Yes. We can... absolutely do a list."

Willa coughs softly. "Translation, we can totally make this happen."

I don't know why I'm so nervous. I taught classes for years at the community center. But having everyone in my new space feels so good and feels right.

There's soft laughter. And God, the sound of people excited while I'm teaching yoga? While my candles are flickering and the salt lamps are glowing in the corners, the whole place smells like eucalyptus and lavender. It feels like magic. The good kind of magic that I dreamed of when I opened up my apothecary shop and dreamed of having my yoga classes upstairs. Everything in one place with people enjoying what I love to do most.

I swallow the ache that hits me out of nowhere and I wish Finn was here to see this. He's working right now and has been really busy. I can't wait to tell him later. He's been my cheerleader through all of this and none of it would be possible without all his help.

I shake that thought off fast, clap my hands, and slide into teacher mode. I am ready to give the people what they paid for.

"Okay, loves," I say, voice going low and warm. "We're going to start slow, no pressure, no pushing, no pain. Your only job is to breathe. In..." I inhale with them. "And out."

The whole room exhales.

And for the next forty-five minutes, I forget about everything else. I'm in a flow state, in my element, just doing what I love. I forget about the mayor and the mean girls who tried to keep me from this. I just move, guide, and soften shoulders with little nudges. I tell people they're doing great and mean it. I love seeing my classes this excited and motivated.

When we hit savasana at the end, half the class melts into their mats, and I hear the ocean through the windows, making it feel even more peaceful.

When we finish, people don't leave.

They linger, talk, and browse the shop. They buy tea and little intention candles, and ask me about class times, requesting morning sessions and inquiring again about the waiting list.

"Do you offer private sessions?" a woman asks me quietly. "I've… kind of been going through it."

My throat tightens when I see the look on her face and how she needs that. "Yeah," I say softly. "Yeah, I do."

Her eyes shine. She nods, like that answer alone is a relief. And this is why I love teaching. It's so good for people. No matter what you're going through, having someone to go through it with you and help you breathe and stretch through it feels like peace, relief, and healing.

The space is alive and my heart feels full. And this is mine. I'm so damn proud of Salt & Root. I'm going to do big things with this place, I just know it.

I'm still riding the afterglow when I head downstairs and wake up my laptop. The wait list is ridiculous with three months out for yoga, six for tarot consults, and three months for tea leaf readings. I refill my water with blackberries and mint, because I am determined to be the healthiest and strongest teacher for all these people putting their trust in me and my business.

The bell above the door jingles. I don't startle, but I can feel the energy shift. I just look up and there she is. Jessica.

Once upon a time, I would have been excited to see her and spilled my guts about everything good and been equally excited about her and everything going on in her life as well. Now, the only thing that drops is my opinion of the universe's sense of humor. You can't trust someone you thought was your best friend.

I take a slow sip of my water. I'm calm, steady, and unbothered. Because that's what I am. An unbothered queen who won't be bothered with petty bullshit behavior from a monitoring spirit like Jessica who is going to get information and report it back to her headquarters.

"Oh," I say, deadpan, like she's the UPS driver and not the girl who set my life on fire by abandoning me for some mean and petty girls who tried to take down my business, my livelihood. "You're…still alive. Good for you."

Her mouth opens and closes again. Opens again. It's like she doesn't know what to say and I didn't give her the reaction she wanted. The loyal friend she used as a doormat isn't here anymore and she's not sure what card to play.

I keep my expression neutral and flat. The kind of neutral that makes *other people* squirm. Jessica always hated silence. She needed reactions like most people need oxygen.

And once upon a time, she got mine. Not anymore.

She looks smaller than I remember. Or maybe I've just outgrown her. Funny how healing does that. It rearranges the scale so the things that used to feel enormous now look like props.

She stands there like she's waiting for permission to speak. I let her wait and I take another drink, tasting blackberries and mint and the peace I built for myself.

If she thinks I'm going to fill the silence, she's forgotten who I am. I'm not her friend anymore. She lost that privilege.

I don't fold because someone looks at me with big, sorry eyes. I don't hand out forgiveness like free samples at Costco. I don't forget the things that burned just because the smoke clears.

She finally exhales, her voice hesitant. "Rowan…hi."

I set my water down and tilt my head a fraction, just enough to be a reaction, just enough to show I *chose* to acknowledge her. "Jessica."

I watch the way her shoulders tense. She shifts like she wants to apologize, confess, or rewrite history.

But the truth happened, and I lived through it and it hurt me. So, I just wait and let her figure out what she really came here for.

Because whatever story she is going to try to tell, I already know the ending: I'm fine. My life just took a turn and it's pretty damn amazing. Finn and I are an item, things are better than ever. My classes are booked out, and my business is booming.

I don't flinch. I don't fawn. I don't soften. She showed me exactly who she was. And I believed her. She looks… nervous, which is new. Because the last version of Jessica I knew was all high ponytail and mean-girl confidence and "I'm just being honest." This version has softer edges. No lip gloss armor. She's twisting her keys in her hands, nervously as she waits to talk to me.

Willa is instantly at my shoulder like a feral guard, ready to pounce. She glares at Jessica. "What do you want?"

Jessica swallows. "I just—I wanted to talk to Rowan, for a second. If that's okay."

I don't answer right away.

Willa leans toward my ear without taking her eyes off Jessica. "Do you want her here? You say the word, and I will escort her little traitor ass right on out to the curb."

I almost laugh. "It's fine," I murmur. "Stay, though."

"Obviously," she whispers back. "I'm not leaving."

Jessica takes a breath and says loudly and not meaningful, "I guess I owe you an apology."

I say nothing.

"I shouldn't have bailed on our trip." She looks at me as if she's trying to gauge how to play on my emotions, but I give her no response.

I fold my arms over my chest and lean on the counter, forcing myself to breathe instead of react. Because the old me would have forgiven her on the spot to make the tension go away. Because I loved Jessica, and she was my friend. But you don't treat your best friend that way and act like it's no big deal.

I'm not doing that anymore. Not accepting the bare minimum from people.

I nod once. "I appreciate you saying that."

But the truth is that I don't really care. I don't need her. I still hurt from her betraying me, but I'm good now.

She nods so fast I'm surprised her ponytail doesn't launch off her head. "No, really—I just—I shouldn't have been such a bad friend."

"Bad friend?" I tilt my head. "That's so cute. No. You were basically a tax fraud in friendship form."

She opens and closes her mouth, like a stunned guppy.

Willa lets out a quiet, unimpressed exhale.

Jessica looks down at her keys. "I know you're probably done with me. I just had to tell you that."

And for a second, I see it. The part of her that's human. Not the version that stood next to Marilyn and Vanessa while they made trouble for me. Just some girl who made bad choices and watched it all blow up in her face. But something about what she's saying and the look in her eyes don't match up. And before, I think I would have totally missed it. But these days, I am trusting my gut and not missing anything.

I smile pleasantly. "Thanks for stopping by."

Her shoulders tense.

"And look," I say, softer now. "We're not enemies. You can come in for books, for classes, for tea. Truly, no weirdness. I wish you well."

She lets out a snarky laugh. "So, I got downgraded to... acquaintance?"

"Congratulations," Willa says dryly. "That's honestly generous."

I almost smile. "Yeah," I say. "Acquaintance is where we're landing."

It feels good to be honest and not pretend. I'm not that person. This is who I am. I'm a straight shooter and I'm going to be honest. Jessica is getting the consequences of her own actions.

"See you around," I tell her.

After she slips out, it's just me and Willa and the soft hum of the shop.

Willa turns to face me fully, hand on her hip. "Do you want me to sage the shop?"

That gets a real laugh out of me. It breaks something loose in my chest. "Sure, and that felt good."

"I'm proud of you," she tells me, giving me a hug. "The old you would have hexed the hell out of her."

I swallow and my throat burns hot. "Yeah, well, I'm evolving, I guess."

She softens. "You did good, Row."

"It felt mean in some ways."

"It wasn't mean." She steps closer and tips her forehead against mine for a second. "It was a boundary. We love boundaries. Boundaries are hot."

I let out a shaky breath.

She pulls back. "Listen to me, because you know I'm right. When people show you who they are, believe them. And when they feel comfortable sitting next to people who try to tear you down? You cut them off. You don't make room for that energy in your life. We are not doing 'let me keep you close so you won't hurt me again.' We're doing, 'godspeed and goodbye.'"

Something in me unclenches.

"I don't want issues with anyone," I murmur.

"Exactly. No drama. Just access revoked." She smiles. "Normalize cutting people off for treating you shitty."

My eyes sting again. I blink up at the ceiling. "Thanks, Willa."

She smiles. "Now. Close up early and go be with your man."

My stomach flutters at the thought of Finn.

"Ah," she says, holding up a finger. "Don't even try it. Lover boy's been circling this block like a shark in a tool belt since 4:30."

Heat rushes up my neck. "Shut up."

"I will not. Go take a break and breathe. I've got your shop for a while. Let him feed your unworthy goblin mouth."

"You're so romantic."

"I know."

"See you at the farmers market!" she calls as I smile and head out.

CHAPTER 23

Finn

HAVE YOU EVER SEEN THE RAIN BY CREEDANCE CLEARWATER REVIVAL

MARILYN'S the last damn person I want to see behind the mayor's receptionist desk as I come in for a meeting that I've been dreading. She's chewing her gum slowly, tapping her pen against a stack of manila folders in an annoying beat.

Of course, she's wearing a saccharine smile that means she's about to say something awful in a nice tone. I hate it when people do that. I don't do passive aggression very well. Just be aggressive for fuck's sake. Why people are like this, I don't understand.

"Well, well," she says, voice high and fake. "If it isn't Finnegan Bennett. What are you doing here?"

I give her a blank look. "Marilyn," I say flatly. "Didn't know you still worked for the mayor, given your close relationship."

"Oh, just helping out until I can go full-time at the Pilates studio," she purrs, twirling her pen, ignoring the jab. "You know me, always keeping busy."

"Busy ruining other businesses, yeah," I mutter.

Her eyes narrow, but the smile doesn't drop. "I'll let the mayor know you're here," she says, pressing the intercom button with one of those super long bright red talon nails. "Finnegan Bennett says he's here for a meeting." She enunciates Finnegan as if she knows that it will get under my skin.

None of this feels right. I don't want to be here. I want to turn and walk right back out to my truck. But I want to figure out what Sammy's up to.

A crackle on the phone, then Sammy's voice, "Send him in."

She leans back, nails clicking against the desk as she gives me a slow once-over, my jeans, work boots, polo shirt. "Try not to track dirt into his office. The mayor's not much for… grime."

I smile sweetly. "Relax. I rinsed off with the tears of people who peaked in high school, like yourself."

Her mouth drops open.

I tilt my head. "Kidding. Sort of." Then I push through the door without looking back. That one was for Rowan.

Sammy Briggs's office smells like expensive coffee and political bullshit and I hate it. This place feels so off and I don't want to be here. The flowers on his desk are fake, the leather chair behind it shines like he polishes it more than he works in it.

He's waiting with that too-bright smile, Mayor Sammy, king of ribbon cuttings and small talk that doesn't equal action. Two men in tailored suits sit across from his desk, flipping through glossy renderings and blueprints that resemble sales pitches more than construction plans.

The door shuts behind me, and for a second, the only sound is the faint hum of the air conditioner.

Sammy stands, all charm. "Finn Bennett. Appreciate you coming on such short notice."

I nod, keeping my voice flat. "You said it was urgent."

"It is." He gestures for me to sit and slides a thin folder across the table. "Before we start, standard procedure. Nondisclosure agreement. Just protects city plans. Won't take a second."

I glance down at the NDA. The top of the page looks routine, but there's fine print halfway down about "project scope participation."

My gut twitches. "This seems extreme."

He smiles as if I just told a cute joke. "It's just protocol, Bennett. A requirement from the city."

One of the men sitting with him, with his slicked-back hair and shiny large watch, chimes in. "Can't show you the magic until the paperwork's official."

I should walk out. But my brain drifts straight home, and I can see her there.

I picture Rowan barefoot in the kitchen that I haven't finished yet, hair up in a messy knot, sunlight spilling over her shoulders. Her laugh echoes off half-painted walls. Her coffee mug resting on the kitchen table. She has plants all over the house and has decorated it to her own style, making it her own.

I picture her leaning over the counter I still haven't installed, taste-testing something she made on the stove, pretending not to notice me staring. I can see her hips swaying to whatever song's playing while she cooks, her soft hum carrying through the house.

That's what all this work is for. Every nail, every splinter, every late-night sanding down trim, it's all for her.

If I can finish it and give her something whole and solid, maybe she'll finally believe and see that what we have is real.

So I sign, hoping to get this over quickly.

"Perfect," Sammy says, snatching the folder back like a magician palming a card. "Now, let's talk opportunity."

He flips the plans around, flattening them on the desk. "This," he says, "is the future of Wisteria Cove."

The drawings stretch across the desk are bright, bold lines carving through the map of downtown. My stomach sinks fast.

What the actual fuck is all this?

Those red lines slice straight through the block that holds Willa's bookstore and Rowan's apothecary. The heart of Main Street looks nothing like it does now. It's full of chain restaurants, all the small-town New England charm gone. It's a disaster, and it's repulsive. I don't want to live in a town that looks like this. If this happens to the town, it'll be ruined.

"What the hell is all this?" I ask slowly, looking around expecting this to all be a sick joke. This isn't Wisteria Cove. This is terrible.

"This is us revitalizing the town," Sammy corrects, grinning. "New sidewalks, new frontage. A modern look for a new era."

Then it dawns on me that these two guys in the suits are the developers. *Lovely.*

The developer to his left adds, "We're introducing commercial chain potential. Tourists love that."

Commercial chain potential. Jesus. I look over and everything that is there now is replaced by bright neon chain stores that is nothing like Wisteria Cove is now. It's terrible and right down the street from my new house that is now rezoned and most of the sidewalk taken out and part of the yard in an imminent domain commandeering.

"That's my house, Briggs," I say as I point to it.

"We're offering an honest and reasonable amount of money for the properties that have to make room for the new businesses."

I skip right past that part, because there's no universe, parallel or otherwise, where I'd ever agree to something that stupid. What really knots my stomach is knowing the town has no clue what kind of chaos Sammy's cooking up behind closed doors. The kind that could gut Wisteria Cove from the inside out.

"You're talking about demolishing businesses and homes," I say, my voice rising. "Shops and homes that have stood for generations. People's livelihoods."

Sammy's smile is all politician-slick. "We're improving everything. Everyone will be compensated. It's called progress, Bennett. We're evolving to better the town."

I arch a brow. "Into what? Strip malls?"

He steeples his fingers, studying me. "Let's just keep all of this professional."

My heart pounds. "You can't just—these are family businesses and homes. On what planet do you think anyone in this town would agree to any of this?"

He leans back, his smile never slipping. "Sometimes you have to make tough calls for the greater good. And for you—well, this contract could mean stability. You want that, don't you?"

Something in my chest ices over. "You don't know anything about me or what I want."

"I know that you signed this NDA. So, you can't talk about this with anyone. Besides, I'm giving you a shot to be a part of this. We're going to do big things, Bennett. I can make you a very rich man."

I glare at him, trying to decide if I should shove his face into the wall or light that NDA on fire and let his whole office burn down.

He waves a hand. "Come on now. I know you can convince the town that this is a solid plan. After all, word is you're with one of the Marens now."

The room goes silent when all three of them see my face. My knuckles tighten on the arm of the chair.

"You ever bring up any of the Marens again," I say quietly, "and this meeting ends with you picking your teeth out of the carpet."

The two developers stiffen and Sammy's grin flickers. "You signed this, Bennett," he says, tapping the folder. "You're in. Try to back out now, and I'll make sure every project your business is attached to gets audited, delayed, or denied. I will ruin you and everyone around you."

He's still smiling when he says it. That's what makes it worse. He's one sick bastard. You know, he made a few mistakes here that he's about to learn from. Number one, anytime anyone tries to strongarm me, it never ends well for them. And anytime anyone threatens someone or the town that I love, well…they're about to meet a new Finn.

I stand and the chair screeches back. "We're done."

"You'll regret this," he says softly in a singsong voice.

"Not as much as you will," I growl, and storm out before I break something I can't afford to replace.

In the hallway, Marilyn looks up when I blow through the door. "Oh," she says lightly, "how was it?"

"Go to hell, Marilyn," I say without looking at her.

"Already here, sweetie," she calls after me. "It's called City Hall!"

This town's about to find out what happens when the wrong people get pissed off.

———

By the time I get to the farmer's market, it's in full swing. Booths line up on both sides of Main Street around the square, string lights glowing against the early evening sky. The air smells like kettle corn, fresh bread, and sea salt drifting in off the bay. Kids run past holding ice cream cones, and the band on the corner is playing something upbeat.

It's the kind of night that makes you forget villains like Sammy Briggs who always think they're untouchable. They're about to learn otherwise.

Rowan's already here, with Willa and Ivy both helping at her booth. The table's loaded with herbs, handmade soaps, and a little chalkboard sign that says Salt & Root Apothecary. She's laughing at something Willa says, her hair twisted up in a messy bun on top of her head. There's a breeze coming in off the harbor, cooling everything down which is a relief because it's been a hot day.

When Rowan spots me, her whole face lights up. "Hey, stranger," she says, stepping around the table and kissing me. "You made it."

"Wouldn't miss it." I slide my hand into hers and pull her toward me.

She leads me through the crowd. Ivy's selling crocheted stuffed animals that her and Junie have been working on. Lilith's at the pie booth, handing out samples of apple pie. Pete waves from a chair behind a cooler of cider, his grin wide and unguarded.

My mom steps out from behind him and her whole face lights up when she sees Rowan's hand in mine. But when her eyes shift to me, her smile falters because she knows me too damn well. She can feel it.

Something's wrong. Because something *is* wrong.

My stomach twists hard enough to make me nauseous, and I force a smile I don't feel. My pulse is hammering in my throat, too loud, too fast. I swear she can hear it.

I squeeze Rowan's hand like it's the only solid thing holding me upright, because right now it is.

I can't tell her or anyone else.

Sammy backed me into a corner so tight I'm choking on it. The bastard really thinks he can get away with what he's doing and he won't. I'm going to protect everyone in this town and make damn sure of it.

The sight of everyone coming together, with laughter, smells, and the town humming with its own heartbeat, hits me square in the chest. This is home. And all these people have no idea that Sammy is trying his best to destroy it.

I've seen the plans, and I know what's coming if I don't stop it. Neon signs for tacky chain restaurants that won't pay what our restaurants pay their workers, chain coffee shops that will take away business from Wisteria Books & Brews, meaning half these people and their livelihood businesses will be gone. And some of them have had these businesses in their families for several generations. These plans will change lives in Wisteria Cove forever. It will ruin it.

And standing here, watching Rowan hand a little girl a flower from her booth, I realize exactly what "re-development" means. It means gutting this. It means erasing everything that makes this place matter. And I would have a part of that destruction.

She glances up at me, smile fading a little, too. "You okay?"

"Yeah," I lie, forcing the word out past the tightness in my chest. "I'm fine."

The lie tastes bitter. It sits heavy in my throat, like gravel I can't swallow. I hate that I'm saying it, hate that I've backed myself into a corner where it feels like the only option.

But what am I supposed to do? Tell Rowan that I took the meeting, knowing damn well what he did to her? Tell her I let myself get blindsided by Sammy Briggs of all people? No. I can't do that to her.

I can't tell her. Not until I fix it. Not until I'm sure it won't break her trust. So, I lie until I can fix it.

She studies me for a second, then nods, though her eyes say she doesn't believe me. She turns back to Willa, and I shove my hands in my pockets, pretending to admire the next booth.

The band begins another song, and the crowd sways in time with it. All I can hear is that one voice in my head whispering, *you signed it. You let them in. You're just as shitty.*

I pull my phone from my pocket and type fast.

> I have to talk to you. I messed up.

The message bubbles for a beat before Remy replies.

> Remy: Where are you?

> Farmer's market.

> Remy: I'm here too. I'll come find you.

I look up. Rowan's laughing again, tucking a strand of hair behind her ear, completely unaware that a group of men with renderings and contracts are already redrawing her world and everything that she has given her life to building.

My stomach knots as I take a breath that doesn't quite fill my lungs and glance down the street at all these faces I know with my mom, Pete, Ivy, Willa, and the kids running wild.

They have no idea.

I force a smile and walk toward the cider booth, because for now, all I can do is wait for Remy and try not to fall apart before he gets here.

I don't have to wait long. Ten minutes later, I spot Remy weaving through the crowd with his usual "don't start" look on his face. He's still in his work boots, a Bennett Tree Farm T-shirt, like he came straight from work.

He scrutinizes me, eyebrows pinched together. "You look like shit."

"Wouldn't be inaccurate by the way I'm feeling."

We move off to the edge of the square, where it's quieter. The music's still playing somewhere behind us, laughter rolling through the air, the whole town glowing like a postcard. Tourists are flooding the town tonight, and the booths are packed with customers.

And I can barely stand it, because I know what those papers in my truck console mean.

Remy studies me as he crosses his arms. "All right. Talk."

I rub my hand over my jaw. "I went to that meeting with Sammy today."

He groans. "Why?"

"I know." My voice comes out tight. "He had developers there. They're planning a full overhaul of Main Street with new shops, new leases. They want to gut it. Rowan's bookstore, Willa's shop… everything is in jeopardy. My house, too. And I—" My throat closes for a second. "I signed an NDA before they showed me the plans. I'm not even supposed to be telling you."

I don't even care about telling Remy any of this. He's a lawyer, although he doesn't practice, he maintains his license and jokes that it's just in case he needs it for any of us. And right now, I'm calling in that brotherly favor.

Remy's eyes narrow. "What?"

"It looked like a standard contract," I say quickly. "Bid paperwork. I thought it was routine. I didn't know they were planning this crap until after they told me everything and showed me the plans. It's awful, Remy. Wisteria Cove as we know it will be gone."

He swears under his breath, glances around to make sure no

one's close enough to overhear. "You have a copy of the paper-work they had you sign?"

"In the truck."

He nods slowly, processing. "Okay. Deep breath. First thing, you didn't commit a felony, so that's good. Second, I can help you figure things out."

I huff out a humorless laugh with relief. "You always know how to make things right."

"I'm serious," he says. "We'll go over it line by line. See what they actually locked you into. If they're planning something that affects public land or existing leases, they can't bulldoze without the board's approval. There are ways around this. If anything, we can get ahead of this."

I nod and swallow a huge lump in my throat, trying to keep my hands from shaking. "They threatened me. Said if I didn't play along, they'd come after me, and all of us. Our businesses are in jeopardy."

Remy's jaw sets. "Typical Sammy."

"Yeah, but I shouldn't have signed," I admit quietly. "I screwed up, Rem."

He looks at me for a long moment, then nods once. "So, we fix it."

I blink at him. "You're not even going to give me hell?"

"Oh, I'm giving you hell later," he says dryly. "But right now, you need a plan, not a lecture."

That gets a small, shaky laugh out of me. "Well, that's a first from my bossy big brother."

"Yeah, well," he says, smirking, "I can't let you drown. Who else would I have to make fun of?"

I grin, but it fades fast as my eyes drift back to the market, where I see Rowan and Ivy laughing at something and Willa leaning over to hand a bag to a customer.

"This place," I say quietly. "If they get their way, it won't look like this anymore. It'll be chaos and soulless. Wisteria Cove will be gone."

Remy follows my gaze, his expression softening. "Then we don't let them win." He claps a hand on my shoulder. "Tomorrow morning, you bring me every piece of paper you've got. We'll read it together, figure out where to hit back."

The knot in my chest loosens a little. "Thanks, man."

He squeezes my shoulder. "You don't thank me yet. Wait till we're done making that snake Sammy wish he'd never met us."

We walk back toward the glow of the market, the sounds of laughter and music mixing with the crash of the tide in the distance. Rowan spots us and waves, her smile bright enough to cut through everything I'm feeling.

I wave back, my heart heavy but steady.

Because whatever happens next, I'm not fighting this alone.

CHAPTER 24

Rowan

AIN'T NO SUNSHINE BY BILL WITHERS

SOMETHING'S OFF WITH FINN, and I can feel it.

He's been quieter the last few days, still sweet, still him, but distracted. His eyes go somewhere far away when he thinks I'm not looking, like he's trying to solve a math problem he can't seem to figure out. I'm beginning to wonder if he's second-guessing us being together. And the thought of that guts me. It's like something you were once holding in your hand, suddenly falling, and you're grasping to catch it before it falls and shatters. Only, I feel like I can't catch it, and the crash is inevitable.

When I asked if everything was okay this morning, he smiled that soft smile and said, "Just work, baby." Which is code for *absolutely not okay*. Kind of like when I'm mad and he asks me if I'm mad and I tell him that I'm fine. Everyone knows that when a woman tells you she's fine, she's definitely *not* fine. And Finn is the most chill person on the planet. And right now, he's not chill at all. He seems anxious. So, yeah. Not okay.

So now I'm standing behind the counter at the bookstore, reorganizing the "Local Authors" shelf, which is mostly just Donna's books, trying not to let the worry consume me.

Willa's restocking novelty cups near the register, humming to herself, when the door swings open and the bell chimes. And in walks the reason my stomach immediately drops. Mayor Sammy.

He's wearing his usual too-shiny smile and too-fancy of a tailored suit, trailed by two men in equally expensive suits. He nods like he's some old-fashioned gentleman, and says, "Ladies."

"Mayor," Willa says, voice tight as she glances my way.

They stroll in like they own the place, heading toward the little seating nook by the front windows. One of the men with him points out toward the street, murmuring about "visibility" and "widening the frontage."

"—part of the redevelopment plan," I hear Sammy say, low and smug as his eyes meet mine and he winks and continues to talk. "First, we'll start buying out leases. Then we'll use eminent domain, if it comes to that. But it won't."

My hands freeze on the stack of books I'm holding. *What the hell are they talking about? And why do they seem like they want us to overhear it?*

Willa meets my eyes over the counter, and we don't move or breathe and we nod to each other and continue to listen and work.

The developers nod, as if this is all perfectly fine—like they're discussing paint colors and not casually dropping that they might *destroy our entire businesses.*

"Won't be long now," Sammy adds, smiling like a villain in a romcom who doesn't know he's about to be taken down. "We've got the right people on board already."

They walk through to my side of the store and point out things. And then they leave. The bell jingles behind them, and for a full ten seconds, it's dead silent except for the clock ticking above the door.

Finally, Willa says, "What the actual hell was that?"

I blink, still processing. "What are they even talking about?"

"I don't know, but I don't like it." Her voice goes sharp. "They're planning something big."

I grab my phone. "I'm calling Ivy."

Within minutes, Ivy's on speakerphone, the sound of kids and chaos in the background. "They said what?"

"Widening the street. Buying out leases. Eminent domain," I repeat, pacing behind the counter. "And they said they've got people on board already."

Ivy swears under her breath. "This is exactly the kind of crap Sammy would pull. Mom and Donna say he's been trying to 'modernize' the town for years."

Willa folds her arms. "We can't just sit here. We need to find out what's going on."

I nod, heart hammering. "I'll talk to Finn tonight and see if he's heard anything."

"I'll talk to Remy," Ivy promises. "I'm hosting a butterfly birthday party at the farm right now. It's starting soon. I'll let you know what Remy says later."

We hang up and sit in shock. Willa helps a few customers and I head over to my shop with a steaming mug of tea and an anxious heart.

———

That night, I find Finn at his house, in the garage, sawdust in his hair and worry lines across his forehead as he bends down, cutting trim pieces.

I'm relieved to see him, but nervous because I have felt him withdrawing, and I don't understand what's going on. It feels like nothing is going right.

"Hey," he says softly, wiping his hands on his pants and leaning in to kiss me. "You okay, baby?"

"No." I take a deep breath. "Sammy came into the shop today with developers. They were looking at Willa's and my shop and talking about how they're widening the street. They mentioned something about eminent domain. And that they've got people on board already."

The color drains from his face. All that warmth that he usually has is gone in an instant.

"Finn," I whisper, my voice trembling before I can steady it. "Do you know what's going on?"

He doesn't answer right away. His jaw works, tight and restless, like he's chewing on words he doesn't want to say. The silence stretches, heavy enough to make my chest ache.

"Row…" His voice is low, rough. "I need to tell you something."

My pulse stutters. "Okay," I breathe.

He shakes his head, eyes closing for a beat. "But I can't."

The floor drops out from under me. "What do you mean?" My stomach twists, a sick rush of dread rising in my throat. "Can't tell me or won't tell me? Because those are two very different things, Finn."

He finally looks at me, and that's when I know that whatever it is, it's bad.

He runs a hand through his hair. "I met with Sammy a few days ago. He wanted to talk about a construction project. I thought it was a city bid, you know, like regular contract work. I didn't know what he was planning until after I signed an NDA. I swear I didn't—"

"You signed *what*? I'm sorry, why would you even meet with him in the first place, Finn?" The words come out small at first, like my brain refuses to process them. "I don't understand." He opens his mouth, but I'm already shaking my head. "You signed a deal with *him*?" My voice cracks down the middle, raw and trembling. "With Sammy? The man who's been trying to tear down my business and now he's messing with Ivy? The man who made Mom cry in a town council meeting a few months ago?"

"Not a deal. Just—" He takes a step toward me, hands out, eyes wide and pleading. "I didn't know, Row. I swear to God, I didn't know what he was planning. I wouldn't do anything to hurt you or your family, you know that."

"You already did." The words hit harder than I meant them to, maybe because they're true.

And God, it hurts. More than Jessica ever did. Because this is Finn. My Finn. The person who's supposed to know me, see me, choose me. He knew what Sammy had been doing with every threat to my business, every petty sabotage, every time Ivy came home shaken, every time Mom wiped her eyes and pretended the town-council meeting "wasn't that bad." He knew all of it. And the fact that he *still* sat down with that man... that he listened, talked, considered signing anything... and didn't tell me? That tells me he knew it was wrong. He knew, and he did it anyway.

My chest tightens, not with anger, though there's plenty of that, but with something sharper, pettier, deeper. A kind of hollow ache that feels like the floor under our friendship just gave out. Because if your best friend can look at the person hurting your family and still choose to be in a room with him, behind your back, then maybe you never meant as much to them as you thought you did.

He flinches, as if I just drove the air out of his lungs. His shoulders tense, breath catching halfway out. For a second, he looks like he might say something, but nothing comes.

Silence fills the room, thick and merciless. I can hear everything—the faint tick of the clock on the garage wall, the hum of the refrigerator he keeps out there for all his drinks. All these tiny sounds of everyday life keep going while mine stops cold.

He says my name, this time softer. "Rowan..."

It breaks something in me, and I can't look at him. Can't breathe past the lump in my throat. The words I want to say, like how much this hurts, how much I love him, how much I wish he hadn't made a deal with the devil, get stuck somewhere between my heart and my mouth.

So, I stand there, silent, while the world keeps moving without me. All I can see is him,—this man I trusted with everything—covered in sawdust and regret, when all I needed was for him to *not work with people who are actively trying to tear me and my family down.*

Just like Jessica. I can't trust anyone anymore.

The workshop feels smaller by the second and I need to leave.

I blink hard, trying to keep the tears from spilling, but one slips free anyway. He sees it and takes another step, like instinct won't let him stay away.

"Don't," I whisper, voice breaking. "Please don't."

He stops cold. And for the first time since I've known him, he looks completely lost.

"Finn, you're supposed to be on *our* side," I say quietly. "And worse, you won't even tell me."

"I'm not helping him. I'm trying to *undo* it."

"I can't do this right now." My throat burns as I shake my head with disgust. "I can't even look at you."

"Rowan—"

"Please." My voice shakes. "Give me space."

He stands there for a second, like maybe he's going to argue, then nods once, slow and broken. "Okay."

The door shuts behind me, and the sound rattles me. I practically jog to my shop, unlocking the door and shutting it. I hit the lock and bury my face in my hands, trying not to cry.

The worst part isn't that he made a mistake and betrayed me. It's that I still love him anyway. I just needed him to choose me. I need him to be my best friend and not like Jessica who chooses other people who try to screw me and my family over. I need people who are loyal to me and won't screw me over with their secrets. This is not the Finn that I know.

The heavy dark wooden door between our shops creaks open, and there she is, my mother in her long dark purple cardigan, hair pinned up with a butterfly barrette, carrying a teapot and a potholder like she's smuggling in a secret. She closes the door behind her with that quiet, decisive click.

Lilith Maren looks around the apothecary, then at me. Her eyes soften immediately. "You've been brooding in here long enough for days, my little crow."

My heart softens at that. She's always called me her little crow as an endearment and it always softens me up. "I'm not brooding," I mutter.

She lifts her eyebrows. "You're drinking cold tea out of a questionably clean beaker and glaring at a pile of rosehips as if they've done you wrong. That's textbook brooding."

A reluctant laugh escapes me. "Maybe I have a reason to be angry."

She smiles, setting the teapot down beside me. "I brought the good blend. A secret blend, and a touch of rose. For heartbreak, exhaustion, and general brooding."

"Perfect," I mumble. "I qualify for all. Secrets are everywhere these days."

She pulls two mugs from behind the counter and slides one toward me, and the smell alone almost undoes me. It's the scent of being cared for—sweet, warm, a little floral, a little earthy. And I need that more than I realized right now.

For a while, we sit there. The candle flickers. Outside, the town hums softly beneath a cloudy night sky. I glance out the back window and a summer thunderstorm is coming in. Fitting for the mood for tonight and hopefully I won't have to water the plants tonight because I don't have the energy to go back over to Finn's for a round two fight.

Finally, she says, "Willa told me about what happened with Sammy and then I'm guessing something happened with Finn because Ivy said that Remy has been assisting him with something he did."

I sigh. So apparently Remy knows and he could tell him but not me. I didn't realize that Remy was in on this too and was helping him. That should make me feel a little better, but it really doesn't.

She hums, patiently, waiting.

I stare into my tea. "He messed up, Mom."

"Did he tell you what happened?"

"Some of it. He says he didn't know what he was signing, that he didn't mean to hurt me." My throat tightens. "And I know him, I *know* he wouldn't, not on purpose. But he still did."

Lilith nods slowly, her eyes soft with understanding. "Love doesn't make people perfect, honey. It just makes their mistakes cut deeper."

I look down at the steam curling out of my cup. "I trusted him. I really did. And you know that I don't trust easily. Finn was my person. The one I thought would never let me down."

She reaches across the counter, brushing a tear from my cheek with her thumb. "And trusting someone doesn't make you foolish, especially when it's someone that you love."

I blink hard, another tear slipping loose. "It doesn't feel like love. It feels stupid. Why would he even entertain the idea of working with that slimebag?"

"I don't know, honey. But I do know Finn. And that man loves you so much. I'd bet everything I have that he'd never do anything to hurt you."

And deep down, I know that's true. I can expect betrayal from a lot of people in this world, but never Finn.

She sips her tea and sits with me, just giving me space to figure it all out with her. Tea has always been the answer to my mom. Bad day at school? Tea. Had a bad dream? Tea. She loves to put together her own blends. And my love for that and apothecary came from her. She taught me everything.

Then she gives me a soft and mischievous smirk and says, "Though I do recall making you a *love potion* before your trip, so maybe part of this is my fault."

I blink up at her, caught off guard. "You *really* did that, Mom?"

She waves her hand like it's no big deal. "Just a little blend for courage and open hearts. Maybe a touch of attraction oil. It looks like it worked."

I groan. "Oh my God, Mom."

She laughs, eyes twinkling. "Well, it worked, didn't it? He fell for you, you fell for him, and it's possibly the best thing that ever happened to both of you."

I cover my face. "That is *not* funny, Mom."

She pats my shoulder. "Sweetheart, you and Finn were always meant to be."

Despite myself, I laugh, tears mixing with it until I'm half-laughing, half-crying.

She pushes the teapot closer. "Drink your tea, my little crow. You can cry, you can curse, and then you can start again. That's what we Maren women do."

I sniffle, sipping. "What if we lose our shops and he has a part in this?"

She smiles, gentle and certain. "Then we'll make another potion."

I laugh again, a small, watery sound that still feels good. "You always know how to fix everything."

"No," she says softly, brushing my hair back. "But I know how to sit with you while it hurts."

The tea's gone by the time she stands to leave. She kisses my forehead, whispers, "You'll find your way through this, my little crow. You always do." Then, she closes the door behind her.

The shop smells like roses and a little bit of hope now. And for the first time all night, I actually believe her. Somehow, everything will be alright.

By the time I reach the top of the stairs, my bones throb with exhaustion. The moonlight spills through the window like a promise that tomorrow will be better, catching the glimmer of dried herbs hanging from the rafters. I collapse into bed, the sound of the waves crashing up against the harbor floating through the windows. The last thing I think before sleep finds me is that even wilted things grow back, given time and light.

CHAPTER 25
Finn

SIMPLE MAN BY LYNYRD SKYNYRD

I WAKE up to the distinct sound of whispering, and pain from my head throbbing.

My skull feels like a tiny, angry construction crew is jackhammering it. Something soft and fuzzy brushes my face, and I realize I'm not in my bed.

"Is he dead?" a small voice whispers.

"No, he's not dead," someone whispers back. "He's breathing."

"I can hear you," I groan. My voice feels rough, like sandpaper, and I've made some bad decisions that involved a bottle of whiskey last night at my shop. A wet tongue slides up my cheek, making me turn my face.

I open one eye and Junie's standing two feet away, clutching a stuffed narwhal. Ivy's behind her, coffee mug in hand, smiling like this is the best entertainment she's had all week. And their blue heeler, Lola, is watching me with concern. Allen is perched on a chair across from me, silently judging me with a glare. He's been out here healing from his neutering, and he's become friends with Lola the dog.

"Hey, buddy," Ivy says, voice far too cheerful for the hour. "You're on our couch."

I grunt. "Yeah."

Remy's at the kitchen counter, leaning against it with that quiet smirk that says *you're gonna get roasted for this*. His mug steams, the smell of coffee filling the room.

"Rough night?" he asks.

"Yeah." I press my palms to my eyes, trying to rub the headache out.

"You showed up around midnight, mumbled something about 'ruining everything,' and passed out on the couch, halfway through explaining it."

"Sounds about right," I mutter.

Junie climbs onto the couch beside me, curls bouncing. "Uncle Finn, you smell weird."

"Thanks, kiddo."

She beams. "You're welcome."

Lola climbs up beside her, tongue hanging out watching our interaction closely.

Ivy looks at us and says, "Junie, Lola, let's go get ready for the day."

Junie grumbles but follows her down the hall, the dog trotting behind them.

Remy finally sets his mug down and joins me at the couch. "All right, what happened?"

"She's pissed." I let out a hard exhale, but even as I say it, the words feel wrong. "She's more than pissed," I admit under my breath, almost to myself. "She's hurt. She feels betrayed. And… she has every right to." I run a hand over my face. "*I* hurt her. And now she needs space. She has every reason to tell me to back off."

The words are heavy, but they feel closer to the truth. I'm not shifting blame. I'm not minimizing her feelings. I'm just finally admitting it: I messed up, and she knows it.

Remy studies me for a second, then nods. "That's fair. It probably feels like a betrayal."

"I would never hurt her. I love her."

"She loves you, too," he says simply. "But she has every right to be angry. You two need to talk it out, figure out what's next. It's all new, you're still learning how to be in it together. Even in the hard stuff."

I glance toward the window. The morning light's filtering through the kitchen, catching on the dust in the air.

Junie's playing with her dog. Ivy's wiping down the counter, pretending not to listen but absolutely listening. And Remy's already pulling on his boots, heading toward the door.

"Come on," he says. "We've got work to do. You can sweat the guilt out while we work on our plan for that asshole, Briggs."

I stand and go to the door where my boots are next to it and Ivy hands me a to-go mug of coffee and a few Ibuprofens. "For what it's worth, she's just as upset as you. But she's not murdering you right now, so that's a good sign."

I snort laugh. "There's that."

"It'll be okay," she promises.

"Hey, Uncle Finn, just say you're sorry!" Junie calls from the kitchen counter.

"I will, Bug. I will."

We head out to the tree farm and the air's cool, heavy with the scent of pine and damp earth.

After a while, Remy breaks the silence. "So. What's your plan with Briggs?"

I shrug. "He can fuck right off."

"Briggs is a moron," he says. "I have an idea to get around it."

"Thank God." I heft a plank onto the pile, jaw tight as we step into the barn.

Remy watches me for a beat. "She'll come around. Rowan's got fire, but she's got a big heart, especially when it comes to a big dufus like you."

I let out a breath, my throat tight. "God, I hope you're right."

He grins, clapping me on the shoulder. "When am I ever wrong?"

I snort. "You want the list alphabetically or chronologically?"

"Easy there," he says, chuckling. "He can't legally make you work for him, and he definitely can't blackmail you like that."

"Yeah," I say, sipping my coffee.

"So, you provide him with the asshole tax. Whatever you would have bid for him, quadruple it. Make it an astronomical number to work with Bennett Construction so that he could never afford you. There's no way anyone on the town board would ever approve that. There's just no way."

"That's a good idea. Play nice. Get as much in writing as I can from him. Meet at the bookstore or somewhere public when I talk to him and have others overhear what's going on so I don't break this ridiculous NDA," I say.

"You could do that. I could get Mom and Pete to conveniently sit at the bookstore, doing their crossword puzzles, and overhear it, then spread the news through town. Once everyone knows about this, he can't sneak around," Remy adds.

"He thinks he's going to pull all of this off, and there's no actual way." I shake my head in disbelief.

"We'll make damn sure it doesn't happen. Period," Remy says as he pulls out his phone.

"Who are you calling?" I ask, rubbing my forehead.

"Mom. I know she'll be in on this. She hates that guy. Schedule a meeting with Sammy for this afternoon at 2:00 p.m. at the bookstore. Pete has a doctor's appointment this morning."

I nod. "Okay." I pull out my phone, and it's dead. "I'm going to head home and get this done. Thanks for letting me crash on your couch."

He claps me on the back. "Anytime."

For the first time since that awful meeting with Sammy, something in my chest eases. The ache's still there, but it's quieter now, dulled by hard work, coffee, and Remy's quiet steadiness.

And maybe, just maybe, by the thought that Rowan hasn't given up on me yet.

———

I let Sammy think I'm on board. I tell him 2:30 at Wisteria Books & Brews, and he actually sounds surprised before he says yes, like a man who thinks he's already won. He gets to be smug all the way until I hand him the bid. Then hopefully he'll lose his shit, and Mom and Pete will hear it all and tell everyone, leaving me not to have broken an NDA, which is what he wants. He wants to be able to come for me. And I won't let him.

I stroll in right at 2:30, and Willa gives me that look that says, "What are you doing here?" Ivy's working the counter over in Rowan's shop, bright and steady as ever, and she gives me a quick wink. Rowan's upstairs teaching yoga, thank God. I need to resolve this issue before I can fix things with her. I owe her a massive explanation on things.

Sammy's there without his developers, a mug of coffee in front of him, watching for me. I sit and then hand him the bid.

"I'm glad you finally came to your senses," Sammy says as he takes the papers out of the envelope and reads through them.

I hammered out the bid this morning. It's absurd. Ridiculously, astronomically high. No sane municipal budget would ever allow it, and that's the point. I signed that stupid agreement because I was foolish, and I let him think he had me. Now I'm here to make sure he doesn't.

He may have caught me at a weak moment, but he won't be catching me again.

Sammy flips through it, brow furrowing. "What is this?" he asks slowly, like he's reading a punchline he doesn't get.

"That's my bid," I say, steady. "Permits, labor, materials. That's what it costs to do this right."

He looks up at me, eyes surprised, turning to anger. "This is— this is way too much. You know we can't hire you for this. You need to come down on these numbers."

"No." The word comes out hard. "I don't have to do anything, Sammy. This is my bid. Take it or leave it."

The muscles in his jaw twitch. He's not used to being played. "This is a waste of my time." He leans forward. "You did this on purpose to sabotage the project. I could have made you a wealthy man. You're going to make me make this personal. If you want to—"

"You want to ruin our town and call it an investment." I cut him off. The heat in my chest is a hard, bright thing. "You pushed false permits on Rowan and Ivy. You tried to choke their businesses with bureaucracy while you were an investor in a competing business. Isn't that a conflict of interest? You're getting a kickback on this project, aren't you? It's all about your pockets, Sammy."

He snorts, voice thinning. "Where are you getting this—"

"I'm getting it from watching you," I say. "I'm not dumb, and neither is anyone else in this town. You aren't getting away with this."

Donna's at the table behind Sammy. She lifts her phone. "I recorded every word you said, Sammy. I have it, and I know what you're doing. I'm not letting you get away with it."

For the first time in the room, Sammy looks pale. His eyes dart to the door, like he's searching for the nearest exit. "You can't record me," he starts. He glances up and sees the camera above us that's always been there.

"Yeah, and when you and your developers came in here to start trouble, that camera caught you, too." I shrug and smile at him. For once, it feels good to watch Sammy squirm since he takes pleasure in hurting everyone else.

Pete doesn't hold back, either. "Come in here and start trouble again," he says. "I'll bury you." It's gruff and ridiculous and exactly Pete, with half protective fury, half old-man stubbornness. "I'm a dying man. No one's locking me up for clocking you, Sammy."

Sammy's lips press into a hard line. He storms for the door.

Donna's already pulling out her phone, fingers moving fast. "Everyone's getting a text," she says. "Emergency town meeting tonight. We're pulling a recall petition. We'll be at the hall by seven." Her voice is fierce and confident.

"Thanks, Mom," I mutter.

"I'm proud of you, Son. You did the right thing. We're finally going to get him out of here. He's nothing but a menace to this town."

The yoga class must have ended because people trickle down in clusters, muttering questions.

"Is Rowan okay?" someone asks. And that makes my ears perk up.

"She said she wasn't feeling well," one student says. "She told us to head out early."

My stomach drops. "Rowan canceled class early?" That's not like her at all.

A woman from the class looks at me with an apologetic face. "Said she'd be back, but she looked pale." She points up the narrow staircase to where her apartment is next to her yoga studio upstairs.

I move up the stairs, and I take them two at a time, and the small world of the bookshop blurs past, the chatter of people below, the smell of coffee.

I get to the door of the small upstairs studio, and the sound that hits me is not talking or the soft hum of wind-down breath, but a retch. My heart thuds so hard it feels like it might hammer through my ribs.

She's sick.

I throw the door open. Rowan is doubled over the toilet, heaving. Her hair is loose, damp at her temples. She looks up at me with red-rimmed eyes and something raw and vulnerable.

"Finn," she manages, voice tiny and ragged. Her hand clutches the rim like it's the only solid thing left. "Go away. Don't look at me like this."

I'm halfway to her before I realize I'm on my knees. I reach for her hair, gentle as I can, and she nods toward me, embarrassed and relieved in one messy breath.

"You okay?" I ask, pulling her hair back.

She shakes her head. "No," she whispers. "I'm not."

I don't know how much of this is the spin of everything—Sammy, the bid, the betrayal—and how much is the physical. I scoop her into my arms like she's the only steady piece I can trust, like if I hold her tight enough, she won't fall apart.

"I'm here," I tell her. "And I'm so sorry."

She leans into me, all shaky breath and exhaustion, the weight of her pressing against my chest like something fragile that finally gave in.

Her head finds my shoulder, and I can feel the tiny sigh she lets out—one that sounds more like surrender than sleep. It's quiet, content, the kind of sound that crawls under your ribs and stays there.

Within a minute, her breathing evens out. She drifts off against me, still clutching a handful of my shirt like she's afraid I'll vanish if she lets go.

I ease her back gently, keeping one arm around her as I grab a towel from the hook near the little sink. I wet it with cold water, wring it out, and crouch beside her again. Her skin is warm, flushed, and a few damp strands of hair stick to her face.

"Hey," I whisper, brushing them back. "Let's get you cleaned up, yeah?"

She doesn't answer, murmurs something sleepy and leans into me.

I wipe her face and the back of her neck, slow and careful, the way you'd handle something precious. When I'm done, I set the washcloth aside and slide my arms beneath her. She stirs but doesn't wake as I lift her and carry her to the little bed tucked against the wall.

"I'm just so tired, Finn," she says as she drifts off.

Her room smells like lavender, like her. I pull the blanket up to her shoulders, tucking it around her as she sighs again, softer this time, almost peaceful.

"There you go," I whisper. "You're okay now."

She doesn't answer, but her lips curve the slightest bit, like she heard me somewhere inside the dream.

I grab her a glass of water from the kitchenette, set it on the nightstand, then stand there for a while, watching her. The rise and fall of her chest, the tiny crease between her brows easing out bit by bit.

I reach out and brush my thumb along her temple. Then I settle into the chair beside the bed, elbows on my knees, eyes on her.

I don't know what tomorrow's going to look like—what we're walking into, what she'll say when she wakes up, but for now, I'll take care of her. She's my priority.

And that's enough to make me believe that maybe, just maybe, we're going to find our way back.

CHAPTER 26

Rowan

LET IT BE BY THE BEATLES

I'M tired to the bone. It's a deep, soul-level kind of tired. The kind where I want to go back to bed and not wake up until tomorrow morning. I must have one of hell of a super bug right now.

It's been a few weeks since everything blew up with Finn and Sammy, and I swear I'm holding the whole world together with herbal tea and sarcasm. My classes are shrinking, my energy is gone, and I can't remember the last time I didn't feel exhausted. It takes everything in me to run my shop during the day and work on my plants at night. Finn has been a lifesaver, helping me with all the plants and even unboxing new orders.

We're okay, but not great. And mostly it's just me. I haven't felt good and he's been busy. Word spread through the neighboring towns as well as Wisteria Cove about Sammy. He was fired and they're looking for a new mayor to step in. Finn's been hired to do so many jobs and he's busier than ever. When he's not working on a job, he's out at his wood shop at Remy's working on projects. It's a busy season.

This morning, I roll out my mat and wait for my students. I light the candles, turn on soft music, and breathe in the scent of eucalyptus and lavender from the diffuser I have going in the corner. Usually, the studio fills up fast with mats lined up.

Students chatter, and the room is full of that little hum of community that I love.

Today there's one person. Doris, a sweet older woman who usually falls asleep during meditation and calls it "nap yoga." I usually let her nap there until she's ready to go home.

She smiles at me as she settles onto her mat. "Where is everyone, dear?"

"I have no idea," I say, forcing a calm tone. "Maybe mercury's in retrograde."

She blinks. "Oh, is that contagious?"

I smile, but it feels thin. "No."

We go through the poses. The room feels too big, too quiet. When class ends, she takes an extended nap. And when she does wake up, I watch her leave, my heart sinking.

By the time I finish cleaning up, the door opens, and my sisters stroll in. Ivy has a tray of coffees. Willa's carrying muffins. They both stop short when they see how empty the shop is.

"Where is everyone?" Willa asks.

"That's the million-dollar question," I mutter.

Ivy looks around, frowning. "Your class is usually packed, and we set up a wait list. What happened?"

Willa looks perplexed. "Is something going on in town today? I haven't heard of anything."

I toss my towel on the counter. "If I knew, I'd fix it. Maybe the universe decided I needed a break."

My stomach twists because something's off. "Do you think that something is going on with the Pilates studio?" I ask, looking up at my sisters who are drinking coffee and eating muffins.

Both stop talking and Willa narrows her eyes. "I smell a rat."

"Let's go see," Ivy says as she grabs her purse. "I'll put a sign up that we'll be back in fifteen."

I grab my bag and we walk down Main Street, leaving Ivy to catch up. The sun is setting and tourists wander between the harbor and the Dairy Witch ice cream shop. Everything looks normal. Which makes the pit in my stomach feel worse. Something is going on, and I just can't figure out what it is.

And then I see it.

Across from the bakery, the brand-new Pilates studio is bursting at the seams. The windows are steamed up. Music pumps through the open door. The sign outside reads:

FREE CLASSES ALL WEEK! COME FIND YOUR BETTER BODY!

And underneath, a printed schedule. Every single time slot matches my yoga classes and more. They have around the clock classes for free.

I stop cold. The classes I was working on the other day when Jessica came to my shop to apologize to me. She must've seen the class schedule since it was right there on the desk. And it's online for anyone to see for that matter. She was never there to apologize.

And there they are, Marilyn, Vanessa, and Jessica, all standing by the counter, laughing with wine glasses in hand like they're celebrating something.

I edge closer, staying just outside the doorway.

"She only had one person this morning," Marilyn says, snickering.

Vanessa giggles. "I almost feel bad. Almost."

Jessica laughs with them. "Maybe she's finally realizing she's not cut out for business. I give her shop another month. Maybe we should make our own apothecary, too."

My throat tightens at the betrayal.

Before I can react, Ivy's suddenly beside me, having caught up. She hears the last part, and her jaw drops.

"Oh hell no," she mutters, and before I can stop her, she pushes the door open and storms inside.

The class full of women on reformer machines turn their heads. Marilyn freezes and Vanessa almost drops her wine glass.

"Wow," Ivy says, her voice shaking with anger. "You think tearing down my sister makes you successful? You're pathetic."

"Ivy," Willa warns softly.

But she's not done. "You've been trying to sabotage her from the start. You're jealous because she built something real. And you —" she points at Jessica "—you should be ashamed. She trusted you. You're a snake."

Jessica looks away instantly, refusing to meet any of our stares. And somehow, that hits harder than anything she's actually done. Coward. That's all I think now when I see her. Not bold enough to own her actions or say this to my face. She's loud when she's whispering behind backs, but silent when the truth stands in front of her. Pathetic.

This is the girl I once loved like a sister and defended, protected, carried through every storm. And she can't even look me in the face.

Marilyn opens her mouth to argue, but I step forward, calm and quiet now.

"Low," I say. "That's low, even for all of you."

Vanessa smirks. "It's called business, Rowan."

"No," I say, staring her down. "It's called insecurity."

The room goes silent.

"I've always encouraged you, supported you, and cheered you all on. I teach different classes, and I've told you more than once that there's room for more than one type of fitness studio in this town. This is absolutely ignorant behavior. And you know what? I'm not worried about it. Karma will take care of this for me. You are all building a business on ugliness and treating other people poorly. And these people taking your classes can see and feel that. You're not fooling anyone. I wish you all the best of luck."

Willa and Ivy glare at them, and I turn to them. "Let's go."

We walk out, heads high, though my stomach is still in knots.

Back at the apothecary, I head straight to the counter, grab a pen, paper, and a Mason jar.

Ivy watches, arms crossed. "What are you doing?"

"Witch justice," I mutter, writing each of their names carefully: Marilyn. Vanessa. Jessica.

I fold the papers away from my body and drop them into the jar, fill it with vinegar and water, screw on the lid, and stick it in the freezer.

"May their intentions freeze solid," I whisper.

Ivy grins, proud. "That's my sister."

A few minutes later, she disappears next door to Willa's. When they both come back, Willa's got that dangerous sparkle in her eye.

"This is retaliation for Sammy," she says. "I'd bet my best wand on it."

"Probably." I sigh, rubbing my temples.

Willa leans against the counter. "You know what the best revenge is?"

"What?"

"Being happy," she says simply. "Doing what you love, better than ever. Let them rot in their own bitterness."

I sigh. "What's that saying? Low hanging fruit will drop on its own?"

Willa nods her head. "Yep. All those people enjoying their free classes will be able to see that they're mean girls and not want to go there. Not to mention most of them overheard them talking about us today and then saw us come in there. Word travels fast in a small meddling town like Wisteria Cove."

"We'll help you plan some new fun classes," Ivy adds. "Candlelight yoga. Yoga with goats out at the farm. Yoga and wine. Something that makes people want to come back and is fun."

I smile weakly. "Yoga and wine sounds about right."

My stomach rolls in protest and I close my eyes as nausea rolls through my stomach and chest.

"Are you okay?" Ivy asks.

I wave her off. "Yeah, I'm fine. I need to eat something, I think. Been too busy to eat today."

Willa grins. "And next time Jessica tries to apologize, don't you dare accept it. Some people aren't meant to be friends. Some people are meant to teach you what betrayal feels like, so you never forget it."

"I'll definitely lose her number. She was never my friend." I look between them, my heart softening. "Thanks."

They both hug me. Ivy squeezes my shoulder. "You're still the best thing this town's got. Don't you forget it."

I nod, but I still feel tired to the bone. There's a deep ache sitting under my ribs.

As they head out, I close up the apothecary and look toward the freezer. The jar gleams in the soft light.

"Good luck," I murmur.

Then I turn off the lights, lock the door, and tell myself I'll feel better tomorrow.

———

The rain starts soft at first, the kind of steady whisper that makes the leaves tremble and the summer air smell like new beginnings.

By the time I make it out to the greenhouse, it's pouring down rain and it's warm, relentless, and beautiful. The roof on the greenhouse hums with it, and the path between the rows of planters has turned to shallow puddles.

I should go home. It's late, and Finn's working out-of-town tonight. His house is dark when I pass it on my way here, the porch lights off, his truck gone.

But instead of curling up with tea and pretending everything's fine, I'm here, soaked to the skin, hands buried in dirt, trying to harvest my herbs.

I took a nap earlier and woke up wide awake. I knew the garden would give me some clarity if I worked through it.

A tray of lavender tipped over in the wind earlier. The mint is flooded. The chamomile is ready to be harvested and dried. I crouch, digging my fingers into the wet soil, my hair plastered to my face.

Tears blur with rain until I can't tell which is which. I've been trying so hard. Working every day to make this business work, to keep the apothecary going, to stay positive while the town seems determined to chip away at me. I wanted to build something for me to give back to the community and help people. And every time I turn around, something is coming up against me and I can't figure out why.

The Pilates girls being petty, Sammy screwing with permits, and the endless whispers about witches and Marens and troublemakers.

And Finn. Things are still weird between us, but better than they were, but still hard. He's been quiet lately, distant sometimes, like he's trying to carry something on his own again. He's been working very hard lately.

Maybe that's why I came out here. Because at least in the greenhouse, I can fix things. And in my life right now I can't seem to make sense of anything.

I sit back on my heels, water dripping off the side of the greenhouse, and whisper, "Was I even supposed to do this? Maybe I'm not cut out for running a business."

The rain answers with angry pelting on the roof of the greenhouse.

I close my eyes and picture Coconut Beach. The sun, the smell of saltwater and sunscreen, Finn's laugh echoing across the sand. Everything was simple there. Just us. Here, everything feels like work.

I swipe at the hot tears that streak my cheeks and reach for another plant, but the soil is too wet, my fingers slip, and frustration breaks through me like lightning. I let out a shaky laugh that turns into a sob.

"Everything's falling apart," I say to no one. "I just wanted to fix one thing."

A sound cuts through the rain. Tires on gravel. A door slamming.

Then a voice. "Have you lost your damn mind?"

I spin around. Finn's jogging toward me through the downpour, soaked from head to toe. His hair's plastered to his forehead, his shirt clinging to his chest.

He looks half furious, half terrified.

"What are you doing here?" I shout over the rain.

"Willa called," he says, tossing the tarp down beside me. "Said you were out here in the rain like a crazy person."

I scoff through the tears. "Of course she did."

He stops in front of me, breathing hard, eyes scanning the greenhouse. "You're drenched."

"So are you," I say. "And it's just a little rain. It's not like it's lightning or anything."

"Yeah, but I didn't plan on swimming tonight."

I look down at the mess of herbs around me. "The wind knocked everything over. I wanted to work on things out here."

Finn crouches beside me, his boots sinking into the mud. Without another word, he starts righting the trays, pressing his big hands into the soil, working quietly.

The sight of him there, mud streaked, sleeves rolled up, helping me, God, it's too much. I don't even deserve him.

"Finn, you didn't have to come out here. I thought you were staying up in Freedom Valley on a job. That's four hours away."

"Yeah, I was. But I missed you." His tone is so soft it almost breaks me.

I reach for a fallen sprig of rosemary, tears burning again. "I'm trying so hard, but I feel like everything's against me. Maybe I'm not good at this. Maybe I'm not meant to have this."

He looks up at me through the rain, and his eyes steady. "You're not bad at anything, Rowan. You just can't control everything. No one can."

I shake my head, voice small. "Why does it all keep falling apart?"

He leans closer, his hand covering mine. "Because you're human. And because you care. That's what makes it hard. But that's also what makes it worth it."

The rain drums louder. My lip trembles. "I just wanted one thing to go right."

He pulls me against him, wet clothes and all, his arms wrapping tight around me. "We're going right."

I let out a weak laugh, half a sob. "Things are weird between us."

He chuckles against my hair. "They're not weird, just busy."

We kneel there for a while, mud between our fingers, rain soaking through every layer, quietly replanting what we can. The world around us smells like wet earth and rosemary and something new trying to grow.

When the worst of it's done, he brushes the back of his knuckles along my cheek. "I've got you."

The words hit something deep in me, something that's been brittle for too long.

I lean into him, forehead against his, the rain still falling around us. "I love you."

He smiles, eyes soft. "I love you so much, Row."

We stay like that until the rain slows to a whisper. The greenhouse glows under the string lights, puddles reflecting tiny pinpricks of gold.

Finn's thumb traces a slow path down my cheek, and the look in his eyes changes with something soft but heavy with something that makes the air go still. The rain hits the roof in a slow rhythm. My pulse matches it.

"Rowan," he murmurs, voice low. He kisses me. It starts gentle, a promise pressed to my lips, then deepens, all the tension and fear and wanting that's been simmering between us spilling out. My hands clutch at his soaked shirt while his slide up to the back of my neck, warm against my skin.

I don't remember how we end up on top of the potting bench, only that his body is solid heat against mine, the scent of wet cedar and rain thick around us. He kisses me again, slower now, savoring, like he's reminding us both that we still fit perfectly, hopelessly together.

His mouth moves to my jaw, my throat, each touch making it harder to breathe. I tilt my head back, eyes fluttering shut.

"Finn," I whisper, barely audible over the rain.

He stills, forehead pressed to mine. "Tell me this is okay, baby."

"It's better than okay. I need you and I need us to be okay."

What happens next feels like an actual storm itself. It's slow, powerful, and indescribable. His hands explore, careful and reverent, until the world narrows to the sound of rain, our ragged breathing, and the soft scrape of his whisper against my ear: *I've got you.*

Later, the greenhouse is quiet again. The rain has eased to drizzle, and we're tangled together, still catching our breath. The plants around us smell of life and new beginnings.

Finn brushes a strand of wet hair from my face. "See?" he murmurs. "We can fix things. Even this."

I smile, resting my hand over his heart. "You're right."

Outside, the first bit of moonlight breaks through the clouds. Inside, the air hums with warmth, renewal, and something that feels a lot like home.

For the first time in weeks, I don't feel like I'm fighting the whole world. I feel like I'm part of it again.

And maybe that's enough for tonight.

CHAPTER 27

Finn

DON'T YOU WANT ME BABY
BY THE HUMAN LEAGUE

THE BACKYARD IS BUZZING in that effortless, golden-hour way only Wisteria Cove knows how to do when we throw a BBQ. Remy set up cornhole and other games, kids are chasing each other through the trees, and the whole place smells like charcoal, pine trees, and the half a dozen side dishes that are enough to feed an army.

It's one of those unofficial Maren-Bennett gatherings with half the town drifting in with coolers under their arms, someone started playing music on a speaker, and now nobody remembers whose idea the BBQ actually was.

That's when Remy wanders over, beer in hand, eyebrows raised at the smoke curling up from the grill.

"You'd better flip the brats before they burn like your love life," Remy says, laughing as he takes a pull from his bottle.

I flip one half-heartedly. "My love life is thriving, thank you very much."

"Uh-huh," he says, peering at the grill. "That brat looks like it's been through it."

I roll my eyes and shove him with my elbow. "You're welcome to take over anytime, Grill Master of the Year."

"Please," he says. "I've been feeding people since before you figured out what seasoning was."

"Yeah," I mutter, "and Ivy still re-seasons everything when you're not looking."

Remy grins. "That's just life. These Maren women run things. We just go with it."

"You're not wrong," I say, laughing, as I flip the brats.

"When are you taking your cat home?" he asks, pretending as if he's not as interested as I know he is. He and Allen bonded and now the cat loves it out here in the workshop mousing. I plan on bringing him back to the house when it's completely done.

"Soon. Just getting the paint done at the house. Almost there."

Things are better with Rowan and me. Remy is usually right about things. He said something last week about how relationships are worth it when you can weather through the hard stuff. And there's always going to be hard stuff. And there's no one I want to do life with, besides Rowan. Including the hard stuff. Having her through the hard stuff, makes life worth it.

Smoke drifts up from the grill, rich with the scent of hickory and summer. The picnic tables overflow with platters of cheeseburgers, foil covered hot dogs, big bowls of macaroni salad, baked beans, buttery corn on the cob, and Lilith's famous peach cobbler cooling at the end like a prize.

Willa's laughing at something Tate said, Ivy's chasing Junie who's running around with a bucket of water balloons, and Rowan's sitting cross-legged on a picnic bench, her hair a mess of curls. She's relaxed and beautiful. She smiles at me and waves.

Remy passes me a plate. "Eat before I catch you stealing bites from the grill again."

"It's called quality control checks," I mumble, mouth already full.

He chuckles. "Pretty sure quality control doesn't require third-degree burns."

I grin, cheeks full. "Worth it. These are really good."

Laughter ripples through the table, the kind that hums low and easy, like summer itself decided to sit down and join us.

Then I catch the tail end of a conversation happening over by the girls.

Ivy's face is pink, and she's biting her lip like she's about to drop a secret. "So, we've been talking about maybe... trying for a baby. I want Junie to have brothers and sisters to grow up with."

Willa gasps, nearly spilling her drink. "Shut up. Us too!"

Tate groans, rubbing his temples. "Do I need another beer before this conversation starts?"

Willa ignores him. "Wouldn't it be so fun if we all got pregnant around the same time? We could raise the kids together. Our babies could all grow up as friends."

Ivy laughs. "Junie definitely needs more kids to play with."

Rowan chokes on her sweet tea, coughing into her napkin. "I'm *not* joining the baby cult."

Willa leans in, grinning. "Why not?"

Rowan waves her hands dramatically, tea sloshing over the rim of her cup. "Because I'm not even convinced I like babies!"

They burst out laughing, and I bite back a nervous smile, watching her from across the picnic table. Her voice has that anxious edge to it when she's trying to make light of something that scares her.

Ivy looks at her and scoffs. "You love Junie!"

"Junie's six," Rowan says, pointing for emphasis. "She's self-sufficient and hilarious. Babies just poop, drool, and scream. I'd probably mess it up somehow."

Everyone's laughing, but my chest goes tight. If Rowan doesn't want kids, I'll find a way to be okay with that. I love her so much, whether we just have a cat, or kids, I just want her.

She's smiling, but there's something behind it that hits me right in the ribs. The way she looks down after she says it, like she believes she wouldn't be good enough.

I take a sip of my beer and... watch her. The way she leans into Willa's shoulder, laughing again, her eyes bright.

She doesn't see how kind she is, how much she already takes care of everyone around her. She doesn't know she's already got that thing moms have, that soft center that makes people feel safe. And no one is more fiercely protective than Rowan.

If there ever was a kid lucky enough to have her as a mom, it'd win the lottery the second it showed up.

Ivy gasps, half laughing, half scandalized. "Rowan! You'd be a kick ass mom! Like nobody would mess with your kids. You'd be full momma bear mode."

Rowan shrugs, fighting a smile. "I mean, I love Junie. What if I get a bad one? Like, a baby who screams every night and hates me?"

Willa laughs so hard she nearly falls off the bench. "There's no way that would happen."

"Hey, I'm just being realistic," Rowan says, trying not to laugh and failing.

Ivy grabs Junie in a hug. "You'd be an amazing mom. The witchy, herb-tea, garden goddess mom. That kid would be so chill."

Rowan snorts. "Yeah, until it starts hexing people at daycare. If we all have kids, you know they're going to be trouble, just like we were."

Everyone bursts out laughing. I'm laughing too, until something clicks in the back of my mind.

She's been tired lately. Sick, even. Falling asleep on the couch after dinner. She swore she had the flu, but it lasted weeks.

And then I realize... I can't remember the last time she mentioned her period.

My stomach drops so fast I swear I feel it hit the damn lawn, and heat rushes straight to my face.

No way. No *fucking* way.

I glance at her again. Rowan, laughing with her sisters, sunlight tangled in her hair, a smudge of barbecue sauce on her tank top she doesn't even know is there. She looks alive and soft and full of this bright joy that always hits me in the chest like a freight train.

And suddenly I can't breathe. Because I know something she doesn't know yet. And the more I think about it, the more certain I am.

"Hey," Remy says, frowning. "You okay? You look like you just saw a ghost."

"I'm fine," I say too fast, grabbing my beer like it can anchor me.

He narrows his eyes. "You sure? You're pale. Like 'saw a pregnancy test' pale."

I choke on my drink. "What'd you just say?"

He barks out a laugh. "I'm kidding, man. Relax. All this pregnancy talk has you crashing out."

But the joke hits too close. Because now my brain won't stop spinning. A baby? With her?

Fear hits first. I'm not ready. I don't know how to be a dad. What if I screw it up? What if I become the man I swore I'd never be? My own biological father who was nothing to us.

But right on the heels of that fear… something else crashes into me. Something that feels a lot like hope.

Because for half a second, my mind paints a picture I wasn't prepared for: Rowan in our kitchen, barefoot, laughing as she leans against my shoulder. A tiny hand wrapped around her finger. Life, loud and chaotic and good.

I don't hate the thought at all. My chest tightens, but not in panic this time. More like awe. Like my heart just expanded too fast and doesn't know what to do with all the new space.

I look at the woman who tore down my walls without even trying and the fear and hope collide so hard I feel dizzy.

Because if she *is*…

If there's even a chance…

Then everything changes.

In the best, scariest, most impossible way.

That night, after the barbecue, I drop her off at the house so she can check on her plants and water them. I tell her I have to run a few errands and head for the drugstore on the edge of town. My hands grip the wheel so tight they ache.

I can't stop thinking about her laughing under the lights, teasing her sisters, saying she doesn't know if she'd even like babies.

God. What if she's really pregnant?

The thought hits me again, harder this time, and my stomach twists. The house isn't ready. The wiring's half finished. There's drywall dust everywhere and the kitchen isn't even done. I wanted it perfect for her. For *us*.

I pull into the drugstore parking lot and sit there for a full minute. Then I mutter, "Get it together," and go inside.

The teenage cashier looks at me like I'm buying explosives when I grab the box. I toss in a pack of gum for good measure. Totally normal, nothing to see here. Mind your business, nosy kid.

On the drive back, I can't stop running through every possibility. What if she's not? She's going to be pissed for me worrying her like this if she isn't. What if she is? And what if she doesn't want it? The feeling hits me in the stomach like a hard punch. Because I want that baby more than anything if she is pregnant. I love kids. I've always been close to Junie. My brother was a single dad for almost five years, and I stepped up a lot during that time to help him.

She said she wasn't sure she ever wanted kids. That she might not be good at it, but she'd be amazing. She already is, she's kind, fierce, and steady. The idea of her carrying *our* baby makes my heart skip a beat. And terrifies me at the same time. I have no idea how I'd make that work, but I know I would. I'd work twenty-four-seven if it meant giving my family what they need. Nothing would keep me from taking care of my family the way they deserve.

But whatever Rowan wanted to do, I'd support her all the way. What we have isn't technically new for me. I've always loved Rowan. But being official is new. I'm worried about how this is going to go.

A text comes across from her.

> Rowan: Almost done. Heading back to the apartment to shower. Meet you there.

By the time I park behind the bookstore, I'm sweating. I sit there a second, staring at the test in the paper bag on the seat beside me like it might bite.

Then I grab it, head inside, and pace her bedroom, waiting for her as I tap the box against my palm, nervously.

The air smells like bonfire smoke, peach cobbler, and a little fresh air from the window she always leaves cracked.

When she walks in from watering her plants, her cheeks are pink. She takes one look at me and freezes.

"Why do you look like you're about to confess to murder?" she asks slowly, her eyes narrowing, suspicious.

I swallow hard and hold up the small box, my hands trembling slightly.

"Neither," I say, my voice tight. "But... we need to talk."

Her brow furrows. "Why do you have that?"

I take a deep breath, trying to steady myself. "Rowan... do we have a baby?"

For a moment, she just stares at me, blinking. Her mouth opens, closes, like she's searching for the words. Then her hand flies to her mouth, and she freezes, eyes wide.

"Oh... oh my God," she whispers, voice shaking. Her gaze drops to the box in my hand. "Wait... that's... I... I'm late."

She presses a hand to her mouth, her breathing quickening. I can see her mind racing, connecting the dots, piecing together the possibility that this is really happening.

The world feels like it's tilted, and for the first time, the full weight of what we might be facing hits both of us.

"You've been sick, tired, and I did the math."

She shakes her head. "It's impossible. I'm on the pill. I take it every day. I never miss it. Sometimes I'm irregular and I've been stressed, so I just figured. I didn't even think..."

"Baby," I say gently, "you need to take this. We need to know."

She groans, bringing it with her into the bathroom. "Don't look."

"Not looking," I promise, hands up, turning around.

A few minutes later, I hear the faucet run. Then silence.

She comes out, face flushed. "I can't look at it." She collapses face-first onto the bed.

I swallow. "I'll look."

She waves a hand. "Go."

I walk into the bathroom and stare down at the test. Two lines are slowly forming, clear as day.

My brain short-circuits, making me feel like every wire crosses at once. I'm equal parts holy-shit-terrified and entirely in love with someone I've never met.

I walk back to the bedroom and drop to my knees next to her on the bed. "Baby, you're gonna be a mom."

She rolls over, eyes wide, tears already welling. "Oh my God."

I start laughing, can't help it, and kiss her all over her face. "We're having a baby."

She's crying and laughing at the same time. "I'm not getting a minivan."

I grin in this moment because that was the first thing she thought to say. "That's fine. I'll build you a custom school bus."

She snorts, swatting me. "No."

I take her hand and press it against my heart. "Baby, we're gonna do this together."

She looks terrified and happy at the same time. "What are we even going to do?"

"Be parents," I say. "Good ones. The best kind."

She shakes her head. "We're a mess."

I laugh softly. "Yeah, but we're a good kind of mess."

She sniffles, still smiling. "You really think I'll be an okay mom?"

I nod, eyes burning. "I know you'll be a great mom."

Her shoulders relax. "There's so much happening really fast."

"Yeah," I whisper, kissing her forehead. "But this—this is the best thing that's ever happened to me, other than you."

I rest my forehead against hers, both of us laughing through tears.

She's warm and soft and shaking just a little. I kiss the top of her head, then her temple, then her mouth. Every part of me is humming with something wild and electric.

"You're really pregnant," I say, still trying to make sense of it. "We're having a baby."

She smiles up at me. "We are."

I press my forehead to hers. "You have no idea how happy this makes me, Row."

Her fingers slide into my hair and she kisses me again. It starts soft, but turns deeper, hungrier, like we're both trying to memorize the moment. It's not about urgency. It's about connection. The way her breath catches. The way my name sounds when she whispers it against my skin.

I kiss her slowly, like she's something sacred. My hands move over her, steady, reverent. Everything feels sharper now, every touch threaded with hope and love. The beginning of a life we made together.

We move together without thinking, like muscle memory, like gravity. I guide her back until we're lost in the dim light of the bedroom. My hands find her waist, her back, the soft curve of her shoulder. Every touch feels reverent, deliberate, like I'm trying to memorize her all over again—the rise and fall of her chest, the warmth of her skin against mine. The feeling of our bodies finally together.

Her breath catches, and the air between us turns thick with

something sacred. It's not rushed or frantic; it's slow, deep, and certain, every movement threaded with meaning.

She whispers my name, and it hits me in the center of my chest. I can't stop looking at her—the way her hair spills over the pillow, the way her eyes never leave mine. It feels like a promise, like the world outside could collapse and we'd still be here, exactly like this.

The world narrows to the sound of her breath, the warmth of her skin beneath my hands, the way she moves with me like she's known the rhythm all her life. Time slows until it's just the two of us, lost in something deep and wordless.

I hold her close, my face buried against her neck, breathing her in. The air between us hums with love, awe, and an exciting promise of a sweet future for us and our family.

When we finally still, I stay there, tracing lazy circles along her back, my heart continuing to race against hers. I kiss her again, soft and certain, and rest my forehead against hers, our breaths mingling in the dark. "We're gonna be parents," I whisper.

She smiles up at me, eyes shining. "Terrifying, huh?"

"Yeah," I say, my thumb tracing her cheek. "But it feels right. Like everything before this just made sense to get to this moment."

Her hand slides over my chest, slow and tender. "Ivy and Willa are going to freak out."

I laugh, the sound breaking through the stillness. "Willa will have color-coded baby spreadsheets set up immediately."

"She'll cry," Rowan says softly. "You know she will."

"She's allowed," I tell her, grinning. "She's gonna be an aunt."

I look down at Rowan's stomach, my hand resting there, feeling something I can't name. Awe, pride, fear—all of it tangled together. "You're carrying our baby," I whisper.

She covers my hand with hers. "We're gonna be okay, Finn."

"We are going to be more than okay," I say.

The night is quiet outside, just the sound of waves and crickets. I pull her closer, kiss her slowly, and hold her like the whole world finally makes sense.

CHAPTER 28
Rowan

COME AND GET YOUR LOVE BY REDBONE

"WHAT ARE you doing up so early?" I ask, still half-asleep as I turn on the kettle, though my hands shake just a little.

Early morning nausea. Except now it has a name. A heartbeat-sized explanation lodged somewhere inside me, throwing my entire world off its axis.

I grip the counter, pretending it's the stupid kettle making me lightheaded and not the fact that my life can be measured in *before I knew* and *after I knew*.

Pregnant.

The word ricochets around my skull like a spell gone wrong. Or maybe right.

My mind spins so fast I can barely breathe. Shock hits first — icy and sharp. Then fear, hot and prickling behind my eyes. Then something softer, something I'm too scared to look at directly yet, something that feels suspiciously like hope.

And threaded through all of it is Finn. What does this mean for him? For us? And the careful, fragile thing we've been building, the thing I was terrified to even say out loud yesterday?

My heart thuds unevenly in my chest, and I swallow hard, trying to act normal, like my entire identity didn't just tilt sideways.

He's sitting at the small counter in my apartment, hair still damp from his shower, scrolling his phone with the most intense concentration I've ever seen on a human face.

He looks up, eyes bright. "Morning baby. Just doing research."

That makes me laugh. "On what?"

He grins and turns the screen toward me. There's an app open with pastel colors and cartoon illustrations. At the top, it says "Your Baby: Week 5."

Finn's off today, which apparently means he's taken "excited dad mode" to a new level. It's adorable, and if I didn't feel so nauseous, I might be more excited myself.

I blink at it. "You downloaded a pregnancy app?"

"Two," he says proudly. "One for tracking progress and one for, like, dad tips. Did you know the baby looks like a tadpole right now? That's crazy, Row."

He says it with full excitement, like we're raising a baby dragon egg, and I can't help but grin.

Morning light filters through the kitchen windows, soft and gold, like lazy magic. The kettle whistles, and I measure out some of my homemade ginger and peppermint tea blend that's saving my life every morning.

I smile, watching him swipe through the apps. "What else did you learn?"

He nods, totally serious. "Apparently, its tiny heart's already starting to form. And this says by next week it'll start to have little arms. Arms, Row!"

My chest tightens in that dangerous, melty way. "You're going to be such a good dad."

He looks up, a soft grin tugging at his mouth. "You think so?"

"I know so."

He sets the phone down and comes up behind me. His hands find my hips, warm and solid, chin resting on my shoulder. "We're both going to be great."

"Yeah," I whisper, leaning back into him. "We will."

He kisses the side of my neck. "You okay?"

I nod, staring at the steam curling up from my mug. "Happy. Terrified. Kind of both at once."

He squeezes me gently. "That's okay. I'm both too."

For a moment, we stand there in solidarity of our unexpected excitement, the ocean breeze flowing through the open window, his arms wrapped around me.

I didn't realize how much I wanted this until it became a reality. Until I saw the joy in his eyes and heard him talk about something the size of a tadpole as if it were already the center of our universe. And it already is. It's crazy how you can love something you've never met. Maybe he's right and I will be a good mom.

He kisses my temple again and murmurs, "I need to check my app and see what it says about breakfast cravings. What can I make you?"

I laugh through the lump in my throat. "Probably dry toast. My stomach is still on hiatus."

"Then toast it is," he says as he reaches for the bread and hums under his breath.

I text my sisters and my mom before I can chicken out.

> Can everyone meet me at the bookstore at 2pm?

> Ivy: I have Junie, and we'll be there. What's going on?

> Willa: Yeah, I'll be working, haha.

> Mom: Ohhh, what's going on?

I am nervous as I stare at my phone for a solid minute before setting it face down on the counter. I'm telling them, and I need them.

It's almost two and I need to head over from my shop. The shops have been busy all day, but we usually have a lull in the afternoon, so I thought this would be a good time to tell them. Willa tried to pry information out of me earlier, but I told her that I would talk to everyone at two.

I'm already jittery when Ivy walks in with Junie skipping behind her.

"Okay," Willa says, setting down her coffee from behind the counter. "You're giving summoning energy. What's going on?"

I pace in front of the counter, heart pounding as I make sure there are no customers around. "We have to wait for Mom."

Ivy looks concerned. "She's freaking out. Did you get a dog?"

Junie gasps dramatically. "You're getting another cat! Allen does need a friend."

"No," I say weakly.

Ivy's eyebrows shoot up. "I can't wait for Mom. I need to know now."

Before I can answer, the bell jingles again, and Mom walks in with that peaceful, witch-in-control energy she always has. "Morning, loves."

Willa looks at her. "Do you know what's going on?"

Lilith smiles. "I have a hunch."

Of course she does. My mom has always had a sixth sense about us girls. This is why I can't keep it from them. I'm surprised they haven't figured it out by now like Finn did.

My throat tightens. "Okay, I'm just going to say it." I take a shaky breath. "I'm pregnant."

For a heartbeat, nobody moves. Then the room erupts.

Willa shrieks so loud that Junie jumps. "WHAT!"

Ivy claps her hands over her mouth. "Oh my God, oh my God!"

Junie's eyes go huge. "You're going to have a baby? Does Uncle Finn know?"

"Yes, he knows," I manage, laughing through tears. "He's the dad."

Junie looks shocked. "Wow. I mean...I have questions. He killed the goldfish he had. So, I'm not too sure about how he's going to do with a whole baby."

Ivy rushes around the counter and pulls me into a hug so tight I can barely breathe. "Rowan! You're gonna be a mom! You made a tiny human!"

Willa's so happy. "This is wild. I was talking about us all having babies, but I didn't think you'd actually go first!"

Junie tugs on my sleeve. "I can babysit! I'm very responsible. Ask my dad. I'm good with Lola."

Mom pulls me in for a hug. "I'm so happy for you, sweetheart. This is wonderful news."

I shake my head, half-laughing, half-nervous. "I'm freaking out. But in a good way. Like my whole body can't decide if it wants to cry, throw up, or dance."

Mom's eyes are warm and shining. "Oh, I remember that feeling. I was scared, too, when I found out about you girls. Every single time. It's supposed to be scary. It's new, big, and messy. But it's also the best thing you'll ever do."

Her thumb brushes away a tear I didn't know was there. "Look at our family, Rowan. Look at what we've built together. You get to add another soul to that. Another Bennett-Maren miracle. How cool is that?"

My chest cracks wide open. "It's... really cool," I whisper.

Willa's grinning through tears. "I'm going to tell Tate we have a green light to try. Our kids are going to grow up together. Cousin chaos!"

Junie pumps a fist in the air. "Cousin chaos! I love it."

Ivy's already pulling out her phone. "We need a group chat. Operation Baby Bennett. And a Pinterest board."

"Not yet!" I say, laughing so hard I can barely breathe. "We still have to tell Remy, Donna and Pete. And let me just get through my first trimester before you start pinning nursery ideas."

Lilith smiles knowingly. "This is good news that Donna and Pete could use right about now."

I nod, feeling the words settle somewhere deep and certain.

"Yeah, that's why we want to tell them so they can celebrate with us."

We are all aware that we're on borrowed time with Pete and trying to live every moment fully with him.

The fear is still there, but it's softer now. It feels more like hope.

Nothing in my life is perfect, but for the first time, it doesn't have to be.

———

Donna's kitchen smells like heaven. And since I've been surviving on toast for days now, my stomach is liking what I'm smelling right now, butter, tomatoes, and love. I'm sure Pete has something to do with it because Donna is not known for being the best cook. I know she's been trying hard to cook with Pete every day. They've made some incredible meals, and I have a feeling this is going to be one that will live special in my memories.

She's got pots bubbling on every burner, wooden spoons scattered like battle weapons, and a mountain of pasta so big it could feed half of Wisteria Cove.

"This is not an impromptu dinner," Finn whispers as he opens a bottle of wine. "This is a full-scale Italian festival."

I laugh, leaning against the counter. "You think she ever does anything halfway?"

Across the room, Donna's fixing a pillow next to Pete and handing him a blanket. My mom sits next to him in a chair and smiles knowingly at us. It's probably killing her she can't talk about this with them, yet.

Pete's thinner now, and paler. But his eyes are still bright, full of that teasing glint he's never lost. Junie's sitting beside him, drawing something on a notepad and explaining her latest invention involving goats, glitter, and jetpacks.

Ivy's next to them. "We're making Uncle Pete a treasure map," she tells me, smiling. "It's going to have the best treasure in Wisteria Cove."

Pete smiles. "It's going to have the best treasure, June Bug."

"Will you tell me where you keep your secret candy stash?" Junie asks.

"What secret candy stash?" Pete asks, and everyone laughs.

The door opens, and Remy steps in, looking confused at the impromptu dinner invite. "What's going on? Why are we having a random Italian feast dinner on a Wednesday? I mean…I'm not complaining, just confused."

Finn looks at me, smiling. His hand finds mine, warm and steady.

He clears his throat. "Because we have something to tell you guys."

Donna whirls around, wooden spoon in hand like a microphone. "You're getting married!"

"Probably eventually," I say, laughing. "But that's not it."

Finn squeezes my hand tighter and says proudly. "We're going to have a baby."

For a second, the whole room goes silent. Everyone looks at each other, probably trying to figure out who already knows and if we're actually serious.

Donna shrieks so loud that Lola barks. "Oh my God!" She drops the spoon and rushes over, hugging us both so tightly. "I knew it! I had a dream about a baby last week, and I said to Pete, 'That's a sign!'"

Pete's eyes are glassy with tears. He smiles so big it feels like something is breaking in my chest. "That's… that's wonderful, sweetheart." His voice cracks on the last word, and I feel Finn's thumb brush over my knuckles. I know he's probably trying to hold this together, too.

"We wanted you to know right away," Finn says softly.

Pete nods, his eyes shining. "I'm so glad you did." He looks at Finn and claps him on the shoulder. "You're going to be one hell of a dad, Son."

Finn swallows hard. "I had a pretty good example."

Donna sniffles loudly and pulls me back into a hug, tears streaming down her cheeks. "I'm going to be a nana again! Oh, I have to start knitting! And baking! And redecorating one of the rooms! We need a theme!"

"You don't knit or bake now, Nana," Junie says, looking confused.

"It's time to learn to do more nana things," Donna tells her, excited, and Junie shrugs.

I laugh through my own tears. "We don't even know what we're having yet."

"Doesn't matter," she says, wiping her eyes. "We're celebrating everything!"

Then she grabs my hands and starts spinning me in a ridiculous, happy dance right there in the middle of the family room. "We're having a baby, we're having a baby!" she sings, off-key and wonderful.

Mom's so happy, too, and she can't stop smiling. Ivy's recording the whole thing, cackling from the couch. Remy's shaking his head, grinning like an idiot. "How about that, a baby," he mutters, but there's warmth in his eyes.

Dinner turns into loud, beautiful chaos. Plates clatter, laughter fills every corner, Donna's garlic bread burns a little, and nobody cares because everyone is together and celebrating good news.

Finn's sitting beside me, his arm over the back of my chair, watching his family with that soft, quiet pride he always gets when he's around them. His thumb brushes small circles on my shoulder as if he's anxious about something and I can guess what that is. It's like the lingering elephant in the room that we have to live as much life as we can with Pete.

Pete tells a story about the time Finn tried to build a treehouse and accidentally nailed his jeans to the ladder. Donna rolls her eyes and threatens to produce the photo evidence when Finn denies it. Ivy and Willa argue over who will get pregnant next.

Tate and Remy are staring at each other and having a silent conversation of 'what the hell is going on here.'

It's loud, messy, and perfect. And it's my family. And this baby is so lucky to have these people.

For a second, I look around the table at my sisters, my mom, Finn's family, this ridiculous group of people who somehow became ours. And I think... this is what life's supposed to be like. Family, fun, and special memories. Love and laughter. The world outside with people like Sammy, Jessica, or the other small-town snakes, they don't matter.

This is what matters.

Finn catches me staring and leans in to kiss my temple, his voice low and steady against my ear. "You okay, baby?"

I nod, smiling as tears sting my eyes. "Yeah," I whisper. "Better than okay."

Outside, the sun dips behind the trees, and inside, the house glows full of warmth, noise, and the kind of love that feels unbreakable.

————

The night air is thick with the scent of honeysuckle and the warmth of summer. Out in the yard, Junie's throwing a rubber ball across the grass, her giggles mixing with Lola's happy barks as the dog bounds after it.

Finn and I sit on Donna's front porch, swaying slowly on the old swing. The wood creaks beneath us, steady and familiar. His hand is warm around mine, thumb tracing small, absentminded circles against my skin.

Finn nods toward the yard. "Maybe we should get a dog," he says quietly. "Think Allen would like a friend?"

I laugh under my breath, leaning into his shoulder. "I think we have enough on our plate right now."

He grins, eyes glinting in the porch light. "I love our life."

Junie squeals when Lola brings the ball back, wet and slobbery, and I can't help but smile. There's so much life here. So much love. I love our life too.

Finn squeezes my hand, and for a second, I breathe it all in, the sound of laughter, the smell of honeysuckle, the warmth of his arms around me, making me feel safe and secure.

I lean my head on his shoulder. "Think Pete was happy?"

He nods slowly, looking out toward the dark tree line with the coast in the distance. "I'm glad we got to share this with him."

"Yeah." My throat tightens.

The swing creaks again as he shifts, turning to face me. The porch light hits his face just enough that I can see the faint smile tugging at his lips.

"You know," he says, "I've built a lot of things in my life. Houses, cabinets, decks. But this…" He glances down at where his hand rests against my belly, his thumb brushing over my shirt. "This is the first thing that feels absolutely right."

My heart stutters. "That's dangerously close to something Donna would write in one of her books."

He grins. "Yeah, well. Guess like mother, like son."

I laugh softly, but it fades when I see the look in his eyes that's the mix of love and awe and something deeper, almost reverent.

"You know I bought that house for you," he says quietly. "Every nail, every board… I wanted it to be perfect because I wanted you to see how much you mean to me, Row. I wanted it to be a place where you'd never question my love for you. You'd feel it there every day."

"Finn…"

He shakes his head. "I always knew it'd be you, Row. I didn't know it'd be this good."

Tears burn behind my eyes, hot and sudden.

He reaches up and tucks a strand of hair behind my ear, voice low and rough. "That house is ours. We're gonna fill it with life. Plants, babies, laughter, and memories. It's gonna be messy and loud and beautiful, and I can't wait."

I laugh through a sniffle. "I love you."

He leans in until his forehead rests against mine. "I love you, too."

The world goes quiet again, just the sound of the porch swing and the low hum of summer all around us.

After a while, I whisper, "If it's a boy…"

He hums. "Yeah?"

"I think I want to name him Pete."

He pulls back just enough to look at me. His eyes go soft, glassy, even.

"Pete," he repeats.

I nod.

Finn lets out a shaky laugh, rubbing his thumb under his eye. "He'd love that."

"I know."

He kisses slow, sweet, lingering and we almost forget we have an audience around us. We finally pull apart and I rest my head against his chest, listening to his heartbeat, steady and strong.

"This," I whisper, eyes closing. "This is what it's supposed to be like."

He kisses the top of my head. "Yeah, baby. It is."

The swing keeps rocking, soft and slow, and everything feels right.

CHAPTER 29

Finn

AMERICAN PIE BY DON MCLEAN

Two Months Later

THE SKY over Wisteria Cove is turning pink when I pull up to our house.

It still feels strange calling it our house, like it's finally ours because I've poured my entire heart and soul into this for almost a year. Every late night, every splinter, every dollar scraped together. All of it for her and our family. I built this when Rowan was just a dream. A dream I wasn't sure I was ever going to have come true. And here we are…

Rowan's in the passenger seat, in one of my flannels, hair pulled up on top of her head, a steaming to-go mug of tea in her hands. She has no idea what she's about to walk into.

When I kill the engine, she looks around. "Why are we stopping here? I thought we had to be at your mom's for dinner."

I grin like an idiot, nerves buzzing in my chest. "You'll see."

She gives me a cautious smile, the one she uses when she's trying to decide if she should trust me or brace herself. "You're not making me help you pick out more things, are you?"

"Nope."

There's officially nothing left to pick out. It's all done. And this week, her sisters, Mom, Tate, Remy, and I have all gotten it cleaned up and ready for her to finally see. I've even snuck a few of her things over here, hoping that she wouldn't notice. It's finally ready for her.

I get out and come around to open her door, and take her by the hand. It's warm from holding her mug.

Inside, the air smells faintly of orange furniture polish, wood, paint, and new beginnings. It doesn't feel like our home yet, but I know it will once Rowan gets to put her thumbprint on it.

Rowan stops just inside the doorway.

Her hand flies to her mouth. "Finn…"

Golden hour light floods through the windows and spills across the honeyed oak floorboards that are finally finished. The walls are painted the creamy white color she picked out, called Betsy's Linen, her favorite. The kitchen gleams, copper fixtures catching the light. Her favorite chipped mug, the one she swore she'd lost is sitting on the counter beside the stove with a brand-new copper kettle. Glass jars line the open shelving, ready for her to fill with all her favorite herbs and tea blends. A fresh loaf of bread is in the wooden bread box, and a candle sits on the counter, its scent of eucalyptus and lavender, her favorite. I wanted it to smell like her shop and remind her of being home. Everyone has worked hard to put the final small touches in place that will make her feel at home.

She takes a few steps in, like she's afraid the floor might disappear if she moves too fast.

"Finn," she whispers, voice trembling. "You finished it?"

"Mostly," I say, trying to sound casual even though I'm nervous. "There's still trim work left at the top of the stairs, and the back deck needs another coat, but it's livable."

She turns in a slow circle, tears shining in her eyes. "It's more than livable. It's absolutely perfect."

My heart squeezes and I shove my hands in my pockets,

watching her move through the space like she's seeing it for the first time. All of the sudden I see her face recognize all of the fixtures and details that she would tell me looked good. I always went with whatever she chose because I knew this would be hers.

In the kitchen, she runs her fingers along the backsplash. "This tile…" She glances at me. "You remembered."

"You said it reminded you of sea glass," I say quietly.

She laughs, soft and watery. "You even got the copper hardware that I mentioned I loved."

"Yeah," I murmur. "I was listening."

Her eyes shine brighter now as she runs her fingers over the big farmhouse sink she told me she dreamed about. "You were listening to everything."

I follow her through the house as she discovers it piece by piece with the built-ins in the living room filled with her books, the window seat I added under the front window because she once said she wanted a spot to read on rainy days.

Every corner has her fingerprints, even though she never touched a single thing here. She's right. I was listening.

When we reach the hallway, she pauses. "What's this room?"

"Open it."

She pushes the door open slowly.

The nursery isn't finished. Just pale green walls she pinned to her Pinterest board with her sisters, a walnut crib, a matching rocking chair, and sunlight filtering through cream gingham curtains her mom made. On the little dresser, I set one of her plant cuttings in a mason jar, roots curling in the water.

Her hand trembles as she covers her mouth. "Oh, Finn…"

I step behind her, wrapping my arms around her waist. My chin rests against her shoulder. "It'll be ready before he gets here," I whisper. "I promise."

Her breath catches. "You already think it's a boy?"

I grin, trying to mask the nerves twisting in my stomach. "Call it a gut feeling, but I think it's a boy."

Rowan raises an eyebrow, smirking.

"But… whatever happens," I add, my voice quieter now, "I just… I want to be there for them. I can't promise anything, and I don't know what's coming, but I'll do everything I can, and I'll love you both enough for two lifetimes. That's what matters."

She squeezes my hand, eyes soft, and I feel a mix of fear and hope twisting together. The rest, the guesses, the excitement can wait. For now, it's about being ready for whatever comes.

She turns, looking up at me. There's so much emotion in her eyes I can barely stand it. "You built this for us."

I nod. "Yeah."

Her tears finally spill. "You remembered everything I ever said I liked. The tiles, the wood color, the window seat. Even the light fixtures. Every little detail."

"Of course I did. I listen to everything you tell me. It's all important to me. You're the most important person to me, baby."

She shakes her head, crying and laughing all at once. "Finn, this is incredible. You poured your heart into this."

"I did," I say, voice breaking. "Every board, every nail, every time I wanted to quit, I thought about you walking through this house one day. And how you'd fill it with plants, memories, and laughter."

Her lip trembles. "You're going to make me cry harder."

"Don't cry, baby," I whisper.

She cups my face in her hands. "You built us a home."

"Yeah," I say softly. "I did."

She kisses me slowly, deeply, and full of everything we've fought through to get here.

When she finally pulls back, she presses her forehead to mine. "I can't wait to start our life here. You, me, the baby… this house. It feels like the beginning of everything."

I wrap my arms around her and hold her close, the scent of new wood and her shampoo filling the space. Outside, the last bit of daylight fades. The house feels warm and inviting, like it's been waiting for her.

We finally make it over to my mom's later that evening, still buzzing from the day and pretending not to be. Rowan's hand is in mine, warm and certain, and there's this extra spark in her—like she's been waiting for the right moment to say something.

Mom opens the door, pulls us into hugs, starts ushering us toward the kitchen... and that's when Rowan tugs lightly on my hand.

"Hey," she murmurs. "Can I... ask you something?"

My heart kicks. "Anything."

She bites her lip—nervous, excited, glowing in this way I've never seen before. "When can we move in?"

I swear the world tilts a little. I brush a strand of hair behind her ear. "Baby, I've been waiting for you to ask."

Her eyes go soft, bright in the kitchen light.

I take her hands in mine. "We don't have to wait. After dinner, we can swing by the apartment, grab your things, and make it official tonight. If you want."

Rowan's breath catches, a small, sharp inhale that feels like hope catching fire. "Tonight?"

"Tonight," I say, grinning like a fool. "Or right now. We can get out of here and I'll carry you over the damn threshold if you ask me."

She laughs, unguarded and happy. "Tonight," she says, squeezing my hands. "Let's do it tonight."

I lean in and kiss her, soft and sure, the promise of everything new and everything ours lingering between us.

And for the first time in my life, when we leave here, it'll feel like we're going home.

Music plays low from the old record player in the corner. Pete's on the couch under a blanket even though it's warm inside, his color pale but his smile bright.

Donna's bustling between the stove and the table, scolding Remy for sneaking bites of the soup. Ivy and Junie are getting bowls down. Lilith and Willa are laughing in the kitchen as they pile bread into a big bowl.

It feels good. Familiar. Safe.

When Rowan walks in, Pete's face lights up like someone turned the sun back on. "There she is," he says, reaching for her hand. "You look beautiful, sweetheart."

She laughs, blushing. "Thank you, Pete."

He pats her hand, then looks at me. "You taking care of her, Son?"

"Trying my best."

Lilith leans over her shoulder. "He's doing fine. She's glowing."

Rowan snorts. "That's sweat. He showed me the new house."

"You finally showed her?" Donna asks, eyes wide. "We've been waiting all week for you to have the grand reveal."

"We're moving in tonight," I say.

Pete grins. "I knew you would. I can't wait to come see it."

After dinner, everyone lingers at the table, full and happy. The chatter softens. Ivy starts humming as she clears plates. Rowan rests her hand over mine under the table, squeezing once. I can feel her heart racing.

"You want to tell them?" I ask quietly.

She nods, smiling nervously.

I clear my throat. "We have something we wanted to share."

Everyone looks up.

"It's about the baby," Rowan says.

Donna gasps. "You already know what it is?"

I chuckle. "Not yet. But we know what we want to name him if it's a boy."

Pete's smile widens. "Oh yeah?"

Rowan glances at me, and I nod. "We'd like to name him Pete," she says softly. "After you."

For a second, no one breathes.

Then Pete's eyes fill with tears. He presses a hand to his chest, voice rough. "You… you'd really do that?"

Rowan nods. "You've been such a light in this family. You've loved all of us so hard. We want our baby to have a piece of you, too."

Donna's crying before he even responds. Ivy hands her a tissue.

Pete clears his throat, trying to joke through it. "You're all gonna make an old man bawl his eyes out at the dinner table."

"Too late," Donna says, sniffling.

He laughs quietly, then looks at both of us. "That means more than I can say. But… there's something I should tell you."

His gaze softens, distant. "When I was a kid, I had a little brother. His name was Chip, and we lost him when we were young, but he was… he was pure joy. I miss him every day."

Rowan's eyes shine again. "Chip," she repeats softly, her hand squeezing mine while she searches my face to see what I think.

Pete nods, smiling faintly. "You don't have to, but… if you ever wanted a nickname, maybe think about that."

I swallow hard, my chest tight. "Chip," I say, testing it. "Chip Bennett. That sounds like someone who climbs trees and builds forts."

Pete chuckles. "Exactly."

Rowan reaches across the table and takes his hand. "I love it. Chip it is."

Pete's eyes glisten. "Then I'm the luckiest man alive."

Donna sets a bowl of rolls down and sniffles. "You've always been that, honey."

Everyone laughs softly, the moment settling in the room, and blanketing us all in peace.

We eat dessert together, sharing stories about Pete's younger days with his first Christmas tree sale, his stubborn streak, the time he and his brother Chip built a chicken coop and accidentally trapped themselves inside. The house fills with laughter and love, and for a little while, the world feels perfect again. Everyone needed this dinner tonight. It feels right.

Later, when Rowan and I step outside, the air is cool and full of honeysuckle.

She takes my hand as we walk toward the truck.

The porch light glows behind her. She rests her hand on her belly, smiling faintly. "Chip Bennett," she says, testing the name.

I slide an arm around her. "Our Chip."

She leans her head against my chest, breathing me in. "He's already so loved."

"Yeah," I whisper, pressing a kiss to her forehead. "He always will be."

The wind shifts, carrying the faint scent of dinner leftover in Mom's kitchen. Somewhere inside, I can still hear Pete's laughter.

And as I hold her there under the porch light, with the sound of crickets and the weight of everything we've built between us, I know one thing for sure.

We're a family.

CHAPTER 30
Rowan

CARRY ON MY WAYWARD SON BY KANSAS

Christmas time, two months later…

SNOW FALLS IN SLOW, lazy spirals, drifting through the air like feathers. The Bennett Tree Farm looks like something straight out of a postcard with rows of Christmas trees dusted in white, wreaths on every fence post, the smell of wood smoke curling through the cold.

It's the kind of perfect snowy day that makes people believe in magic.

And for the first time in a long time, I'm not sprinting between yoga classes and inventory spreadsheets and working in my shop.

Thankfully Marilyn, Vanessa, and Jessica have laid off of me and I haven't heard from them. I do my thing, and I guess they're doing theirs. I don't really know because I'm too busy with my own world to pay attention to what anyone else is doing.

My life… feels steadier now.

The shop is thriving and the holiday rush hit early this year, and thanks to my new herbal apprentice, Grace, the shelves actually stay stocked. The customers keep coming, curious and loyal, filling the place with chatter and warm air and the smell of tea and cinnamon.

The yoga studio is gentler these days. I'm not teaching every class anymore. Leslie, one of my long-time students, stepped in to run the early-morning sessions, and she's somehow even more Zen than I am. I still teach my candlelit evening class and now that I'm pregnant, my new "Mama Flow" class once a week. It's small, cozy, supportive. A circle of women who move slowly, breathe deeply, and whisper little hopes into the universe.

I've never felt so much support.

But standing here, surrounded by snow and trees and the sound of Junie giggling somewhere behind us, I can admit... maybe I do glow a little.

Or maybe it's just happiness.

Maybe this is what it feels like to build a life that isn't held together by fear and survival, but by love, help, and actual breathing room.

I rest a hand on my belly without thinking, the tiny flutter inside reminding me that everything in my world is shifting—my business, my body, my future—and somehow, I finally feel ready for it.

Finn's hand is warm against the small of my back as we walk between the trees. He keeps close, like he's afraid I might slip on the snow, even though I've told him three times now that I'm fine.

"You're walking in boots that have less traction than a baby deer," he says, tightening his arm around me, anyway.

"I'm pregnant, not fragile," I mutter, even though I secretly love it when he gets all protective over me and our baby.

He grins. "You're both."

I bump him with my hip. "Keep it up, and when this baby comes, you'll be on diaper duty for the next decade."

His laugh fogs the cold air. "Deal."

The farm feels even busier this year. Still full of families bundled in scarves, kids tugging sleds, Ivy and Junie handing out cocoa from the farm stand near the barn, but underneath it all, there's a softness. A missing heartbeat.

Pete's not here, and when I'm reminded of that. It still hits me with a punch to the heart.

He passed in early October, just as the leaves turned. Peacefully in his bed, Donna said. And reminded up until the last day how much he meant to each and every one of us, Remy said. But I still feel him every time I walk into Donna's house and at every family function we've had ever since. Our missing heartbeat. I still half expect to hear him say, "Hey, sweetheart," when I walk through the door. And when he doesn't, my heart feels so sad.

Finn squeezes my hand gently, like he can feel where my mind's gone.

"Hey," he murmurs. "What are you thinking about?"

I nod, but my throat feels tight. "Just thinking about him."

Finn looks out over the rows of trees. "He'd tell us to stop moping and pick the damn tree already."

I laugh softly. "That sounds about right. And he'd call you a lunatic for wanting to put a tree in every room of the new house."

"Hey. I can't help it that I'm excited for Christmas." He grins. And he is excited. Finn is over-the-top with holidays. He wants to go big on every decoration, dinner, and tradition. And I love it. Life with Finn is never boring and always full.

We finally find the most beautiful tree. A tall, full pine with just the right mix of wild symmetry and the perfect evergreen smell.

Finn circles it, inspecting it like he's choosing lumber for the perfect project. "You sure this one's not too big?"

I tilt my head. "You can handle it, big guy."

He smirks. "You're saying that because you know I'll try to prove you right?"

"Obviously."

He shakes his head, laughing, and hoists the saw from his shoulder. Junie runs over from where she's been helping Tate and Remy tag trees, her cheeks red from the cold.

"Uncle Finn, can I help?" she asks.

"Absolutely," he says. "You're my number-one helper."

She beams and together they cut the tree down, both of them cheering when it tips over into the snow.

I watch from the sidelines, heart full. Finn scoops Junie up and spins her around, her laughter echoing through the cold air.

For a moment, the grief softens. The world feels whole again.

By the time we haul the tree back to the truck, the sky's gone that soft pink-gray that means more snow's coming.

Ivy waves from the cocoa stand, calling, "You picked a good one! I can't wait to see it later!"

"Thanks!" I call back. "I've got the soups in the slow cookers and everything will be ready."

Finn loads the tree with his usual efficiency, brushing snow off his jacket.

"I can't wait to get home and decorate our first tree."

He grins, a little proud, a little nervous. "And our first dinner party in the house."

I look up at him, at the red in his cheeks, the snow in his hair. "It's perfect, Finn."

He leans down and kisses me, soft and slow, right there in the cold.

"Yeah," he says quietly against my lips. "It really is."

By six o'clock, the house is glowing with a new Christmas candle lit, the fireplace crackling, the smell of comfort food filling the cozy kitchen.

Our kitchen table looks ridiculous in the best way. Everyone brought a themed board.

Remy and Ivy made a "Pizza Board," complete with mini calzones and garlic knots shaped like snowflakes.

Willa and Tate showed up with a "Fondue Board," which is really just melted cheese and a borderline sinful number of different types of bread.

Donna, Mom, and Junie made a "Dessert Board" that looks like Willy Wonka and Santa had a sugar-fueled fever dream.

Finn and I made a fruit, nuts, and cheese "charcuterie board," but it's really Finn showing off his woodworking because he built the board out of walnut and branded Bennett into the corner. The rest of them don't know it yet, but he made them all one too, customized for them and wrapped under our new tree and ready for them to open. This was such a hit, we might do board nights more often.

Everyone's laughing and talking over each other. The fire pops. There's music playing, Donna's holiday playlist, the same she made for the party. She's struggled a lot the past few weeks, but she is keeping busy. We all know that we got much more time with Pete than we thought we'd have and for that we're grateful.

Junie's sitting cross-legged on the rug with Lola, sneaking her bites of cheese. Allen is perched on the back of the couch, glaring at everyone, but secretly, he likes the company, I can tell.

I can feel Pete here. In every laugh, every spark of warmth. He's in this family still, tucked between all the love he helped grow.

Finn sits beside me on the couch, his arm draped over the back, thumb rubbing slow circles on my shoulder. He's been doing that a lot lately—little touches, quiet reassurances. Protective and reassuring, and sometimes I think just for him.

I'm showing now. Not a lot, but enough that my sweater doesn't hide it anymore. Every so often, I catch him looking at my belly like it's the most sacred thing on Earth.

I rest my hand over his and whisper, "Stop staring at me like that, weirdo."

He smirks. "Can't. That's my kid in there."

"You're ridiculous."

"Yeah," he says, kissing my temple, "and completely in love with you."

I look around at the people we love—our family, our friends, our town—and feel something settle deep in my chest.

This is it. The life we built, the one we fought for.

When dinner slows down and everyone's on their second round of hot cocoa, Finn stands and clears his throat.

"Alright, listen up," he says. "We have an announcement."

Donna gasps dramatically. "You're eloping!"

"No," I say with a laugh. "Although that would be less stressful than dealing with planning a future wedding."

"Hey," Tate says, "speak for yourself. I'm officiating when you do it, whether you want me to or not."

Finn squeezes my hand and looks down at me, eyes soft. "You wanna tell them?"

I nod, heart racing a little.

"It's a boy," I say.

The room explodes. Cheers, squeals, laughter.

Donna bursts into tears immediately and covers her mouth. Mom hugs Ivy, who's already crying into Remy's shirt. Willa throws an arm around Tate and yells, "Another Bennett boy, look out world!"

Junie jumps up and down. "I called it! I said it was a boy!"

I laugh through the noise, wiping tears from my eyes. "You did, Junie."

Finn raises his voice over the chaos. "We've officially picked his name."

He nods, his voice softening. "His name will be Peter. But we'll call him Chip. It's what Pete wanted."

The room goes quiet. Donna covers her mouth. Mom's eyes well with tears.

Remy blinks hard, then nods slowly. "Chip," he says quietly. "That's perfect."

Willa sniffles. "I love that so much."

Junie runs over and wraps her arms around Finn's legs. "Chip's a good name. Like a cookie. Or a superhero."

Finn laughs, his voice catching just a little. "Yeah. Exactly like that."

Donna steps forward, tears streaking her cheeks. "He'd be so proud of you two."

Finn nods, pulling her into a hug. "We hope so."

"He is," she says firmly, pressing her hand to her heart. "I can feel it."

After dinner, we all gather around by the tree Finn cut earlier today for pictures.

Finn wraps his arms around me from behind, his hands resting on my belly. The lights twinkle across the branches, soft and golden.

Willa's setting up her phone on a tripod, trying to get everyone in the shot. "Okay, smile! No one blink! Finn, stop whispering in her ear, you're making her blush!"

"I'm not doing anything," he says, voice full of mischief.

"Liar," I mutter, elbowing him.

He laughs, kissing my cheek just as the flash goes off.

Junie's giggling. Tate's holding Lola like a baby. Remy's pretending to look annoyed while secretly smiling.

The picture ends up perfect, a little crooked, but completely real life.

Later, after everyone's gone home and the snow's still falling, Finn and I sit on the couch in front of the fire. The house smells like pine and cinnamon. The tree glows in the corner, bright and beautiful. I can't stop looking at it as I rub my belly.

He stretches his arm along the back of the couch, pulling me against him. "So, Mrs. Almost Bennett," he says, voice low. "How do you feel about our first Christmas in this house?"

I tilt my head toward him. "Happy and hopeful."

He smiles softly. "Yeah. Me too."

The fire crackles. Outside, the world is quiet and white.

I look down at our joined hands over my belly. "He's gonna know love, Finn. So much of it."

Finn presses a kiss to my forehead. "He already does."

We sit there for a long time, just listening to the crackle of the fireplace, the faint whirl of the furnace, the heartbeat of a house finally alive.

I think about everything it took to get here. The heartbreak, fear, and rebuilding.

The girl who once doubted she was meant for love now has a home, a partner, a baby on the way, and a family who refuses to let her fall. And the man who believed in it all before any of it ever even existed. Or maybe it did exist and he just felt it before I did. Either, way, I'm so grateful.

Hope feels different now. It carries more weight and it makes me feel full.

Finn's fingers brush the back of my neck. "What are you thinking about?"

I smile, leaning into him. "Just... how lucky I am."

He laughs softly. "Pretty sure I'm the lucky one."

"Wrong," I whisper. "It's me."

He kisses me, slow and sweet, like he's sealing a promise.

Epilogue

Rowan
Sweet Child O'Mine by Guns N' Roses

THE CONTRACTIONS STARTED AT SUNRISE. At least I think they are contractions. They haven't been dramatic, just that deep, slow ache that feels like my body's politely warning me it's time.

But I ignore it. Because, honestly, who has time to be in labor when there are seeds to plant? I have things that have to get done before Chip gets here. He's just going to have to wait.

The greenhouse smells like damp soil. Sunlight filters through the glass in streaks of gold, lighting up the rows of herbs I've been tending for weeks. I'm hunched over a tray of seedlings, muttering to myself about moon cycles and germination rates, pretending like my insides aren't twisting in rhythmic waves.

I'm fine. Totally fine. Except for the part where I have to stop every five minutes and brace a hand on the potting bench, breathing through the pain like some amateur in a prenatal yoga video. And I'm not fine. I'm freaking the fuck out. I am scared to be a mom, scared to go into labor. So, if I just keep on planting my seeds, maybe I can trick my body into this not really happening.

"Rowan," Ivy calls from the doorway, sounding suspiciously calm. "What… exactly are you doing?"

"Planting more seeds." I wipe my forehead with my sleeve of my jacket that no longer zips thanks to my massive round belly. "I just need everything ready."

Ivy blinks. "You're in labor, Row."

"No, I still have five more days," I reassure her and myself.

"You're contracting," she corrects. "You're also sweating and making weird noises."

Remy appears behind her, looking concerned. "Where's Finn?"

"He's working. I don't want to bother him," I say, scooping dirt over the seed tray. "And I'm not having a baby right now. Even if I were in labor, my book says early labor can take hours. Maybe even days. I have things to do first."

Remy stares at me like I've grown two heads. "You're gonna have that baby in this greenhouse if you keep this up."

"I am not," I shoot back.

Ivy looks at Remy with concern and back at me. "You're seriously in so much denial right now."

"It's fine," I say, because the alternative, acknowledging that this is actually happening terrifies me.

Remy mutters something about not being qualified nor wanting to deliver his brother's baby.

Another contraction hits hard, bending me in half. I grip the edge of the potting bench and focus on breathing. The baby's moving lower, and everything feels hot, heavy, and unreal. I try to keep planting seeds in the dirt through it, but my eyes are wide with the pain that shoots through my rock-hard stomach.

When it passes, I straighten, forcing a smile. "See? Fine. Totally fine."

Remy looks ready to lose it. "Ivy, call Finn, your sisters, Donna, and your mom."

"Don't you dare!" I shout.

She pulls her phone out of her pocket. "Rowan—"

"I said I'm fine."

Remy rubs a hand down his face. "You women in this family are going to be the death of me."

"I thought you liked strong women," Ivy teases.

"Yeah," he says. "Strong. Not crazy."

"No," I protest weakly. "My book says—"

"I don't care what your book says," he interrupts. "Your book also told you not to drink caffeine during pregnancy, and I've seen you down coffee like a trucker on a night shift."

I glare at him. "Low blow. I mostly drank tea."

Ivy looks up from her phone. "Finn's five minutes out."

"I'm not leaving."

Remy throws up his hands. "For God's sake, woman!"

Ivy sits with me, helping me scoop dirt in and whatever else I tell her we need to do, probably hoping we can be done so we can get to the hospital. Really, I'm stalling.

Finn pulls up fast and brakes harder than usual, gravel crunching under the tires. The truck isn't even fully stopped before he's out the door and sprinting toward me.

He looks wild, not in a panicked way, but in a *locked-in, nothing-will-stop-me* way. His jaw is tight, like he's holding himself together by sheer force. His eyes sweep over me, sharp and wide, taking in every wince, every breath, every tremble I can't hide.

"Baby—" His voice breaks on the word, and he swallows hard, throat working like he's trying to shove his own fear down before it touches me.

I open my mouth to tell him I'm fine, that I can walk, that this contraction isn't that bad—

Because as soon as he reaches me, another one hits.

He steps in close, brushing a shaking strand of hair off my face. "You're okay," he murmurs, but it sounds like he's saying it to himself too. His hand shakes when he cups my cheek. Just barely. But I feel it.

And then in one smooth, determined motion, he scoops me up

bridal-style, like I'm weightless. His arms are tight, protective, solid as the heartbeat I can feel pounding against my ribs from his chest.

I can see everything on him now: The fear in the tightness around his eyes. The awe in the way he keeps glancing down at me and the excitement trembling beneath it all—the kind that says *holy shit, this is happening.*

"Finn—" I gasp through the contraction.

He holds me closer, jaw clenched, breath uneven but steadying for me. "I've got you. I've got you, Row."

He heads for the truck with long, urgent strides, tightening his grip every time I tense. And even though everything hurts and my heart is racing, I focus on the fierce determination etched across his face, on the way he looks like he'd carry me through fire if he had to.

And somehow…even in the pain, I feel safe. Because there's no one I would ever want to do this with than him. And right now, Finn looks like a man who would fight the whole damn world just to get me and our baby safely to the other side of this.

"Finn, I can walk, you know."

He smirks. "Nope. You're gonna have this baby in a hospital, not in your greenhouse."

"Thank God," Remy mutters, following behind us.

"I have time!" I protest. "And I need to finish up that tray."

"Nope," Finn says. "We're going to the hospital."

Junie's waiting by the truck, holding her stuffed narwhal and looking way too excited for someone witnessing my unraveling.

"Is Aunt Rowan having the baby now?" she asks.

"No," I say at the same time Finn says, "Yes."

Junie's grin widens. "Cool. Can I come?"

"Sure, June Bug," Finn tells her. And I realize that he's shockingly calm.

"Why are you so calm?" I ask him.

"Because I know that you're going to be just fine. And we get to meet our baby boy very soon, so that is exciting. And I'm not calm, I'm excited."

"You're freaking out," Remy mumbles. "He always gets eerily calm when he freaks out."

"Shut it," Finn grumbles to Remy, who slides into the backseat with Ivy and Junie.

"Stop looking at me like that," I mutter as Finn buckles me in. "I'm fine."

He brushes my hair off my forehead. "You're amazing, and you're in labor."

"You guys don't know that for sure," I say weakly, and then another contraction hits, sharp and deep.

I grip his hand so tight he winces as I moan.

Junie leans forward from the back seat. "Don't you want me to meet my cousin?"

I try to smile through the pain and grit my teeth. "Of course I do, sweet girl."

"Then stop being a silly goose and have him already."

I burst out with a laugh, which turns into a groan. "I think I'm working on that."

The drive to the hospital is a blur of contractions, annoying music, and Finn whispering encouragements that sound more like reassurance to himself.

"You're doing so good, baby," he says, voice rough. "You got this."

"I hate you right now," I pant. "You did this to me."

"Understandable." He nods.

"What did you do, Uncle Finn?" Junie asks.

Remy says, "Nothing. Aunt Rowan is just in a lot of pain."

"Your kid is aggressive," I moan.

Finn laughs softly. "He's just excited to meet you."

By the time we pull up to the hospital, the contractions are right on top of each other. Finn runs around to my side, lifting me out.

Inside, everything happens fast—nurses, paperwork, questions, monitors. I barely hear any of it. Finn never leaves my side. He's holding my hand, brushing hair from my face, whispering how proud he is of me. I honestly couldn't have done any of it without him.

At some point, I start crying, but not from the pain—though there's plenty of that—but from fear.

He leans close, forehead pressed to mine. "Hey. Look at me. I'm here."

"I'm just pretending it's not happening because I'm scared," I whisper.

"I know," he says softly. "But it's happening. You're already the best mom."

I needed to hear that, needed the reassurance.

The next hour blurs into light and noise and pain and breath and Finn never lets go of me. He wipes my face with a cold cloth, whispers encouragements, cracks terrible jokes, kisses my knuckles, and is everything I could have ever hoped my partner would be.

When it's finally over, I feel relief and an emotion I couldn't begin to describe other than just...motherhood. The feeling of your heart outside of your body just beating there in another human form that you already love with every piece of your soul.

Finn's standing beside me, his hair a mess, his eyes red, his whole face soft in a way I've never seen and he's holding a tiny bundle in his arms.

"Hey, Momma," he murmurs.

I blink through happy tears as he places our baby in my arms.

He's small, pink, and perfect. His little hands curl around my finger like it's the only thing that exists and his eyes search until I swear they lock on mine. I fall in love harder than I ever thought possible.

"Hi, Chip," I whisper, voice breaking. "Welcome to the world."

I glance at Finn, tears blurring everything. "He's perfect."

He smiles, kissing my temple. "Yeah. He is."

We sit there like that for a long time, the three of us wrapped in soft hospital light and something sacred.

The nurse finally asks if we're allowing visitors because I think she is legitimately afraid that they're going to break the door down from the lobby at some point. They're all chomping at the bit to meet Chip. We give the go ahead and wait for them all.

Junie comes in first, with Remy and Ivy behind her. "Where's my cousin?" she says.

I lift Chip so she can see. "Right here."

Her eyes go wide. "He's so tiny!"

Finn laughs. "He'll grow fast. You'll have to teach him all your tricks."

She nods solemnly. "Okay. But not the one with the bad tricks."

"Good plan," Ivy says, laughing.

Remy squeezes Finn's shoulder, eyes shining. "He's adorable."

I glance down at Chip's dark hair and dimpled chin.

Finn chuckles softly. "He's got your stubborn streak already. I can tell."

"Good," I whisper, stroking our son's cheek. "Nothing wrong with being strong."

Donna and Mom arrive next, crying and cooing, crowding around the bed. Mom kisses my forehead. "You did it, my girl."

Donna's wiping tears, staring at Chip like he's a miracle. "Look at him. He's perfect."

Finn clears his throat, voice low. "He's Pete's namesake."

Donna nods, tears spilling again. "Then he's doubly perfect."

That night, when everyone's gone and it's just us, the room is dim and quiet. Chip's asleep in the bassinet beside the bed, making tiny noises in his sleep.

Finn stands at the window, looking out at Wisteria Cove.

"You okay?" I whisper.

He turns, smiling softly. "More than okay."

I reach for his hand. "Come here."

He crawls into the narrow hospital bed beside me, wrapping his arm around my shoulders, and we watch our son sleep.

After a while, he says quietly, "You were amazing today."

"I was a mess."

"You are brave," he says, pressing a kiss to my hair. "The strongest person I've ever known."

I rest my head on his chest, listening to his heartbeat. "You were pretty brave and strong, too. I'm so glad I get to do this with you."

He laughs quietly. "I was just trying to keep up with you."

Outside, a light spring rain falls. Inside, our little family is safe, warm, and whole.

I breathe a sigh of relief into Finn's chest, whispering, "He's really here."

He kisses my forehead. "Yeah, baby. He's here. And now we're a family."

Bonus Content

Want more of Finn and Rowan? Check out this bonus scene for
Hexes & Honeysuckle when you sign up for Erin's newsletter!
Scan the QR code to get your bonus scene:

About the Author

Erin Branscom is a creator of happily-ever-after's, crafting spicy, Hallmark-like romances that make readers fall head over heels for charming small towns. When she's not writing heartwarming stories, Erin can be found anywhere there are dogs, with a cup of coffee in hand, or lost in a good book. As a passionate Scorpio, she brings intensity and heart to everything she does. Dive into her world and discover love, warmth, and a touch of spice in every story.

Acknowledgments

To my family. I love you all and you are my reason for working hard every day. I'm so thankful for all of you and your support. To all my readers, thank you for always showing up for me and being excited!

Freedom Valley Series
Falling Inn Love
Baked Inn Love
All Inn Thyme
Love Inn Books
Forever Inn Love
Snowed Inn

Bridger Falls
Forever To Me
Wild As Her
Always You
High Road

Wisteria Cove
The Pumpkin Spice Spell
Mistletoe & Magic
Hexes & Honeysuckle

Cozy Creek Collection/Standalones
Fall Too Well
Bagpipes & Buns

You can find all of Erin's books on her website:
Erinbranscom.com

Love small town books
and want more?

After a one-night stand with the town's grumpy bar owner, I should have walked away. Instead, I stayed—and now I'm falling for the former country music legend hiding in Bridger Falls, Wyoming.

Walker was the last person I expected to end up with after leaving Nashville. But there he was, behind the bar, pouring whiskey, looking like sin in flannel, and making it way too easy to forget why I swore off love.

He's done with music. I'm done with love. But when our pasts come knocking, and the whole town watches, pretending we're nothing isn't an option anymore.

Now, we're tangled in lyrics and late-night kisses, chasing melodies and breaking every rule we swore to keep.

This was never supposed to be more than one night.

Some people belong to the past, but some are meant to be your forever.

Walker & Violet's story is a spicy, small-town western romcom with a grumpy bar owner, steamy songwriting sessions, and a love story too big to stay unwritten.

Start reading it now FREE on Kindle Unlimited, ebook, paperback, or audio.